BLEACH
Can't Fear Your Own World

contents II

SHUHEI HISAGI

Assistant captain of Ninth Company. Editor-in-chief of the *Seireitei Bulletin*. His interests include guitars and motorcycles from the world of the living.

Shunsui Kyoraku

He succeeded Genryusai Yamamoto as Captain General of the Thirteen Court Guard Companies. He has been friends with Ukitake since they were at Shinoreijutsuin Academy together.

Kisuke Urahara

The former captain of the Twelfth Company and founding chief of the Department of Research and Development. He provides Ichigo and the others with transcendental engineering ideas.

Soi Fon

Captain of the Second Company and commander-in-chief of the Secret Remote Squad tasked with assassinations and intelligence. She respects Yoruichi Shihoin.

Nanao Ise

Assistant captain of First Company. She has constantly been at Kyoraku's side as his second-in-command since her days in the Eighth Company.

Tier Halibel

An Arrancar and the third Espada. She took over governing Hueco Mundo after Aizen left.

Mayuri Kurotsuchi

Captain of the Twelfth Company and chief of the Department of Research and Development. A mad scientist whose internal observations and research continue even in the midst of battle.

MAIN CHARACTERS

Grimmjow Jaegerjaquez

An Arrancar. He developed an obsession when he was an Espada after losing a fight to Ichigo Kurosaki and wants to settle things.

Nelliel Tu Odelschwanck

An Arrancar. She lost her memories and powers but regained them after meeting Ichigo Kurosaki.

Kaname Tosen

Former captain of Ninth Company. He sided with Aizen to betray the Soul Society because a close friend of his was killed by a Soul Reaper.

Sosuke Aizen

Former captain of Fifth Company. He betrayed the Soul Society and engaged in a war against the Thirteen Court Guard Companies. Currently imprisoned in Mugen.

Shukuro Tsukishima

A Fullbringer and member of Xcution. He tormented Ichigo with his powers to alter the past.

Kugo Ginjo

A Fullbringer and the first deputy Soul Reaper. He led the Xcution group and fought against Ichigo and his team but was defeated and died.

Aura Michibane

A mysterious woman who introduces herself as a representative of the religious group Xcution, which shares the name of the Fullbringer group Ginjo created. She attempts to contact Yukio.

Giriko Kutsuzawa

A Fullbringer and member of Xcution. He can manipulate time constraints.

Kukaku Shiba

Ganju's older sister and a fireworks expert living in the Rukongai. She helped Ichigo and his friends with her unique spiritual powers.

Yukio Hans Vorarlberna

A Fullbringer and member of Xcution. He stole an immense fortune from his father and now runs a large corporation.

Shinji Hirako

Captain of the Fifth Company. He has an aloof personality but a quick mind. He led the Visoreds to battle Aizen.

Ganju Shiba

Kukaku's younger brother. He rides a boar. He originally hated Soul Reapers but ended up fighting alongside Ichigo and the others.

Kensei Muguruma

Captain of Ninth Company. He was Hollowfied during Aizen's treachery. He was reinstated to his position after fighting against Aizen as a Visored.

Hiyori Sarugaki

A former Twelfth Company assistant captain. After fighting alongside Hirako as a Visored, she's been staying in the living world.

Cirucci Sanderwicci

An Arrancar. A Privaron Espada. She was defeated by Uryu in the battle in Hueco Mundo but, like Dordoni, was resurrected as a zombie.

Dordoni Alessandro Del Socaccio

An Arrancar. A Privaron Espada. He lost to Ichigo but was resurrected as a zombie by Mayuri for the fight against the Vandenreich.

Charlotte Chuhlhourne

An Arrancar. Even after being turned into a zombie by Mayuri, she still has absolute confidence in her own beauty.

Luppi Antenor

An Arrancar. The former sixth Espada. Though he died after Grimmjow attacked him, blowing away the upper part of his body, he is brought back to life as a zombie.

Meninas McAllon

A Quincy. She possesses superhuman strength. It was thought she'd been rendered incapable of battle by Liltotto, however...

Liltotto Lamperd

A Quincy. Her beautiful appearance hides a wicked tongue. She survived Auswählen but was defeated in the battle against Yhwach.

Candice Catnip

A Quincy. Uses lightning as a weapon. Her whereabouts are uncertain after the Auswählen.

Tokinada Tsunayashiro

A member of the Four Great Noble Clans. Part of the Tsunayashiro family.

Hikone

A beautiful child who follows Tokinada.

Ichigo Kurosaki

The main character of the original story.

Can't
Fear
Your
Own
World

II

Tite Kubo
Ryohgo Narita

VIZ MEDIA   SHONEN JUMP

"THAT'S WHY
YOU SHOULD REMAIN
A SEATED OFFICER."

"POWER
IS NOT THE MOST
IMPORTANT THING
FOR A WARRIOR."

"IT'S THE FEAR
OF BATTLE."

"IT'S BECAUSE WE KNOW THE FEAR OF BATTLE THAT WE ARE ABLE TO GRASP OUR SWORDS AND FIGHT FOR THOSE WHO ALSO FEAR BATTLE."

"THOSE WHO DON'T FEAR THE VERY SWORD THEY HOLD ARE NOT WORTHY OF HOLDING ONE."

—Former Ninth Company captain
Kaname Tosen

INTERLUDE

WHO WAS THE "SOUL KING"?

Before the Soul Society was created by his magnificence, what did the world look like?

It was a question that had come to the minds of many of those living in the Soul Society at least once. Even residents of the Rukongai, who did not have the word Soul King in their vocabulary, wondered what kind of person ruled over the Soul Society. Excepting those who had to put their every effort into simply surviving day to day, most had probably wondered what great presence ruled over the Soul Society and the world of the living. Along with their surprise that an afterworld actually existed, many of those who came to live in the Rukongai from the world of the living were curious to know who ruled over the Soul Reapers, who proclaimed themselves to be "gods of death." Yet they, much less the Soul Reaper "gods" themselves, for the most part had no idea what the "Soul King" was. In practice, most accepted the Soul King as a nebulous symbol of the world and an absolute presence.

≡

The aristocracy was no exception. In the past, a certain boy from the nobility asked his father this:

"What is the Soul King?"

The father looked down upon the boy as he answered.

"The Soul King is, in practical terms, the linchpin of the world, the cornerstone that controls the universal flow of konpaku. If the Soul King were to disappear, the three worlds—the Soul Society, the world of the living, and Hueco Mundo—would likely crumble immediately."

"In that case, what was the world like in the time before the linchpin was established?"

After asking that, the boy was harshly scolded by his father.

"That time, or any history prior to the Soul King's birth, did not exist," he said.

"Even considering such a thing is not allowed," the father reiterated, his face pale. It was the obligation of those with wisdom, words, and power—in other words, the "Soul Reapers"—to be thankful for and constantly revere the Soul King for endlessly existing as the world's absolute pinnacle.

The boy pretended to accept that answer. Even in his youth, the boy's instinct told him that adults spoke in lies. Among the Five Great Noble Clans, the Tsunayashiros were confident that they held particular power. Though he was a member of that clan, the boy looked down upon his own family.

He looked down on his own family as it continued to indulge in pretentious luxury and as it frivolously squandered a history built up through time and complacency. They were evil—simply despicable.

As he forced himself to temper the flames that smoldered within his heart, the boy continued to quietly bide his time.

≡

Many moons passed. A crude laugh slipped from the mouth of the man who had once been that boy, "Ha ha."

In the Tsunayashiros' innermost library, which was a secret among secrets, this man who had just solved a cipher text carved into a stone monument, felt certain.

"Can...can this really be?! It is just as I imagined. No, it's even more than I imagined!"

His family truly was made up of hopeless villains who were not even worth despising.

"We record the crimes of our ancestors here."

After he had read the totality of the cipher text that began with that preamble, he sliced it apart with his own zanpaku-to.

"Guh ha ha ha...ha ha ha ha ha! I see... These are the dark innards of the Soul Society—and of the Tsunayashiro family!"

After he had laughed for some time, the man said to himself, "I never would have thought they would leave behind a monument like this. Was it so they would not forget their own sin? No, they likely left it behind as some sort of threat to the other clans. Oh, yes! It is exactly as I expected! It's proof that the world works just the way I had guessed!"

The world was rotten, just as he had suspected, and it was even less salvageable than anyone could have imagined. With that truth before him, the man who had continued to foster the sentiments of his boyhood was so incredibly pleased that he just couldn't help it. Then, he was thankful for the world. He was thankful for the million-year-old history of the Soul Society. He was thankful for the Tsunayashiro family that had sustained the petty evil of their bloodline.

They had done well creating a world filled with deceit. He turned theatrically to face the ceiling of the library and allowed his mouth to contort into a smile full of all-encompassing gratitude and affection.

"This is truly amazing! Yes, I am grateful! I am grateful for my distant ancestor's sin! Because they hid it, I am able to dedicate my joy to the great malice that has been left unpurified for a million years!"

After the man had laughed for some time, thinking of what he could do because of that, he resolved himself.

If the world is duplicitous, then I should be duplicitous as well.

The Tsunayashiro family, which exists for nothing more than the sake of being despicable, ends here.

What meaning is there in an evil that exists only to be looked down upon and despised? It was all a fraud.

What am I to do if I am unable to go along with the lie?

Ahh, I will sing to the tune of my passions as my heart desires.

I may be destroyed by the Quincies, squashed by the Hollows, or sabotaged by my own hubris.

If the final days of the Soul Society are upon us, then I vow to bring about evil until that day.

There will be no necessary evils. My malice will be entirely needless as I laugh at this world!

What a joyous day!

The Soul Society's history has validated that my malice is just!

The man, his soul etched in this way, left the hidden archives behind, his smile transforming into something wicked. The events of the day had given the man a modest goal. That was all that had occurred.

The man had simply reaffirmed himself, nothing more. Though he did not know whether he had been born with them, he had decided that all those things within him—his appetite, his malice, his sadism—were sanctioned. No trigger or tragedy had turned the man evil. He would tyrannize others entirely of his own volition and indulge extravagantly in it. Nothing whatsoever had changed in the man in the moment he had seen the Soul Society's sealed past. There hadn't been the slightest murkiness about Tokinada Tsunayashiro's true nature. His true self hadn't changed—he had simply been given different *options*.

Had he not seen the writing etched in stone, he might have gone through his life as a high-ranking noble who devoted himself to injustices of ambition and hubris of the furthest extremes. But now he had a goal—a goal to satisfy his desires to the maximum extent possible—and a playground in which to set his malice free.

Thus it could be said that on this day the world had changed—a momentous change in the direction of vile evil that profited no one.

Then time flowed onward.

≡

CURRENT DAY, KARAKURA TOWN

Just after everything had been swept into this strange maelstrom, but when it was yet much too late to do anything over, a single Soul Reaper cast himself into the center of that malice.

This was a Soul Reaper who was far flung from the aristocracy, with origins in the Rukongai. Nevertheless, this man, who came to work as the assistant captain of the Ninth

Company—an important office even within the Thirteen Court Guard Companies—after building himself up through training and hundreds of battles, was attempting to step into the Soul Society's karmic fate that had continued uninterrupted for a million years.

Whether he realized he was involving himself in a grand plot that encompassed all three worlds or not, that very Soul Reaper flinched, wide-eyed, at the relic of history that had appeared before his eyes.

"Are you serious, Mr. Urahara? Is this actually from the legendary Galmuna Ecstasy...?"

"Yeah, isn't it a beauty? I was reminded of it when Mr. Sado mentioned that you were interested in it, so I did what I could to get my hands on it."

"I never could have imagined I'd be able to hold it in my own hands like this... Is it the real deal?" the man with a giant scar running down his face inquired, cradling an electric guitar that was white and brick red in color.

Facing him was a man wearing a cloth hat, who pointed at the guitar with the tip of his cane as he nonchalantly replied, "Yes, that's a replica of a replica of a replica, but that just means it's gone full circle and has its own unique charm. In other words, it's a genuine, bona-fide reproduction."

"Doesn't that just mean it's a plain old replica?!"

"Now that's just amateur thinking!"

"Huh?"

The man with the hat turned a serious gaze upon his bewildered companion as he emphatically explained. "It just means that many artisans have given the original prototype a tune-up. That guitar is a mirror reflecting many souls. It's a replica that's surpassed mere imitation. Occasionally this process births something original onto itself that transcends even the genuine article. Through human workmanship, the legend reaches the promised land. Can't you feel those vibes just oozing out of it?"

"I-I see..."

"Just take a look at the way it shines even thirty whole years after the legend! Look at these marks scratched on the back that prove the event! Doesn't it seem fresh—like it all happened just yesterday? An original simply wouldn't compare to this! The whole reason it's such a once-in-a-lifetime marvel is *because* it's fresh off the line!"

"Well, when you put it that way..."

As the other man once again began to inspect the guitar, the man in the hat attempted to forge ahead with his business deal, pouncing on the opportune moment.

"What do you think? How about I give you a discount right now and set the price to just three months' worth of your salary?"

"Isn't that kind of pricey?!"

"That's because I crafted this with my own two hands. I have to figure that labor into the price. This guitar can even function as a zanpaku-to sheath."

"So it's got a practical use? Well... But..."

The man's name was Shuhei Hisagi.

He was the Ninth Company's assistant captain as well as editor-in-chief of the *Seireitei Bulletin*. The man, who was a Soul Reaper and a journalist, was most certainly approaching an "answer," as well as the center of a sinister malevolence, though he himself had yet to realize that fact.

After faltering for some time, he murmured a response with a determined look in his eyes.

"Would you also...issue me a loan?"

A girl and a boy of around middle school age were watching him from a distance with expressions filled more with pity than exasperation as they muttered, "C'mon, that guy's getting ripped off again."

"He's such a good customer..."

CHAPTER SIX

KARAKURA TOWN, MITSUMIYA

IN THE PAST FEW YEARS, the land of Karakura Town has become extraordinarily important to the Soul Society. It has been known as a Jureichi—a concentrated spirit zone—for quite some time and has even been in the sights of Sosuke Aizen. Karakura Town is the place where Isshin Shiba once met a human woman during a conflict, resulting in the birth of the man who would change the history of the Soul Society. But even before that, the town was known as a place to be wary of because it often spawned Hollows. Whether it has any relation to those things is unknown, but a unique shop that can be found in no other place exists on this land: the enigmatic candy store known as Urahara Shoten.

Even among the residents of the neighborhood, not a single person has certain knowledge of just when the store first appeared; however, none find that odd, and the shop seems to meld into the scenery of the town without the slightest sense of being out of place.

The primary minders of the store include an incredibly large and brawny man, some children who are believed to be relatives, and a mysterious man who occasionally makes an appearance and wears a hat pulled down over his face.

The residents of Karakura Town know the store as a place that carries an extensive range of sweets, including trendy confections, sweets bundled with toys from small manufacturers that are only familiar to connoisseurs, and truly suspicious, odd candies that do not seem to be sourced from legitimate manufacturers. The store is seen as a hidden gem that only a few candy collectors in the know are aware of, essentially an old shop set on a road with little foot traffic.

However, there are a select few who recognize the shop as something else. To those who know about the existence of Hollows and Soul Reapers, this store serves an entirely different purpose. The place is both a temple to run to when one finds oneself in a troublesome tango with a dangerous spirit and a place in which one can sever ties with any previous mentality one has conformed to during the peaceful days until that moment.

Karakura Town's underground bigwig uses the store to manage spiritual issues related to the town's being a Jureichi. This man, once the captain of the Soul Society's Twelfth Company, is the sweets shop manager whom the surrounding residents know as a curious man who looks dapper with his pulled-down hat. However, all those who are aware of the man's true power know him as the one who established the Seireitei's Department of Research and Development and its first director: Kisuke Urahara.

"So, I was thinking that's how I'd introduce you, Mr. Urahara."

"Oh, Mr. Hisagi...I'm impressed you could keep a straight face reading that all the way to the end." Kisuke Urahara—the man who wore his hat pulled far over his eyes—held a folding fan over his mouth as he responded to Shuhei Hisagi, who had deliberately read the entirety of a preprepared manuscript.

"Huh? Was there something that shouldn't be in it?"

"No, I wouldn't say that, but don't you think that introduction is aimed more for people in the world of the living? I'm not sure the people over there would have much interest in Karakura Town."

"Ah... I wanted to use this as an opportunity to explain what Karakura Town is again, but I also didn't know how much I could write about your past with the Soul Society..."

Hisagi apologetically lowered his head. To him, Urahara was someone who had saved the Soul Society from crisis countless times. Since he had also been a superior among superiors in the

Thirteen Court Guard Companies, Hisagi just couldn't operate on equal footing with him. As an assistant captain, he had looked into the man's personal history from several hundred years ago. Urahara had been banished from the Soul Society due to a false accusation, which was why they were having this conversation.

"No, no. Looks like you went out of your way on my account. Sorry about that."

"The article is a little long, so I think we'll need to cut some of it when we run it in the magazine."

"Well, of course you'd need to. Oh, but I'm tickled by the phrase 'enigmatic candy shop,' so maybe you could just leave that in there. One way you could go is to pair it with the text 'mystery market.' Also, you can describe me as a 'shady guy' rather than 'mysterious'..." As he said that, Urahara once again turned his eyes to the copy and addressed Hisagi. "So 'Isshin Shiba once met a human woman'... Seems like you're being pretty discreet about this too."

"Yes. I didn't know how far I could delve into that. Well, it doesn't directly relate to you, so I think we'll probably cut it."

Isshin Shiba was Ichigo Kurosaki's father. Though Hisagi was aware from his news coverage that Isshin's wife, Masaki Kurosaki, was a Quincy, he hardly thought that would be a matter he could casually disseminate, so all he could do was represent it in this way.

Though Ichigo himself might not have cared, if it was picked up on by those in the aristocracy who still believed Ichigo Kurosaki was an "outsider," even after all this time, there was a chance they would make some sort of false charge against him. Though the war was over, the Soul Reapers still were fundamentally hostile to the Quincies. Since there were also supporters like the Ishidas—a father and son pair who had lent Ichigo a hand in the decisive battle against Yhwach—the issue might have resolved itself with time. However, at the moment it could be said that making it known to the world that Ichigo Kurosaki's mother was a Quincy would be premature.

"Well, putting that aside, I'd like to thank you for your cooperation today."

Hisagi once again bowed his head to Kisuke Urahara after pulling out an interview recorder that made use of a spirit recording bug. As Hisagi lowered his head humbly, Urahara snapped his folding fan closed and handed the reporter a sheath of papers he pulled from his chest pocket.

"Well, I get it. I've got the answers to everything you wanted to ask, compiled right in here."

"Huh?! But you didn't have to go out of your way..." Though hesitant, Hisagi accepted the papers and ran his eyes down a page. "'The secret formula! How to make Urahara Shoten's original candy, the Hollo-hollo-hollow! First, combine a massive amount of sugar and salt in equal quantities and knead it together with a good dose of honey. This is the most important point! When you add a ton of vegetable oil and butter at this moment, it'll transform the flavor! You'll be crying yourself hollo-hollo-hollow!'"

"Wow, I didn't think you'd actually read that out loud."

Pressing his folding fan against his lips, Urahara slid away backwards. When Hisagi had finally internalized the contents of the page, he uttered, "But this is just some candy recipe! And it seems ridiculously unhealthy too!"

"Yes, it's our secret trick. We can't let it get out of the shop primarily because of those issues with health and flavor!"

"You should have just kept this thing a secret!" Hisagi replied, putting the recipe into his equipment bag nevertheless. "Well, I might be able to use this for news content at some point, so I'll accept it anyway."

"Oh, so that's what you're going to do? Well, you can have it, but you really shouldn't try it yourself. Mr. Hirako will complain about it no matter what it tastes like, so that's what I'd recommend."

"Please, give me a break. I'm going to be the one Captain Hirako yells at if I do that." As Hisagi spoke, he remembered that he'd had a similar conversation with Hirako himself right before coming here.

"Well, if you're headed to Kisuke's then you'll also get to see Hiyori. If you do, make sure to tease her for me."

"Come to think of it, does Miss Sarugaki live around here?"

"You mean Miss Hiyori? I think she's been working part-time for the neighborhood Odd Jobs Service lately. I'm guessing that if you take a march around town, you'll spot her Reiraku spirit ribbons."

"I see. Thank you."

He had said *I see* since he had been directed by Hirako to "tease her for me"; however, he didn't have a particular reason to go and see her.

Well, wait a sec. I might be able to interview her to get a different point of view.

As Hisagi was thinking that over, Urahara once again spoke while opening his folding fan. "But, to be serious, there isn't anything I can tell you about that war at this point."

"What are you talking about? Because of the pill you made that covered us in Hollow reishi, they couldn't steal our Bankai—and we were able to get into the Reiokyu because of you too."

"Yes, that's why I have nothing else to talk about beyond those facts. I just happened to use a preventative measure I'd cooked up when the moment presented itself. That's all. Actually, I'm the one who should be grateful for being put in a situation where I could implement my plan."

Although Urahara waved his fan as he spoke, Hisagi knew better. The "preventative measure" he happened to have was just one of a thousand—or ten thousand—such plans Urahara had stored up. Or it could have been that he responded to the situation at hand by spontaneously coming up with yet another brilliant tactic.

In order to carry out such a plan, just how much wit and knowledge, not to mention skill and experience, would one need?

There were many people other than Hisagi who wanted to understand the secret essence of Kisuke Urahara, this man of multitudinous mysteries, and what it was about his inner workings that gave him the ability to come up with an infinite number of strategies.

But trying to ask the man himself would likely result in noncommittal answers as he tried to elude the questioner. Moreover, trying to get answers from Yoruichi Shihoin or Mayuri Kurotsuchi, who knew about his past, would present an even more difficult path.

I feel like they'd find a way to dodge any question.

After hearing that Hisagi would be interviewing Kisuke Urahara, Shinji Hirako had said to him, "That guy's not the type who would ever give a direct answer in an interview," and Hisagi could practically sense the aura of total evasiveness coming from Urahara's demeanor. Though one might at first mistake his responses as yielding, one would eventually realize they represented a clear warning for people not to trespass carelessly on his territory. But if Hisagi surrendered now, there wouldn't have been any point to his getting formal permission and sealing away a part of his power in order to come here to the world of the living.

Hisagi steadied his breath slightly, then said with a serious look in his eyes, "Mr. Urahara... No, *former* chief of the Department of Research and Development, I came today to expose your past."

When Urahara heard that, the man narrowed his eyes ever so slightly at Hisagi. However, it wasn't enough to constitute a change in expression, and after a moment, he grinned and shrugged.

"Please don't show me your scary side all of a sudden like that, Mr. Hisagi. What'll you do if Jinta bursts out crying from where he's watching from behind the sliding door? He might start wetting his bed again."

In the next moment the sliding door slammed open and a boy with grim eyes who looked to be about middle school age came in, roaring with rage.

"I wouldn't cry and I haven't ever wet my bed, ever, you crummy shopkeep! I'll pummel you!"

Jinta Hanakari, the boy with sharp features and red hair swept to the back of his head, tried to leap right into the room, but a brawny arm seized him around the neck and he ended up writhing in midair, immobilized.

"Ow ow ow. Tessai, you little...!"

"*Hmph*. You cannot threaten others with violence, Mr. Jinta—especially not in front of a guest."

Holding up the struggling Jinta with a cool expression on his face was a bespectacled giant sporting a brawny physique. Then a girl who also looked to be middle-school age peeked out from behind the man called Tessai and started to tickle Jinta while he was held captive.

"Ha ha ha ha gaha... U-Ururu, you better not be doing that to my feet again... I'll kill ya—*ha hwah*!"

The girl he had called Ururu was dexterously tickling Jinta's feet with her own hair as the boy suffered all manners of agony. The girl continued to tickle Jinta as she turned to face Hisagi, dipped down into a bow, and said, "I'm sorry. Jinta's body went through a growth spurt, but the same can't be said for his brain..."

"Oh...uh, I don't mind."

After bowing her head one more time, Ururu next turned to face Urahara. "Mr. Kisuke, I'm going to get the bulk purchases done."

"Yes, thank you. We've got to stock up on five hundred kilograms of bouncy balls, so please take Jinta with you to carry the goods."

When Urahara said that with a bright face, Jinta attempted to shout in protest, "*Grr*...what the heck is with that?! Five hundred kilograms is just comical, no matte—*hya ha ha ha ha*!"

But with Tessai locking him at the neck and Ururu tickling his feet, Jinta was carried away before he could get his mouth to form a decent reply and was dragged out of the shop.

"Yes, if it's comical, then please laugh your heart out as you do your work. Give it your all!"

As he watched Urahara see off the boisterous group, Hisagi released a large sigh.

"I'm not sure how to put this, but they seem like they've simultaneously changed and stayed just the same... Though when I first saw them, it seemed like that Jinta kid was the one teasing the girl."

"Well, this is when they're going through growth spurts, and Ururu is actually three years older. He used to make fun of her for having 'hair like a cockroach,' so do you think tickling him with her hair is revenge for that?"

"I'm not sure there's any point in asking me that." Though Urahara was clearly attempting to redirect the conversation, Hisagi decided to go along with the shopkeep. "Soul Reaper or human, I just don't get the way kids think."

Then, nonchalantly, he attempted to extract a bit more from Urahara. "The way their Reiraku feel... They both seem to have unique ones."

"That was a bit obvious for a leading question. Since we've been used to Mr. Tosen's interview style, don't you think that's a crude way to try to get at people's weak spots?"

This counterattack struck a painful spot for Hisagi. It was true that the former editor-in-chief Tosen would have either asked about it straightforwardly, without dancing around the point, or he wouldn't have touched on the matter at all.

Although Hisagi personally was curious, he didn't actually want to know what the true nature of the boy and girl was, and he had sensed Urahara's unwillingness to talk about it.

However, Hisagi could be calculating in his own way. His strategy was to touch upon something that was difficult to talk about in the beginning, then, as though in exchange for retreating from that line of questioning, he would jump right into a topic that was just a slight degree less sensitive. It was a risky strategy that could result in the interviewee indignantly cutting off the interview at the beginning. However, after the last few minutes of their conversation, Hisagi had realized he wouldn't be able to draw out information from Urahara using conventional methods. Although it wasn't his true nature, he hardened his heart and devoted himself to being a reporter.

As though he had seen right through the young man's stern resolve, Urahara said, "So? What do you think those two are?"

So that's how he wants to do this.

Hisagi was bewildered when Urahara said that, as though the shopkeep were testing him instead of the other way around, but he offered the first reply he could think of. "Gikongan… I guess they wouldn't be, though."

"Well, the temporary souls in Gikongan generally don't grow. Though they will 'learn' to a certain extent from the user's position and commands, there are limits as far as that's concerned."

"You said they're generally like that, so that means there are exceptions."

At that moment, Hisagi recalled the stuffed lion toy that made frequent appearances in the Soul Society and looked serious as he said, "For example, a mod soul."

"Oh my, you're sharper than you seem, Mr. Hisagi. But that doesn't mean you're right."

"Well, other than that...the only thing I can think of is that they're something like Miss Nemu from Captain Kurotsuchi's..."

Urahara opened his folding fan in front of Hisagi's mouth to stop him from continuing.

"Whoa there. If you say something like that, Mr. Kurotsuchi will use them for his experiments. Their insides are quite different from Nemu's. I'm sure that Mr. Kurotsuchi already knows that and is imagining my bitter expression as he dances for joy about Nemu's growth, thinking, 'I've surpassed Urahara.'" At that moment, Urahara snapped his folding fan shut and shook his head.

"Well, I guess he wouldn't actually be able to imagine that."

"Why is that?"

Urahara grinned like a mischievous kid at Hisagi's question and replied with what could be taken either as the truth or a joke.

"That's because I've never genuinely been bitter in front of Mr. Kurotsuchi. ♪"

≡

THE SOUL SOCIETY,
DEPARTMENT OF RESEARCH AND DEVELOPMENT

"What's wrong, Captain?" Assistant Captain Akon asked quizzically when Twelfth Company Captain and head of the Department of Research and Development abruptly paused at his work.

"I suppose you could say something foreboding is bugging me." Looking unamused, Mayuri resumed his work. "The quantum spirit bugs I inserted in my cerebellum are throbbing. I'm sure it's just the jealous ramblings of some banal scientist, going on illogically."

While ignoring the "bugging" that was no metaphor, Mayuri turned his eyes to the image receiver in front of him. What was displayed there appeared to be the Rukongai as seen from high above. If a person from the living world were to see it, they would have likely concluded it was a shot of a desolate village taken from a satellite or airplane. However, the Soul Society naturally had no satellites in the air.

When Akon saw the image, which was leagues more sophisticated than the best satellite surveillance images from the living world, he was half impressed and half dubious, remarking, "That's pretty precise, though I should expect that from you. But why'd you go to all that trouble to devote yourself to building a surveillance system from scratch? It would've been a heck of a lot easier to just build it on top of the Visual Department's system... Actually, wouldn't that have been more efficient?"

The Visual Department—that was the general umbrella organization that managed the visual surveillance system that spread like a net primarily over various places in the Soul Society and the living world and, in recent years, even a section of Hueco Mundo. Its ties ran deep with the Department of Research and Develoment, and by joining forces, they could access all types of intelligence from various sources and use that as a basis for analyzing the current state of affairs.

For starters, Hiyosu from the Department of Research and Development, who had been analyzing the information coming in through the Visual Department, was able to find Rukia Kuchiki operating in the living world using a gigai. Thus this collaboration was recognized as being extraordinarily important, continuously recording the turning points in the Soul Society's history.

Because of that, no one outside the Visual Department or Department of Research and Development other than a select group could access the information. Since the Department of Research and Development so frequently used this data, and because of the crucial nature of the research, it was even jokingly remarked that the Visual Department was already a part of the Department of Research and Development.

So why was Mayuri creating an entirely separate surveillance system from the Visual Department at this time? He had certainly improved the resolution of the visuals and performance of the other sensors substantially, but wouldn't it have been easier to just update the versions they already had?

That question floated in Akon's mind as Mayuri gloomily replied, "We're going to cut the Visual Department out of the Department of Research and Development's work."

"Huh?"

"Though we'll continue to pretend we're using it like we have been all along. The data coming from them is less reliable than a drunkard's gibberish."

Though Mayuri had spoken abruptly, Akon didn't seem all that surprised. As though he recognized that this was business as usual, he spoke in an indifferent tone. "Ahh...well, if it's about reliability, I don't even have to think twice to know that the system you created is better. Did something happen?"

"Blind faith is a poison that weakens performance. Please just say 'Though we put together our flawed minds and inspected it, the mechanism that Mayuri Kurotsuchi created was undoubtedly better in every way.'"

He felt that even if he were to say that, the captain would respond that the time he spent deliberating over something so obvious was a waste. And then Akon realized that even thinking about it now was a waste of time, so he simply nodded obediently and asked again, "Is it because of that whole incident with the aristocracy interfering with the surveillance system?"

Just the other day, the Soul Society's surveillance system had picked up an odd spiritual pressure, but one of the Four Great Noble Clans had directly notified them that the individual responsible was not to be interfered with. Akon and the others could hardly believe that the captain would simply comply.

When he reflected on it, he realized that the captain would most certainly create his own surveillance system in response to something like that. In fact, he had once inserted bugs and germs into relevant Soul Reapers and people in the living world for surveillance purposes, so in a sense you could say the Department of Research and Development already had their very own private intelligence system set up.

"They so blithely attempt to joke about it. Really, now. They must be idiots if they think that just because they're backed by one million years of history they can manipulate those who are far more resourceful on a whim."

"I'm sure the Visual Department is having a heck of a time being on the receiving end of that." Akon shrugged, at which point Mayuri turned his eyes to the scientist and said, "What are you saying? There are no whims here—they're in on it."

"Excuse me?"

"Ah, I see. You never had any interest in the constitutional government. You should dedicate this to mind regardless— in order to continue with your research undisturbed, you need the skills to lead the incompetent around by the nose. Really, now. Though it's required for the sake of a functioning society, it is an obstacle to freely implementing my ideas, and that just shows that the laws are still far from maturity." Mayuri's complaint displayed extreme insolence toward all of the Soul Society. He went on indifferently in response to Akon's questioning, "Right now, decorative aristocrats are taking turns operating the Visual Department, but it was established and is managed behind the scenes by the Four Great Noble Clans."

"That's...the first I've heard about that."

"If I were to be even more precise, there is one family in particular among the four that is involved."

Mayuri adjusted the coordinates depicted on a screen and continued both tediously and politely, "If we call the Shihoin family the Tenshi Heisoban because they are the heavenly defenders of the realm, and they have the role of managing the arms that the Soul King supposedly bestowed on them, then the Tsunayashiro are the ones managing the past itself. Before the establishment of the Dai Reisho Kairo Underground Assembly Hall's Great Archive for gathering and accumulating information, the Tsunayashiro family were the sentries recording all history."

"They're the sentries of history?"

"If you're researching a specific bit of history, you're required to get their permission to research the historic

remnants, and passages for publication are heavily censored. I have also heard that the historian's whereabouts became unknown in a considerable number of cases."

Without scorn or resentment, Mayuri spoke dispassionately of this issue with the Four Great Noble Clans.

"I believe that striving throughout your life until you get results is itself a talent. I don't exactly intend to ridicule those historians, but if they had really wanted to pursue the truth, they should have prepared numerous countermeasures. To the degree that it's insufficient, working on 'The Soul Society's Million-Year History' or suchlike is a troublesome barrier that stands in front of the work of us researchers. Then again, as I said earlier, such a barrier means nothing to a clever person such as myself. Muttering that last bit to himself, Mayuri turned his eyes to a specific place on the monitor. "There, I've found our guinea pigs. I'm heading out to the experiment without a moment's delay. I will leave analyzing the data to you, Akon."

Mayuri had simply run an automatic tracking and recording program through the surveillance system and was heading out to the actual place himself.

While executing his orders, Akon threw just one more question at the captain as though he were still curious. "Captain, at least tell me the ending to your lecture. Why are we separating from the Visual Department?"

"It's simple." Mayuri shrugged as though nothing else could be done about it and didn't even turn around as he answered,

"The man who has the slacker job of managing the Visual Department, a man who was ridiculed by the aristocrats he came from, killed all the leaders of a single family and became the head of the Tsunayashiro. And I have come to the conclusion that this man will hinder my research. That's all there is to it."

≡

THE RUKONGAI

"We're being watched..."

On a road at the outskirts of the Rukongai, Kugo Ginjo was heading over to the Shiba residence where he was free-loading. He kept his gaze facing forward and muttered in a voice that only his companions, who were walking behind him, could hear.

"An enemy?"

"Hm. I can think of several people it could be."

Shukuro Tsukishima and Giriko Kutsuzawa, who had heard the muttered warning, replied in a way that would likewise prevent their watcher from catching on that anything was out of place.

"It's just a hunch, though. I feel something unpleasant in the air, like back when I felt something off about the deputy badge."

Ginjo put his hand to the pendant on his chest with an instinctive motion.

"I guess the most rational explanation…would be that the upper crust have come to erase nuisances like ourselves since that Hisagi assistant captain guy actually went and investigated us?"

"That may be the case. Though I think a bit too much time has passed for that to be the cause."

Ginjo internally agreed with Giriko. Based on Hisagi's personality, he likely went inquiring to the "Captain General" immediately after the fact in search of the truth. It had been several days since then, and if they were really serious about crushing Ginjo and the others, they'd had many earlier chances to do it. Or, if they had waited this long to do it, there was a chance they'd worked out a plan to strike at their weaknesses. Either way, Ginjo had the thought that he shouldn't let his guard down, but…

Their attacker did not give him the chance to mull it over any further.

Something came flying down the horizon—a flash of lightning.

To be more accurate, it was a single, extremely ruthless arrow entirely covered in high-voltage electricity.

"Hey, you freakin' serious?"

Though it was much slower than an actual lightning bolt, the reishi arrowhead was quick enough that it could

appropriately be said to be going at "lightning speed." Even
if he could just barely sidestep it, there was no way he would
be unharmed if he were to get caught up in the electrical
discharge. But Ginjo used the large sword that had appeared
in his hand to cast away the reishi that filled the air as well
as the lightning, causing it to disperse. He readied his sword
in the direction from which the lightning-imbued arrow had
come as a bold smile formed on his face.

"Hah. That's pretty slow for lightning. Was that supposed
to be your most lethal move or something?"

Though Ginjo was provoking this enemy that had yet
to make an appearance, Giriko spoke indifferently from a
slight distance away. "Hm. Lightning is far from the speed of
light, though people mistakenly believe it to be. Then again,
atmospheric pressure and the humidity in the air influence
its speed and can easily effect a change. Really, now, speed is
so fickle compared to the flow of time."

"Why're you spouting weird trivia all of a sudden?"

While vigilant of his surroundings, Ginjo at least replied
after the interruption. However, Tsukishima, who had at
some point leaned back against a nearby tree, butted in again.
"Believing that the flow of time is fixed is such a blind assumption. It's not just some scientist's theory. We all know about
how Dankai messes with time and about Yukio's Fast Forward."

"You think that way, Tsukishima, because you simply
have not entrusted yourself to the god of time in a true sense.

Relativity and playing with time and space is meaningless compared to the flow of time that dwells within you."

"Okay, like I said—what're you two babbling about?"

Ginjo was exasperated as he turned to glance at the two of them, but once he saw what they were doing, he smiled to himself. Going with the flow of the conversation, Giriko had naturally picked up his pocket watch, and Tsukishima had already closed his book on the pretense of starting a conversation with Giriko and had his hand on his bookmark. Ginjo had no idea how much the enemy knew about them, but at least all three of them were holding their weapons.

"Well, they're not coming to attack us. In addition to being dull, that thing might be slow to recharge. That technique just wasn't anything to write home about…"

Ginjo stopped short in the middle of his comment. Though he had been joking around, his caution hadn't wavered for even a second. That was exactly why his spine froze when he suddenly heard a voice call out to him from behind, "And who exactly…are you calling dull?"

It was a young woman's voice. At the same time, a spiritual pressure that was different from any Soul Reaper's or Hollow's swelled from the middle of Ginjo and his two companions. She must have used something like a strange coat equipped with optical camouflage, or perhaps she pulled it off using some other method. The woman, who had appeared abruptly almost as though she had *oozed* out from the shadows themselves, was wearing white plasma all over her body.

Her white Western clothing, which was wide open at her chest, seemed as though it had been modified to fit her tastes; its design showcased her stomach, including her belly button. They could see traces of experimentation all over her, including on her exposed skin, but Ginjo had no time to concern himself with those details.

Just then the woman who had appeared from the shadows yelled, in a voice mixed with scorn and irritation, "In that case...you should all hurry up and die already!"

Accompanying her violent words, a small bolt of lightning stretched into the sky from her raised hand, and instead of an arrow clad in electricity, a genuine flash of lighting roared as it came down on Ginjo and the others.

≡

KARAKURA TOWN, URAHARA SHOTEN

"Now then...since you cleared everyone out, can I assume you'll give me some answers?"

They were in Urahara Shoten after Jinta and the others had left. In response to Hisagi, whose question was asked in a grave tone, the shop's owner shrugged.

"Well, who knows? I may simply be trying to evade your questions in a more flamboyant way."

"Please rest assured that no matter how much you jest here, I'll make sure every person who reads the *Seireitei Bulletin* will think 'Kisuke Urahara is a hero'!"

"Isn't that more or less fraud?"

When he teased Hisagi in his usual way, he hid his mouth with his folding fan, and his eyes narrowed sharply behind his hat as he looked in Hisagi's direction.

"Actually, it appears the person hiding their sentiments and true thoughts is you rather than me. Did something make you panic? You're making the same face as a trainee coming across their first Hollow right now, Mr. Hisagi."

"What?! That's just..."

As though something had come to mind, Hisagi froze for a while. Though he felt guilty about asking questions that pertained to his own circumstances in a formal interview, if he was going to pause here because of that, he might as well go for it.

Hisagi made up his mind.

"From here on, half of this is relevant to my work, but the other half is relevant to my own interests."

"I see. I've never made a distinction between personal and business matters, so I don't mind. Just give it to me straight."

"Actually...before I put this interview into the article, I'm going to have to publish a special edition."

"A special edition?" Urahara snapped his fan closed, and a bold smile spread over his face. "Is it...about the unveiling of the new Tsunayashiro family's head?"

"Huh! You already knew?!"

"Nah, I just happened to hear from Miss Yoruichi that the head of house was changing."

At that point, Urahara turned his eyes down and something like self-derision seemed to resound in his next comment. "She said it seems the new head of the Four Great Noble Clans is quite the overachiever or something."

"So you know something about him then...about Tokinada Tsunayashiro."

"Hmm. Well, it's not as though I've had direct contact with him, and I think Mr. Kyoraku would actually know a lot more about him."

Though Urahara averted his eyes for a moment, he didn't try to redirect the conversation and replied nonchalantly to Hisagi, "I know about the ties between Mr. Tosen and Mr. Tsunayashiro, but it happened a long time before I became a captain... Well, I can give it a guess, but making speculations about a person's past is pretty rude."

"I'm having a hard time being convinced about his past too, but I didn't want to ask about that. I just ran into a Soul Reaper kid who was involved with him, and that kid just didn't seem normal, so I'm looking for a lead about who that could have been."

"A Soul Reaper kid, you say?" The smile disappeared from Urahara's face as he replied with interest.

"Yes, and I don't mean like Captain Hitsugaya either—that kid acted like a normal kid, mentally."

"Oh? Don't you think it's unwise to bring up Captain Hitsugaya as your example?"

"W-well... Please don't tell him..."

"Oh, sorry. Please go on. No need to get distracted. I'm quite fine with you just telling me what you saw as your eyes perceived it."

Though Urahara said that lightheartedly, Hisagi felt as though he could sense the intent it contained—Urahara wanted exact data, free of any individual speculation. So he quietly inhaled and matter-of-factly described his experience.

He talked about how he had heard about the Tsunayashiro family directly from Captain General Kyoraku.

He talked about how he had departed to head over to the pharmaceutical clinic that was run by Hanataro Yamada's older brother Seinosuke Yamada in order to get an interview.

Then he talked about how he had met a child Soul Reaper who went by the name of Hikone Ubuginu.

He talked about how, though the kid had been severely injured, this child claimed to be Tokinada Tsunayashiro's servant and how, when Hisagi had tried to restrain the kid, Hisagi himself had been rendered helpless before he knew it by the child's martial arts. Hisagi went on without hiding anything.

Several minutes passed.

Urahara listened to everything, nodded several times, and then spoke in a reminiscing tone. "So Mr. Seinosuke Yamada, huh… Yes, I knew him from when I was back on that side. He was the Fourth Company's assistant captain."

"To be honest, I've never seen kaido like that. Hanataro Yamada also has amazing abilities, but the man really did just feel like Hanataro's older brother. Though he doesn't have the same bearing or speak like his brother at all."

Listening to Hisagi's character sketch, Urahara had started to draw on his memories of his former colleagues from the Thirteen Court Guard Companies.

"That man certainly has remarkable skills. He might even be the same type of person as me. It's in his nature that he can't feel satisfied unless he's prepared countless strategies in order to reach his goals. However, I did things with my own life in mind… In other words, in order to win a battle, Mr. Seinosuke was different from me in that he did things only for the sake of the patient in front of him."

"Doesn't that make him a model doctor?"

"But when it came to anything other than helping the injured and sick before his eyes, his ethics were pretty screwed up… He was always getting into quarrels with Miss Unohana over that. But these were only superficial disagreements; they really did have respect for each other. I think you'd find that the veteran soldiers still trust him."

Urahara's eyes narrowed behind his hat.

Feeling like things had taken a turn from the expected, Hisagi hesitated to utter his next words. With Hisagi wavering in front of him, Urahara mumbled half to himself, "I see... so that's how far the Tsunayashiro family is willing to go. But the Hollow element wasn't supposed to be a requirement...or maybe they were trying to achieve something different..."

"Huh?"

When Hisagi tilted his head quizzically at the inscrutable mutterings that he heard, Urahara whacked his own hat with his fan and said, "Oops. Sorry about that. Just got lost in my thoughts."

"Not at all. It was my first time feeling a spiritual pressure like that and I was so bewildered that I..."

"Are you sure it's correct to say it was your *first* time feeling something like that?"

"Huh?"

While Hisagi was bewildered, Urahara began questioning him instead. "You can't think of anything at all? When it comes to people with diverse spiritual pressures mixed together, I believe there's someone you're already aware of."

Hisagi suddenly recalled the very thing he had read out loud a bit ago.

Shiba once met a human woman during a conflict, resulting in the birth of the man who would change the history of the Soul Society.

"Being acknowledged by Unohana is nothing to scoff at."

Though Hisagi once again felt admiration for the impressive Seinosuke Yamada, Urahara seemed as though he intended to put a damper on that and with a sardonic smile he added, "Having said that, it was true that he was deliberately mean, and the Fourth Company soldiers' apprehension was nothing to scoff at. After Mr. Seinosuke was headhunted, I heard that the Captain General had this in mind when he appointed a more approachable kid as assistant captain. I was already here by then though."

Urahara stopped talking for a moment and, after thinking things over for a few seconds, returned to the information Hisagi had given him.

"So, you said you felt an odd spiritual pressure coming from this Hikone kid?"

"Y-yes, I did. But I wasn't sure whether you'd believe me after what I told you... I was so flustered back then, I couldn't really tell for sure, but now that I think back on it, it felt like there was something mixed in with his Soul Reaper spiritual pressure."

"Something was mixed in there, you say?"

"It was like I felt hints of Hollow and normal human in him, and even something like Quincy...and he came out of a hole like a garganta rather than a Senkaimon to begin with. It was kind of like he was this ridiculous patchwork of stuff, and even Hanataro Yamada was saying that treating him was difficult because of that."

"Ichigo...Kurosaki."

"Yes. Though in general his spiritual pressure is fundamentally made up of human and Soul Reaper, there're Hollow and Quincy factors hidden deep within him. You know that as well, don't you?"

"Now that you mention it, Yamada was saying the kid was just like Ichigo, but he meant it in a different way..."

But what does it mean?

I heard that Kurosaki has two sisters, but it's not like Hikone is one of them.

The issue isn't whether or not they're similar. There's something fundamentally different between Kurosaki's spiritual pressure and the kid's.

As though to reassure Hisagi as he was immersed in thought, Urahara threw him a lifeline. "Well, I don't think that's any reason to fuss about Mr. Kurosaki. Actually, there was another Soul Reaper with a similar nature."

"Huh? Who was that?"

Hisagi's eyes grew wide with surprise. He breathed out quietly and waited for Urahara to speak, the tension showing on his face.

"Though they're not strictly the same...there used to be someone who had the essence of a Hollow, the powers of a Soul Reaper, and another, different power, all at once."

"There *used* to be? So he's not around anymore?"

"That's right, not over here."

"'Over here'?"

Urahara matter-of-factly continued, describing to the dubious-looking Hisagi a person with a nature similar to Hikone's and Ichigo's. "I heard rumors that he assisted Mr. Kurosaki at the Reiokyu. Do you happen to know about that? Well I would think someone in your position would have seen his wanted posters, at least..."

"There's no way."

"After all, it seems that his cadaver rather than his konpaku was once taken to the Seireitei. It would be odd if you hadn't heard of him, actually."

However, that wasn't a lifeline at all—instead it drove Shuhei Hisagi's mind even deeper into uncertainty.

"This Deputy Soul Reaper, Kugo Ginjo... Just how much do you know about him, Mr. Hisagi?"

CHAPTER SEVEN

THE RUKONGAI

THUNDER and a blinding flash swallowed their surroundings.

"Hah. How'd you like that? How's it feel to be scorched by someone you misjudged as weak?!" muttered the woman in the white Western clothing, still enrobed in lightning.

The woman was Candice Catnip, and she was one of the Quincies that had infiltrated the Soul Society. She currently found herself in an extraordinarily complicated position, albeit only from her perspective. Viewed objectively, she amounted only to a prisoner who had been captured by the Soul Reapers and put into forced labor.

Until half a year ago, she had been a Stern Ritter who belonged to the Vandenreich. After being defeated by the Soul Reapers, but before she could be absorbed by Yhwach's

Auswählen, she had been "retrieved" by Torue and others from the Twelfth Company.

At present, she had been half zombified by Mayuri Kurotsuchi as a functioning specimen and was turned into the Department of Research and Development's registered bloodhound through their "equipment." Rather than being simply a prisoner, she and the other captured Stern Ritters were being treated exactly like guinea pigs. Naturally, the Quincies weren't obediently following orders, but Mayuri Kurotsuchi was extraordinarily adept with the "carrot and stick" approach to manipulation. He had eroded away the roots of their minds from their very foundations. And so, in Candice's case, she had been ensnared using a poison-filled "carrot."

$$\equiv$$

SEVERAL DAYS AGO, DEPARTMENT OF RESEARCH AND DEVELOPMENT

"My, my, aren't you stubborn? You're still not in the mood to cooperate." Mayuri Kurotsuchi was expressionless as he uttered these words with the test subject in front of his eyes. He was looking at a gigantic cylindrical tube. It was half full of some sort of liquid and a woman whose bottom half was submerged in the liquid yelled angrily, "Why would you ever think I'd yield to you under these circumstances? Huh?!"

Facing Candice, whose entire body was wrapped in chains to seal her, with tubes and electrodes and such attached to her limbs and the back of her neck, Mayuri Kurotsuchi nonchalantly said, "What strange things you say. If you're able to raise your voice like that, you should realize that's the best kind of welcome a test subject could give."

"Well, at least I realized you're a crazy sadist way before this."

"So close. If you put it in modern terms, you would call me a scientist, not a sadist."

"So you're not going to deny you're nuts..."

"From an ordinary person's point of view, the acts of a genius will naturally seem odd. Though it makes me feel such pity for those who can only quiver in fear and reject any new endeavor they encounter. Humoring every single one of them is just a waste of time."

In response to Mayuri, who was serene but arrogant, Candice *tsked*.

"So? What, you want me to cry tears of gratitude to the Soul Reapers who healed my wounds and just become your pawn?"

"We didn't really heal your wounds, to be precise. It's more accurate to say we 'rebooted' what was almost a corpse. Well, while you were half dead, we more or less finished our experiments, including dissection."

"Wait...what did you just say?! Dissection?!"

"As far as we see it, we saved you from a heartless owner who, far from abandoning you, was about to mercilessly devour you, so I don't think it would be out of order for you to offer a word or two in gratitude."

She glared at Mayuri as he said that, and she bluffed with a smile.

"Hah...all you did was uncollar a hunting dog. I haven't sunk low enough to choose scum like you as my new owner."

"I am so upset you think I'm scum. I am known as a prominent gentleman even among the Thirteen Court Guard Companies, so I would hate to rough up a lady."

"And you think this *isn't* roughing me up, you bastard?!"

Ignoring her objections, Mayuri sighed dramatically and continued, "We've already long finished our research into you Quincies, rare species that you are. Though it was somewhat difficult analyzing the Quincies, who received the divided power of that subspecies Yhwach...or would it be more accurate to say 'pure breed'...finalizing the results was easy enough because we had enough samples. Had we not, we would have simply analyzed you until you were nothing more than goo, like our past samples."

Mayuri recalled the numerous ghastly experiments done on Quincies in the past—the days of experiments that had, at times, involved chopping Quincies up, or mashing them, or drilling holes in their skulls while they were still living, or having Quincies roast their own children to death.

No one else could possibly know whether Mayuri didn't conduct those experiments on Candice at present because it was unnecessary in his opinion or because he had had a change of heart concerning experiments. To Candice, who in fact had no idea about the preceding Quincies' terrible fates, those words seemed like yet another bluff.

"I have no idea why this is happening, but if you're done analyzing me, you can hurry up and off me already. But don't think I'll go down without a fight. I'll turn you all into cinders before I go! I'll start with that Ichigo Kurosaki for making a fool outta me!"

Though she spoke those words in a tone of simple banter, Candice's eyes said she was completely prepared to fight until her final moment.

"That man is already long gone from the Soul Society. And he's so naïve that if he saw your current circumstances, I wouldn't put it past him to complain that I was being unreasonable." Mayuri lightly brushed off the woman's death stare and started to slowly slide "carrots" into his words. "In any case, we have no need for specimens for internal research. However, if you are uncooperative in the next battles...In other words, if you don't work with us to evaluate your performance in battle, we will need to stock up on replacements."

"Replacements...?"

When Candice seemed dubious, Mayuri turned an ogling glance toward her and continued. "It seems that the zombie girl and the little glutton girl you were working with have been sneaking around Hueco Mundo of late. Well, we have finished our research into zombies and have our conjectures about the gluttony ability, so I don't have any particular interest in them."

"What..."

At first she hadn't understood what he was saying, but her memory immediately made the connections and the flame of hope that had long disappeared in her once again began to quiver.

"Hey...wait. Lil and Gigi are alive?! Then is Bambi too?!"

"Yes, the bomb girl seems to be still zombified, however. Really, even after showing their faces to me, I cannot believe they wouldn't realize that I inserted tracking bacteria into them. Quincies truly are a heedless bunch."

Mayuri grinned ominously, and Candice hid her faint joy under a veneer of irritation as she raised her voice. "If that's the case, why're you leaving them alone? Other than you, the other Soul Reapers don't have a reason to leave them be, right?"

"Though it is exceedingly unfortunate for me, the Captain General and the others accepted their offer to set up a united battlefront against Yhwach during the war. That means they no longer see them as a hostile force. My, my, though they did it for the purpose of defeating Yhwach, I believe they are being incredibly generous."

"A united front? So they betrayed his majesty?"

Candice was bewildered by the many facts he had relayed to her that she was hearing for the first time.

However, since she had a very clear memory of the sensation of Yhwach attempting to steal her power in the end, she guessed what happened in her own way.

"Actually, I can't believe his majesty actually tried that with us... If that's the case, knowing Lil's personality, she's definitely capable of it..."

As Candice muttered, deep in thought, Mayuri continued to speak. He converted the poison he had inserted into the conversation disguised as information into a sweet treat.

"What do you think? As I am someone who is known to have love running through his veins in place of blood, if you will tell me that you will cooperate, then..."

"I wouldn't be opposed to returning the specimens that have completed their experiments to your fellow Quincies."

≡

PRESENT DAY

In fact, Candice Catnip hadn't believed what Mayuri said. In the first place, she didn't trust Soul Reapers, and of them she especially did not trust Mayuri Kurotsuchi. However, she pretended she was going along with what he was telling her and believed there was significance in having a means of contacting the outside world.

There was a chance she would be able to contact Meninas McAllon, who had also been captured, so they could work together, and she thought the Soul Reapers might leave an opening, perhaps allowing her to reverse the situation if she were able to get into contact with Liltotto and the others who were outside.

Of course, she understood that was overly optimistic, but for Candice, it was enough reason to become a temporary puppet of the Soul Reapers—even if all of that had been a part of Mayuri Kurotsuchi's calculations.

That was exactly why Candice didn't make any adjustments of her own to the work she had been given.

"Render the Fullbringers powerless and secure their bodies."

Though Candice had fought Hollows and Soul Reapers constantly as a Quincy, she didn't know much about Fullbringers. She recalled that Liltotto had once mentioned something about them, but she had judged them simply a minority group with a couple of powers, not even qualifying as a hostile force, and she hadn't really listened.

However, Candice had no intention of letting that cause her regret. No matter what kind of enemy they were, they wouldn't amount to anything against her lightning, and she was confident there was no way they would be able to defend against it. Then again, her confidence had been smashed to smithereens once before in the war with the Soul Reapers, primarily by Ichigo Kurosaki. That was the exact reason why, when her first arrow was blocked by the large sword, the electronic limiter on a girl who was known for her short temper quickly went out of order.

In addition, she would use the equipment that Mayuri had prepared as a base for the shadow teleportation that was characteristic of the Vandenreich, in order to strike her targets with a massive hit of lightning from a short distance.

Though its power had decayed after her Voll Stern Dich had been stolen, she still hit them with her "Electrocution" force, which surpassed the power of natural lightning.

≡

Mayuri Kurotsuchi, who was observing that lightning from a distance, narrowed his eyes and shook his head.

"Good grief, it seems she did not properly understand what 'secure the bodies' means."

She had released the lightning with the intent to reduce her opponents to cinders. Hearing the roar that tore through space itself a few seconds later, Mayuri sighed dully, "I don't remember preserving her so sloppily that it would result in brain decay."

The deep voice of a man emanated from behind him. "Didn't I tell you so? That tomboy doesn't seem to have any grace, so delicate strategies just aren't her thing..."

"Who gave you permission to speak?"

Mayuri pressed a button in his hand without turning, and there was the sound of an electric shock whizzing behind him, then the shrieks of several men and women rang out in unison.

"Ha ha...In the face of ultimate beauty, a shock like this is the same as a spotlight!"

"Grr... Don't make such a fuss of it! Why must we be dragged into this and receive an electric baptism?!"

"Actually, why's Charlotte so ecstatic when she's the main one who got it?!"

"Just when I thought I was getting used to it, he increased the voltage, didn't he...?"

The four of them, who were wearing white Western clothing and exhibited characteristic scars, each praising themselves and complaining, were:

Charlotte Chuhlhourne

Dordoni Alessandro Del Socaccio

Cirucci Sanderwicci

Luppi Antenor.

They were powerful Arrancars who normally wouldn't have existed in the Soul Society. They had been treated as the living dead in the Department of Research and Development for much longer than Candice and the others and were used as both the subjects of experiments and as hunting dogs in the Kurotsuchi Corpse Unit. Their reactions to this situation were varied, with Dordoni and

Cirucci doing the job as though it were their own contract work without submitting mentally, Luppi accepting it half out of resignation, and Charlotte enjoying herself to a certain extent.

"In any case, did we really need to come all the way out here?"

Mayuri casually replied to Dordoni's question without taking his eyes off of the lightning. "You are like suppression equipment for any Quincy subjects that malfunction. Have you realized how generously lenient I am to allow you to breathe air from the outside?"

"If you just need them suppressed, why can't you just use that lightning or poison you're so proud of?"

"Hey, stop saying weird stuff to provoke him. What good will goading him into another shocking do?"

Cirucci voiced her complaints as Luppi scolded her. Meanwhile, a short distance away, Charlotte was posing for mysterious reasons.

"Actually, what about that promise to let us see the orange-haired niño?"

In response to Dordoni's comment, Mayuri shrugged as though he found the thing tedious and replied, "I plan on bringing him along soon. In fact, the target we are capturing this time is a Deputy Soul Reaper like Ichigo Kurosaki... and he is also the man whose thread of life Ichigo Kurosaki himself severed."

When he heard those words, Dordoni's face scrunched.

"Oh... If he killed a human like himself rather than Hollows like us, does that mean he left his naïveté behind? In that case, I can't call him a niño anymore."

"He is a unique specimen to call a human. If I were to elaborate, he is the man who cut down the Quincy Uryu Ishida."

At that point, Cirucci, who hadn't been very interested until then, spoke up. "What?! You're screwing with me! There's no way that irritating four-eyes Quincy could have been killed off so easily by such a nobody!"

"Ah, then that just proves he isn't such a nobody. Well, that is exactly why I ordered the Quincy corpse to go retrieve him this time around."

As Mayuri continued his observations, Luppi looked toward the place where the flash of light had come from and murmured to himself, "There's no retrieving any bodies— they'll be cinders by now."

However, Mayuri showed no obvious sign of being flustered.

"This is quite entertaining, isn't it?"

"Huh? What is that?"

Then, as the smoke rose from that spot and the afterglow that had burned into their eyelids started to fade, the corpse company, starting with Luppi, opened their eyes wide when they saw the vision that replaced it. Mayuri smiled merrily as he compared the scene to the data that flowed from his observation equipment.

"If that's just a fraction of the Fullbring power, it really has caught my attention."

≡

What is this thing?

What am I seeing right now?

Candice, who had been certain of her victory, broke into a cold sweat immediately.

Though it wasn't as powerful as it had once been, that lightning should have been powerful enough to turn even a reasonably strong Soul Reaper into ash. However, when the lightning that she had called forth settled, the forms of the three men who seemed to have survived the lightning strike emerged. But that wasn't what had struck fear into Candice. What had left Candice flabbergasted was the gigantic, thick-rooted tree that seemed to stretch into the air as though it were stabbing at the heavens that had abruptly appeared by the men who were her targets. Though Candice had been the one to surprise attack them, she had at least known her own surroundings. That thing hadn't been there just before she had unleashed her Electrocution.

Damn it! Most of the lightning strike was redirected into the tree!

Most of the thunderbolt that surpassed natural lightning had been absorbed into the ground through the gigantic tree, and the man in the black jacket had brushed any extraneous lightning that broke away using his large sword just as he had before. Before she could take in what had happened, a blade closed in before Candice's eyes.

"*Guh!*"

Candice narrowly leapt backwards as the place she had been was sheared by the blade of the large sword, which glinted silver.

"Huh...?!"

An electric chill ran down Candice's spine.

As she twisted her body and leapt to the side, the attack unleashed by the sword ripped through the reishi in the air and grazed her. The slashing attack plunged through the smoke that came from the gigantic, lightning-singed tree, and eventually pierced the side of a distant hill and blew part of the slope away.

"That was...Ichigo Kurosaki's attack just now!"

"Hunh...? You've fought that guy, little lady?" The man who had unleashed the air-rending slash raised an eyebrow, then he smiled as though to provoke her. "So that's how you dodged it. Got pretty lucky there, didn't ya? You better thank Ichigo for that."

"Whaaaat?! You want me to thank *who*?!"

Though just moments ago she had escaped life-threatening danger, Candice became enraged and lightning coiled around her entire body.

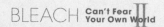

"Oh dear. Aren't you a short-tempered little lady?"

Sighing as he leapt back to make some distance between them, Ginjo glanced at the large, scorched tree standing next to him.

"We've been pretty reckless in our own way."

When Ginjo spoke those words to him, Tsukishima shrugged lightly and replied, "That wasn't anything. I just *nurtured a tree* in my spare time while I was reading. I tried everything I could do while it was a sapling."

"Just how many years ago did you insert yourself into it?" Ginjo said, exasperated.

When their opponent had appeared, Tsukishima had turned his bookmark into a sword using his Fullbring and used his Book of the End ability to cut a tree near him. He inserted himself into the tree's past and gave the tree a twisted form of nourishment in order to turn it into a massive giant.

Tsukishima had used his unique ability in a way that broke the rules and that only had an effect on his target, and the woman who had attacked them seemed unable to comprehend what had happened. If she'd heard the conversation that had just occurred, she might have been able to guess at what his ability was, but the would-be assassin seemed unable to read their lips as a result of the blood rushing to her head.

Well, I'm sure she'd just throw up her hands if we told her all of it was an act.

After their conversation, Ginjo once again guessed at what the woman could be. "You don't look like a Soul Reaper. Since you use a bow, you seem to be a Quincy, but...if you're one of the survivors of those that fought the Soul Reapers, then I don't get why you'd want to attack us. Have you got a connection with Xcution in the living world?"

For the last few days, Ginjo and the others had been going around talking to the newly dead from Japan who had come to the Rukongai in order to gather information on a religious group called Xcution that had recently become well-known in the world of the living.

He had formulated his own theories about it, and since they had been attacked right as he was considering how to contact Yukio or Riruka in the world of the living, he thought that if the enemy wasn't a Soul Reaper, it wouldn't be odd if she was related in some way.

"Why are you spouting nonsense?! No tree is going to protect you now! Just be good and turn into cinders already!"

The Quincy had recovered from her confusion and started a rapid-fire attack using her bow clad in lightning, so Ginjo and the others didn't have time to leisurely analyze the identity of their opponent.

Unknown to Ginjo and the others, lurking a slight distance away, a shadow was carefully observing Candice and the Fullbringers' fight.

"Good grief, that idiot's completely forgotten she's supposed to capture them. I hope I don't get treated like an incompetent by that perverted scientist with her."

The man was wearing the same kind of white clothing as Candice—he was NaNaNa Najahkoop. He was close to being a corpse after one of the Stern Ritter Bazz-B had served him a fatal wound, but Mayuri made him into one of the "rebooted" Quincy.

"Well, make sure to make a good show of crushing each other."

Though he hadn't shown any rebellion toward Yhwach until the very end, now that Yhwach was gone, he prioritized surviving and biding his time for a chance to escape.

"Since I can 'observe' tons."

Being able to see the outside, collared or not, was an opportunity for him, and in order to fully take advantage of this ability, he intended to observe as many Soul Reapers as he could.

The ability of The Underbelly, his "U" Schrift that he had received from Yhwach, Morphine Pattern was a technique that searched for holes in the spiritual pressure of his opponents and could force those to open wider in order to stop the spiritual pressure's operations. Though it had been powerful enough to paralyze all four of Sosuke Aizen's limbs, when he tried to use it against Mayuri, the result had been Mayuri declaring, "There's no point in observing me. Changing your spiritual pressure pattern every second is fundamental."

Since he couldn't actually follow along in his observations with the fluctuations in the patterns, Najahkoop had ended up getting an electric shock from the equipment Mayuri had inserted into the Quincy's body. So, unable to come up with a way to get out of there, he was stuck in his current situation.

"But are those guys what they call Fullbringers?" Najahkoop muttered dubiously about the Fullbringers that Mayuri had ordered him to observe.

"This is my first time seeing them, but...there certainly is something Hollow-like mixed in with the patterns of their spiritual pressure..."

≡

THE WORLD OF THE LIVING, KARAKURA TOWN

"Please wait a moment, Mr. Urahara. Why are you bringing up his name now?"

Urahara saw the agitation on Hisagi's face and pointed it out readily. "Oh, were you acquainted with him? When Miss Kuchiki and the others came to give Mr. Kurosaki his Soul Reaper powers, I believe you weren't present, were you?"

"Well, I just happened to run into him in the Rukongai earlier."

"That's quite the coincidence. He's basically living as a human, so you wouldn't feel anything odd from his spiritual pressure unless you were to fight him."

It really was exactly as Urahara said. When he thought back on it, he normally couldn't tell that there was some other element mixed into Ichigo Kurosaki's spiritual pressure, and it wasn't as though he had the analytical abilities of someone like Urahara or Mayuri Kurotsuchi.

Under these circumstances, he would need to decide whether to believe what Urahara was saying. But if he were to doubt the man now, then the whole entire interview would be pointless. Hisagi resolved himself to his fate and decided to continue his conversation with Urahara on the assumption that what the man was saying was true.

"Does the Fullbring ability have anything to do with this?"

"Yes. Would you like me to review things just a bit from that point?"

When Urahara brushed the edge of the tatami mat, a giant whiteboard dropped down from the ceiling. Alongside unintelligible equations, the board featured sinister-looking drawings of Soul Reapers and, at the top, the title "Strange! Thrillingly Grotesque! How to Make a Demonic Soul Reaper (temp.)!"

"Oops, sorry."

When he pressed a corner of the board, somehow the writing and diagrams that had just been there all neatly disappeared, leaving nothing but the board's pure white, shiny surface.

"All right. First, about the Fullbringers..."

"What was that just now?! You tried to cover it up all casually, but that's a little much!"

"Well, it's quite embarrassing. Demonic Soul Reaper is just a temporary name, so don't worry, I'll come up with a more stylish name to rival the Karakurizer."

"That's not the issue! What even is a Karakurizer?! Also, that just made me remember! After the war ended, Miss Shihoin was looking terrifying as hell, going around asking everyone who went to the Reiokyu 'Did you see me when I fought the last battle?' And when anyone was careless enough to say they did, she seemed to kick them around until their memories were oblivion! Does that have anything to do with this?!"

As Hisagi masterfully employed his great sense of intuition, Urahara averted his eyes and chuckled loudly.

"Well, I was certainly in dire straits after that, but it's not directly related. I suppose you could say that putting my craft to use is all in a day's work..."

Though there were some things he still wasn't clear on, the information on the whiteboard was already gone. Though he believed that Urahara's intention was to calm him, Hisagi had to stop himself from saying something sarcastic.

"Sorry... Please tell me what the Fullbringers are."

"Then how about I get the easy stuff over with first?!"

Hisagi, now calm, watched with unamused eyes as Urahara started to write text on the whiteboard in a carefree manner.

"So in this world, there are several intelligent races. To put it in broad terms, those are the humans, Soul Reapers, Pluses, and Hollows, I suppose. Well, putting aside that Hollows were originally human konpaku, fundamentally, Fullbringers are derived from humans."

"So does that mean they're mutations?"

"I suppose you could say they are forced to mutate through external forces. To put it generally, Mr. Sado and Miss Inoue are also included here."

"Huh?"

When the names of people he knew came up, Hisagi seemed somewhat puzzled. He had heard that they could use skills—Orihime through her hairpin and Chad through the skin of his arms. But what Hisagi had never guessed was that those things would connect them to the Fullbringers.

"But I heard that their powers came from the influence of being near the Hôgyoku..."

"Yes, that's why the events leading up to their becoming that way are slightly different from other Fullbringers. However, only the mechanism was different and their origins and the results are the same."

Drawing a diagram on the whiteboard, Urahara continued with the explanation.

"Fundamentally, Fullbringers were still in the womb when their mothers were attacked by Hollows. If they are able to survive that attack and are safely brought into the world, the children are influenced by the Hollow factor, and it is thought that the possibility their Fullbringer abilities will awaken in the future is high."

"I feel like I've definitely heard that somewhere before... But I'm impressed they'd be able to survive a Hollow attack." Hisagi recalled a time when he had been attacked by a Hollow while powerless, and put that misgiving into words.

"A Soul Reaper or Quincy likely came to their rescue in the nick of time...at least, that would be the conclusion one might naturally come to. But if that were the case, then how aware would the Soul Society have been...about the fact that the children of those pregnant women they had just saved had the potential to become Fullbringers?"

"Oh."

"I also have been gathering all kinds of information on Full-bringers since I learned of their existence, but could it be possible that the Soul Reapers, who have fought Hollows for tens of thousands of years, would not have noticed that before me? I had Miss Amakado look into it, but what seemed to be proof of just that, which had just recently been at Dai Reisho Kairo, seems to have disappeared."

"Well, they're only obligated to keep information about

the Soul Society over there, so I don't think they'd have much on the living world…"

As though to interrupt Hisagi, Urahara brought up the name of a certain organization…

"But how about the Visual Department?"

The temperature in Hisagi's heart plummeted. Over the last few days, he had looked into many things in his own way. Among those were activities relating to the time period when the Tsunayashiro family had established the Visual Department.

"Is that why you're telling me about this now?"

"It wouldn't be strange to think you'd know something. Well, I'm not the one who needs to do the rest of the work now—that's the job of a journalist with a backbone."

"So then the Fullbringers…or rather Ginjo and the others… are also involved with the Tsunayashiro family in some way?"

What came to Hisagi's mind was the reason Ginjo had given him for why the Fullbringer betrayed the Soul Society. If the Tsunayashiro family were involved, he could understand why Kyoraku had told him he wanted to "wait a bit.

"Whoa there, don't have such a stern expression! Jinta might actually wet his pants if he came home to that!"

While jokingly scolding Hisagi, Urahara continued to speak as though he were a child up to some sort of trick. "But a guess is nothing more than that. This is all the information I can give to you as of *right now*. I have several other conjectures, but in the unthinkable chance that I'm mistaken, I'd be causing a great deal of trouble to many people. On account of that, I'd like a bit more information to settle my guesses."

"In other words, you want information from me too?"

"I've asked Miss Yoruichi for the same. I'd like data from all angles. As a matter of fact, what you just told me about that child Hikone was an extraordinarily useful data point. Thank you very much."

"I feel like you're getting the better of me, but I understand. If you're willing to put your trust in me as a journalist and a Soul Reaper, then I'll do what I can."

With that acceptance from Hisagi, Urahara opened his folding fan and put on his businessman's smile.

"Well, what do we have here? Looks like we've got ourselves a deal! I suppose we'll be badgers in the same hole for many years to come!"

Was I being a little too hasty...?

With that thought, Hisagi mentioned something that suddenly came to his mind. "Actually, what's the relationship between Fullbringers and Hollows? Oh, I don't mean their origins, but their current power dynamic..."

"Their parents were attacked by Hollows, so I'd guess there would at least be some ties between them. I'm sure that Hollows also vary in whether they'd be cautious or amused upon seeing humans with the same traits as them."

Urahara shook his head as he thought of the Arrancars he knew.

"Well, ultimately we have to take it on a case by case basis."

"Since there has been an increase of fairly thoughtful Arrancars lately."

≡

THE SOUL SOCIETY, THE RUKONGAI OUTSKIRTS

At the far reaches of the Rukongai, piercing thunder rang out countless times.

Of course, the neighboring residents hadn't approached after the first lightning strike and everyone had sequestered in their homes to hide. Naturally, the lightning had been observed from the Seireitei, but Mayuri had recently put in a "Petition to perform Department of Research and Development experiments," so none of the Soul Reapers came to check on what was happening.

Given that, because of the continuing, bombastic thunder, Ginjo and the others had missed hearing something incredibly important: the sound of the gigantic tree, which had been standing upright just moments before, being snapped by something's fist.

"No, no, Candy."

Along with the leisurely voice of a woman, *something* came fluttering down from the sky.

"Your orders were to capture them, so I think you'll get in trouble if you burn them..."

Ginjo and the others, who realized that a shadow had appeared over their heads, looked up to see a Quincy holding the broken tree in one hand and dropping it.

"Hey, how can you be so stupid strong?" Ginjo asked in exasperation as the lightning-scorched tree came down on him.

With a rumble, the ground quivered and a dust cloud rose around them.

"Are you an idiot, Minnie?! We'll get in trouble if you crush them too!" Candice opened her eyes wide as she yelled at Meninas McAllon, the holder of the "P" Schrift for "The Power," who had appeared as her reinforcement.

"But if all I do is crush them, I think that weird scientist would still be able to do somethin' with them..."

"Then he'd be able to fix them up even if I burned them! Well, it doesn't matter. Anyway, we need to use this chance to try getting in contact with Lil and the others..." Just then, a crushing sound resonated from the tree on the ground.

"Huh?!"

"No way! Nobody other than Minnie can do something like that..."

Just as the name suggested, Meninas's ability, "The Power," was unadulterated and mighty brute strength. In a simple contest of strength, Meninas's power was analyzed to likely be unbeatable even by Kenpachi Zaraki, but in the

next moment, a "power" that rivaled hers slung the scorched tree into the air.

"Ah!"

Meninas and Candice dodged it narrowly. In front of their eyes was a man whose silhouette had completely transformed from earlier.

"*Phew...* Looks like this time we're just facing some strong-armed blockhead."

Based on his eyepatch, it seemed as though this was the slim man who had been wearing a gentlemanly outfit until just a moment ago.

However, his height currently seemed to exceed five meters and his silhouette had transformed into that of a huge Hollow with swelled and distorted muscles. He looked strong enough that they guessed that not only had he stopped the gigantic tree, but had also thrown it back at them.

Facing the eyepatch-wearing man who had become a beefcake in front of her, Meninas, who had been called "a strong-armed blockhead," vacantly said the first thing that came to her mind: "I think swelled-up muscles like those are gross..."

"When you really go all out, Minnie, your arms and everything end up looking like that too..."

For his part, Ginjo scowled when he saw his companion Giriko's transformation.

"You stop making a big show of things too, oi. Actually, what was that about 'this time'?"

Come to think of it, I never asked Kutsuzawa how he died.

As Ginjo considered that, Giriko acted in a way that was the reverse of his usual calm, gentlemanly self, speaking excitedly about his powers. "Ginjo, I made a mistake. In order to properly wear the god of time's power on my own body, I must have a clear offering of time to give!"

"R-right."

"Yes, what governs over my Time Tells No Lies is *time*! I will offer the vast amounts of time that Tsukishima inserted into that gigantic tree to the infinite torrents of time, and pure strength has roosted within me! I will not make the same blunder as before! Now, let me thoroughly demonstrate this power I have received from god!"

"Why're you getting so worked up about this...?"

Beside Ginjo, who was at a loss as to how to react, Tsukishima smiled thinly as he shook his head.

"What am I going to do after you've gone and offered the past I inserted?"

Just as he and Giriko had expected, the gigantic tree that had been thrown into the air had, at some point, shrunk back into a small tree and was shattering into pieces as it fell. Taking that as a sign, the enemy Quincies started to make their move.

"Your blustering ends now! No matter how this goes, you're all getting the death penalty!"

"Again, I don't think we can kill them when we're on a mission to capture them…"

Candice poked fun as Meninas started to thrash the man with the eyepatch who had become a giant clad in muscle armor. Her arm, which swelled like a gigantic log and creaked with strength, swung down diagonally as though it were spring-loaded.

"*Mgh!*"

Though he wrapped his enlarged hand around it, the gigantic man's balance crumbled under the attack that had come at him with the force of a cannon.

"Oho, if you're able to make me stagger, then you can at least talk."

"I haven't actually said anything though."

Meninas tilted her head quizzically for a moment, then unleashed several consecutive attacks using her arms as the upper half of her body turned. The man with the eyepatch continued to receive and handle them without breaking a sweat, as the ground started to crack beneath them. When Giriko's gigantic knee sank into it for a moment, Meninas found a good opening to add on a powerful strike. However, in response the man straightened his leg all at once and released his power into the ground as though he had been waiting for it.

"Feel it with your own body! Know that you cannot budge the flow of time with strikes that lack reverence to god!"

"*Uh!*"

What came in the form of a simple diagonal shoulder tackle from below was accompanied with a sound like the impact of a train striking a large cow as it blew Meninas high into the air.

Giriko tried to use his Fullbring right away, on the ground and atmosphere, but countless arrows pierced him and at the same time, high-voltage lightning rushed through him.

"*Mgh?!*"

"Hah! You know what a giant is? A good target!"

Though even more arrows came flying, Ginjo, who had come out in front, brushed them all off.

"You're being too careless, Kutsuzawa. Making yourself big just makes you a more convenient mark for the Quincies."

"Not at all. There's no need to worry about me. The power I gained through the contract should hold back even the pain from a lightning strike."

It seemed he really hadn't taken much damage from the arrows that pierced him. However, on the other side, Meninas also looked unfazed when she landed after being blown high into the sky.

"Guess that's all there is to it...I'll make a distraction. While I do that, Tsukishima, you *insert* yourself into one of them."

"Yeah, all right. If I look into their pasts, I should be able to figure out exactly what their goal is."

Ginjo, who had judged that if they kept things up it would simply be a battle of wills on both sides, planned to coordinate and end things early, but...

He sensed a strong presence rising up from the distance, one that seemed to be ridiculing the fight itself.

≡

"Captain! We've found an anomaly in the reishi! Three spirit miles to the west-northwest...a garganta's about to open!"

When Mayuri heard the radio report from Rin Tsubokura, he turned his eyes dubiously in the specified direction. A garganta—it was the method of transportation characteristic of Hollows. Its peculiar shape brought to mind a jaw opening in the atmosphere.

"An Arrancar, then. I've seen this turn of events before."

Just glancing at the data that had been sent over to him, Mayuri immediately knew the identity of the foe they were dealing with.

"It isn't that plaything of the Four Great Noble Clans. This one is a genuine Arrancar."

Mayuri's eyes narrowed then, and as though he'd had a sudden memory of someone's face, he continued in a disappointed tone, "Good grief, Ichigo Kurosaki isn't even here. Every last one of them is such a nuisance. Really now."

≡

The garganta had opened far into the west. The white silhouette that had appeared there manipulated their body through the Soul Society exactly like one of Candice's bolts of lightning—just like a predator rushing directly into the savannah after spotting its prey.

"Huh!"

"Uh?!"

They had likely noticed the strong presence of Arrancar approaching them. The Quincies and Fullbringers who had been battling at the outskirts of the Rukongai simultaneously turned their attention toward it. It was a presence too formidable for them to ignore and focus on their fight. More importantly, it was heading straight toward them with seemingly malicious intent.

Before Ginjo and the others could prepare themselves and attempt to figure out the identity of their opponent...

There was wind.

A blue-haired beast surrounded by a surge of wind tore strikingly through the air of the battlegrounds. Bulldozing through lightning and the gigantic boulders the Quincies had thrown and turning them into powder on the way, the figure rushed into the middle of the battleground. Then the wind subsided and within the thinning dust storm a single Arrancar revealed himself.

"What is with this?"

The Arrancar, who was muttering as he showed up, didn't seem very interested in the cautiously steeled Quincies and Fullbringers before him.

"I came here 'cause I thought I felt the presence of something *mixed*, but it ended up being *neither* of 'em."

He observed Ginjo as though appraising him, then eventually, as if remembering his purpose there, the Arrancar who had caused everything to freeze said arrogantly, "Well, never mind. Kurosaki wasn't the target today."

Grimmjow Jaegerjaquez.

His sudden appearance had turned this into the most chaotic location in the Soul Society at present.

Soul Reapers.

Quincies.

Arrancars.

Fullbringers.

Each of these groups had once been an enemy of Ichigo Kurosaki, and they seemed to be meeting here in the Soul Society, the base of the Soul Reapers. Was it a coincidence or was it an inevitability?

Grimmjow, who had appeared as though he were drawn to the center of calamity, made a single demand to Kugo Ginjo, whom he had determined was the strongest of the lineup currently in front of his eyes.

"You better hurry up and tell that kid Hikone that I came to finish what the little brat started."

CHAPTER EIGHT

HUECO MUNDO

"...GRIMMJOW DISAPPEARED?"

They were in Las Noches, the place in Hueco Mundo that Aizen had once held as his base. Although their fights with the Soul Reapers, starting with Ichigo Kurosaki, had left the walls and spires caved in here and there, the Arrancars were still able to take up residence in the place and make it their base. In a corner of what had once been their royal castle, Tier Halibel questioned Rudobon emotionlessly as she listened to his report.

"Do you know where he was headed?"

"Yes. He was witnessed using a garganta, so I believe he must have been heading to the world of the living or to the Soul Society."

Then another woman's voice rang out from behind Halibel. "He couldn't have gone out looking to fight Ichigo, right?"

The woman was Nelliel Tu Odelschwanck, who had come to discuss the future path of Hueco Mundo and the Arrancars.

"If Grimmjow rampages in the world of the living, we'll have a disaster on our hands. We must stop him immediately, or else..."

"Most humbly, Lady Nelliel, may I propose that Lord Grimmjow is the type to wait prudently for his opportunity, despite how he may seem. If he were truly only wishing to enjoy a fight for pleasure, I believe he would likely have already visited Karakura Town in this last half-year."

Nelliel seemed somewhat puzzled at Rudobon's response.

"You think so...? He looks to me like he pretty much acts according to his mood."

Halibel then voiced her own opinion of Grimmjow. "He must have his own conception of pride. He was defeated in a battle in which each side's self-respect was on the line. He wouldn't simply attack without just cause."

"Either way, he seems to act on his feelings in the moment. Well, be that as it may, he really did back down without a fight when I told him to earlier, I suppose..."

When they had reunited with Ichigo in the Soul Society, Nelliel had been incredibly wary of Grimmjow starting a fight with Ichigo, but she recalled that in the end, they had been on the same side despite being enemies.

Normally, she would have thought she would need to use everything in her power to stop Grimmjow, but it was somewhat unexpected to Nelliel that Grimmjow would have laid down his arms before she needed to intervene.

"Grimmjow is a man with strong animalistic instincts. For him to leave Hueco Mundo, the territory he is supposed to protect, he must have had a good reason."

When Halibel said that, Nelliel remembered something more. During the war between Quincies and Soul Reapers, when Grimmjow had sided with Ichigo, Ichigo had asked him, *"Why are you on our side?"* Back then, the simple reply Grimmjow let slip was, *"If Hueco Mundo's gone, where would I kill you?"* From his words back then, Nelliel could conclude that his priority was to settle things in Hueco Mundo.

Is it because Hueco Mundo is more advantageous to Arrancars?

No, Grimmjow isn't the type to consider that.

Or perhaps it is that he has strong feelings about it too.

Maybe he senses the Hollow factor with its roots still firmly set inside Ichigo.

That was exactly why Ichigo Kurosaki was able to demonstrate his maximum strength in Hueco Mundo, where the Hollow factor was dense. He likely thought that there was significance in defeating Ichigo while in that state. Or was it just for the simple reason that he wanted to be somewhere spacious where they could unleash their power to its fullest extent, without anything getting in their way? Nelliel tried to hypothesize what was going on in Grimmjow's head from all vantage points, but she realized that no matter how she sought to find the answer, the man in question wasn't around.

"So where has Grimmjow gone, and what's he up to?"

"He either went to crush the surviving Quincies or went in pursuit of that odd Soul Reaper from before."

"Then he *has* left his turf."

"In other words, he probably has a 'good reason.' In truth, I also was concerned about that Soul Reaper child."

Halibel remembered the Soul Reaper-like boy—or girl— who had cut in during their fight with the Quincy survivors and a faintly somber expression came over her face. She remarked, "More specifically, it was the zanpaku-to that Soul Reaper held that concerns me."

≡

THE SOUL SOCIETY

Naturally, the spiritual pressure from the strong Arrancar that had appeared from the garganta did not go unnoticed by the Seireitei either, and several of the Soul Reapers in the vicinity of the east gate sensed the appearance of the Hollow. The seated classes in particular, which excelled at detecting spiritual pressure, recognized that the Hollow was clad in a spiritual pressure greater than a Menos Grande and

immediately informed their superiors as they broke out in chills. In the end they were informed it was part of an experiment being conducted by the Twelfth Company; many Soul Reapers were relieved, though some portion of them were instead seized with a strong sense of anxiety upon finding out the Twelfth Company was involved. Someone in the captain class directly sensed that spiritual pressure.

"Hm? What's that? I'm suddenly feeling a tremendous Hollow spiritual pressure."

Shinji Hirako, captain of the Fifth Company, turned his eyes in the direction from which he had sensed the spiritual pressure with a repulsed look on his face.

"This spiritual pressure...I've experienced it in the past in Karakura Town as well."

He mulled this over with Momo Hinamori by his side. She had gotten the particulars through communications with the observation room but seemed troubled and glowered as she said to Hirako, "Captain, I just made contact with the observation room of the Department of Research and Development, but their response was that it's part of an experiment and not an issue..."

"Ah, of course. So it's one of the Twelfth Company's usual experiments then. I'm sure they've just called in an Arrancar for a tea party or something. Oh, the Department of Research and Development has it so easy now that they don't have someone like Hiyori as their assistant captain and lab chief... There's no freaking way that's the case! Are they idiots?! A garganta opened and an Arrancar-level Hollow has made its way in! No problem, my ass!"

After this angry bout of sarcasm, he gave the flustered Hinamori her instructions. "Well, in any case, a normal soldier going up against an Arrancar is pretty much suicide. I'm going to the place in question myself, and I'll leave reporting that to the Captain General to you, Momo."

"Y-yes, sir! Captain Hirako, please be careful!"

"Well, frankly, I think facing the Twelfth Company would be much more dangerous than any Arrancar."

≡

At the same moment that Hirako sighed with apprehension, a particular Arrancar wore delight on his face.

"He's here..."

An Arrancar with the physical appearance of a young boy spoke up in a voice filled with childlike joy. "Oh...sorry, everybody. Looks like I'm going to meet my goal before anyone else."

A sadistic smile came over Luppi's face as he turned and spoke to the Arrancars behind him. Though his eyes glittered like those of an innocent child who has found some treasure, the spiritual pressure that oozed from him was intermingled with blatant, murderous rancor.

"That spiritual pressure…it couldn't be Master Grimmjow's?!"

In lieu of a reply to Dordoni, Luppi kicked at the ground forcefully.

"Hey! Hold it! If you act on your own, then he'll do it again…!"

Although Cirucci tried to stop Luppi, anticipating an electric shock from Mayuri would be forthcoming, before they knew it Luppi had already leapt up and broken away to a distance where their voices would reach him. However, there wasn't any sign of an electric current running through him or through Cirucci and the others. When the Arrancars turned toward Mayuri suspiciously, they saw he held his finger over the button as he smiled good-naturedly and said, "Hm… He's out of line, but I'm interested to know why that Arrancar is here…as well as how the Fullbringers and Quincies will act when faced with multiple Arrancars."

Then, muttering to himself as well as to the Arrancars behind him, he said, "If you'd like, I also wouldn't mind if you all got involved in the fight."

"Oh, it's not as though we're battle-crazy. Whether there's a reason to fight is dependent upon whether there's beauty in it… Grimmjow is a bit too crude to show beauty. Well, I suppose once you're at my level, he might seem beautiful like a wild rose."

Mayuri ignored Charlotte's opinions as he watched Luppi leave. Then the scientist smirked and he turned his attention toward Grimmjow.

"That Hollow seems to have been in league with Kisuke Urahara…He couldn't possibly be pulling the strings behind the scenes, could he?"

☰

URAHARA SHOTEN

"Come to think of it, Mr. Urahara, do you still have ties to those…Arrancars?"

Hisagi had suddenly thought of and posed this risky question to Urahara; it was about the alliance that Urahara had arbitrarily made with Arrancars themselves when he had gone to Hueco Mundo. In the worst-case scenario, it could have resulted in the Soul Society charging him with another crime. However, there was no question that in the huge battle that followed, the Arrancars had been a factor in the Quincies' defeat. Though he didn't know about Central 46, Hisagi judged that Captain General Kyoraku wasn't likely to reproach him about it, so Hisagi asked the question as a Soul Reaper.

"Well, in order to keep the peace, you need to keep a couple of channels of negotiation open. Unlike those nice Quincies who believe in total Hollow erasure, a Soul Reaper's ultimate goal is supposed to be to keep the balance."

"At the same time, they're also the group responsible for slaughters here in the past. Are you convinced it was right to do that?"

"Hueco Mundo's currently being run by moderates like Miss Halibel and Miss Nelliel. Mr. Grimmjow is certainly belligerent, but, well, he's not the type who rampages for no reason."

As a matter of fact, the activities of Yammy, an Arrancar who went on a massive murdering spree in Karakura Town, had ceased. It was said he fought Byakuya Kuchiki and Kenpachi Zaraki, so the probability that he would have survived such a battle was low. Hisagi felt slightly troubled accepting this in order to keep the conversation going.

"To be honest, I feel conflicted about that. Though I've certainly taken to heart the teachings that Hollows are not absolutely evil and are instead souls that Soul Reapers should purify…"

"The Arrancars that Sosuke Aizen had as his pawns are an exception?"

"I'm not that easily convinced. Whether they're Hollows or humans or Soul Reapers…they were the ones who worked with Aizen in order to damage the world."

The moment he said the words "Soul Reapers," Hisagi thought of a specific person, but he kept it close to his chest. Urahara, seemingly not noticing Hisagi's behavior, didn't tease him and answered indifferently, "The strong Arrancars in Hueco Mundo are the aggregations of several tens of thousands—or hundreds of millions—of konpaku. Whether it's the result of them all mixing together, or the result of one strong individual overtaking the will of the others, the resulting Arrancars have their own beliefs. That's exactly why, if we can understand their way of thinking...even just a tiny fraction of it, if there's a part of them that agrees with us, negotiations are possible."

Hearing that, Hisagi recalled the Arrancars he had fought in the past. There were certainly some who were more humanlike, rather than like the Hollows who were thoughtless and had lost all sense of logic. And if they weren't distinguishing between friend and foe he could at least have had a conversation with them, even if they rubbed him the wrong way. And above all, even the man he had thought was correct in his convictions had turned himself into an Arrancar in the end, hadn't he?

At that point in Hisagi's thoughts, Urahara stated the conclusion that followed, "Of course, knowing that, when they become your enemy, you must cut them down without hesitation. That's what the Thirteen Court Guard Companies teaches, isn't it?"

"Yes...It is."

Once again burdened by this reality, Hisagi drew a breath. It forced him to recall memories of the moment he had cut down a certain enemy. The memory revived itself vividly from within Hisagi—the feeling of thrusting his zanpaku-to into the head of his opponent to take him by surprise and simply reaping a life.

As though testing Hisagi, Urahara spoke out loud the name of that enemy: "You can't possibly be having regrets, can you, about killing Mr. Tosen?"

Hisagi sensed that the tone of Urahara's voice had changed. This question was not being posed by the owner of Urahara Shoten but by a former Thirteen Court Guard Companies member, and one who, though imperfect, had served in the past as a captain.

"No, I don't have any of those."

Hisagi didn't hesitate for a moment to speak those words as an actively serving assistant captain.

"If I regretted it, then I would have already put down my zanpaku-to."

Though there was no doubt in those words, Hisagi hadn't been able to come to terms with the way things were to the extent that he could abandon all his feelings either.

With his eyes turned slightly down, Hisagi reproached himself about his own incompetence.

"It's just...I still think about how I could have persuaded him to see reason, even now. I don't regret anything, but I don't want the same thing to happen ever again. I don't want to say this, but if someone other than me had..."

"Let's stop right there. Thinking about other possible paths does connect us to the hereafter. But seeking that from others is pointless."

Urahara cut off the conversation and bluntly admonished Hisagi, "That 'someone other than you' wasn't there at the time. The people who had the right to change something were only the ones who were there. You stuck with your own principles. Don't you think that's enough?"

"..."

"Well, Mr. Kurosaki, Miss Inoue, and the others could certainly have different principles than those of the Thirteen Court Guard Companies, but I think that itself is a strength of theirs that's different from ours. Protecting the thing you want to protect in the end is what we deem satisfactory."

So what I want to protect, huh?

In response to Urahara's words, Hisagi once again considered what he had protected.

What I wanted to protect was not Captain Tosen. It was his teachings...

It was what he had taught me as part of the Thirteen Court Guard Companies about how a Soul Reaper should be.

The Court Guards—they were the ones who protected the Seireitei.

The Seireitei—so named, the court was where things were governed and judgements were given. It truly managed the world expansively—in other words, it represented justice. It was the conviction of the Soul Reapers that protected the fairness of the world.

In the end, that was why he had ended up killing Tosen. He had believed that stopping Tosen was the legacy of the teachings he had received from him as a Soul Reaper.

The issue wasn't whether he had been right or not, and as he had declared to Urahara, he had no regrets about the killing of Tosen itself. That was because he realized that to give in to regret would be a slight to the Soul Reapers he fought alongside as well as to Tosen himself.

However, despite that, the fact that Hisagi had been the one to cut Tosen down was engraved on Hisagi's soul and was slowly working its way into him, giving him a continuous, vague sense of dread.

Since he had killed the very person who had guided his life, he felt like he himself might end up changing. Or that he might already have changed without even knowing it.

Hisagi could not deny the chill that had coiled around his spine, and he steadied his breath. "No, what's different is my weakness. That's exactly why I have to apologize to Kurosaki and the others…"

He realized at that moment that something was amiss. At some point, Urahara had come to be holding the sword cane that was his zanpaku-to, and he seemed tense as he stared off in an entirely different direction.

"Huh? Mr. Urahara?"

"I'm sorry to interrupt, Mr. Hisagi."

He apologized lightly, but his gaze, which seemed to be directed far into the distance, was filled with caution.

"Have you prepared for Gentei Kaijo?"

"Huh?"

When Soul Reapers with powers above the assistant captain level headed into the living world, they were required by law to seal away part of their powers. That was a measure to prevent their strong spiritual pressure from having an ill influence on spirits in the living world, and Hisagi, who hadn't intended to battle, had that measure put into place already. As a result, Hisagi's spiritual pressure had dropped to 20 percent of its usual strength. He immediately realized that Urahara was asking whether he could release that seal, and the string of tension wound its way around his mind.

"Is it...an enemy? If we're up against a dangerous opponent, I'll request a Gentei Kaijo immediately."

"I'm still not quite sure whether they harbor any ill will, but...it seems we're surrounded."

"You mean they're surrounding the shop?"

Though he could feel the disruption of an eerie spiritual pressure when he searched for it, he couldn't find specific Reiraku. However, though the storefront was small, if they were surrounding it, then there would be just that many presences. The memory of when he had been surrounded by huge Hollows revived itself in Hisagi's mind. He recalled

the pain and fearsome time when he had lost his friend Kanisawa. However, Urahara's reply caused his memories to fade instantly.

"No... If they'd come that close, I would have noticed them a while ago."

"Huh?"

"It isn't the store they've got surrounded."

Urahara stood up slowly and quietly opened the sliding door.

"*Something* is surrounding all of Karakura Town."

≡

A CERTAIN PLACE IN THE SEIREITEI

"Now what could this be? Who would have thought an Espada would leap right into the palm of my hand?"

A man with a mirthful smile on his face was encircled by many monitors in a dark room. At first glance, the place seemed to be the Twelfth Company's observation room, but the equipment in the room seemed more out of place than it would have been in the Department of Research and Development.

Tokinada Tsunayashiro, who was the one and only person with absolute control over that place, looked at the reishi signals on the monitors with interest as he said to himself, "That's an Arrancar that came during the Quincy attack. I'm not sure whether to call this a coincidence or an unexpected inevitability."

When Tokinada quietly stood up, he held his hand over the flame of a candle nearby. Then he spoke to something on the other end of the candlestick, which appeared to be a communications device.

"Hikone."

He spoke plainly, and the candlestick's flame flickered immediately.

"Yes, Lord Tokinada!"

A voice whose innocent tone didn't seem to fit the place's atmosphere reverberated from the candlestick.

"Did you call me?! Mr. Yamada was kind enough to heal me completely! I think that I will be able to fulfill your expectations this time, Lord Tokinada!"

"Don't be foolish. You haven't betrayed my expectations. If I expect you to fail, then you will fail perfectly."

"Lord Tokinada?"

"Your earlier defeat only served to fuel you and Ikomikidomoe." Though you may become almighty, you are not omnipotent. In order to avoid a fatal blow due to self-conceit, you must experience defeat at least once. Your fight in Hueco Mundo a while ago was only that."

Snickering, Tokinada asked Hikone, "Do you resent me because I expected you to lose, Hikone?"

"No! I'm not very smart, so I don't really understand, but if you say so, Lord Tokinada, then I am very happy! I'll make sure to live up to your expectations from here on out too, Lord Tokinada!"

"I see. I wouldn't have minded whether you scorned me or not. After all, you are the future king. Seeing, hearing the name of, or being aware of the presence of a worthless aristocrat like me will likely become annoying to you. Remaining in your memory, if only because of spite, is preferable to that."

"What are you saying?! I would never forget you, Lord Tokinada! Especially since I never would have been born if it hadn't been for you, Lord Tokinada! And you were the one who said we should be equals earlier, Lord Tokinada!"

Tokinada sensed not only denial in Hikone's words but also a plea, and his smile twisted all the more sadistically. "I see. Thank you, Hikone. I'm glad to hear from you that you would like us to be equals as well."

"Yes, Lord Tokina—"

However, at that moment, as though to cut off Hikone's joy-filled voice, an entirely new voice came over the communications device from the other side, butting in.

"Don't make me laugh."

It was a voice of bleak and dour scorn.

"If you think you are equal to this brat, you haven't put even a shred of thought into it."

Far different from Hikone's brilliant, cheery voice, the speaker's tone was filled with suspicion and malice.

*"Stop that, **Ikomikidomoe**! How could you say that to Lord Tokinada?"*

Following that were some moments filled with the sounds of a conflict, and just as those sounds eventually settled down, Hikone's voice came across the communications device.

"I apologize, Lord Tokinada! I finally got him to be quiet!"

"It's fine, Hikone. Ikomikidomoe was never an Asauchi you yourself set free into a zanpaku-to, after all. Just like my Kuten Kyokoku—Heaven Mirror Valley—and the Ise family's Hakkyokenn—Eight Mirror Sword—it's something you inherited from others. I think it will likely take a bit more time for the blade to understand you."

"I don't mind even if it doesn't understand me! But I would be so sad for you to be misunderstood, Lord Tokinada!"

"I see. You're so kindhearted, Hikone. However, I am not the one who will use Ikomikidomoe. Actually, I cannot use it."

Though Tokinada spoke as if he were soothing a child, his eyes shone with the glint of a sadist preparing to torment a small animal. The voice-only communications device couldn't convey that and continued to deliver Tokinada's casual voice to Hikone in the child's distant location.

"I think the only ones able to handle that zanpaku-to would likely be someone like you or Ichigo Kurosaki, or…well, actually…" His next words were deliberate. "Perhaps Kugo Ginjo might also be able to use it."

"Mr. Ginjo? I've heard his name before! Is he strong?"

"In that case, why don't you check for yourself? Actually, that's another reason I contacted you."

Tokinada checked on the observations he had from a part of the Rukongai—where an eddy of spiritual pressure had been jumbling together for some time—and urged Hikone to take voluntary action.

"At this moment, an Arrancar man you previously fought against has arrived. In addition, Ginjo and the others are there."

"What?!"

"This is your opportunity to demonstrate to them you are the king. You should fly to their location and show them this time that you are capable of being king."

Hiding the rapacious smile behind his words, Tokinada gently persuaded Hikone.

"I expect you to win this time, Hikone."

"Please leave it to me, Lord Tokinada!"

After directing Hikone to the aforementioned location, Tokinada extinguished the flame of the candlestick that had been acting as a communications device, and the room echoed with words he spoke to himself. "Ikomikidomoe… what is most important is that it seems your 'nurturing' is going well."

Recalling the vehement voice that had come through earlier, Tokinada looked over the many measurement devices
and smiled—sneered—savored.

Then, as he looked at another set of equipment observing
a place that was entirely separate from the Rukongai, where
Hikone had headed, Tokinada's eyes narrowed faintly as he
said, "So they've made their move in Karakura Town. I see.
What a prudent decision."

He was looking over the vast amounts of data pouring in
through the Visual Department's equipment about Karakura
Town, an important sacred ground in the living world.

Analyzing the flow of reishi from the entire town,
Tokinada again muttered to himself, "There is likely no other
opportunity to seize that Jureichi other than this.

"This is the only opportunity—when Ichigo Kurosaki is
out of town."

≡

THE SOUL SOCIETY
THIRTEEN COURT GUARD COMPANIES,
FIRST COMPANY BARRACKS

"Thank you for the report. We will launch an investigation
from our side as well, so please wait for word from Captain
Hirako in a station nearby, Momo."

"Y-yes, sir!"

After watching Hinamori bow in a flurry and run off, Shunsui Kyoraku, the Captain General of the Thirteen Court Guard Companies, exhaled quietly and muttered to himself, "Seems like this really has become an ordeal, hasn't it?"

Having uttered his favorite phrase, assistant captain Nanao Ise picked up the documents and reported, "There certainly was an advance petition from the Twelfth Company to use Quincy and Arrancar *corpses* for an experiment. I believe that is likely the usual 'Kurotsuchi Corpse Unit' though...

"Oh...that. I'm dubious about how humane it is. Well, it's not like pretty words will serve all our needs, though. It was enough that he cured Captain Hitsugaya and the others from zombie-ism."

"But, according to the information from Assistant Captain Hinamori just now..."

"Yeah, it's likely that Arrancar is separate from the ones that the Twelfth Company is keeping. Though I can't sense the spiritual pressure myself from here to confirm it. Well then, I wonder who has come here and with what purpose," Kyoraku said anxiously, then gave instructions to Okikiba, his other assistant captain.

"Anyway, Okikiba, if you could please get word out to the Second Company immediately and have them dispatch the Survey Company. If the Twelfth Company complains, I don't mind you bringing up my name and pushing this through by telling them it's an order from the Captain General."

"As you wish."

Though his instructions to the older Okikiba were casual in tone, Kyoraku's eyes reflected his determination to protect the Seireitei as the Captain General. It wasn't simply the sparkle of optimism—his look also included the conviction to sacrifice something in order to protect everything else. He looked ready to endure whatever came his way.

"Good grief. It's been half a year since the war, but it's something I still haven't gotten used to."

Since becoming Captain General, Kyoraku had come to learn more and more about the world.

He came to know realities that were wide-ranging, from understanding the Seireitei's dark side to purposefully sacrificing a part of the Rukongai in order to protect the world's balance. And in this way he continuously encountered an infinite menagerie of things he had more or less expected and things that were entirely outside of his imagination.

So old man Yama was the intermediary between us and the world and under this pressure for a thousand years.

How must he have felt when giving the order to execute Rukia Kuchiki?

How must he have felt when he decided to treat Inoue as a traitor after she had gone to Hueco Mundo?

How had it felt when he had sacrificed his own arm?

How had he felt when he turned his zanpaku-to on Kyoraku and Ukitake while shouldering the Soul Society's laws?

These were things he couldn't know now that he had arrived here in the present, and old man Yama loomed too large in his mind for him to imagine it. There was no need for him to walk the same path as Genryusai Yamamoto. However, as long as he was the Captain General, it was assured that the time to make a choice would come. There would likely be many occasions when he wouldn't have enough time to prepare himself. Just as in the past, when he had thrust the possibility that resided in Ichigo Kurosaki's future at the children who were the boy's school friends.

How much would he forsake in order to protect the Seireitei or the world?

Old man Yama was way too serious, after all. He might have been prepared every day of his life for what was to come.

Beneath what had seemed to be callous decisions there had likely been hundreds or thousands of other choices. Kyoraku, who had come to represent the very thing those choices had protected, smiled painfully as his reverence for his mentor continued to grow even deeper.

"Now that I'm in the same position, just when I thought I'd arrived at where he was, it feels like he's so far away. You really were such a strict teacher to your pupils, old man Yama."

≡

THE WORLD OF THE LIVING, URAHARA SHOTEN

"Kurosaki's not here?!"

Hisagi, whose distress was obvious in his voice, was met with an indifferent confirmation from Urahara. "Yeah, did I not mention that? Mr. Kurosaki has been on a trip with family and friends since yesterday."

"On a trip?! *That's* why he's not here?!"

When the town was first being confined by a mystery presence, before Hisagi had requested more detailed information, he had proposed, "First we should get word out to the Soul Reapers in charge of this sector. I don't want to involve them if we're the ones being targeted, but since we don't know what they're after, let's at least get in contact with Kurosaki and the others." However, when he then came to learn that Ichigo Kurosaki was absent, his spirits were dampened right away.

"Actually, I'm surprised that you didn't know, Mr. Hisagi. Miss Kuchiki, Mr. Abarai and the others are supposed to be traveling with him."

"Now that you mention it, I feel like I haven't seen Abarai and the others for the last few days..."

"It's a Jureichi in western Japan. It's not as important as Karakura Town, but it's probably the third most likely place in Japan for spirits to gather. Mr. Kurosaki and his younger sisters ended up going there..." He seemed to be distracted by his preparation to deal with whoever was surrounding the town—Urahara directed only his voice at Hisagi in explanation as he fumbled around briskly with some sort of apparatus. "Apparently there was some trouble going down over there. It wasn't much of an emergency, but when Mr. Isshin heard that his daughters were in danger, he tied up Mr. Kurosaki and ran over. Well, if Mr. Kurosaki had heard what happened first, he would have headed there on his own accord anyway."

"You mean Isshin, the former captain...?"

Hisagi had broken into a cold sweat when he heard about the overly aggressive response of the former captain of the Tenth Company, but Urahara cackled as he responded, "Well, that guy was adaptable enough to break out of the Soul Society after all."

"I think you're pretty quick to adapt too, Mr. Urahara."

"Regardless of that, when Miss Inoue and the others heard the news, it seems they headed to the Jureichi after them. So I think they won't return for a few more days. Well, I'm sure they'll come back once they realize we're in a state of emergency, but without spiritual tools or equipment it's a heck of a distance to travel to get back."

"Then that means..."

When he considered this new information in light of their current situation, Hisagi's instincts as a Soul Reaper and a journalist brought him to a single suspicion. Before he could even say it out loud, Urahara gave voice to the same conjecture. "It seems almost as though it were arranged this way, doesn't it?"

"How can you so easily..."

"Though it is a spiritual spot to begin with, it's not as though many Hollows would show up on that territory. If that weren't the case, Mr. Isshin never would have given his permission for them to go on the trip. Although there's also the possibility that the trouble there really did come up coincidentally and that they chose to rush in and make their move intentionally when Mr. Kurosaki left town. Though I think the chances of that are low."

"For sure. It's common sense to conclude that the situation over there was caused by the people who are attacking here."

Though it wasn't as if there was no chance that the attackers had come completely by coincidence during the time that Ichigo wasn't in town, Hisagi didn't think there was much point in following that possibility and decided to put it aside for the time being.

"But you didn't head over there?"

"No. I promised to be interviewed by you today, after all."

"Huh?"

Hisagi suddenly felt an inexpressible guilt budding inside of him, believing that had Hisagi not planned the interview that day, Urahara would have accompanied the others on the journey and they might have already solved whatever the superficial trouble was by now. However, seemingly unable to countenance Hisagi's clear distress, Urahara quickly revealed this to be a joke.

"That's not entirely true. To be accurate, I thought it was suspicious, so I purposefully decided to stay behind. It just felt like there was the distinct air of an intentional ruse to lure Mr. Kurosaki and the others out of town, so I thought it would be better if at least I stayed in town."

"Then did you know that something might happen today?"

"Things would have been better if I had been off the mark, though. It's in my nature that I can't help being unable to ignore a possibility once it's occurred to me."

At that point, Urahara straightened his hat and once again directed his eyes outside.

"Well, in the end, it looks like I was right again."

At the same time he stepped out onto the porch, something that looked almost exactly like the static on a TV screen coursed through the sky above the yard, and a boy's voice, which sounded as though it were coming through a machine, echoed across that disordered space.

"Been a while, Kisuke Urahara."

"Oh my, quite a shock to find out it's you."

"Don't lie. One such as yourself must have guessed it was me a long time ago based on the manner of the town's confinement."

In response to the boy's exasperated voice, Urahara flipped his fan open and replied, "Yes, of course I had figured it out some time ago! You feel like giving me any more praise?"

"You really are good at annoying people, aren't you...?"

In response to this voice, which exhibited faint traces of both annoyance and awe, Urahara's eyes narrowed below his hat, and he poured salt on the wound.

"Now that I've got you all annoyed, if you'd be so kind as to spill the beans about what's going on, it would save us so much effort..."

Hisagi had his doubts as to whether the kid would talk after being antagonized in this way, but he was sure that this was some sort of an Urahara-style negotiation tactic, so he forced himself to be still.

However, there was no way the kid was going to go along with such provocation, and instead of explaining the situation, he revealed himself through a projection on a rectangular screen that appeared in midair.

"Sorry, but I've got my reasons."

Hisagi didn't recognize the face and asked Urahara, "Mr. Urahara, do you know this kid?"

"Yeah. I think you'll know his name as well. Especially since you did all kinds of research into Fullbringers yourself, in your own way."

Staring into the face projected in the air, Urahara once again queried the boy.

"So, you'll give us an explanation then...President Yukio Hans Vorarlberna?"

CHAPTER NINE

THE RUKONGAI

"WHAT'S THIS? You seem pretty ambitious for having just shown up."

Looking at the Arrancar man who had appeared abruptly, Ginjo was cautious even as he muttered lightly to himself, "Actually, there was talk that some Hollows came by during the Quincy war...since you mentioned Ichigo Kurosaki, you must be one of them, right?"

The person who confirmed his suspicion was Tsukishima, carrying the bookmark he had turned into his Fullbring, which was in the shape of a Japanese sword.

"You must be Grimmjow Jaegerjaquez. He was one of the mid-class Arrancar Espada in the ranks that served under Sosuke Aizen."

"You know him... Wait, of course you wouldn't."

"Right, I've just seen him from inserting myself into Orihime Inoue's past. Back then he was someone we could have easily defeated."

Though he said that in a quiet voice, Tsukishima's stance revealed no trace of carelessness. Observing that, Ginjo understood the Arrancar before his eyes was no ordinary opponent.

What a nuisance, especially when we're in the middle of a fight with the Quincies.

If it ended up being a three-way fight, even if they were more powerful, they wouldn't be able to predict which direction the fight would take.

In that case, would it be better for us to draw him to our side? No...he'd probably start something even if we took no action.

In any case, it seemed unlikely that the Quincies, who believed Hollows existed only to be destroyed, would suddenly team up with one of them. Judging that, Ginjo decided to simply observe for a while, but...

The Arrancar himself wasn't looking down at the Quincies but at Tsukishima and the others as he said, "Hunh...? You over there, what'd you just say?"

"You mean me?"

"I've got no idea who you are. What was that you were saying about who you could have easily defeated?"

So he heard us?

"Ah well, you've got sharp ears."

Ginjo sighed lightly and shrugged as he said in an

intentionally friendly tone, "That right then was his idea of a joke. Don't worry about it."

"Oh was it? You know what I think about that?"

The Arrancar named Grimmjow snorted lightly.

"It ain't funny."

Just as they saw his eyes narrowing, he sped up in a single breath and appeared right where they were.

"Huh!"

He kicked at the reishi in the air like a wild animal and drew on his outstanding spiritual pressure's trail to make his form disappear. In the next moment, the piercing sound of a collision echoed in the air around them as the reishi in the place turned into a harsh wind and stirred up.

"Stay out of my way."

Before they knew it, Grimmjow had unsheathed his zanpaku-to. Ginjo used his own large sword to stop the blade, which appeared to be aimed at Tsukishima. Grimmjow asked him with annoyance, "Are you...a Soul Reaper?"

"Used to be. Now I'm just a wanderer."

Amidst the sound of crossing swords, they exchanged these brief words.

He's fast.

It wasn't that Ginjo couldn't follow the action with his own eyes, but he felt a slight sense that something was off. In terms of speed, he was at about the same level as a skilled Soul Reaper's shunpo.

However, the Arrancar's spiritual pressure seemed to waver momentarily, as though its moving essence were like a mirage or hologram, as though it were capturing him in an optical illusion.

Whether out of instinct or due to his collective experiences in battle, Ginjo ended up stopping the blade in the nick of time, still trying to address his immediate sense that something was wrong here. Though he'd assumed they would fight right away, Tsukishima had initiated the opening in a split second, and Grimmjow leapt far back from the two. After confirming his opponent had indeed distanced himself, Ginjo put his sense of something being "off" into words: "That guy has some strange moves."

Tsukishima easily answered Ginjo's suspicion. "It's sonido. It's a method of movement unique to Arrancars that allows them to slip past our and other Hollows' spiritual pressure senses."

"I see. Actually, they weren't Arrancars, but...I think I might've seen some Hollows in the past that did something similar when they got stronger."

There were many Soul Reapers and Quincies who had learned techniques to move quickly, called "shunpo" and "hirenkyaku" respectively. Shunpo was considered the standard, but when a hirenkyaku's power consumption was efficient, there were subtle differences that could be perceived. Additionally, the high-speed movement possible through Fullbring could be described similarly.

"Hah...surprised you know that much. You've got a pretty annoying way of moving yourself."

The high-speed movement possible through Fullbring enabled control over the reishi dormant in the ground and the power to increase the ability to move itself. Unlike shunpo, it would disturb the surrounding spiritual pressure to a minimal degree and could be said to be similar to sonido in that it was covert and allowed one to take an opponent by surprise.

Meanwhile, it didn't seem Grimmjow's attention had been captured entirely by the method of movement as he turned his eyes to a small amount of blood oozing on his wrist and smiled brutishly.

"Ah, looks like you tore through my Hierro. Not too shabby, *Tsukishima*."

Tsukishima's blade had apparently reached Grimmjow, and the scratch that he had given the Arrancar began to form a trickling red line.

"Huh?"

Grimmjow glanced at Tsukishima with the look of a beast of hunt that had decided the prey that had injured him was worth the fight. However, in the next moment there was a change in him.

"Tsukishima..."

When Grimmjow realized he'd uttered the name of a man he himself had only just met, he felt suspicious.

"Did you *insert* yourself?"

Ginjo merely shrugged as though they had saved themselves some hassle. Though it was faint, Tsukishima's blade had made a small mark on the Arrancar.

To Ginjo and the others, that meant something even more significant than the fact that they could get through the Hierro and hurt him. Tsukishima's ability, the Book of the End, could insert him in an opponent's past even with a faint wound. Ginjo, who knew about power that was corrosive to the point of being fiendish, sighed in a show of disappointment, but...

"Well, in the end..."

A sword flashed next to him, and the dry sound of metal clanging echoed around them.

"...That was close. Hey, what's going on here?"

"I'm sure I inserted myself."

Just barely defending himself against Grimmjow's attack as the Arrancar closed in on them again, Ginjo questioned Tsukishima. This time it was the other man's turn to shrug.

"It's not really that much of a mystery. Regardless of the past, someone who wants to kill me now will still want to kill me."

In the past, when Tsukishima had inserted himself into Byakuya Kuchiki's history as his "savior," he had had the experience of the Soul Reaper not hesitating at all to cut him down. That was why he didn't seem all that fazed by Grimmjow's behavior.

"When I insert myself into wild animals' pasts, much of the time their animal instincts guide their actions more than their memories of the past. Unlike with Byakuya Kuchiki, that's probably the reason this didn't work."

"So human empathy won't get through to Hollows then."

Though Ginjo was cracking jokes, the effort he put into the clash of swords hadn't been disturbed, and in that moment he started to pour spiritual pressure into his large sword.

"What're you complaining about? We're in the middle of a battle to the death!"

"I'm about to cut you down. Shut up and listen."

When Grimmjow's mouth warped fiendishly, reminiscent of a predator baring its fangs, Ginjo released the spiritual pressure he had stockpiled in his sword at high density.

He was using Getsuga Tensho at point-blank range.

"Huh?"

Grimmjow had likely been able to narrowly avoid it because the experience had been engraved into him during his battle with Ichigo Kurosaki. He felt a sense of déjà vu from the spiritual pressure that passed by his side, which he had retreated from reflexively as he questioned Ginjo with narrow eyes. "Your spiritual pressure... You part of the same tribe as Kurosaki? You don't look like you're related."

"What, you know Kurosaki too? I don't know if it's a small world or if he just gets around."

Meanwhile, the two Quincies were struggling with what to do next.

"What the heck are they doing? They go back and forth between losing interest and really getting into it."

Candice and Meninas, who were watching the Arrancar that had made an abrupt appearance, were trying to figure out the exact nature of their opponent, but before they could ask the Arrancar himself what he was seeking, he had started his own fight with the Fullbringers. Casually observing the fight, Meninas mulled over how things had flowed until then and guessed out loud. "Hmm...I think he's trying to use a power like Pepe's."

Candice recalled their former brother Pepe and his fiendish ability, "The Love," which made those who were struck by it love him unconditionally. Even if it wasn't exactly the same, they judged that the Fullbringer had attempted to use a similar psychological control mechanism and that it hadn't worked on the Arrancar.

"So he must've messed up. Pathetic."

Though Candice snorted, she suddenly felt suspicious and turned to Meninas. "Wait. That Mayuri scientist guy must know about that ability, right? Why didn't he mention it before?"

"Who knows... I think Lil would've known though."

"Yeah, Lil...I'm pretty sure she could have..."

In the Vandenreich, where they called each other

brethren but were essentially striving to outmaneuver each other, Liltotto was one of the few people they could trust to have their backs. They imagined what the bitingly sarcastic but skilled info analyst would have said about this.

Candice murmured at the Liltotto she drew in her mind: *"Don't you think he probably put you up to it so he could see what happened?"*

"...I could believe it."

Though it wasn't Liltotto herself speaking—it was nothing but an opinion originating in Candice's own imagination, essentially her own thought—she really could see a man like Mayuri Kurotsuchi doing such a thing.

"Huh? Believe what?"

"Talking about it won't change anything. More importantly, what do you want to do? We could find an opening and fry those guys, Arrancar and all, with my blitz."

"Like I said, I don't think you can burn them."

Thus they spent another moment on an exchange they had gone over already any number of times...

A different voice broke into their conversation.

"That's correct. You can't do that, you two. You've got to have on your listening hats when someone tells you something."

"Huh?!"

Candice and Meninas spun around to find a boy they had seen before their fight started. Though he had the appearance of a young boy, the girls knew that he wasn't in fact the age he seemed.

"You're one of that scientist's minions…"

"What a terrible thing to say. Sure, I've resigned myself to being a minion, but you're in the same boat, aren't you? Not that it matters now."

"What? Did you come here to light a fire under our asses or something?"

"Ah ha ha. No, nothing like that."

That boy-shaped Arrancar, who was one of Mayuri's pawns, wore the grin of a mischievous kid. "I came here to tell you two to keep out of this."

"Hunh?"

As the Quincies puzzled over what he was saying and whether this constituted a new instruction from Mayuri, the Arrancar—Luppi Antenor—grinned widely as he continued, "Oh, sooorry. Maybe that was too difficult for your wee brains? I'll put it more simply."

"Are you trying to pick a figh…"

Whenever Luppi seemed to be trying to provoke them, the blood rushed to Candice's head.

"I'm the one who kills that leopard Grimmjow."

"Huh…?"

Still wearing that joking smile, Luppi's words were layered with dark murder. At the same time he had spoken, ominous Hollow spiritual pressure began to eddy around

him. Then, with Candice and Meninas, who had unintentionally taken a step back, in front of him, the boy who had
unsheathed his zanpaku-to at some point held it lightly as
he spouted his incantation thick with bloodlust.

"Strangle—Trepadora!"

≡

"Oh dear, we can't have that. I'm surprised he'd show his
hostility so openly. Youth can be so lovely, but at times it
fails to be beautiful..."

"Actually, that Luppi seemed in pretty high spirits when
he ran in..."

Behind Mayuri and the Twelfth Company that was
still observing, the corpse unit that had been left behind
whispered to each other as they also felt Luppi's spiritual
pressure.

"Does he even have a chance? I heard that Grimmjow
didn't even lift a finger and still beat him."

This was spoken by Cirucci, who was blind to the fact
that she was fixated on the Quincy Ishida who had beaten
her. Dordoni harrumphed as he stroked his beard and
answered, "Indeed. However, I did not witness it myself. I
heard that though it was like a surprise attack, after his
chest had been pierced from the front, his upper body was
burned away by a Cero."

"If that's what happened, I'm impressed he survived without super-fast regeneration."

"He died. That's why he ended up in the same position as us. Though I do not know what treatment was undertaken by Lord Szayelaporro after his corpse was recovered... If he wasn't changed from before, then the result would likely be the same. However..."

Dordoni attempted to connect what was being said to his own training and education—

"Stop saying such idiotic things. A single sample is more than enough if you're going to just regenerate something," Mayuri butted into their conversation without a second thought, not even looking at them as he concentrated on his observations. "Though it seems that so-called scientist Espada did some fiddling around of his own."

With a suspicious smile lingering on his lips, Mayuri told the somewhat obvious *experimental subjects* the truth. "Though it was a joke, I still operate you under the Kurotsuchi Corpse Unit name. Of course I've modded you to be much higher performance."

≡

A Hollow's spiritual pressure?
Did someone follow me?

The moment Grimmjow felt the rising spiritual pressure behind him, he was slightly shaken. He had sensed that spiritual pressure before. But there was nothing in his memory that immediately connected to it. That was because Grimmjow, for whom "survival of the fittest" was a foundational belief, had no use for remembering the spiritual pressures of enemies he had eradicated in the past.

—That ain't Nelliel or the others.   —Yet, this spiritual pressure...
—I remember it from somewhere.   —No...
—I'm sure I killed him.

However, it was true that because this was someone who had disgraced him, there were faint remnants of the other Arrancar in the corner of his mind. That resulted in him feeling slightly baffled, and Grimmjow's movements were slowed by a moment.

The Fullbringers he was involved with had also noticed the abrupt appearance of strong spiritual pressure and turned their gazes in its direction as they muttered, "Another one?"

Grimmjow distanced himself from Ginjo and the others temporarily as he tried to look that way, but...

He realized that the spiritual pressure was exhibiting a peculiar movement.

A Cero…

No! This guy's about to…

It was likely the bestial instincts that dwelled inside of him that made him do it. He momentarily ignored Ginjo and the others as he turned his back and unleashed a Cero with all his strength.

Revealing his weak point to an enemy might have been perceived as reckless at first glance, but in the end, Ginjo and the others didn't attempt to pursue him. That was because when Ginjo and the others saw what was closing in on them, they dedicated all their efforts to avoiding it as well.

There was light.

It was a warped torrent of power—a hollowed spiritual pressure within a bright stream of light. Though it likely shared the same roots as the Cero Grimmjow unleashed, the volume of reishi and its density was much greater than any common Cero and it was strong enough to warp the existence of the space itself as it cut through the Soul Society's sky.

The wake of that light wriggled black like a heat shimmer, whether due to heat or the reishi themselves being disrupted. Though the Cero he himself had unleashed had been obliterated, his slight sway at the recoil allowed Grimmjow to narrowly evade that.

It was at this moment that he recognized the spiritual pressure of the enemy Hollow that had appeared behind him,

and his confusion cleared away as he looked for the source of the trail of light.

"So it's you... I was wondering who it was."

Grimmjow's look was a mix of exasperation and annoyance as he addressed the Arrancar boy who had appeared from the settling dust. The boy smiled with murder and wild joy on his face and he said, "Oh, sooorry. I was concerned that the king of the beasts might've forgotten all about me, so I thought I'd need to introduce myself."

The Arrancar's form was humanoid, but warped. Though his base body hadn't changed, there was a revolving dish on his back that looked like a fusion between a mechanical gear and a creature, with eight, long feeler-like organs wriggling from it. The feelers were as big as large logs and each one of them writhed powerfully like large white snakes with wills of their own.

"I'm so happy you remember me, Grimmjow."

The Arrancar, who had gone into his Resurrección state, was clad in even denser spiritual pressure than when Grimmjow had known him in the past. Although his bearing was similar, his appearance had changed so much that if Grimmjow hadn't seen him straight on he might not have recognized him.

"Yeah, but just in case, maybe I'll tell you my name again. I think you'd forget it anyway in about three steps." The Arrancar didn't hide his animosity at all, yelling his name as though to provoke Grimmjow: "It's Luppi Antenor. Don't go and accidentally call me the 'ex'-sexta, all right?"

"Who cares? What use is it now to bring up your name?"

Grimmjow sneered as he spat out his response, and Luppi's smile disappeared for just a moment as he gritted his teeth until they ground together. Then he smiled once again.

"You should be quiet and just try to remember—you've got to at least remember the name of the one who kills you."

"Who's that? That just now wasn't a normal Cero..."

The moment the Arrancar who had appeared after Grimmjow had unleashed "that," Ginjo felt his internal alarm bells going off based on his experience during his Deputy Soul Reaper days. That was exactly why Ginjo had been able to dodge it and had enough time to see the way Tsukishima had dodged it as well.

"What the heck was that, Tsukishima? The way you just dodged it...it was like you knew something about it."

"Well...but it's my first time seeing him actually release it."

Tsukishima, who knew more about Arrancars and Espadas after inserting himself into Grimmjow's past, squinted his eyes as he gave a name to "that" phenomenon.

"It's a Gran Rey Cero."

Though Tsukishima retained his usual faint smile, beneath that he was scowling slightly and continued as though to urge Ginjo to be cautious. "It's a special Cero that only Espada can use. Do I even need to mention the kind of power it's capable of?"

Shrugging, Tsukishima turned his gaze to a midsized hill some distance away. When Ginjo saw that it had been cleanly gouged in part by the light ahead of him, he also shrugged as though to match Tsukishima and smiled boldly.

"I see. Apparently even the Hollows have evolved since the time I knew them."

While the Fullbringer men who had many similarities with Hollows were talking on the side, a pronounced amount of spiritual pressure screeched between Grimmjow and Luppi.

"Still, I'm impressed you dodged that just now. I guess savage meat-eaters have sharp intuition, if nothing else..."

"You sure have got a lot to say. You spooked or something?"

"I've always been the one to talk. Perhaps you're the one who's scared, since you don't know why I'm here."

Grimmjow and Luppi provoked each other. However, they were keenly attentive as each probed the other's spiritual pressure. The two, who were accustomed to battles, knew with a single glance that the power of the other was different from what it had been in the past. At that point Luppi started to talk about their past interactions as though to muster up his own hatred. "Did you think I was dead? Well, I suppose I was. It would be only normal to die after having something like that happen, wouldn't it?"

It wasn't intentional but entirely coincidental when Luppi narrowed his eyes and said the *same thing* that Grimmjow had once said to Ichigo Kurosaki. Unlike Grimmjow, who had spoken with glee to Ichigo, Luppi said it with gloomy, pent-up hatred in his voice:

"Like I would die before killing you, Grimmjow..."

"Hunh...stop spouting words you're not fit to say." Grimmjow accepted the acrimony straight on as his mouth once again contorted to say, "I haven't got a clue why you're alive and can't say I'm interested in knowing."

Then he condensed his own spiritual pressure in his right hand and instantly let loose a Cero.

"But who could've guessed you'd come looking to get killed by me again! What a friggin' celebration!"

"What was that? Are you underestimating me?"

Rather than a Gran Rey Cero like the one Luppi had just shown off, Grimmjow had unleashed a regular Cero. Luppi had judged that Grimmjow was underestimating Luppi's Resurrección form and immediately tried to inform the other Arrancar of his error by sweeping away that Cero with a tentacle, but—

"Huh!"

Just as his sight was obscured by the scattering Cero, Grimmjow had disappeared.

"Like I'd let you!"

He had used sonido, which was made for slipping by an opponent's spiritual senses to launch a surprise attack. What resurrected itself in Luppi's brain was a memory of the time when Grimmjow had used that method to quickly draw near him and pierce his chest. He caused his tentacles to spin and created a protective sphere around himself. However, it occurred to him within an instant that this was a stupid plan.

"No, I've..."

He realized that putting all eight appendages into defense had created a lethal opening, and he also knew that his mind had reacted instinctively after recalling the moment he had been killed. As the fear rose up in Luppi, he cursed himself and Grimmjow.

"Grimmjow!"

Grimmjow had in fact exploited that momentary opening to its fullest extent. He poured blood from the wound Tsukishima had cut earlier into the palm of his hand, where he would launch his Cero. Then, in the next moment, a flash even greater than the one that had been released earlier swallowed the tentacles rotating around Luppi...as well as Luppi himself.

It was a Gran Ray Cero.

In the aftermath of Grimmjow's attack, which had been strengthened by the blood mixed into it, the space surrounding them once again began to warp.

"Oh ho, he's getting all flashy... Gauging its power, I'm guessing it'd put up a good fight against my Getsuga!"

At Ginjo's words, Giriko, whose body and clothes had at some point reverted to their normal state, responded, "Hm. The volume of spiritual pressure itself may have been greater, but taking into consideration speed and the number of moves, I think even you would have been able to cope with it quite well enough."

"You think so?"

Bewildered by Giriko, who had finally regained his tone and enthusiasm, Ginjo once again analyzed the situation. "So, what do we do? Should we make ourselves scarce and retreat from this mess for now? That is, if there isn't anyone waiting to ambush us..."

The two women who seemed to be Quincies were distracted by the Gran Rey Cero. This was a natural response, since getting hit by any stray attacks likely would have meant death for them, but Ginjo had discerned that there was something else behind the women, something that was calmly observing them. It felt similar to the time when Soul Reapers had been assigned to keep a lookout on him through the Deputy Soul Reaper badge.

Though Ginjo had in fact systematically probed the surrounding spiritual pressure and found what seemed to be several "observers," he didn't sense any of them going on the move just yet. Instead, he realized that the situation had now changed.

"A Soul Reaper is heading over here. And also someone else…" Ginjo suddenly scowled. "What? This spiritual pressure is…"

As though he had seen something mystifying, he turned his attention to the spiritual pressure that was still distant. However, he immediately rejected the conjecture he had arrived at as a result.

"Ichigo…? No, it couldn't be."

"What? Looks like you got a little sturdier."

After the light and dust had cleared, Luppi was visible, with several tentacles burned to a crisp by Grimmjow's Gran Rey Cero.

In the past, that would have obliterated him.

After being defeated by Ichigo Kurosaki, Grimmjow had continued to challenge, defeat, and eat hostile Menos Grande and Arrancars in order to exact his revenge. Since he could boast that his spiritual pressure had grown since then, he turned cautious eyes at Luppi, who withstood an attack that held his power.

I see. Something in his body must have been tweaked.

Seeing the stitch marks that ran down Luppi's face, Grimmjow was convinced of that.

Those straight, parallel scars weren't the type that would be made during a battle. Though there was the possibility they were the result of torture, they seemed too neatly stitched back up for that to be the case.

Actually, that Urahara guy did something similar to himself.

Grimmjow concluded that Szayelaporro must have carried out a unique procedure on Luppi while that Arrancar scientist was still alive—if it wasn't Kisuke Urahara or someone else—and smiled boldly as he continued to provoke Luppi. "I was hoping I'd obliterate you down to your toes this time so you couldn't come back to life."

Glaring at Grimmjow's jeering remark, Luppi's face transformed from a sour expression to an unbelievable grin, and he opened his arms with newfound excitement.

"Ha ha ha! You really are so irritating, Grimmjow!" His voice danced with a joy that belied the hostility of his words. "I'm glad you're your usual self... I finally feel like I've actually been 'reborn.'"

≡

A CERTAIN PLACE IN THE SEIREITEI

"Whoa, whoa, whoa. That idiot Mayuri is trying to pass this off as 'just an experiment' right after such a flashy rampage? That's like a slapstick joke! What am I supposed to do if my zanpaku-to reads the air too accurately and ends up transforming itself into a comedy prop?"

Using shunpo to travel quickly, Hirako headed to the closest Seireitei gate and winced at the spiritual pressure that had already started to accumulate in the air.

"That's not just any normal Cero I feel. Are they trying to destroy the sun or something? Well, if they're the same as when I met them last time, it should be fine as long as I put on my mask..."

Though he spoke lightly, Hirako was already calmly calculating whether he could hold them back based on the spiritual pressure he could feel all the way from there.

"Hm?"

At that moment, Hirako noticed something. Though it was quite far away, there was spiritual pressure that seemed to be heading to the place where the Arrancars were rampaging, just like he was.

"Is it the Second Company moving under Captain General Kyoraku's orders? Nah...that ain't it."

Though he had predicted that the Second Company would be on the move as a result of Hinamori's report, Hirako was dubious it was them; that would've been too strange. The nature of that spiritual pressure he sensed just seemed odd.

"Well, for starters, it doesn't feel the same as a Soul Reaper's."

At its base, it had the same nature as a Soul Reaper's spiritual pressure. In the living world, where he would have been able to visualize its Reiraku, he thought it likely would have been red in color, but if he were to be exact, the red would be interwoven with more complex colors.

"Are they the same as the Visoreds...? No, that's not it either. It's something completely different."

Hirako almost stopped, but he couldn't just abandon his path toward the Arrancars, so he kept heading in that direction as he tried to cross paths with the other presence that was coming through.

After adjusting his speed in order to slip into the path of the mystery spiritual pressure, Hirako could see it clearly.

"Huh? Who the heck are you?" Hirako muttered unintentionally, still moving at high speed.

A lone child wearing clothing similar to a shihakusho had made an appearance. That Soul Reaper, who could easily be perceived as either a boy or a girl, noticed Hirako running beside them and put on a happy smile, remarking, "Whoa. You're not from the Thirteen Court Guard Companies, are you?! It's nice to meet you. My name is Hikone Ubuginu!"

The child's shunpo didn't miss a beat as they politely greeted Hirako. Though he was taken aback for a moment, when Hirako realized the person he had come across was someone he could at least communicate with, he felt relief—and, simultaneously, a strong sense of caution in his chest.

What is with this kid? That's some spiritual pressure.

Sensing the volume of spiritual pressure coming from the child's small physique, Hirako guessed that Hikone was in fact something else in the form of a child.

Of course, I couldn't claim this kid is on the same level as Aizen or Ichigo, but... I am at least sure the kid's dangerous.

This was an enigmatic Soul Reaper who possessed a spiritual pressure that was anything but ordinary. If this was what the child was like when not fully developed, what would they be like as an adult? Pondering this, Hirako decided that for the time being he would try to converse with the kid in order to tease out more information.

"Well, I was wondering about your name, but there's something else I wanted to ask you about. Those clothes look very similar to a soldier's garb, but they're not from the Thirteen Court Guard Companies, are they? In fact, you don't have a company number."

"You're right! I am Lord Tokinada Tsunayashiro's retainer!"

"A re—what now?"

Though he poked fun at the child's old-fashioned word, Hirako's caution had immediately heightened when he comprehended the name he'd just heard.

Tsunayashiro! So this kid is related to the Four Great Noble Clans!

Though Hirako had spent some time slipping away to the living world, he was a veteran in the current Thirteen Court Guard Companies. Because of that, he was one of the people who fully understood the Four Great Noble Clan's absolute power; he knew they weren't all openhearted like Yoruichi Shihoin or unfailingly loyal like Byakuya Kuchiki.

And among them, the Tsunayashiro family was like all the negative aspects of the Seireitei aristocracy rolled into one.

He decided he wanted to avoid getting involved if at all possible, particularly after briefly recalling that he'd heard the Tsunayashiro family had distanced themselves from the Thirteen Court Guard Companies because of an incident from several hundred years ago involving a slaughtered colleague.

I'm pretty sure that was the incident involving Tosen. This won't do. All I can sense is trouble.

Regardless, it wasn't as though he could wave goodbye to Hikone here and now, so he continued to speak in a friendly manner to draw out more information. "Well, sure. So what business does a distinguished retainer of the Tsunayashiro have in the Rukongai? There are some fearsome ghosties rampaging around there right now, you know?"

"Yes, sir! I know those ghosts! Just before this they almost killed me!"

"What?"

Hikone had answered without missing a beat, and Hirako gaped in exasperation. He had started to feel somewhat frightened about Hikone's potential. Though Hirako was moving at nearly his top speed, the child was not only keeping up with him but didn't seem even the slightest bit out of breath.

"What is going on here? The observation room staff are practically stealing their salaries if they haven't noticed everyone coming in willy-nilly like this."

"No, I went to Hueco Mundo on my own! I went to become the king of Hueco Mundo, but the Arrancars got mad at me and beat me up!"

Hearing Hikone saying such preposterous things, Hirako could barely keep himself from reflexively blurting out, "This must be a joke."

It'd be great if it were just a joke, but I think this kid is being serious.

"Why would you become the king of Hueco Mundo? Aren't you a Soul Reaper?"

"Yes! I'm going to become king of the Soul Reapers... I'm going to be the Reio!"

"What now?"

"That's why Lord Tokinada said I have to be respectful to the Zero Company and Thirteen Court Guard Companies that will protect me in the future! That's why I honor everyone in the Court Guard! Oh, and I'll become king of the humans too! Lord Tokinada said he would let me! I'm so happy!"

Hikone had the expression of a young child anticipating a present from Santa Claus, and Hirako narrowed his eyes, feeling a chill.

Nope, nope, nope. This isn't any ordinary trouble—this is the eye of a hurricane.

If some random kid had said such things, this all would have seemed like a silly joke. But the unnatural vacillations of the spiritual pressure from the Soul Reaper keeping pace with him made Hirako's instincts scream that the child spoke the truth.

In that case...it makes no difference whether I retreat or keep on going. If I'm actually in the eye of the storm, then I might even be able to change something.

I've seriously drawn the short straw here. I keep doing that, don't I?

Hirako composed himself and let out a short sigh. "Hey now, are you sure you should let the cat out of the bag regarding such important matters? Won't you get in trouble with Lord Tokinada?"

"No, it's fine! I was really worried before, when I spoke about it without thinking, but Lord Tokinada said, 'I don't mind if you speak candidly about it, since everyone will soon know.' And he gave me permission!"

"Everyone will know about it?"

"Yes! Lord Tokinada ordered me that if anyone laughs or puts up a fuss, I must use force to convince them! But... you're not going to laugh about me saying I'll become king?"

Hikone asked him in such a nervous tone, Hirako felt an instinctive unease as he answered honestly, "Laughing about that would be idiotic. But it's also not something to be angry about."

Hikone's face sparkled happily. The child looked at Hirako in a way that made him feel empty somehow and said, "That's good! You seem like a good person, so I didn't really want to use my sword on you!"

Hikone glanced at the zanpaku-to hanging at their hip. Although Hirako felt a sinister air from the unusual zanpaku-to, he decided now wasn't the right time to ask about it and inquired about something else instead. "Oh, sure... So are you a boy or a girl? I can't tell from how you look."

Hirako had asked straightforwardly; Hikone continued to smile and replied, "Yes. Lord Tokinada said, 'You are the beginning and the end, so you need no reproductive function, or gender, or development. That is the way you were made'! So I don't really know!"

"I see. Well, the inner workings of living things are complex, after all. I'm sure that must be a factor."

Several disturbing pieces of information embedded in the words Hikone had just uttered caused Hirako's distrust of the man named Tokinada Tsunayashiro to skyrocket.

Though it seems this kid isn't actually a bad apple.

At the same time, there was no reason for Hirako to let down his guard when it came to the kid in front of his eyes.

With someone like this, the fact that they don't have bad intentions is actually worse.

Hirako didn't relax the speed of his shunpo as he felt the presence of the Arrancars he was steadily approaching and scowled as he said to himself, "How am I supposed to deal with this situation once I get there...?"

≡

THE RUKONGAI

Grimmjow had once completely stopped Luppi Antenor's enterprises as an Arrancar. Grimmjow's arm had been restored by Orihime Inoue, who had been forcibly summoned by Aizen. The skin on his back and the No.6 carved there was restored right on the spot. That occasion had made Luppi and Grimmjow both sexta Espada simultaneously, but the redundancy was put to rest just a few seconds later. Feeling perplexed and irritated, when Luppi had tried to ask what Grimmjow's intent was in restoring the number on his back, he had ended up stabbed through the chest in an unambiguous response.

"Just this. Bye bye, ex number six."

Grimmjow's words and an enormous spiritual pressure that rose from inside his chest: those were Luppi's final memories as an Espada.

I had a thirst.

When he had been brought back to consciousness by Mayuri Kurotsuchi, he seemed somewhat removed, but Luppi hadn't forgotten that hatred from his previous lifetime. He hadn't forgiven anyone who had looked down on him or embarrassed him in the past—not a single one of them. He schemed and planned in secret, waiting for his chance to take revenge.

I had a thirst.

That was how he thought he had felt, at least.

When he was deployed to an actual battle as part of the Kurotsuchi Corpse Unit, he ended up doubting himself.

Toshiro Hitsugaya.

In a past battle in Karakura Town, that was the name of the first opponent who brought Luppi down. Luppi had learned the Soul Reaper's name after being resurrected. He remembered well the words he had yelled when he had withdrawn from Hitsugaya.

"Don't forget my face. Next time we meet, I'll twist your little head off and smash it!"

He hadn't just been bluffing—his words were loaded with heartfelt hatred. Though he had been careless, Luppi himself recognized that his opponent had been strong. However, even with that understanding, he decided it was something

he must do—that, in order to remain himself, he needed to tear that captain in a child's body into shreds.

An incurable thirst.

Their opportunity for a reunion had come even sooner than he could have imagined. As part of the Kurotsuchi Corpse Unit, he had been thrust onto the battlefield with Dordoni and the others fighting against Toshiro Hitsugaya, who had unexpectedly appeared before them as one of the Quincy's pawns. As a result of the Quincy's abilities, the Soul Reapers had been turned into zombies and made a stand as peerless, atrocious enemies. However the moment he had seen that, Luppi realized the urge to destroy in his heart was cooling.

What?

Why are you already broken?

You were supposed to be my plaything. I was supposed to break you!

The Soul Reaper who had appeared after that was another he remembered fighting—Rangiku Matsumoto. In the past, when he had confronted her in Karakura Town, he had commented that she had a "killer body" and tried to skewer her with an untold number of needles. Luppi's taste in bodies hadn't changed since then, but since she had been turned into a moving corpse, her mind was of course completely broken. Although he had fought under Mayuri's orders, the excitement and urge to destroy that he'd experienced in the past were gone, and he didn't even experience the glee of crushing someone weaker than him.

An unfulfillable thirst.

The husk company, huh?

After the war with the Quincies was over, and even after he had heard that Hitsugaya, Rangiku, and others had been returned to their previous states, he hadn't been driven by the will to go kill them again.

That might be right for the way I am now.

It's like I don't actually feel like I'm living...

He spent his days working behind the scenes to capture newly born Hollows with unique abilities and doing odd jobs for the Department of Research and Development.

Lately, he hadn't been put under restraints except while working, but that was probably just because the surveillance system that Mayuri Kurotsuchi made had become foolproof. Based on Mayuri's personality, Luppi understood that it wouldn't have been odd for Mayuri to have inserted a self-detonating bomb inside the Arrancar. However, even without that, had Mayuri, for example, ordered him to fight Toshiro Hitsugaya, he doubted his heart would have leapt.

The thirst.

It spread.

While obeying the instructions he was given, his days were filled with insatiable thirst. But there was nothing to thirst for. There was nothing he wanted to fill the hole that had opened in him as a Hollow. What had withered away might have been his desire itself—the one fundamental nature of a Hollow.

Though doubt floated into his mind, Luppi didn't care. If things kept up like this, he would just end up being used as a tool by the Soul Reapers until they were done with him, and both his mind and body would shrivel up and vanish. All he felt was resignation.

Yeah, I thought I would dry out and shrivel up, hollowly withering away, and that I'd have the sorry fate of turning into the sands of Hueco Mundo in the end.

On this day, just when he had been wondering what meaning there was in continuing to live out the dry days like this—when he had sunk into a negativity his previous self could never have conceived of...

Grimmjow appeared in front of his eyes, and all of the *thirst* disappeared.

There was dread of the one who had killed him.

There was hatred for the one who looked down upon him.

There was joy in finding the thing he needed to *destroy*.

The emotions that seemed to have run dry burst forth from inside of him. It was almost as though the piece of himself he had lost—his hole—was overflowing from a well deep within.

The Gran Rey Cero that Grimmjow had released severely damaged several of his tentacles. Though Luppi's main body was bleeding, he didn't flinch. Rather, as though his anger about the injury had amplified his spiritual pressure, the speed of his feelers increased. Grimmjow spoke even more boldly and provokingly despite being outnumbered and continuing to receive blows. The slashed feelers spurted blood that spattered on Grimmjow's cheek.

Luppi instantly transformed each of his eight tentacles into bristling expanses of needles and sharp blades, rotating them rapidly like helicopter blades in order to strike Grimmjow.

"Cut it out with those weak attacks!"

For his part, Grimmjow purposefully leapt around in the intervals between the attacks. Swiftly kicking Luppi away, he tried to follow up by releasing another Gran Rey Cero, but—

"Huh!"

As Luppi collapsed, the tips of his eight tentacles released a stream of Ceros, one after another. Of course, the singular rays alone didn't have the power of a Gran Rey Cero, but as if he had learned from Grimmjow's technique of increasing their spiritual pressure by mixing his blood into them, he was able to produce flashes that were denser than a common Cero and assaulted the enemy Arrancar with the force of a Bala bullet.

"Like I said, that's weak!"

Grimmjow stopped repelling the attacks, and with no thought of getting injured, he unleashed his words.

"Grind, Pantera!"

≡

HUECO MUNDO

"Are you really going to go too, Halibel? Do you really think it's okay to leave Hueco Mundo alone?"

"I'm just going to gauge the Soul Society's intentions. I'll leave it to you to get Grimmjow back."

As she was replying to Nelliel, Halibel had opened a garganta under Las Noches's canopy.

Their continued investigation confirmed that the trail of Grimmjow's spiritual pressure led to the Soul Society. Though they needed to bring him back before it became a bigger problem, it was likely that all of them moving at once would be seen as a hostile act by the Soul Society.

Halibel, who understood that there was no point in creating a meaningless dispute with their current forces, had decided that the minimum number of people—that is, just herself—would head out to "negotiate" with the Soul Society. Her Fracciónes—Apache, Rose and Sun-Sun—were persistent in attempting to accompany her, but in the end they stayed behind once convinced that they were needed to defend the place in Halibel's absence.

"Leave it to me to protect the place. Lord Halibel, please try not to overextend yourself…"

The anxiety that wavered in Sun-Sun's seemingly composed voice was likely rooted in an incident in her past when she had been captured by Yhwach. Knowing that, Halibel felt bad about her own feeling of inadequacy and attempted to assuage Sun-Sun and the others.

"Sorry. In order to make sure that never happens again, I need to do this now."

Speaking directly to the Fracciónes, she brought up a speculation that had been building in her mind. "It's possible that Soul Reaper child…could become an *enemy* like Yhwach if we don't do anything."

As Halibel and Nelliel disappeared into the garganta, a girl who was observing the flow of their spiritual pressures from a distance quietly muttered, "Looks like they've made a move…"

In response to Liltotto Lamperd—the girl with the serious tone of voice—Giselle Gewelle, who was fooling around with the zombified Bambietta Basterbine behind Lil, blurted out in a lighthearted way, "What? Did they, seriously?"

"Wuh…Candy…Minnie…where?"

Bambietta had spoken unclearly, as though she were sleep-talking, and Liltotto brought up a conjecture in response to the delirious comment: "Are they headed to the living world or to the Soul Society? If this is related to that weird Soul Reaper, then it's probably the latter. In that case, this might be our chance to get back together with Candy and Minnie."

"So, what are we doing? Are we just going to go?"

"Yeah, but we'll wait a while before we get really rowdy. First we need to figure out where Candy and Minnie are, while those Hollows are distracting the Soul Reapers."

And then the survivor Quincies were also on the move.

They were unaware that those they had gone to aid, Candice and Meninas, were in fact in the midst of a battle with "those Hollows."

≡

THE SOUL SOCIETY, FIRST COMPANY BARRACKS

"I'm going to head out for a bit too. Could you keep an eye on things here, Nanao, my dear?"

With Kyoraku in front of her, putting on his woven hat, Nanao asked curiously, "What? Where are you heading to? I didn't think you had plans for anything like that today..."

"To Central 46. I'm making a quick stop at the Gilded Seal Aristocrat Assembly."

"What?!"

When Nanao realized the significance of where he was going, she looked at Kyoraku nervously.

"Don't look so scared. It's not like I'm heading to my death or anything."

"That is true...but I thought you still needed more time to prepare?"

"Yeah, I wanted to dig around a little more, to be honest. But after hearing that report from Momo, I felt a little uneasy."

Kyoraku quietly turned his eyes down and smiled as though to comfort Nanao.

"Well, Ukitake might get mad at me about it."

"You mean...Captain Ukitake?"

In response to Nanao's words, a pained smile came over Kyoraku's face. "Since he was such a people person. Well, I think that's the good part of Ukitake that I myself was lacking."

Reminiscing about the deceased, Kyoraku turned to memories further in the past.

"This is from back in the day, but Ukitake, that Tokinada, and I were classmates at Reijutsuin. Tokinada didn't stand out and was neither praised nor scolded by old man Yama. He just went through life like a shadow... Ukitake would talk to him like he was normal. I think Ukitake might have thought they were friends. Even after we graduated—until that thing happened...no, maybe even after that too."

By "that thing," he was likely referring to the incident in which Tokinada had slaughtered his wife and colleague. Nanao, who had inferred that, didn't inquire about it and quietly waited for Kyoraku to continue.

"Just because we were graduates of the same class, Ukitake gave the benefit of the doubt to Tokinada. Ukitake thought if Tokinada just had a change of scenery, if he just got some sort of opportunity, he could definitely be reformed. He said he was sure Tokinada would confront in his heart the crime he had committed."

"Well..."

"I wasn't able to believe that. But I also hadn't been able to kill Tokinada back then. The time has come for me to take responsibility for not making a decision. That's all there is to it."

Though she felt disquieted when he said the words "back then," Nanao felt that Kyoraku's resolve was held in that short phrase, and she didn't question his intentions.

"Not only did I push work on him he would rather not have done, I'm starting to wonder if it might just have ended up a fool's errand. I might have done an injustice to Hisagi."

As he was saying that, Okikiba, who had finished giving instructions to the Second Company, had come back.

"Hey there, Okikiba. I'm heading out for a...what happened?"

Kyoraku noticed Okikiba's grave expression, and the second assistant captain seemed tense as he gave his report. "It seems that Shuhei Hisagi, who headed to Karakura Town, has applied for a Gentei Kaijo."

"...A Gentei Kaijo? Things can't be going smoothly."

"Apparently it's because an unidentified enemy force has appeared...but according to the observation room, the communication was interrupted when they were about to give him permission. Furthermore, all of the observation equipment for Karakura Town has been shut off, and Karakura Town is currently in isolation as a result..."

Faced with a report that was even worse than he had imagined, Kyoraku appeared somber. He kept his composure as he replied, "What happened to private Yuki Ryunosuke and Shino Madarame, whom we dispatched to Karakura Town?"

"Yes, communication with them has also been cut off."

"Please get in contact with the Soul Reapers in the surrounding towns and instruct them to report on the current situation... Nanao, I'm sorry, but since our problems on both fronts have intensified, would you go too?"

"Yes, sir!"

Nodding intently, Nanao and Okikiba left the room to prepare. After he saw them off, Kyoraku wore a more serious expression than usual as he muttered, "Looks like things have taken a turn for the worse...

"Tokinada might have already got the jump on us."

CHAPTER TEN

KARAKURA TOWN IS BY NO MEANS a deserted rural town. Located in the heart of the Tokyo suburbs, a railway runs through its center. It boasts a population of over a hundred thousand and a general hospital beside Main Karakura Town Station that is larger than those in neighboring towns. Because of that, nonresidents and residents alike use the station, and a large number of people travel in and out of the town.

In order to protect the town from Aizen in the past, the Soul Reapers orchestrated a ruse to transfer its hundred thousand inhabitants to the Soul Society, though many Soul Reapers found that unfathomable given the labor it involved and the fact that ordinary humans were fools. It had been a large-scale operation in which Soul Reaper craftsmen had worked together to temporarily halt trains and cars from entering or leaving the town; oversaw the surrounding region's electricity, water, and sewage lines to ensure there was no mishap; and even manipulated the memories of vast numbers of residents in the area surrounding Karakura Town.

As a result, the Soul Reapers had successfully implemented their ploy to deceive the world while isolating Karakura Town. Though there had been sacrifices, when the Seireitei considered the goals of Aizen and the Arrancars, they had gotten away with minimal casualties.

And now Karakura Town was once more isolated from the world.

The isolator's goals were unknown.

If a wall that divided the dimensions of reality physically existed, it would have appeared as what now divided the town—a gloomy virtual reality curtain of static that was imperceptible to the ordinary human eye.

However, the isolation was permeable. The trains did not stop. Cars made their way across the city limits of neighboring towns as usual and the same was true of pedestrians. Sparrows and other birds flitted across the sky and the flow of the rivers hadn't even stalled. It was just a normal day. Despite that, the town most certainly had been isolated.

"Huh? The TV isn't showing anything!"

"Hello? Hellooo? Huh? The line cut out..."

"I haven't got a signal.

"I don't either."

"I give up. I can't get my email to work..."

"*Are you kidding me? The connection dropped right when I was about to win?!*"

Such statements were heard across Karakura Town.

All manner of communications devices and signal-receiving equipment that connected the town to the outside world ceased to work, and electronic communications outside the town were cut off entirely.

However, that was only the case for mere minutes.

First the TV signal returned—then the radio, the landlines, wireless, the internet, and the cell phones each came back in turn. The people were mystified but explained away the phenomenon in their own ways, as an outage at the relevant facilities, and went back to their daily lives. They did not notice that in those brief few minutes, their communications devices, easily over a hundred thousand in number, had all been tagged. And that based on that tag, a portion of those devices hadn't reconnected even after the minutes had passed.

"Huh...that's strange..."

When Ururu said that, Jinta replied in a pained voice, "What's so strange? You know what I think is strange? The situation I'm in right now!"

Ignoring Jinta, who held half of the five hundred kilograms of bouncy balls by himself, Ururu wondered aloud to Tessai, who walked next to her, "Mr. Tessai, my cell phone isn't working anymore."

"Heh! You probably visited a dirty site and broke it buh buh buh boo boo hya ha ha! Stop! Wa—! Wait! Why you little...! Don't tickle me right now!"

Ignoring Jinta, whose knees were shaking and on the verge of collapse, Tessai answered Ururu. "Hm? Perhaps it's electromagnetic interference?"

In contrast to Jinta, who lugged two hundred fifty kilograms of bags on his back, Tessai was easily carrying the same weight using just one arm. He used his free hand to pull out his own cell phone and checked his signal.

"You're right. My phone isn't connecting either."

After manipulating the phone in several ways, Tessai knitted his eyebrows together.

"This is no normal interference, it seems. I also sense a strange disturbance in spiritual pressure... We should get back to the shop quickly."

"Karakura Town should be right ahead of here... What the heck is this?"

There was a boundary line along the west side of Karakura Town. A young Soul Reaper in charge of the next town over had arrived at the site.

"Right after the Seireitei sends out an emergency communication... Was this a Hollow's doing? Or a Quincy's?" The Soul Reaper muttered to himself in front of the peculiar barrier.

The film, which was projected into the sky like a hologram, emitted static as it cut through the town. However, cars, passersby, and even trains were plunging into the membrane and passing through as though nothing were amiss.

"All right! The hell with it!"

Though he faltered at first, the proactive Soul Reaper finally took a step directly into that membrane.

Then...

"Hm? What? I went through it just like normal..."

Just as he said that, he noticed another Soul Reaper right in front of his eyes.

"Who're you? I thought Karakura Town was managed by a young guy and a girl?"

In response, the middle-aged Soul Reaper, who sported graying hair, posed a question back to the young Soul Reaper: "I'm the Soul Reaper in charge of Kagamino City, east of here. I'd actually like to ask you the same question. You just came out of Karakura Town, didn't you? What's going on in there right now?"

"What?"

At that point the young Soul Reaper realized something was off. The scene around him was entirely different from before he'd gone through the membrane.

"Where am I? Where's the station?"

"This is the east side of Karakura Town. Do you mean Main Karakura Town Station? You weren't...on the west side of the town, were you?"

That was when they both realized it—the membrane functioned differently for normal humans than it did for Soul Reapers. Then, simultaneously, they were both concerned for the well-being of the Soul Reapers inside.

"You think they're okay? I don't think those in charge of Karakura Town are that strong..."

"In any case, we need to report this to the top. But, you know, Karakura Town has Ichigo Kurosaki, former captain Isshin, and also the former captain Urahara. I'm sure he'll be able to figure out a solution."

They didn't know.

They had no idea that Ichigo Kurosaki and Isshin Kurosaki were both currently out of town, and in their place an assistant captain was there—one who couldn't compare with either of them in terms of firepower.

≡

URAHARA SHOTEN

"Yukio Hans Vorarlberna..."

For a moment, Hisagi was bewildered by the long name, but he had certainly heard it while interviewing others about Ichigo Kurosaki. And he remembered it was a name he'd heard recently.

"Yukio and Riruka transported us there directly. We were crossing a pretty dangerous bridge, you know?"

"Huh! Aren't you one of Ginjo's people?"

"Possibly. So who're you? I haven't got any business with anyone except Mr. Urahara, to be blunt."

Hisagi clenched his hands into fists as he replied to the boy who spoke indifferently through the airborne monitor. "I'm the Ninth Company assistant captain of the Thirteen Court Guard Companies, Hisa—"

"Oh, I really don't care. Doesn't seem like there's much point in knowing anyway."

"What?! What's with you?! All you had to do was be patient for a little longer and listen! You're doing exactly the opposite of what that Ganju guy did!"

Ignoring Hisagi, who stomped his feet, Yukio turned to Urahara and started to address him. "Guess it's been half a year. I'd like you to come with me for a bit."

"Oh, I would have gone to you if you had rung me up in advance. Besides, I've more or less guessed what you want."

"Oh, have you…"

In contrast to Yukio's narrowed eyes, Hisagi's eyes were wide with surprise as he asked, "Are you serious, Mr. Urahara? You know what this guy wants…?"

Urahara snapped his fan closed and smiled boldly. "The president of Y-Hans Enterprises, which has scaled up rapidly with gaming projects as its foundation while also focusing on the entertainment industry as a whole, could only be seeking one thing from me."

Then he opened the fan he had just closed with a flashy sound and declared, "Of course! You must be scouting me!"

"Whaa...?"

Hisagi looked as though he had no idea how to react, while Yukio was entirely expressionless. Ignoring the two, Urahara continued shamelessly, "Well, I suppose you could say I have an eye for trends, as the owner of a humble candy shop who develops his own new products. If I dare say so myself, I thought a large corporation would set their sights on me eventually. But it's a problem for me if you think I'm only motivated by money. If you want to buy an old town worker's soul, I'd rather you offer good faith over cash. Yes, to put it in practical terms, how does seven percent of the company shares sound?"

"So you just wanted money after all! Seven percent?! That's audacious! And is Karakura Town even considered old town?! Also, it's not like a small-time candy store would be developing their own in-house product line in any case!"

"Mr. Hisagi, you're really so polite when you make fun of people, aren't you? Mr. Vorarlberna, you should take notes."

Urahara spoke without any shame whatsoever, but Yukio didn't become exasperated or angry; instead he remarked indifferently, "You really are frightening. Wouldn't want to come across someone like you in a PvP game.

"What's gotten into you all of a sudden?"

"While you were making dumb jokes, you were observing all of my reactions, weren't you? You were trying to upset me from the moment you started making a fool out of that guy, weren't you?"

"You're giving me too much credit. Do I look like such a villain?" Urahara smiled wryly as he pulled his hat low over his head and glared up brazenly from under its brim at Yukio beyond the monitor. "It's the nature of my business to size people up, but it's not as though I can see everything."

Seeing Urahara deftly dodge this jab, Yukio sighed and said, "Uh-huh. But you at least know that I'm not here to recruit you, right? This is the main deduction phase. Can you guess my goal even though I haven't given you the main evidence yet?"

"I'd like to say I've seen through you already, but I'm still not certain I have. How many questions do I get? At the very least, since I know you're not here to murder us and don't bear us any hostility, I'm now hoping to get some extra time."

"Huh?"

So he's not hostile toward us?

Come to think of it, I definitely don't get the sense that he's attacking.

Hisagi could tell that Yukio's power was to fuse the digital virtual world with the real world, based on the monitor that had appeared in midair and the phenomenon of static noise that had started to flicker around the shop. Because of that, he was cautious of the possibility that Yukio could rewrite his body's information as he used his spiritual pressure senses to search for Yukio's actual whereabouts. While he certainly didn't feel like he had been attacked, he remembered being manipulated in the past, when a Quincy named Pepe had attacked him without his knowledge, so he couldn't let his guard down.

Damn it, why'd I remember that? Why did I let that bizarre old man do that to me...

When he remembered the time he had temporarily "loved" the Quincy due to the brainwashing power of Schrift, he shook his head and scowled.

"Mr. Urahara, you said this guy isn't hostile... Well then, why'd he go out of his way to cut off Karakura Town?"

Though he had already sent in the requisite message to request a Gentei Kaijo from the Soul Society, he still hadn't received a reply. It was likely that the transmission had been jammed somehow, but he had no way of checking whether it had been cut off just like the town. Though Hisagi had trained to battle while holding back a vast majority of his power, as was now the case, even an Adjuchas-class Hollow would have forced a tough fight on him.

"Yeah, it was definitely me who cut off the town."

Yukio himself was the one who replied to Hisagi's question.

Hisagi looked at Yukio doubtfully, but even his intuition didn't sense that the kid was hostile. As Hisagi was trying

to figure out what Yukio's goal could be if that were the case, Yukio continued. "That's right, no hostility here...from me, that is."

At around that time, there was a change in the place. Hisagi sensed the faint disturbance of spiritual pressure behind him as he silently leapt forward and turned back to the spot where he had been standing. Right at that moment, human figures that had appeared from the midair static were standing there, lashing the air with oddly decorated, expandable batons. Though the batons were not blades, the force with which the blunt weapons were brought down was such that one wouldn't go unscathed if they connected with one's head. Given a Soul Reaper's physical resilience, they probably wouldn't have done much harm to him, but he knew these weren't just normal batons.

More importantly, when Hisagi saw the figures holding those batons rush out of the static, one after another, to surround him, he concluded that the situation had long since progressed into a battle. The reason he'd been able to dodge them instantaneously while listening to Urahara's joking around was likely due to his many years of experience battling as a Soul Reaper. Hisagi reached for the hilt of his zanpaku-to as he observed the group of people who had appeared in front of Urahara Shoten.

This isn't any Hollow or Quincy spiritual pressure.
Are these guys...humans?

The group of men and women were not even the konpaku of the deceased, and the colors of their spirit ribbons marked them as people no different from any others who lived in the world of the living. Because they were all wearing homogenous black suits etched with white patterns and identically colored gas masks on their faces, Hisagi couldn't see their expressions.

If they're human, it's not like I can cut them down just like that.

But even if they're just humans, being outnumbered like this is still a problem...

Hisagi attempted to use shunpo and hakuda in order to stun them all, but...

"Huh?!"

The moment he went around behind his opponents using shunpo, he felt something strange afoot and immediately leapt back a step. In that instant, a baton grazed the tip of his nose. The moment he had circled around them into what should have been their blind spot, they had attacked him with a precision that made it seem as though they had eyes on the backs of their heads. Furthermore, their movements seemed much faster than a normal human's, even out-stripping those of a general Soul Reaper soldier.

What is with these guys?!

Did they use spirit senses to figure out where I was?

Soul Reapers and Hollows, as well as some special humans, could use spirit pressure senses—which were often

referred to as spirit senses—to deduce the spiritual pressure of others. Despite that, Hisagi was hard-pressed to believe that normal humans who lived in the living world were capable of that, so he suspected there was a chance the people he faced might possess powers. Naturally, his opponents gave him no time to investigate. While dodging the baton strikes of the group attacking him continually from all sides, Hisagi sensed a subtle, strange change taking place in his body.

What is this?

Am I getting slower...?

Even taking into account that he hadn't obtained a Gentei Kaijo, it felt as though his reaction times were about ten percent slower than usual. His body lagged just a moment behind the reactions in his mind.

Urahara, who was watching Hisagi, narrowed his eyes and muttered, "Poison... No, this is konpaku and reishi subjugation, I think."

"Huh?! What's going on, Mr. Urahara?!"

"Of course, that gentleman wearing all black just grazed you with a baton, right? It feels as though your spiritual pressure has been slightly disturbed since that moment. It's likely a Fullbring that uses contact as an operational trigger." Urahara described in detail the conjecture brought about by his observations.

"I see... I knew I could depend on you, Mr. Urahara. I can't believe you're cool-headed enough to think that through in the middle of a fight like this...huh?"

Dodging the attacks, Hisagi had been impressed. But he couldn't help but notice the significant difference between his circumstances and Urahara's.

"Wait... Am I the only one being attacked here?!"

All of the black-clad people in gas masks who had appeared around the shop were attacking only Hisagi and made no attempt to approach Urahara, even though he appeared defenseless at first glance.

"Well, I wonder what could be going on here? I suppose you could say we just have different aptitudes?"

"Doesn't it seem unfair?! Hey...this is Yukio's doing, right? What's your deal?!"

Hisagi shouted at the image projected in midair, but Yukio seemed bored as he answered, "Weren't you listening? Didn't I just say my business is with Mr. Urahara?"

"You mean your 'business' wasn't to make him disappear?"

"If it were, I'd already have launched a surprise attack. Do I look like the type who'd openly announce his intentions before attacking?"

Looking at Yukio, the static flickering in midair around the screen, Hisagi clucked and said, "No, you don't." Then he hit a human dressed in black who was assaulting him with the back of his palm.

"Then why are you attacking me? Although, in light of what Ginjo told me, I understand why anyone who's friends with him would hate Soul Reapers."

Because of the Soul Reapers' betrayal, Ginjo's former Fullbringer friends had been slaughtered. Hisagi wouldn't be surprised if any Fullbringer who had heard about this from Ginjo would consider Soul Reapers as sworn foes, to be taken down at any opportunity. Maybe Urahara wasn't being attacked because they knew he had been exiled from the Soul Reaper's world? Hisagi speculated that that was the case as he parried the black-clothed group's attacks, and faint surprise showed on Yukio's face as he heard the Soul Reaper's words.

"Oh? So Kugo went so far as to tell you about that?"

He started to show an interest in Hisagi for the first time, whereas before he had been about as interested in him as a stone by the roadside, and he said, "I doubt that Kugo would have folded to torture and interrogation. How do you know him?"

"We shared a drink once... We're neither friends nor enemies right now."

"Oh...?"

"Well, I would describe it as the relationship between a journalist and their subject... Hey, if you're interested in what I have to say, would you at least stop these guys?!"

Hisagi parried with his attackers, ultimately leaping high in the air to escape them. He solidified the reishi at his feet in a spot the people could not reach and stood in the air. Hisagi stared at Yukio's projection on the screen, which was now at his eye level, and took stock of the situation.

*Well, I'm glad I wasn't in a gigai. If an ordinary human saw
me flying through the air...*

*Wait a sec! If they can see my spirit body, then does that
mean everyone down there is a Fullbringer?*

Supposing that all the people in black were Fullbringers,
there was a possibility they could even leap up to his level.
Realizing this wasn't a situation where he could catch a
breath, Hisagi rose up even higher, then once again looked
down at the group in black below him.

At that moment, a voice resonated from below and in
front of him.

"What a surprise..."

"Huh?!"

A tremble ran down Hisagi's spine.

"I never expected the Soul Society would hire journalists..."

The whispering sound of the voice felt to Hisagi like
it had the power to make his brain melt, and he momentarily forgot he was standing in a battleground. The very
odd-sounding voice and the fact that it seemed to emanate
from a place that was absent of spiritual pressure made
Hisagi, who was used to battle, wary.

"Who're you? You don't seem like a Soul Reaper or
a Hollow..."

When Hisagi slowly lowered his gaze, a beautiful young
woman appeared before his eyes. She was wearing a suit that

had both a dignified and seductive air and emitted an aura of enigmatic charm.

"Are you a Quincy? No...that's not it. If you're in league with Yukio, I guess that makes you a Fullbringer."

"You're exactly right... No."

She stopped speaking, and the moment he looked down the woman disappeared as though she had been dispersed into the air.

"Huh?!"

Hisagi was in shock. Just as he was thinking it was some sort of illusion Yukio had created, he realized an arm was wrapped around the upper half of his body.

"Uh... Huh?!"

He didn't feel as though anything were touching him. Hisagi's keen spiritual pressure senses didn't detect anything at all out of place, and as he turned, shaking off the arm in a panic, his hand cut through empty air. However, his eyes most certainly saw a slender arm gently hugging him close from behind. And as though to prove it wasn't a hallucination, a woman's beguiling voice resonated in his ear, "I suppose this is when I'm supposed to say 'exacta,' Ninth Company Assistant Captain?"

"What...?!"

Hisagi's suspicion of his enemy rose by several degrees. This peculiar expression, "exacta," was the favorite phrase of the Arrancar Findorr Calius, whom Hisagi had fought previously in this place—or, to be more accurate, in a replica town modeled after Karakura. He had told Yukio his title earlier, but this meant that the woman must have inside information about Hisagi. On top of that, she knew about the particulars of the battle he had fought here. And if she could get so close to Hisagi in midair, without revealing any indication of her presence, he couldn't underestimate her as an ordinary human.

"You sure have done your homework. What, are you a fan of mine or something?"

He couldn't underestimate her—even if she was an alluring woman who shook Hisagi to his core.

"Yes, I suppose I am... I've wanted to get close to you ever since learning about you... Would you believe me if I said that?"

He couldn't, even though her flattery was charming and her voice shook him to his core.

"L-like I would!"

He just barely managed to maintain his senses as he leapt back and put his hand on the hilt of his zanpaku-to.

That was way too close. If Captain General Kyoraku and Captain Muguruma hadn't warned me, I'd have been in hot water.

Recalling the time he had been assessed as "most likely to fall prey to a woman attacking his weaknesses," he felt clear headed, as though he were sitting under a waterfall.

It was like someone had peered inside Hisagi's head and was giving an unwelcome warning echoing up from below, "Are you okay, Mr Hisagiii?! Be careful not to fall for a honey trap!"

Urahara had called to him from below. Hisagi's face burned red and he objected, "Why's that the image people have of me?! There's no way I'd be fooled by that! I mean, I am an assistant captain!"

If the situation weren't what it was, Hisagi would have been nearly crying with the force that he was yelling. The woman spoke to Hisagi in a way that wasn't quite joking or serious. "Oh, how unfortunate. It would have been so much easier if I could have used seduction to avoid a fight."

Smiling bewitchingly, the Fullbringer woman stared at Hisagi and cocked her head to the side.

Get ahold of yourself! Don't let her get in your head! Right, think of Rangiku!

Without showing his internal unease, he feigned coolness and answered, "Too bad for you. I won't deny that you're charming, but you can't seduce me when you're not even dressed as boldly as Rangiku."

"Mr. Hisagi, I'm sure you think you're playing it cool, but if Miss Matsumoto heard you say that, she'd be grossed out and bring her heel down on you."

"Huh? What did I...?"

Hisagi was brought back to his senses by what Urahara had said, and his ears even turned red as he took in his surroundings.

The woman floating in the air chuckled as she looked at Hisagi, opened her arms and remarked, "Aren't you an amusing person? I hope the other Soul Reapers have a sense of humor like you do."

Then she made a flourish with her hands as though she were directing an orchestra.

"I'd like to take this occasion to introduce myself... I am Aura Michibane."

Her dancing fingers were like puppet strings controlling a doll and had a certain kind of beauty.

"Though I am but a handmaid serving a god that governs death, I am pleased to make your acquaintance."

"Huh?"

A god that governs over death?

Does she mean us Soul Reapers? What does she mean about being a handmaid?

As Hisagi mulled over his skepticism about this woman who called herself Aura, about how she acted and what she was saying, he noticed something was out of place around him. Just as he realized that the spiritual pressures of the people on the ground had changed, they all foisted their extendable batons up in the air. The scene, which looked exactly like plants extending their vines toward the sun, gave him a bad feeling. Then the bad feeling manifested.

The patterns on the batons gained form and rose into the air. They immediately started swelling and turned into large feelers that attacked Hisagi where he stood.

"Wha...?!"

Symbols and letters reminiscent of a divination circle swarmed and wriggled like a single living organism. Hisagi, who had been expecting them to release a Cero or something similar, was taken by surprise. He immediately unsheathed his zanpaku-to and cut away several feelers that were approaching him. However, the patterned limbs he cut away immediately recombined and once again attempted to attack.

"It's like a swarm of bugs. What's going on here?!"

Though Hisagi continued to dodge and slash, given the fact that his continued efforts made no impact, he determined that he would run out of steam before making any difference. Additionally, as Hisagi crossed swords with the patterned limbs he had sensed another danger. Whenever he cut the swarm of letters, his zanpaku-to's spiritual pressure would warp unexpectedly. It was almost as though the edge of the sword itself were becoming duller, and it felt similar to just before when his own physical abilities had felt decayed.

"Damn it... This feels a lot like the time when I got done in by Ayasegawa..."

Hisagi had once crossed swords with Yumichika Ayasegawa when Ichigo Kurosaki had first visited the Soul Society and caused mayhem. The result was Hisagi's crushing defeat.

Ayasegawa's secret weapon was Ruiirokujaku's ability to absorb spiritual pressure. Even now, Hisagi vividly

remembered the sensation of being rendered immobile after his spiritual pressure had been absorbed by blades of light that fanned out like the feathers of a peacock.

But this is different from back then. It isn't that my pressure is being absorbed so much as...it feels like I'm being held back.

I guess this is the "reishi subjugation" thing Mr. Urahara mentioned earlier. What a pain.

Though his spiritual pressure was unchanged, he couldn't help but feel an eerie dullness, as though his blade had sunk into a swamp. It was likely due to the special ability of his opponent, but he couldn't grasp anything about how it worked at all.

Is this like Kira's Wabisuke...? If it is, waiting it out probably isn't a good plan.

The thought of a zanpaku-to that multiplied the weight of anything it cut crossed Hisagi's mind. "Ah well..."

Then, facing Aura and the people in black on the ground, he issued a warning. "I don't know exactly what your aim is right now...but from now on I'm going to operate on the assumption that you're an enemy."

"Oh, I had no idea you could look so fierce."

Realizing Hisagi's bearing had changed, Aura's eyes narrowed as she replied, "If you would be so kind as to promise us that you won't interfere, we wouldn't be opposed to immediately lowering our weapons."

His demeanor was different from earlier when Urahara had been joking around. He met hostility with hostility and wore the expression of a Soul Reaper who would cut them down, human or not, without faltering. Although he thought it was likely that the captains who considered themselves the most aggressive—or dutiful—likely would have told him his resolution had come too late, Hisagi once again solidified his determination to cut down the enemy before his eyes. It might have been the influence of Tosen's teachings—and because Hisagi understood his blade was an object that could kill—but he deliberately gave those who stood in his way a final warning. "Who wouldn't interfere when they're being attacked? What're you trying to do, isolating the town like this in the first place?"

"We are laying the foundation..." Aura lowered her hands as she answered Hisagi.

As she did that, the wriggling swarm of patterns around Hisagi visibly settled and swayed to the right and left from a safe distance.

"The foundation for...?"

"Karakura Town is the world's most prominent Jureichi—you are aware of that, yes?"

"Well... No, you couldn't possibly..." When he arrived at the only logical guess about what their intentions were, Hisagi's voice went rough. "You're not trying to make an Oken are you?!"

An Oken—that was a key to the Reiokyu created from a Jureichi of one spirit mile radius and a sacrifice of a hundred thousand konpaku. Thinking back to the past, when Sosuke Aizen had invaded Karakura Town in order to destroy the Reio, he could guess that was more than enough reason to single out the town. However, Aura slowly shook her head at Hisagi's loud accusation.

"I suppose...that's close, but not quite right."

"What...?"

"We do not intend to sacrifice innocent people's konpaku, and we have no need to create an Oken." A daring smile formed on her face. Aura confused Hisagi with roundabout phrasing. "Our goal is...to make Karakura Town the true capital, where the king will sit."

"Huh?"

For a moment, Hisagi didn't understand. He felt as though she were making a facetious joke or just spewing random words to confound him. He would have been able to comprehend effortlessly if she had said that she was killing all the humans in the town to make an Oken, but when she said she intended to make this town the king's capital, the meaning of that sentence was too much for him to wrap his head around.

Aura kept speaking through Hisagi's befuddlement. "The Reiokyu and Las Noches—the thrones placed in the Soul Society and Hueco Mundo will serve as wings, and in turn, it will serve as their wings to lift up and create the perfect throne. That was the decree given to us by heaven."

"What're you saying? Actually...who's this 'king' you've been going on about supposed to be?"

That was the only question that mattered at that moment.

There's no way she means Aizen, right?

Or maybe it's Yhwach? No, I'm sure that Kurosaki killed him...

Several names came to his mind, but a young face floated in a corner of his consciousness as his thoughts spun with images and memories.

A...A king...?

"*...said...make...into...king.*"

I'm pretty sure that's the kid from the aristocrat's Shino-Seyakuin clinic...

Although he had just described the child to Urahara, he couldn't immediately find the connection. The existence of the child had been baffling in many senses, but he could hardly think this had anything to do with something as absurd as making Karakura Town a king's seat. However, when he recalled the details of that earlier conversation, Hisagi's heart began to chill.

"*And...Lord Tokinada said that he'd even make someone like me into the king!*"

"Oh!"

The twisted puzzle piece made an unpleasant sound as it began to snap into place in Hisagi's mind. He didn't know

whether it was fate, coincidence, or the manipulation of some unknown force, but Hisagi groaned as he muttered the name from his memory, "Hikone...Ubuginu?"

"Huh?"

At that point, Aura's smile faded for the first time. "What a surprise. How do you know that respected name?"

"You couldn't be...one of Tokinada Tsunayashiro's underlings?"

"Though I said I was a handmaid, underling...isn't quite the right word. That aside, are you sure about this? Are you sure one such as yourself should be calling someone from the Four Great Noble Clans—from the Tsunayashiro family— by name without a title?"

Though Aura spoke as though to provoke him, Hisagi wasn't swayed.

"I haven't got any reason to call him lord...not anymore."

"Actually, Mr. Hisagi, I don't think you call Miss Yoruichi or Mr. Kuchiki 'lord' either..."

Urahara muttered that from the ground, where he was listening in on the conversation, then Yukio said from beyond the screen as though following suit, "You're not going to go help him? I believe Aura will be fairly tough to go up against solo."

Watching the projected image intermittently mixed with static, Urahara used Benihime, which had been turned into a sword cane, to poke and prod at the ground as he responded,

"Not a chance. I'm more inclined to being a history buff and providing healing-specialized support, you see. Though he's capricious, Mr. Hisagi is much more suited to the attack."

"Hmm? Doesn't seem like he'd do much DPS though."

"He does tend to be more of a tank. His resilience against death is what really pushes him up above the rest."

The space was filled with static and the sound of the cane's prodding, and Urahara intently observed the group in black on the ground. Ever since they had ejected the tentacle patterns from their batons, they'd simply continued to stare at the sky motionlessly, slowly releasing the spiritual pressure they had.

"But what a vulgar thing you've done. Are you sure that you and the possessed can manage this?"

Accepting Hisagi's hard look with a smile, Aura, whose internal response to Urahara's words was inscrutable, raised her voice slightly as she addressed him. "You... truly are a frightening person, Kisuke Urahara."

"Oh, so you heard me?"

"Did you already comprehend my Fullbring's special ability?"

"Huh?" Hisagi seemed surprised and turned toward Urahara, while keeping a vigilant eye on his surroundings.

Fullbringers each had their own unique abilities. For example, based on the research he had done, Hisagi knew the man named Tsukishima, who was with Ginjo, was able to insert himself into others' pasts, and though he could only

do it to one person at a time, he had the terrifying ability to alter a person's history itself.

If the woman in front of him was also a Fullbringer, then he could believe the writhing letters and symbols around him, as well as his own delayed reactions and his zanpaku-to's sluggishness, was her doing.

Hisagi waited for Urahara's reaction, a pause that should have meant an advantage in the progress of the battle; however...

"Well of course not. Don't joke around like that." With a loud laugh, Urahara answered Aura's question. "You aren't using a single special ability, now are you?"

"..."

"Well, to be more precise, I suppose I should say that you can't use one..."

≡

KARAKURA TOWN

Gripping his Soul Pager, the Soul Reaper boy complained to his companion in a tearful voice. "Ahhh, what should we do, Shino? We definitely aren't getting through to the Seireitei!"

"Stop with that whimpering! Anyway, all we can do is leave town for now or head over to Mr. Urahara's and ask him about it."

In their attempts to process the situation after noticing the membrane of static covering Karakura Town, the Soul Reapers in charge of the town, Ryunosuke Yuki and Shino Madarame, had been busily engaged. Not only were they unable to receive any communications whatsoever over the Soul Pager, they had also heard that Deputy Soul Reaper Ichigo Kurosaki and his friends were currently out of town. The upshot was that they'd now have to purify all the Hollows themselves.

"There's a possibility the Quincies might be up to this... I wonder if we could go to Mr. Ishida's father at the general hospital and consult with him."

"I see him in front of the hospital sometimes, but to be honest, his eyes are so piercing that I can't approach..."

Shino sounded miffed as she pouted, "What is with you? You once said I got my big bro Ikkaku's piercing eyes—are you implying that I've been unapproachable this whole time?"

"Uh, you're an exception, Shino! Isn't that obvious?!"

"A-am I?" Shino was taken aback by Ryunosuke's firm assertion.

"I mean, it's you, Shino. Your shiny forehead is a lot more like Mr. Ikkaku than your eyes, plus my eyes are drawn to it, so if I can just loo—"

Scowling, Shino punched him directly in the face mid-sentence and started walking.

"We're leaving now."

"No good... We really can't get through."

Traveling along a railroad track using shunpo, the two had reached the boundary line that ran along the riverbed of the neighboring town. However, things didn't look good from there.

Though normal people and cars were going along their merry way across the town boundary and through the "membrane," the two couldn't make their way through it at all. When they tried to cut it with their zanpaku-to, their blades weren't able to penetrate it, and they confirmed that they were dealing with a barrier so firm they couldn't even scratch it using their shikai.

"The trains are getting through on their tracks as usual, so how about we try that?"

In response to red-faced Ryunosuke's suggestion, Shino exasperatedly replied, "Yeah, are you okay with that plan knowing that if we're still unable to get through, we'll end up hitting the wall traveling at the speed of a train?"

"That'd probably kill us, wouldn't it?"

"Looks like the only thing we can do is go over to Mr. Urahara's place. It's on the other side of town, but if we use shunpo we should be able to get there right away..."

Shino stopped talking at that moment. Something like static coursed through the air around them, and as though bubbling up from cracks in the floor of the world, several men and women clad in black appeared. They wore black gas masks on their faces, and though Ryunosuke and Shino were unaware of it, they were dressed exactly like the group that had appeared around Urahara Shoten.

"Huh?! They're wearing masks... Are these humanoid Hollows?! W-we should scram, Shino!"

Yuki, mistaking them for Vasto Lordes-class Hollows, reflexively grabbed Shino's hand to run, but Shino snatched her hand back and forced him to wait.

"Get a grip! Sure, these guys made a weird entrance, but they don't have Hollow spiritual pressure. Plus, their masks aren't white."

"Th-then do you think they're Quincy?"

"No... Well, I can't actually say for certain."

The Quincies had engraved a significant trauma within Shino's konpaku. Her beloved and respected superior Hidetomo Kajomaru had been slaughtered before her very eyes, and the Seireitei, the place they were meant to protect, was reduced to scorched earth, stained with blood and covered in wreckage. Though Shino's soul had been crushed with fear and she had lost her will to battle, she just barely maintained her attachment as a Soul Reaper and had trained with Ryunosuke to begin again, eventually arriving at her current state.

Right, if even Ryunosuke continued on as a Soul Reaper, then how can I let this break me?

Though Ryunosuke was currently trembling, he had survived that battlefield alongside Shino. True, he had looked

like he was about to cry, but if he hadn't been there with her, Shino's life might have been cut short at the hand of the Quincy. Then again, when she saw Ryunosuke trembling beside her now, she couldn't help but wonder if his surviving the battle had actually been a miracle, an anomaly. Regarding her colleague, whose courage was questionable, Shino felt a renewed resolve to maintain a level head as she questioned the black-clad, gas-mask wearing people who had appeared before her eyes. "So? What are you guys supposed to be? If you can see us even though we're not in gigai, I guess we can assume you're not just any normal humans, right?"

Shino composed herself so she could unsheathe her zanpaku-to at any time, but the people in black were silent, simply readying their extendable batons and attacking Shino and Ryunosuke with mechanical movements.

"Huh?! You're not even going to bother talking to us?!"

Even as they attacked her directly and more rapidly than she had expected, Shino was able to use her zanpaku-to, which she had immediately unsheathed, to stop their batons. Meanwhile, Ryunosuke screamed, "Wuu-aaah!" and slipped past the groups' attacks, trying to make a break for it.

"Ryunosuke! What do you think you're doing?! You've got to actually fight!"

"B-but they're not Hollows—they're humans, aren't they?! Are we even allowed to cut them with our zanpaku-to?!"

"If they can attack us when we're in our spirit bodies, it's not likely that they're normal humans…right?"

At that moment, Shino realized that something was off. In the same way that Hisagi had noticed it at Urahara Shoten, the spiritual pressure her zanpaku-to released started to dull.

"Huh?! My zanpaku-to…"

Taking advantage of her moment of unsteadiness, one of the people in black hit Shino hard on the back.

"Guh…!"

"Shino!"

"I'm fine. This is noth…ing…"

Shino then felt as though her whole body had been caught in a giant spider's nest. The movement of her body creaked and slowed like a machine that has run out of oil. Though there was nothing wrong with her mentally or physically, it seemed as though a strange pressure were impacting the flow of spiritual pressure that connected them.

"What…is this…?"

As though they had verified that Shino was weakened, the people in black took their distance at once and raised their batons in front of them. The patterns etched into those weapons floated up and turned into feelers that all flew through the air to attack Shino simultaneously. Uncertainty accosted Shino about whether she could evade this attack in her current condition, as the unfurling, arcane attack grew close, but she kept a steady grip on her sword to meet it.

"Shino!"

Ryunosuke attempted to run to Shino's location to protect her, but before he got to her there was a roar and the tables turned. Before the patterned limb could reach Shino and Ryunosuke, a red humanoid figure seemed to drop from the sky and kicked at the ground with the force of a cannon. The dirt, sand, a cloud of dust, and, almost as an afterthought, the people in black scattered high into the air.

"Huh?!"

"Waaaaaah?!"

Shino covered her face as a cloud of dust came at her, and Ryunosuke fell over from the impact. Once the dust died down, a lone girl was standing there.

"Who do you think you are, coming around and oozing your disgusting spiritual pressure on my turf? C'mon..."

Shino and Ryunosuke immediately understood the girl was someone to reckon with.

"Are you a Soul Reaper?"

Her spiritual pressure certainly was very like a Soul Reaper's. However, they could sense something not quite right about it.

The girl, who wore a red tracksuit, shouted irritably at one of the figures in black who was silently trying to stand, "Who said you're allowed to stand?! What're you doing taking that risk, baldy?!"

During this irrational rant, the girl kicked a rock at the person in black. Shino watched the rock, which was about the size of a fist, make a direct connection, knocking down the person in black once again. She cautiously began to speak. "Uh, um! Thanks for saving us from a tough spot! Are you part of the Thirteen Court Guard Companies?"

"Hunh? No way, you dunce. I'll tell you this, I didn't save you for nothing."

The girl, who turned toward Shino and stared her down, righted her hat, which read "UNAGI," and pointed at her own chest with her thumb.

"I'm not a Soul Reaper. I'm an Odd Jobs Service apprentice who happened to be passing by, Lord Hiyori Sarugaki!"

"What's an odd jobs service...?"

"You're an apprentice...?"

While Ryunosuke and Shino tilted their heads quizzically, the girl with the Kansai accent went on with a sour look on her face, "Any other time, I wouldn't take any job to help Soul Reapers since I hate them. Well, the situation being what it is, I'll make it cheap."

"Huh. Why're you talking like we're going to pay you...?"

"Shuddup, stupid! Ikumi told me to 'Take a job, no matter what it is!' What am I supposed to do if I don't get paid?!"

"I don't know what to say about that..."

Shino and Ryunosuke, not knowing how to respond to the girl's somewhat unreasonable yelling, glanced at each other. However, the situation did not allow them to continue

the idle chitchat. New static ran through the sky and even more people in black appeared from the resulting gaps.

"Eek! There are more of them—Are there are even more, Shino?!"

"What's going on here? What is with these guys?!"

If they attempted to simply cut them down with their shikai, would there actually be an end to it? Ryunosuke guessed that they couldn't know how many more were left and that there was a chance they'd end up in a stalemate. He lowered his head to the girl who had called herself Hiyori.

"Um, so I'll pay you. So, two for Urahara Shoten in Mitsumiya, please!"

"Why're ya saying it like that?! I'm not a taxi! You underestimate me, baldy?!"

"Eek! I'm sorry!"

"Well, it's fine... But you want to go to Kisuke's of all places, huh?"

Swinging her zanpaku-to, which she had taken in her hand at some point, she cut at the ground, raising a cloud of dust and putting the people in black in check. After picking up Shino and Ryunosuke with power that they never would have expected based on her small form, Hiyori didn't even give the two time to scream. She used shunpo to leap. Then, sensing a spiritual pressure similar to that of the people clothed in black who were popping up all over the town,

Hiyori scowled in annoyance and recalled the man who had once been her superior.

"Having to rely on that half-comatose lantern face is no joke...but in this situation it's the right thing to do."

≡

URAHARA SHOTEN

"What's wrong? Whether it's 'exacta' or 'no es exacta,' I'd be so happy if you could confirm whether I'm right."

From below the darkness of his hat, Urahara's sharp eyes glinted down at Aura. Though he smiled, there was something in his expression that said he could stab and kill his opponent in a moment and no one would blink an eye. When Aura saw his face, she felt shivers down her spine but appeared somewhat cheerful as she said, "How curious. I didn't think I'd given you that much information."

"You did end up doing that today though, didn't you? The religious group called Xcution started to throw its weight around right after the Quincy attack on the Soul Society. Did you think I'd ignore you?"

Urahara flipped his sword cane onto his shoulder and laid it on with a lightly teasing tone. "Well, I think you did a pretty good job, if I may say so myself. After all, I couldn't collect any info on you except your official records as

leader, Miss Michibane. But...after putting that information together with the dark underbelly you just showed me a hint of, I've started to get an idea of what's going on here."

"You are stunning, aren't you...?"

Aura ignored Hisagi, who stood in front of her, and dedicated most of her focus to the conversation with Urahara.

"What more could I have expected from the very man who created the Hogyoku himself, eh? We really must get you over to our side."

"..."

"The Hogyoku?"

The Hogyoku—the moment the term came from Aura's mouth, Urahara's smile disappeared, and he went silent. For his part, Hisagi wrinkled his forehead and spoke up. "What's that got to do with anything?"

"Well, but now we're getting into territory that's not appropriate for a so-called journalist to hear... So if you would, please take your leave."

Aura politely bowed in midair. Not knowing what his opponent's true motive was, Hisagi didn't know what his next move should be.

"What? Did you think I'd just go home when you asked me to like none of this was happening?"

"No... I wasn't asking you. I was threatening you that I would eliminate you by force if you go one step further, Assistant Captain."

Though Aura coquettishly cocked her head ever so slightly to the side and smiled, in the next moment, the blade of a zanpaku-to was at her throat.

"Oh!"

"You're underestimating me. Even without Gentei Kaijo, my shunpo speed won't be diminished."

By gauging when Aura would blink, Hisagi had closed the distance between them using shunpo and thrust his blade at her instantly. After seeing the zanpaku-to at her own throat, Aura gave Hisagi a look of honest admiration.

"What a surprise. It's almost as though you're an entirely different person than when you were being teased like a child earlier."

She still hadn't lost the smile on her face.

"You seem calm. You think I'm not the type to kill a woman?"

"No... As far as I am aware, you are a very Soul Reaper-like Soul Reaper. If there is a reason to kill someone, you would likely kill them; old and young, men and women alike, with no mercy, based on your internal sense of justice."

Suddenly the temperature of Aura's smile fell, and she stated a fact in a tone that would make the listener's heart freeze over.

"After all, you...killed your own teacher for the sake of the justice you believe in."

Hisagi's eyes then narrowed faintly. The surrounding spiritual pressure twisted severely, and those with

heightened spiritual pressure perception would likely have noticed that the air around Hisagi seem to quiver. Regardless, Hisagi's blade did not falter. Without creating a single opening, he kept his zanpaku-to on his opponent's throat.

"Ah, it seems that did not anger you."

"It's the truth. And also..."

What crossed Hisagi's mind were the words of the terrible criminal who had given his "teacher" the finishing blow.

"Forever is a word that shouldn't be uttered so lightly. Even Tosen's conviction wasn't eternal, after all.

"I did not kill Tosen as punishment for defeat.

"It was my version of mercy."

"Compared to what that Aizen said, that's not even a challenge."

"You really are such a funny person. How about this...would you join me?"

Aura proposed this carelessly, and Hisagi's forehead furrowed as he responded, "Do you comprehend the situation you're in? The only reason this sword hasn't gone through your throat by now is so that you can undo the barrier over this town."

Actually, it's weird how calm she is.

Guess I'll try shaking her up a little.

"According to Mr. Urahara, you haven't used any unusual powers yet, so was that strange letter tentacle thing that suddenly appeared one of your friend's powers? In any case, you better not get up to any tricks."

After hearing what Urahara said earlier, Hisagi had determined that the woman in front of his eyes wasn't able to use her unique ability as a Fullbringer. Though he didn't know how Urahara had come to such a conclusion, based on previous experience, Urahara's guesses weren't off.

But it's weird…

Even though I can see her in front of me, I'm definitely not sensing any normal spiritual pressure from this woman.

It's not as though there's no pressure at all, but it's almost like it's really weak.

Are all Fullbringers like this? I feel like Ginjo and his gang had more substantial spiritual pressure, but if she has the ability to erase her presence then the fact that she even came out into the open where we could see her is weird.

Or maybe she just hadn't used her ability yet. Even if those weird patterned limbs were her power, he was prepared to cut off her head if she made any moves. Yukio's capabilities were certainly a worrisome element, but if they were in league, he couldn't make any bad choices here. Although he did speculate that…

"Just as Mr. Urahara said earlier, I am the one organizing the religious group Xcution. Those on the ground are believers…or rather, they were heretics who opposed us—though they are being very cooperative right now."

"Huh?"

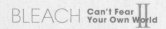

When Aura started talking of her own accord, Hisagi was befuddled and unable to gauge his opponent's aim. He had thought she might be intending to surrender, but he stiffened his guard even more, realizing that he couldn't be careless.

"Our believers currently number seven hundred seventy thousand."

"Seven..."

Hisagi had envisioned a small organization somewhere on the order of a hundred or so people when he heard she was the leader of a religious group, and the true number rendered him speechless. It was far greater than he expected, and it took him aback; Hisagi was unable to weigh whether his opponent's words were fact or bluff.

"Though it is a modest assembly, not even in league with the top five new religions in Japan...if you consider that it's only been a few years since it was established, you might say that's an odd number. Do you know how I gathered so many believers?"

"Can't say I do... The sects of the living world are none of my concern. I haven't got a clue how you're gathering people. Is there someone in your group who can brainwash people or something?"

"It would have been much easier if we had. Even if Mr. Tsukishima had still been alive, having him insert his book-mark into a hundred thousand people at a time would be quite difficult, of course."

"Hurry up and give me the answer. If you're trying to buy time, it's a wasted effort."

Hisagi was in fact starting to believe it was a tactic to buy time, but Aura broke into a smile before his eyes.

"The answer is simple."

She then pressed her neck into the blade.

"Huh! What are you...?!"

Is she trying to commit suicide?!

No, then it'd be all over after I caught her konpaku. There'd be no point in it!

What is she thinking...?

If he drew away his sword now, it would give her an opening. If that was what she was aiming for, it was sloppy. After wavering for a moment, Hisagi tried to pull away his sword and pin her down before the wound became fatal, but in the next moment, the woman's neck, which had been pressed to his zanpaku-to's blade much closer than he had imagined, easily slipped across it. Her head simply separated from her body and fluttered through the air.

Even as the woman's head left her body, her smile still did not vanish. Hisagi was so captivated by the scene that he didn't even notice that he hadn't felt any resistance on his zanpaku-to. Then the same beguiling voice from earlier came from the severed head that had been separated from its lungs.

"I simply created miracles. Right in front of people's eyes."

"What...?!"

Passing by Hisagi's side as he gaped, Aura's body grabbed her head and simply put it back where it had been. Moving gently, she turned to Hisagi, placed the palm of her hand against her forehead, and cocked her head to the side. There was no evidence of a cut, graze or even the remnants of trickling blood to be seen. Her neck extended as gracefully and flawlessly as silk. "Wha...what's going on?! You just..."

"Cut my head off?"

Aura spread her arms again to the left and right and started to manipulate the patterned limbs that unfurled around her. They were whipping around faster than before and the limbs themselves seemed to have more than doubled at some point.

"It was cut off. But I just reconnected it again."

"Was it super-fast regeneration? You're not a Hollow, are you?"

"Of course not. However, you're not far off the mark, even though you are wrong."

A somewhat lonely smile formed on her face as she manipulated the throng of patterned limbs to dance toward Hisagi.

"I am a Fullbringer. I was born with the Hollow factor gnawing away at my body, after all."

Hisagi was buried in red-black limbs until he simply disappeared beneath them.

Having observed these goings-on, Yukio determined that this was the moment—

"Reap, Kazeshini."

The surroundings billowed from attack, as the patterned limbs that Hisagi had been immersed in were cut away. Hisagi, appearing from within the scrum, gripped his zanpaku-to in its shikai form and murmured in annoyance, "They definitely grind at my spiritual pressure when I cut them."

The zanpaku-to he carried was made up of two giant, adjoined sickle blades made to rotate to bring about the image of a sickle and chain. The other end of the chain was also equipped with an identical double sickle. Hisagi held each of the blades' grips in his hands as he once again confronted Aura.

"Oh!"

The smile disappeared from Aura's face and she started to look cautious.

"I see... Now that I've seen it with my own eyes, you really do have a magnificent zanpaku-to. It's rare for one to have two swords."

"No good's going to come of praising me...plus, Kazeshini isn't two swords."

The number of Soul Reapers with a dual-sword style zanpaku-to was incredibly small—it was rare to the point that some said one could count how many had existed throughout the entire history of the Soul Society. The well-known ones were Captain General Kyoraku's Katenkyokotsu and the former Thirteen Company Captain Jushiro Ukitake's Sogyo no Kotowari. It was said that such zanpaku-to were so rare, they were one of a kind. It was true that Ichigo Kurosaki had commanded two swords using his Hollow and Quincy powers, but that information was only disseminated to a select group among the Soul Reapers. Hisagi didn't explain why Kazeshini didn't count as two swords as he slowly turned his blade toward Aura.

"I'm going to check and see if your 'miracles' or whatever are real."

Before he had finished speaking, Hisagi threw one of his zanpaku-to blades. The point of the blade rotated rapidly and turned into a disc of silver light as it leapt at Aura. But the blade flew past her and traced a rapid arc in the air as it went around her back.

"Huh!"

Hisagi moved around in the opposite direction of the disc's path to Aura's side and passed by the blade he had released himself as he made the chain cross. He used shunpo as he instantly created a circle with the chain in order to wrap up Aura. Then, after Kazeshini wrapped the chain around Aura several times, it once again fluttered back into his hand.

"Binding Spell sixty-two, Hyappo Rankan!"

After wrapping Aura in the jet-black chain, Hisagi had also used a binding spell on her in an attempt to completely restrain her. Countless points of light flew at Aura and stabbed through the chains that wrapped around her, fastening them in place.

"Give up. Magic tricks won't work on a Binding Spell."

Hisagi pulled on Kazeshini's chain as he tried to extract what Tokinada was scheming out of her. However, the chain's resistance suddenly disappeared.

"Huh?!"

He seemed to see Aura's body waver like smoke, and then she simply slipped right through and dangled below Hisagi. On top of that, the linchpins of light that he was sure Hyappo Rankan had released had vanished.

"What's going on here?"

If all she had done was simply pass through his blade, he would have thought it was just a trick or an illusion. However, she had been able to get past the chains that were wrapping her and even the Binding Spell, and so the only conclusion he was left with was that this was some sort of special power.

"Mr. Urahara! She's definitely got to be using some kind of abili—" Hisagi stopped mid-yell, suddenly looking below. "Huh?"

Urahara, who should have been observing them from in front of his shop, had disappeared. And by the time Hisagi scanned his surroundings, Kisuke Urahara had long since finished his work.

"Huh?"

Urahara, who had come around behind him, stabbed a thin, needle-like object deep into Hisagi's arm. As his brain

registered what was happening, the pain in his arm rushed throughout his entire body.

"Gah...Mr. Urahara?! What did you..."

"Excuse me, Mr. Hisagi." Urahara answered Hisagi's misgivings with his usual smile and without any remorse. "That was an emergency measure to forcibly remove your Gentei Spirit Mark."

"Huh? Oh..."

"The pain will go away soon, so please just deal with it a little longer."

Hearing Urahara's words, Hisagi realized that the place he had been stabbed was where he had placed a Gentei Spirit Mark in order to seal away his spiritual pressure. In that moment, power overflowed from Hisagi's body, and the atmosphere surrounding him was inundated, reverberating with spiritual pressure.

The Gentei Spirit Mark limited a Soul Reaper's powers to match the scale of the living world. That spirit mark, which sealed his spiritual pressure down to 20 percent of its power, wasn't something that generally could be removed of his own volition. The mark, which took the shape of a white poppy, the Ninth Company's insignia, was part of a system linked to the Seireitei's jurisdiction department through a special procedure and could not be lifted without permission for a Gentei Kaijo through a Soul Pager. However, Urahara had employed some kind of technique that used a single needle to remove the seal.

"Well, I thought it was possible, but that was pretty rash…"

"The ones who came up with this Gentei Kaijo system was the Department of Research and Development, you know? It's not as though I wouldn't be able to lift it… Oh, I'll make sure to explain to Mr. Kyoraku so that you don't get punished for taking it off yourself."

Urahara simply stood in front of Hisagi as he held his hat in his palm and said, "Let's do this together. It looks like she hasn't yet shown us everything she's got."

"Yes, sir!"

Though Urahara's tone was light, Hisagi sensed from Urahara that he couldn't refuse. If Urahara made the suggestion in that way, he was merely stating a fact.

So that means this woman is strong enough that we need to face her together, and I needed a Gentei Kaijo…

"Oh… But you know, that woman's power…"

Hisagi stuttered awkwardly, thinking that Urahara was, for once, wrong in his estimations, but Urahara didn't seem to mind at all and actually responded in a supremely self-confident tone, "Yes, Mr. Hisagi. Because of you, I've been able to confirm it. It's exactly as I thought."

"Huh?"

"She can't use a Fullbringer's characteristic power. All she can do is use Soul Subjugation, which is one of the foundations that Fullbringers share."

"What does that mean?"

Hisagi knitted his brows, unable to follow the conversation as Urahara described his suppositions about Aura Michibane's powers in a casual tone. "A Fullbringer controls the reishi that dwells in material, and they twist and manipulate the material, or sometimes the laws of physics themselves. On top of that, sometimes they can take something they have a special attachment to and change it to create an ability of their very own. But she doesn't have that."

"Huh? Well, she's been doing tricky stuff for a while..."

"Those are all basic Fullbring abilities...they're just at an unusually high level. She is directing the water and the earth to move and even controlling the cells in her own body and the atmosphere itself. She's controlling her blood and skeleton...no, she's manipulating her body at the brain and blood cell level to make herself look like smoke, even as she's still living—though I think those things are beyond common Fullbringer knowledge."

At that point Urahara stopped talking and looked at Hisagi, whose expression showed he wasn't getting it. He decided to rephrase it in a simpler way. "If I were to compare it to a Soul Reaper, it's like instead of using a zanpaku-to, she's using kido and hakuda skills on Sosuke Aizen's level... do you get it?"

"Ah!"

It was then that Hisagi understood just how dangerous the Fullbringer who stood in front of them was. However, it seemed that Urahara had set his sights even further ahead, and he turned his sword cane zanpaku-to Benihime at the woman as he voiced his suspicion. "However, that is not the issue. If she is here and she has over seven hundred seventy thousand followers, then... where are those believers right now and what are they doing?"

Rather than addressing Hisagi, it seemed he was directing the question to Aura herself where she stood some distance from them. In response to the one who had understood her true nature, rather than answering the question, Aura smiled cautiously.

"Kisuke Urahara...you really, truly are a terrifying person, aren't you?"

Her smile felt as gloomy, heavy, and cold as a riverbed in winter, and Hisagi, who had thought until that point that they were fighting on equal footing, felt a chill run through his body.

"That is exactly why we want your abilities. So that you can create a new Hogyoku...and elevate our offering of Hikone Ubuginu into a true god."

≡

As he watched what was happening in the space he had created, Yukio sighed quietly and muttered, "I'm not going to interfere directly, so do your damage—both of you."

Then he resumed his mission in order to go about fulfilling the role he had been given. He did it even though it meant betraying the very thing he was supposed to protect.

CHAPTER ELEVEN

DESTRUCTION.

That was the form of death *they* ruled. In short, *their* existence was burdened with contradiction—they were slaves to their everlasting impulse for destruction, repeatedly causing destruction because they sought freedom. *They* were the ones who had once fought each other for the rank of "6."

Grimmjow Jaegerjaquez.

Luppi Antenor.

Their personalities were entirely different on the surface, but in both a passion flowed in their foundations like magma. The Octava Espada had once said to Luppi, who had become the Sexta after Grimmjow had committed a blunder:

"The form of death that represents you is likely the same as Grimmjow's. That is the precise reason why you were chosen to succeed him among Dordoni, Cirucci, and the other candidates.

"And don't try to tell me you had no idea. The only way you can establish a connection with anything is through destruction. If the holes bored through us Hollows are what we lack, then you—or rather you both—can only use destruction as a means to fill that void.

"The reason why you hate Grimmjow from the bottom of your heart is simply because you hate others the same way you hate yourself.

"Actually, you are the legitimate Sexta, especially now. You should pity him.

"Well, if you accidentally kill Grimmjow, I will make good use of his corpse, so you should feel content in following your desires.

"Because as long as you carry that number, you are disposed toward an existence that causes *destruction*."

≡

THE RUKONGAI

After Aizen's departure from Hueco Mundo, the Espada numbers no longer held meaning, and what remained for *them* was the form of death called destruction.

"Ha hah! I won't let anyone get in my way. I'll tear you apart—eight against one!"

Swinging around his mangled tentacles and splattering his opponent's blood, Luppi hit Grimmjow multiple times in succession. Grimmjow, who through his Resurrección had transformed into a beastlike form, continued to use both his clawed hands and the occasional Cero to evade the surging wave of attacks that consisted of strikes, slashes, and the odd Cero.

"*Tsk*... There's no fun in killing a weakling who couldn't even leave a scratch on me."

"In that case, you can die bored."

Luppi used his four inner tentacles in an attempt to pin Grimmjow from four directions. He used his four remaining tentacles to release Ceros blended with his blood. Grimmjow, whom he faced, purposefully went out in front of him and slipped past the tentacles.

"But, you know what, I've got a reason to kill you."

Then, using his claws, he swiped away the Ceros that had been released from the remaining four tentacles and went right for Luppi's chest.

"Ah!"

"I'll crush anybody who underestimates me, no matter who they are!"

He tried to drive his sharply honed zanpaku-to claws into Luppi's chest like he had in the past, but...

"Gotcha."

Luppi smiled boldly and stepped forward, purposefully impaling his own abdomen with the claws.

"What?!"

"You'll crush anybody who underestimates you, eh? Yeah, what a coincidence."

Grimmjow had not only missed the vitals he had been aiming for but had been enclosed with Luppi in the eight tentacles like a carnivorous plant taking its prey.

"That's what I intend to do too, Grimmjow."

Wrapping his body around Grimmjow, he shot out Ceros all at once.

"Like I'd let that happen!"

At the same time, Grimmjow inhaled and let out an explosive roar interwoven with spiritual pressure, and from the armor that had opened up on his arm, he unleashed a Garra de la Pantera—lumps of spiritual pressure in the form of expelled claws.

Next, their attacks blended, and explosive flames and sprays of blood covered the vicinity.

"These guys are reckless. Seriously, fights between Hollows are pretty rough," Ginjo, who had been watching the state of the fight, muttered to himself as wind from the explosion swept up a cloud of dust and impaired his vision. From beside him Tsukishima said, "I'd say you're pretty reckless yourself."

"Stop spouting nonsense. I'm always about safety first."

"We'll leave it at that then. More importantly, looks like they're about to get here."

"Yeah. Well then, guess there's no telling what's gonna happen under these circumstances."

As Ginjo turned his eyes to the fight between the Arrancars, he was wary of the Soul Reaper who was heading toward them, as well as the other presence that seemed like it had intersected with that Soul Reaper.

"We should really start thinking about temporarily withdrawing soon. Even if we try disappearing into the chaos, we could end up goners in an instant if we try our luck and get hit."

"*Tsk...* I thought I got you just now."

After the cloud of dust dissipated, Luppi appeared from within it with a bloody, sarcastic smile, his tentacles even more torn up than earlier. Next, Grimmjow appeared, covered in cuts but not out of breath.

"That's my line. You toughened up suddenly. It ends here."

Grimmjow clucked his tongue, but he was grinning as he started to pour his spiritual pressure into his claws to deal the finishing blow. However—

"*Tsk...* I thought I got you just now."

"Huh?"

"*Tsk...* I thought I got you just now."

"You off your rocker or something? What're you saying?" Grimmjow asked dubiously, as Luppi repeated the same words over and over again. But...

"Huh?!"

He realized that the spiritual pressure he had been collecting in his claws had been reset, and then he knew for certain that something strange was happening.

"I thought I got you just now."

"Thought I got you just now."

"I   thought   I" "Th ou ght" "ought" "ught" "…"

While listening to Luppi's words repeat, he was overcome with the feeling of every nerve in his body going numb.

"Oh, sooo sorry. Did I forget to mention it? All of that blood I showered on you is chock-full of this super special poison," Luppi said with a smile that was both coldhearted and innocent when Grimmjow suddenly collapsed onto his knees.

"I dunno how it works exactly, but apparently it's a fearsome poison that causes your mind to repeat the past over and over again. And while that's happening, your body is fully paralyzed."

Luppi staggered, riddled with wounds himself, approaching Grimmjow one step at a time. He knew Mayuri Kurotsuchi had hidden that poison in their bodies. In fact, he had already demonstrated its results on Rangiku Matsumoto's zombie when he had fought her. Though whether the poison would work on a Hollow had been a gamble, he'd felt confident that Mayuri Kurotsuchi would have considered that contingency and had purposefully fought in a way that would shower Grimmjow with his blood.

"Ah ha ha. This isn't how I wanted things to go down..." Luppi ridiculed himself for being prepared to fight until his last as he looked down on Grimmjow. "But this is the first time I've felt alive in a while. I'm grateful, Grimmjow, even though I'm gonna kill you."

Then Luppi filled each of his eight tentacles with spiritual pressure, preparing to release Gran Ray Ceros from each of their tips. However, something wildly unexpected occurred at that moment. Grimmjow, who he was sure had fallen prey to paralysis, slowly stood up.

"What...?"

"*Tsk*...looks like you've actually got you...Luppi!"

"Impossible! How?! How can you stand?! Even captain-class Soul Reapers were no match for that poison!"

≡

"Ah, so that Arrancar has some tolerance," muttered Mayuri Kurotsuchi, who had been observing the events from afar with deep fascination.

"Tolerance? To the captain's poison?"

When Akon, who had stayed back at the Department of Research and Development, asked that through the communications device, Mayuri responded with an explanation of the situation that was interwoven with complaints about Luppi. "Really, what a thoughtless man. I need to establish a point in the past to go back to for the drug to demonstrate its absolute efficacy. Well, in any case there should have been a great many other types of paralysis drugs hidden in him as well."

Mayuri was intrigued as he watched the spiritual pressure data on Grimmjow and muttered to himself, "It seems he has been subjected to some kind of peculiar poison that elongated his life. Just contemplating such a poison is truly tantalizing."

≡

Grimmjow was once almost poisoned to death under the powers of a Quincy named Nakk le Vaar; he had become more resilient to poison after that experience, though he himself didn't realize it. Usually Mayuri would have immediately made "adjustments" to nullify that resistance had the captain been by Luppi's side. However, Luppi showering Grimmjow in poison hadn't taken the Arrancar's physical function away—he was even capable of standing on his own.

"Pretty sneaky thing you did there. Well, who cares? If somebody like you wants to kill me, take whatever shot you can."

It wasn't as though the poison hadn't had any effect. Though he was probably in the worst possible physical shape, Grimmjow still had a ferocious smile on his face and a thirst to continue the battle.

"I'll crush every piece of you—including that arrogant little face of yours."

Though Luppi had been uneasy when his opponent had stood back up, he regained his composure once he saw that terrible look.

"Ahh, poison just really isn't for me. Guess I'm no Szayelaporro."

While rotating his eight shredded tentacles, he started to stockpile spiritual pressure as though in preparation to release another Gran Ray Cero.

"All right, Grimmjow, challenge accepted."

Then a wicked smile, just like his opponent's, appeared on Luppi's face, and in an unusually rough tone he announced his murderous intentions. "With an enemy like you, I've definitely got to crush you head-on!"

It was a Gran Ray Cero octet.

Inferring that an extraordinary attack was likely on its way, Grimmjow once again tried to intercept it using a countermeasure.

The technique he used was a Desgarrón.

Grimmjow distilled spiritual pressure even denser than a Gran Ray Cero in the tips of both sets of claws, forming gigantic, piercing talons that towered over him to the left and right. Though no one could know which of them would be the more powerful, what was obvious was that the impact of either of their spiritual pressures would blow away everything around them.

"That's going to give us a little trouble. We're retreating."

"What the hell is that?! Are they trying to drag us into this too?!"

Ginjo and Candice yelled simultaneously and started to gather their companions in order to get away from the two Arrancars, but—

That *thing*, which flew in as though taking their place, inserted itself between Grimmjow and Luppi, instantly upsetting the spiritual pressure in the vicinity.

"Wha?!"

"Huh?"

Luppi and Grimmjow's concentration was broken by the shift in spiritual pressure, and they both stopped using their abilities.

"Who the hell are you?" Luppi asked, though he did not call off the spiritual pressure he had gathered in order to launch the Gran Ray Ceros. The mass of strange spiritual pressure that had leapt in began to speak.

"Ow, ouch, ouch! I just can't get the hang of landings..."

Muttering to itself in a tone that was entirely unfit for the current circumstances, *it* directed a smile that held not a shred of ill will at Luppi and introduced itself. "Yes! My name is Hikone Ubuginu! I was told by Lord Tokinada to come here to meet him...umm... Mr. Grimmjow!"

When Hikone heedlessly spoke, confusion filled Luppi's eyes as he looked at Grimmjow.

"Ahh, uh… Is this kid your reinforcement or something?"

"Hell no," Grimmjow readily denied, then stared straight at Hikone. "Wait, I don't remember telling you my name earlier. How do you know it?"

"Yes! Lord Tokinada told me! You're number six in the Espada, right?!"

When Luppi heard that, his eyes narrowed faintly. Grimmjow, on the other hand, didn't seem to care about Espadas or the Sexta anymore and reacted to something entirely different.

"Toki-nadah, huh? You mentioned him last time too, didn't you? Is that the Soul Reaper boss or something?"

Next, they heard another voice coming from behind Grimmjow. "Wrong, you numbskull. Though he is up there. Kyoraku is always our head."

"You're…"

He was a blond Soul Reaper who wore a captain's coat over a standard shihakusho. Though his hair and attire were different, Grimmjow immediately recognized him.

"That spiritual pressure. I remember it. You're one of the guys who got in the way of my battle to the death with Kurosaki in the living world."

"You're mistaking me for someone else."

"You screwing with me? Then who're you supposed to be? The kid's guardian or something?"

"I'm sure I already told you… 'What's it to you?'"

"You are definitely the ass from back then."

Grimmjow, who had heard the same phrase several years ago, let his mouth contort fiendishly and clucked his tongue, then said with glee, "Hah! I've got people to slaughter coming at me one after another! If Kurosaki showed up, that'd top the whole thing off!"

But Hikone easily refuted Grimmjow's suggestion. "Mr. Ichigo Kurosaki isn't coming."

"Hunh?"

Hikone brushed off the hostility of Grimmjow's stare and continued casually, "After all, Mr. Ichigo Kurosaki should be busy in the living world! Apparently he is risking his life fighting for his sisters! Isn't that amazing? It's so honorable!"

Hearing that, the blond Soul Reaper said dubiously, "Hold up, hold up—just wait a sec, lad. How would you know something like that? What did you say was going on with Ichigo?"

However, before Hikone could reply Grimmjow went on the move. He pointed his left hand at the blond Soul Reaper and his right hand at Hikone and Luppi as he shot Ceros in both their directions.

"That was close! What was that?! I thought that Ferris wheel was supposed to be your enemy!"

As the Soul Reaper grumbled and narrowly evaded the attack, Grimmjow bared his fangs and sneered, "Quit your lame yapping. I'm gonna kill all of you no matter what happens. You got no problems with that, right?"

"Did you just call me a Ferris wheel?"

Luppi, who had instantly used his tentacles to defend against the Cero, glared at the Soul Reaper and Grimmjow but then noticed Hikone between them.

Huh?

This kid didn't even try to dodge and he's unscathed?

Luppi felt a foreboding chill run down his spine. It wasn't just Luppi—Grimmjow, the blond Soul Reaper, and even the distantly spectating Quincies and Fullbringers all sensed a massive, overbearing power, as sweat oozed from their palms.

"Hey, what the hell is this kid even?" Grimmjow asked. The blond Soul Reaper shook his head and replied, "I wouldn't tell you if I knew. To be honest, I want to know too."

A single zanpaku-to reflected in their eyes. The sword that Hikone had unsheathed was an eerie hue, strangely white for a blade. It didn't seem to glint so much as blot out the light itself with a white cast. Unlike Sodenoshirayuki, which was a full-bodied white from its hilt up, this blade contained a sinister black motif intermingling with the whiteness here and there that made the Soul Reapers and Quincies feel a rudimentary fear, while it made the Arrancars and Fullbringers feel a clear and fundamental sentimentality.

"This presence...it's a Hollow's, isn't it?" Luppi asked his enemies without thinking, and Grimmjow replied in annoyance, "No doubt about it. This kid's zanpaku-to is the same as *our side*. It even opened up a garganta."

"Hikone, was it? What is that zanpaku-to?"

I'd prefer it to have been a trick of my eyes, but...

That zanpaku-to just ate a Cero, *didn't it?*

Starting with Arazomeshigure, there were several zanpaku-to known to be able to absorb reishi attacks. However, he didn't think this one was the same as those. Hirako's spiritual senses felt that the sword itself had taken in the spiritual pressure like a living creature sipping water. Hikone smiled happily upon hearing Hirako's question and innocently replied, "Right, I'll introduce you too, Mr. Hirako! This is the zanpaku-to Lord Tokinada granted me!"

"He *granted* that thing to you?"

As Hirako pondered the many ways that sounded like a complete joke, a voice that bewildered him all the more came from the base of Hikone's hands.

"How deplorable."

"Hm?"

"How could a fellow Hollow's spiritual pressure amount to this, even after breaking their masks?"

Those words were cast out by the zanpaku-to to Luppi and Grimmjow.

"What is Barragan doing? Has he been sealed away like me?"

Hirako had thought at first that Hikone's voice had just changed, but he instantly discounted that possibility. That was because there was spiritual pressure mixed in with the voice that made the atmosphere itself quiver, and it had a pronounced Hollow nature to it.

"What the heck is that zanpaku-to?! Is it externalizing itself?!"

"Quiet, Soul Reaper. I am not a zanpaku-to. I am... I am..." the zanpaku-to that was about to speak its name paused, then its voice turned resentful and irritated. **"Cursed...Soul Reapers...you did that to my name..."**

"What was that? A sword cracking a joke to itself is just so creepy, it isn't even funny."

As Hirako was dubious on the sidelines, Grimmjow and Luppi each started shouting.

"What're you complainin' about?"

"Anyhow, we've gotta assume that you're picking a fight with us based on what you just said, right?"

They turned their bloodthirstiness toward the zanpaku-to—or rather, to the thing that seemed Hollow-like—that had just sneered at them.

"Ah! Sorry! This little one recently developed the ability to speak, but it never has anything nice to say!" Hikone humbly apologized, but the child then blurted out something strange with a bright expression. "But I'll be so pleased if you fight me with everything you've got, even if it's out of anger!"

"Hngh?"

"This time I'll break your spirits and force you to acknowledge that I'm the king! Please expect great things! I'll give it everything I have!"

After so innocently provoking them, Hikone Ubuginu sonorously recited their own zanpaku-to's—or rather, the zanpaku-to-like thing's—release words.

"Mark their funeral, Ikomikidomoe."

Spiritual pressure rose up like a tornado and turned into an eerie wall of intermingled light and shadow covering Hikone's surroundings.

"Huh?!"

As the only one who had faced Hikone before, only Grimmjow noticed that strange atmosphere.

What's going on here? That's not the same as the bankai from before...

The bankai he had heard in Hueco Mundo had been the words "revolve around the stars." Back when the kid had shown off the zanpaku-to's ability, the sword had transformed into something that resembled a Hollow's arm that seemed to act of its own accord as it mowed down the surrounding enemies. Though the ability had been simple, its atrocious power was unparalleled to the point that many Vasto Lorde-class Arrancars had been overcome after a few swipes and ended up withdrawing. However, the difference wasn't only the words of the bankai.

The hell...? The density of this spiritual pressure is also on a different level than it was back then!

Several seconds passed as he had attempted to quell his doubt, and the tornado of reishi dispersed. What appeared from within the tornado that they had to *look up at* left everyone there at a loss for words.

"The hell is that?"

Even Ginjo and the others were able to clearly see it from their current distance. It would be hard to avoid noticing it.

The scene might have been familiar to Soul Reapers and Arrancars. This was because they had encountered Hollows that size in the past, such as the characteristically one-eyed Menos Grande gathering called Fura or the Espada Yammy Llargo, who after unleashing his anger, had become a non-standard size. However, even taking that into account, considering the fact that *it* preserved the spiritual pressure density of a humanoid Vasto Lorde, *it* was obviously an abnormality. The thing, which seemed to overwhelm both their vision and spiritual pressure perceptions, stepped firmly onto the land of the Soul Society while inhaling the dregs of the tornado. It was larger than a common Menos Grande and was a creature with an ominous yet beautiful form, like an Adjuchas. Furthermore, they could see that the shihakusho-wearing child who had appeared just earlier was riding it.

"That's not some ninja's frog. That thing's too dangerous to keep as a pet."

Meanwhile, the Quincies were also bewildered at the sight of the giant monstrosity.

"Is that thing bigger than the bankai of that wolf guy Bambi did in?"

"More importantly, something's bugging me..."

In response to Candice, who was gaping in shock, Meninas voiced a single response:

"Yeah, I know."

Candice broke into a cold sweat as she completed Meninas's thought. "Why does that Soul Reaper-looking kid riding on top of it have infusions of *his* spiritual pressure?"

≡

"Looks like the bait worked," Mayuri Kurotsuchi muttered to himself, grinning broadly.

Then, operating the communications device equipment in his ear, he gave instructions to the distant NaNaNa Najahkoop. "It's your time to shine. You may use one of your few redeeming qualities to strip their konpaku bare."

"That was an unnecessary dig. Well, I'll get it done. Was your target that weird kid and the monster all along, not the Fullbringers?"

"Analysis of the Fullbringers was naturally part of my goal. Originally, I was planning on analyzing those 'odds and ends' a little later. However, since baiting him was so easy, either something must have come up that made time of the essence, or he sent them knowing it was a trap."

Mayuri narrowed his eyes and uttered the name of a certain man as a sneer formed on his face.

"If it is indeed the latter, you must have entirely under-estimated me, Tokinada Tsunayashiro."

≡

AN UNDISCLOSED LOCATION IN THE SEIREITEI

The place was a certain establishment in a concealed underground area of the Seireitei that was exclusively used by nobles. This establishment was the gathering place of all direct data from the Visual Department— it was where every bit of the visual observation data of not only the Seireitei but also the entirety of the living world and, in recent years, parts of Hueco Mundo was gathered and stored. In a passageway that connected the establishment to the ground level, a man wagged his head vaguely at a collection of people who were blocking his way.

"The fun was just starting though. You've come to bother me at just the wrong time," Tokinada said with a tone of heartfelt disappointment, though his eyes revealed an irrepressible smile of joy. "So? What in the world do you intend to do? I'm afraid I'm slow on the uptake about these things, and I'd like an explanation."

The people in front of his eyes consisted of a petite Soul Reaper wearing a captain's coat and a group clothed fully in black waiting behind her—they were the Secret Remote Squad's first unit, the Punishment Force.

"Lord Tokinada Tsunayashiro, we have received word that someone is scheming to assassinate you. Until we eradicate the threat, we would like to take you into our custody."

"Oh, I see. So we've come to this." Tokinada shrugged with an unpleasant smile on his face. "Attacking from behind is Kyoraku's way of doing things. It looks like he still hasn't made any progress on laying the groundwork to unseat me as head of family. So, he figured out that I'm a step ahead of him, and he's trying to buy himself some time."

"Excuse me, but I do not understand what you mean to say, sir."

"Shouldn't you, though? Please stop your unskilled attempt at trying to fool me, ninth generation Fon. I can see right through your forced civility. I don't think superficial respect suits the Secret Remote Squad."

"How you jest."

Though Tokinada provoked her, Soi Fon did not display any change of expression whatsoever. Intrigued, the man who was the chief of the Four Great Noble Clans continued to toy with the lesser noble from a family of assassins.

"Of your older brothers, two of them passed while running errands for the Tsunayashiro family, did they not? Well, now that things have come to this, one could say they died in vain, but at least they fulfilled their role as pawns."

"I humbly accept your words of appreciation." Smothering her heart, Soi Fon responded mechanically. Seeing that, Tokinada's lips twisted, and he lit the fuse of what would be a bomb for her.

"I said the respectful facade was unnecessary, didn't I? The only ones you truly respect are the Shihoin household—especially that runaway Yoruichi, who isn't even the head of house anymore, isn't that right?"

"..."

Soi Fon's expression did not budge. However, Tokinada, who had sensed the faintest waver in her spiritual pressure, continued to throw words at her to salt the wound. "Oh, yes, that's it! Maybe if I were the one to take Yoruichi as my bride, you would show me true respect as one of her own? We're both part of the Four Great Noble Clans—don't you think we're a suitable match? The man who thoughtlessly killed his own wife and the woman who, incited by Kisuke Urahara, thoughtlessly betrayed the Soul Society. Indeed, don't you think we really are a perfect match?"

Snap—the sound of something breaking rang out.

Soi Fon's spiritual pressure started to waver, and the still expressionless Punishment Force behind her tried to hold Soi Fon back. In that moment, the voice of the person in question suddenly echoed through the passageway.

"Now now, you must not think much of me if you'd take me as a wife just to get on Soi Fon's nerves."

"Huh?"

When Soi Fon spun around, Yoruichi Shihoin was there, clothed in black.

"Ms. Yoruichi!"

"Oh, looks like you've overheard some embarrassing things."

In response to Tokinada, who was clearly not embarrassed, Yoruichi declared, "Since I couldn't possibly bear the unthinkable possibility you would actually propose to me, I'm just going to say it. If I were to be tied to you for life, I'd rather leave the Soul Society again and elope to Hueco Mundo."

"Ms. Yoruichi! Please let me come with you for your honey-moo—I mean when you elope!"

Soi Fon said that with a serious expression, and Yoruichi almost closed her eyes as she sighed, "Soi Fon, your brain just stops working the moment I show up, doesn't it?"

"Yes, ma'am! Thank you!"

"That wasn't praise! Actually, the Punishment Force is pretty amazing, considering they're waiting on standby with such straight faces. I suppose you really trained them well."

"Yes, ma'am! Thank you!"

Exasperated with Soi Fon, who had made an about-face from mechanical silence to acting like a talking toy that parroted the same words over and over again, Yoruichi once again addressed Tokinada. "It seems that I'm being targeted by assassins as well. I was so frightened that I thought I'd enter into Soi Fon's protection along with you. You wouldn't mind, would you?"

Tokinada was silent for a while, then eventually put on a sarcastic smile and let escape a loud sigh.

"So Yoruichi Shihoin, who holds no zanpaku-to, and the ninth generation of the Fon family, who specializes in martial arts. I see, I see. It seems that you've heard of my zanpaku-to's *ability* from Kyoraku, that chatterbox."

"How rude. I've got my own zanpaku-to. It's just that I'm much stronger at fighting in combat. That's why soothing my sulking sword is part of my daily routine."

Ms. Yoruichi comforts her zanpaku-to every day?

Imagining that, Soi Fon felt terrific jealousy for Yoruichi's zanpaku-to, even as she remained vigilant around Tokinada and would not say such a thing out loud.

While Soi Fon skillfully compartmentalized her thoughts, the Punishment Force calmed their spiritual pressure like the surface of a body of water in order to protect Tokinada.

Tokinada lingered in thought for a few more moments, then smiled in a remarkably vulgar way as he accepted the request. "Why not? In that case, I will ask you to guard me. I was very uneasy being alone anyway."

"You were uneasy?" Yoruichi asked.

"Yes. Lately I'm continually being attacked by assassins. And my guard Hikone is not here right now. On days like this, when I walk around without any guards in front of me—"

In the next moment an explosion echoed, and a gigantic hole ripped open in the ceiling.

"Huh?!"

A group of men and women whose faces were entirely covered by cloth appeared from the hole. They didn't give even a passing glance around as they rushed to the place where Tokinada and the others were, gripping their zanpaku-to that had already achieved shikai.

Assassins?! Wait, was he serious?!

No, they must be Tsunayashiro's people!

Though Soi Fon wasn't sure which was true, in either case her only prerogative was to keep an eye on Tokinada and protect him. Determining that, Soi Fon's expression instantly returned to normal, and she gave minimal instructions to the members of the Punishment Force under her command. "Get in formation and engage!"

"Oh, I'm so frightened. Assassins are so terrifying. I suppose I must also cross the boundaries of social status and fight alongside a lesser noble such as you."

Sneering at Soi Fon, Tokinada smiled and reached a hand to the zanpaku-to at his hip.

"Offer, Kuten Kyokoku."

Thus, near the center of the Seireitei, the curtains rose on a tragedy that the aristocracy had created. Perhaps it could be said that this was an overture to the further chaos that would ensue.

CHAPTER TWELVE

FULLBRINGERS.

Since ancient times, they were those born at the nexus of human and Hollow relations. Those who knew the truth of the Fullbringers' birth were few. The Fullbringers themselves had been granted their powers, which they absurdly did not know the significance of, through a circumstance they had no control over—as a result of their parents being attacked by Hollows. There were even some who overindulged in their powers, believing them to be useful. However, what they knew was only the surface.

The ones who continued to use their powers just as they desired, without knowing their significance, would eventually begin to destroy themselves. Those who didn't indulge their desires still had powers that others did not and eventually became so unstable that most ended up trying to hide from the world.

Specifically, the unique power they possessed of using their Fullbring to manipulate any object they had an attachment to could seem like just the kind of power that would be bestowed upon them by god. That, or the power could be thought of as a god in and of itself. It was no exaggeration to say that they seemed able to rearrange parts of the world's state of being itself. It was almost as though they had the privilege to shout their objections against the system someone else had created.

They had attachments to what was around them. In other words, the Fullbringers' characteristic power was something that simultaneously caused them to rise above the physical world and the chain that kept them connected to the world they ended up floating above.

So what became of those who lacked attachment?

A Fullbringer who had not a shred of sentiment, who refused to have connection, affection, or hate for the world, for anything around them, or even their lives themselves— Where would such a Fullbringer land?

Aura Michibane was one answer to such a question.

She was a rare second generation Fullbringer. Though her father had been a Fullbringer, her mother had been a normal human. She was the realization of the feelings between her Fullbringer father and human mother. They had been tied by love through hardships that common people did not know, and they were each other's destiny, but her merely human mother had been attacked by a Hollow. Her Fullbringer father had made full use of his powers to force the Hollow to withdraw, but Aura's mother had sustained a deep wound during the incident. Though she delivered the baby safely, in exchange, the wound had taken her life.

Maybe the Hollow was attracted because I'm a Fullbringer and my blood was mixed in her? It was a question that had tormented Aura's father, and he continued to search for a way to erase that power from himself even after Aura was born. It was possible that it wouldn't just be him. He was afraid even Aura would be rejected by the world.

Then, when a decade or so had passed, Aura's father turned a gleeful expression to Aura, who had grown rapidly, and spoke to her.

"Rejoice. You and I might be released from our curse. There's this Deputy Soul Reaper named Kugo Ginjo and he's gathering people. I don't know what a Deputy Soul Reaper is supposed to be, but we can trust this man, as he claims that he can absorb our Hollow power from us. First, we'll check if it works on me. If nothing bad happens, then after that...

"Aura, you'll be able to live a normal life."

Listening to him with hope and joy, and also a fragment of unease, Aura thought:

I wonder what normal is. Why would I want that? Isn't Hollow power the basis of the Fullbring power my dad taught me? Why would I give that to someone else? Do I have to erase

it? If I do that, I won't have anything else. What does it mean to
live normally?

Does that mean I'm not "normal" now, Dad?

Aura, who had been confined to a basement by her own father, suddenly had these thoughts.

Aura's father might have been broken by his wife's death. Though he had confined his own daughter underground, it wasn't as though he had been violent to her or neglected her upbringing. She was someone he needed to protect, and the offspring that his beloved wife had given a part of her life to. In other words, she was something that gave his life meaning. He had to protect her—from Hollows, from inquisitive human eyes, from the world that treated them like blasphemy itself.

For Aura, who had been raised in a water tank room in the basement of their house, the world consisted only of that space and her father. Aura's father, believing that knowing about the world would only bring her unhappiness, wouldn't even give Aura a single book. He didn't teach her about television, of course, or that there was anything beyond the room. He only taught her the basics of how to read and write, the laws of physics, and about her Fullbring, so she could protect herself against a Hollow.

To her, that was the entire world.

Though it was unobstructed, the world did not spread any further than that for her.

A world where she could not even identify the passage of time.

A colorless world.

A world without freedom.

A world where she could not know hope or despair, or the difference between them.

The one and only thing that moved her was her father's cooking. Though she had memories of her father's meals being delicious, before it could become the cornerstone of a Fullbring through attachment, her father went to see the man named Ginjo.

And he had never come back.

Even Aura, with her meager knowledge, quickly understood that something abnormal had occurred. However, she wasn't able to determine what to do in that situation.

They say that starvation is one of the particularly painful types of human suffering. To Aura, who had never experienced any scarcity of food to eat, even while she was confined, the pain she experienced then for the first time was more than enough to break her immature mind.

The reason she didn't break completely was likely because of the blessing of her father teaching her the basics of her Fullbring, or possibly because of the grace of the certain skills that had always been within her as a Fullbringer. Regardless of which it was, before she reached the point of no return, she was able to escape the situation.

When she had reached the limits of starvation, she raised her hands to the tanklike walls of the room she was in and brought out its soul using her Fullbringer powers, enslaving it, and then, in the next moment the wall that had been restraining her—the reinforced glass of the tank—turned into sand and disappeared in front of her.

She stepped out into the outside world on uncertain legs from her room in the basement. Still not realizing she was in the inside world of the house, she used her Fullbring to destroy all seven locks that had been placed on the door and kept walking. The first part of the world she grabbed was a food item from the kitchen. Realizing it was one of the components of the meals her father had made for her, she gobbled it down on instinct and then immediately spat it out because of its rancid taste. Ironically, it was her own body that ended up rejecting the one and only part of the world that she had an attachment to. Had that one moment not transpired, she would have awakened to *food* being the attachment for her characteristic power and likely would have been able to live out her life as a "normal" Fullbringer.

She might have met the man named Kugo Ginjo. She might have fought Ichigo Kurosaki or found true salvation. However, that did not happen.

Nothing ever made its way into the girl's world that was a tether she could attach to. Perhaps, though they had a twisted relationship, her father might have been her tether, but he had disappeared from her world as well.

When she actually left the house for the world outside and collapsed on the ground, she was lucky to have been found by a passerby and was put directly into the care of the police. When they found evidence of her having been confined in the house, society was up in arms about the abomination of a man who would lock up his own daughter. But even that uproar immediately quieted, and the girl named Aura was forgotten by the world.

Not wanting to give her the name of the father who had kept her imprisoned, she was taken in by the Michibane family on her mother's side and lived her life as "Aura Michibane" thereafter.

≡

Several years had passed since then, and she had blended into society. Then again, it wasn't quite correct to say that she blended in. She had erased herself completely and lived like a weed on the side of the road.

She was very beautiful, and it wouldn't have been unusual for her to have attracted the attention of both men and women. Considering that she hadn't drawn looks despite that, it was possible her Fullbring might have also had an influence on her surroundings.

She didn't intend to hide from the world. It was just that she was unable to hold any interest in it and had settled into it in that manner almost naturally.

When it came to her father, the one and only person she had trusted, others had continuously vilified him, telling her he was a "bad person" and saying "Forget that man." Based on the information that she had gathered since then in open society, she also realized that her father had indeed been abnormal. She came to that realization as she was growing up, but Aura no longer cared about it. To her, that cramped water tank room had been the first true world, where she had never come to find an attachment. She could only view this supposedly stimulating new world beyond it as just an extension of the water tank.

Though broadly speaking, there was nothing that she had an attachment to in order to mature her Fullbring, when someone asked Aura whether she had attachments, she had this single reply:

"What's most important to me is the Fullbring that my dad taught me. That was what saved my life. Because of it, I can keep living. I need nothing else. I don't care about my father. But the Fullbring that my dad taught me is everything to me."

Then the one asking the question nodded in satisfaction as he said, "I see. I see. So that's the upbringing you needed. It's pretty funny."

That man, whose face wore a vulgar smile, was something different from the humans surrounding her; she had realized that immediately. One day, *it* had suddenly appeared in front of her. No one else could see it. It was something similar to the white monsters that occasionally tried to attack her. The man, who was dressed in an odd manner, as though he had come from another era, observed her appraisingly as he spoke. "So you could even hunt a huge Hollow at that age. I find it so very intriguing that you were able to do so using only basic Fullbringer abilities."

As he spoke, the man kicked the wreckage of the white monsters Aura had just dealt with a moment ago, which were scattered around him.

"Who are you? Are you not a human?"

"Oh, me? How rude of me. I'm what you people would call a god. I'm something called a Soul Reaper—a god of death. Did your father not tell you about those?"

Soul Reaper.

Memories came up inside her. The absolute entities that ruled over death she had read about in books on the outside were not what came to mind. Instead, she thought about the last words her father left her with:

"There's this Deputy Soul Reaper named Kugo Ginjo, and he's gathering people."

"Ginjo?"

Aura muttered the name, and the man who had called himself a Soul Reaper laughed mockingly.

"Ha ha ha ha ha! So that's what you think! So close! So very close! I wonder if it would have been better if I had been. For both you and Kugo Ginjo."

"Who...are you?"

In response to Aura, who asked that with no hint of emotion and simply had suspicion in her words, the man's mouth twisted in delight all the more as he sang out his own name. "My name is Tokinada—Tokinada Tsunayashiro."

"Tokinada...?"

"That's impertinent for such a human. You may add 'lord' to my name. It's Lord Tokinada to you. Though I'm under house arrest, the living world has been so interesting lately that I just ended up slipping out and coming here. Well, it's good evidence to show that the main family does not pay attention to me."

Aura didn't pay any particular attention to the man who had started talking about things she didn't understand at all and that she hadn't even asked about, but right after that, the matter he talked about did firmly end up drawing Aura's attention. "Oh, right, right. This isn't about my name and circumstances so much as who I am."

Still wearing a friendly smile, the man calmly told her the truth.

"That's a simple matter. I'm related to the family that gave the order to kill your father."

"Huh?"

Aura's face, which had been like a mask until then, crumbled noticeably.

As though he were enjoying her reaction, the Soul Reaper named Tokinada continued, "Officially, your parents' whereabouts are unknown, but they're actually dead. You could show me some gratitude for saving you a hopeless search. I'd even enjoy it if you cried and yelled. It'd give me a brief amount of amusement if you were to cry out that I'm an enemy of your parents and if you tried to kill me. Would you like to try your hand at seeing whether kido or Fullbring is more powerful?"

"I don't understand. Your family killed my dad? Why?"

"Hm? Right, the reason, the reason... If I could say there was no reason, I could have further denigrated your father's memory, but I suppose I'll tell you the truth."

Tokinada slowly walked around Aura as he observed the fluctuations in her spiritual pressure. Although he saw bewilderment, he did not sense any turmoil from emotions like anger or grief. Staring at her as though he were ogling some rare beast, Tokinada answered her question. "It was to retrieve something—something that was originally our property has fused to your father's and your konpaku."

"What?"

"Well, does it matter what it is? What's important to you right now? One of the members of the hateful family that is your enemy, that stole the world in your cramped fish tank, is in front of your eyes right now."

When Aura heard those words, she narrowed her eyes.

"You know...about my past?"

"Yes, naturally. I was watching. There was likely some factor hiding on your mother's side as well. Two generations and Fullbringers at the same time is exceedingly rare. I took the opportunity to observe. So, what will you do? If you want a duel, I'll accept. Of course, I'll defend myself."

"I don't need that. To be honest, I'm not interested."

When Aura swiftly shook her head, Tokinada laughed.

"Ha ha ha, of course, of course. That *is* your personality, isn't it? In the past when I tried this tactic on a man who was the exact opposite of you, who had wallowed in sentimentality, I used a more elaborate scheme. Yes, the memory of that man glaring at me with unseeing eyes still makes me giddy even now. Though it seems you couldn't even begin to comprehend how that feels."

In speaking about someone who wasn't even present, Tokinada seemed to intend to make a fool of Aura. Responding without anger or fear, Aura indifferently asked about her own fate. "Are you going to kill me too?"

"Yes, eventually. Depending on the situation, I might just overlook you."

"Eventually?"

While she of course felt no emotion toward the man in

front of her eyes who had just declared he would kill her, Aura could not gauge what the man's motivations were and was bewildered. Perhaps that bewilderment itself was something like the only emotion that Aura allowed herself. Tokinada did not lie about his goals as he described them to her. He declared his intentions in the knowledge that he would revel in the results, regardless of her reaction. "That factor that resides in you would be much more entertaining if it were operating independently than if I were to retrieve it as a part of you. Furthermore, you seem like you'd make a useful pawn."

"A pawn. You want me to be that for you? For what purpose?"

"You have no attachment to this world, right? In that case, why not remake the world anew? If we create a new world, you might even be able to find an attachment there."

Aura, who couldn't comprehend the world at that time, didn't know whether or not he was all talk. Like the snake that had originally tempted mankind, Tokinada used words like threads to entangle her little by little.

"Though the heart and left arm ended up returning to the Quincies...the thing inside you is also rather unique. I would certainly like you to become my pawn. I'll give you whatever you desire—to the extent I am able, that is."

"There isn't anything I want right now."

"In that case, you can think it over until that time eventually comes. Also, if you are to become my pawn, then work on your manners. Even a fake smile will do. A faint smile from you could likely seduce men and women alike."

He spoke crudely, but she ignored him and asked insistently, "What's inside of me?"

In response to that question, the man grinned and informed Aura of a fact.

"It's an organ of something called the Reio, the thing which we call his Saketsu."

CHAPTER THIRTEEN

THE PAST, A CERTAIN PLACE IN THE SOUL SOCIETY

"GAH..."

Blood and an anguished cry came out of Shuhei Hisagi as he fell to the ground on his knee.

"What's wrong, Shuhei? Weren't you going to teach me about having the 'right' to do something?" This question was delivered harshly by the Ninth Company Captain, Hisagi's superior Kensei Muguruma, who was looking down at him.

"I'm still getting started..."

Spitting out the words through gritted teeth, Hisagi stood up. "What? You still wanna go? I'm getting hungry and you'll just end up dead, Shuuheiii." The self-proclaimed "Super Assistant Captain" Kuna Mashiro at his side fussed from under her mask.

At the time, they were resisting the Vandenreich. Captain General Genryusai Yamamoto had been killed by Yhwach, and the unease that accompanied their defeat seemed to spread among the Soul Reapers like a plague. Four of the captains' bankai had been stolen, and they didn't even know how to begin fighting.

That was when Muguruma had commanded Hisagi, "Perform bankai."

"I didn't lose my bankai this time, but that may not be the case next time."

"The more guys who can do bankai, the better."

He had heard that the Department of Research and Development was currently researching a way to prevent bankai from being stolen. However, they had no idea whether that research would be complete before the next invasion or whether the stolen bankai could be taken back. Either way, if they could just formulate a countermeasure bankai it would undoubtedly be a major turning point in the war.

Though Hisagi wasn't against the plan itself, Muguruma's scheme was to awaken Hisagi's bankai by having a Hollowified Mashiro attack him aggressively.

She was at the same assistant captain level as Hisagi, but she was tenacious and had been working with Hirako and the others in the living world as a Visored. She likely couldn't have been outclassed by a powerful captain when she was Hollowified. Despite her power, she was distinctly uncharitable. Continuing to battle her despite the difference in their abilities was essentially putting Hisagi's life in danger. The basic plan was to make him learn bankai under threat of death. And Muguruma hadn't chosen that method of learning anticipating automatic success.

In the past when Ichigo Kurosaki trained in order to bring out his mask—which was his Hollow power—he'd used a dangerous method that would cause the Hollow in him to take over his body if he made even one misstep. Muguruma had been involved with that effort, and as a result, Ichigo Kurosaki's power increased by no small amount. Normally it took a long time to achieve bankai, but if they wanted to shorten that time, Muguruma knew that they needed to act accordingly.

If he couldn't withstand it, then Hisagi would likely die in the next battle.

Although there were methods to use other than bankai if one did not have one, Shuhei Hisagi was not a skillful enough man to pull those off. Yet Muguruma knew that he had abilities worthy of being an assistant captain. In truth, Muguruma had complex feelings about Kaname Tosen, who had been his subordinate, and he had trained up the young boy who had been crying in the Rukongai to this level. That was exactly why Muguruma had purposefully invoked Kaname Tosen's name so harshly.

"Do you doubt that she'll really kill you?"

"I ain't soft like Tosen."

The assistant captain was perplexed by the question but reacted instantly.

"Hold on, Captain Muguruma."

"I looked up to you. And I respect you too."

"But…"

"You got no right to badmouth Captain Tosen…!"

By then he had gone through over half a day's formal combat training with Mashiro, but…

"I never had a right to badmouth Tosen, you say? Don't be soft. Whose fault is it that he's getting badmouthed? I'm saying *you're* half-baked."

With Muguruma's attempts to rouse him, Hisagi stood even straighter.

"I already knew that…"

Though it sounded like he had conceded, Hisagi's eyes were not dead. If anything, they transformed with the resolve to challenge the deepest pits of hell.

"But I simply can't condone anyone badmouthing him."

"You're being unreasonable."

"Yeah…I am."

Hisagi staggered as he stood up and once again bowed his head to Muguruma and Mashiro.

"Captain, thank you very much. You too, Kuna."

"Why do you say that?"

"Because I'm not the only one risking their life."

"*Hmph.*"

When Muguruma heard that, he averted his eyes uncomfortably. A bankai could be obtained by toeing the line between the zanpaku-to's externalization and submission, and it was the deepest power a zanpaku-to held.

Because of that, in the middle of attempting the process of submission it was possible to roughly estimate what kind of bankai it would be and when it was learned, so the user could often naturally handle the power. However, when suddenly attempting to bring out a bankai's power like this, there was the chance that the bankai would rampage.

If a bankai like Mayuri Kurotsuchi's Konjiki Ashisogi Jizo Matai Fukuin Shotai's "Spray lethal poison in a hundred-mile radius" were to be invoked and Hisagi were unable to completely control it, Mashiro and Muguruma would die.

Even if it didn't come to that, since bankai often had special abilities, even if the user did have complete control over theirs, getting anyone in the surrounding area caught in its power was a concern. Hisagi had realized that was exactly why they were training so far away from the Seireitei, and he had thanked Muguruma and Mashiro for putting themselves in harm's way despite such a risk.

"That's quite immodest of you. If your bankai runs wild, I'll be fine."

"Could you quit saying stuff to demoralize me?"

"But you know, I hope it's not like that Sakanade thing."

"Sakanade...? Is Captain Hirako's bankai that dangerous?"

In response to Hisagi's question, Muguruma awkwardly tutted and shook his head.

"If you don't already know, then forget about it. You just don't tell people about other people's bankai."

"Right..."

He remained curious, but if a bankai's ability was revealed to the enemy, there was a chance they could come up with countermeasures, and since it was common to hide one's bankai's nature, Hisagi didn't pursue it further. Though there were some who were cocky and didn't hide their bankai in order to prove they could resist whatever counterattack they faced, those who did so were often Soul Reapers who didn't shirk their self-discipline. As though to change the subject, Muguruma started talking about Hisagi's bankai.

"Well, if we're talking seriously, I think your Kazeshini already packs a punch as a shikai. If you make it a bankai, there's a chance you might not be able to make adjustments. That's why I've left this to Mashiro, since she can probably deal with it."

Mashiro, who had been listening in but seemed bored up until that point, pouted and complained to Muguruma, "Huh? What the heck? But then *you're* not doing anything, Kensei! I'm actually the only one who's been battling all along! You're the one who's supposed to be a captain! It's unfair! Unfair! Unfair gorilla!"

Mashiro kept repeating "gorilla, gorilla," and although a vein started pulsing on Muguruma's forehead, he used all his power to ignore her and took a deep breath as he turned back to Hisagi with a serious look on his face.

"To phrase it another way, it's actually a wonder that you haven't been able to acquire bankai up until now. If you know how to use your shikai, then you can at least have a conversation, right?"

"Yes..."

With a zanpaku-to, the user would answer the call inside the zanpaku-to, and by calling the sword by its assumed name, they should be able to turn an Asauchi into a shikai. When that happened, they could talk to the soul in the zan-paku-to—or rather what perhaps could be called the true form of the zanpaku-to—in a mental realm. In Hisagi's case, since he could use a shikai with no issues, all he had to do was externalize the true form inside the zanpaku-to in this world and use force to make it submit, but—"To be honest, even though I've talked to Kazeshini, I don't think anything I'm saying is getting through. Actually, it will barely show me itself even in the mental world and just appears in the form of a black shadow or a black puddle or a black twister every once in a while."

"That's an odd one."

"In the past, it externalized once when we were in the middle of a huge conflagration, but it looked a little different, and for a moment I had no idea it was Kazeshini."

"Right. I don't know the details, but it seems you were once forced to make it externalize."

Hisagi didn't speak more about the incident itself and instead focused on Kazeshini's nature.

"Maybe it's because it knows I might not like its form, but it won't really talk to me. Every so often when it does speak, all it says is disturbed stuff like, 'Give me blood,' or 'Offer your life.' I know it's not fundamentally a bad guy, but honestly I have some reservations. I'm worried that if I understand it completely...that maybe I'll end up tainted by it."

"Are you scared?"

"I can't say I'm not."

As he spoke, Hisagi regarded Kazeshini, which he had made into shikai during training. Muguruma thought for a bit then muttered as though talking to himself, "You can't know for sure that a zanpaku-to's words are really what it thinks."

"Huh?"

"Well, whatever path we take, it's clear we won't make it in time using the usual methods."

Muguruma simply approached Hisagi and brought his hand up to his own forehead—then making a motion as

though he was tearing at his own face, he pulled a Hollow mask out of thin air and equipped it.

"Wha...?!"

The air creaked, and Hollow spiritual pressure coursed past Hisagi's spiritual pressure perception. Adding to the Hollow spiritual pressure from Mashiro, who had had her mask on until then, the dense pressures sandwiched Hisagi and resonated around him.

"Huh? Are you taking over, Kensei? Then can I go get a snack?"

"No, you idiot."

Dismissing Mashiro's words, he hit Hisagi with a spiritual pressure filled with the brutal thirst for blood.

"From here on out, we're going to tag team."

"Huh!"

In Hisagi's mind, the image of death came to him even more clearly than when he had been fighting Mashiro. Rather than the deaths of those in the living world, he imagined the death of his konpaku itself. All of his memories and experience would disappear, and he would turn into scraps of reishi on a journey to nothingness. For a moment, Hisagi's mind flashed back to a certain scene...

This scene, the clearest vision of death that had been burned into the foundation of his very konpaku, came back to him. It was the scene of death itself that came to mind every time Hisagi confronted fiendish Arrancars, Aizen, or formidable enemies like the Quincies just now.

It wasn't the time he had been attacked by a Hollow in his youth, or when he had almost been butchered by a monster called Ayon, or when he was almost killed by the bankai of Chojiro Sasakibe that had been stolen by the Quincies.

It was the time when, after being attacked by countless huge Hollows, he had lost a friend named Kanisawa. What allowed him to move through that fear were the teachings of Kaname Tosen, but even now, that scene still came back to him.

What this meant was that the spiritual pressure of Muguruma before him was just as dangerous, and Hisagi's instincts were warning him that he was on the brink of death. When Hisagi started to freeze up, Muguruma spoke to him with his mask still on. "So you're afraid of your zanpaku-to? That Tosen guy also said something like that. He was always blathering on about how that was why he could fight."

"…"

"I can't clear away your fear. But if it's like Tosen said, and you can fight because of your fear…"

Readying his zanpaku-to, which was in a knifelike form, Muguruma hit Hisagi with even stronger spiritual pressure.

"Then prove it."

As he thought of the man who had once betrayed him and killed his friends, he took that action to check whether

that man was a reviled enemy even now or the teacher that had raised the man called Shuhei.

"Prove whether you're worthy of talking about Tosen or not."

Then time flowed onward.

≡

THE PRESENT,
KARAKURA TOWN, MITSUMIYA

In Karakura Town's western area, where Mitsumiya ward was located, there was a candy shop with a peculiar atmosphere called Urahara Shoten. Normally it was bustling with the traffic of children and other customers. But presently, perhaps because something like a barrier to drive people away had been invoked, one couldn't even glimpse a cat strolling on the road. Instead, a group of figures clothed in black were in formation around the shop. Nearby, a girl in a red tracksuit held two Soul Reapers on her shoulders.

"What's that? What're they fighting against?"

"Huh?"

After hearing what the girl in the red tracksuit—Hiyori Sarugaki—had to say, Ryunosuke Yuki held back the urge to throw up and looked up at the sky even though his head was spinning

"*Ahh*?! What is that thing?!"

In order to understand what was happening with Karakura Town after it had been abruptly spiritually sealed, they went to the front of the shop where Kisuke Urahara should have been. Instead they witnessed a somewhat bizarre battle scene. Kisuke Urahara and Shuhei Hisagi were there.

They were the former captain and founder and chief of the Department of Research and Development, Kisuke Urahara, and the current assistant captain and editor in chief of the *Seireitei Bulletin,* Shuhei Hisagi.

They were flamboyantly leaping through the sky and violently battling *something* whose nature they did not know.

"Mr. Urahara, I'll ask again. Are you sure this isn't some sort of special ability like a bankai?"

"Yes, it's something like kido. It's a basic ability that any Fullbringer should be able to use. There is likely iron or rust or something that she's mixed with her blood to raise the quality of the konpaku. She's moving it using the Fullbringer ability Reishi Subjugation."

"She's subjugating reishi. That's definitely a concept we don't have."

"But it's a little different from the Quincies' reishi enslavement. The size of those things is nothing to trifle with, but if you get swallowed up by something like that, your body and your zanpaku-to might end up 'subjugated.'"

They were confronting countless reddish black gigantic *dragons* that had been formed from a spurt of blood. These

were not Western dragons, but the type of dragon from Eastern legend that looks like a gigantic snake with arms and legs. The five dragons had turned into red-black silhouettes in the light gray sky they were coursing through.

"It's pretty unbelievable, though..." Hisagi muttered, looking at the gigantic dragons floating in front of him.

When he looked closely, he saw they were a gathering of letters and patterns, but like a school of fish in the sea, they were packed together and wriggled in unison to create the form of one living creature—the writhing body of a dragon. A jaw the size of a large truck's payload closed in on Hisagi and Urahara in an attempt to swallow them. Urahara just barely dodged it and made his shikai-state zanpaku-to glisten.

"Kamisori Benihime."

The red slash that appeared from the sword's tip easily chopped off the dragon's head. However, the cut wafted like smoke and regenerated as though it had never been cut in the first place.

"Shibari Benihime."

This time, a black kimono sash stretched out from the zanpaku-to and wrapped around two of the dragons, forming a lattice net.

"Hiasobi Benihime Juzutsunagi."

In a moment, the black lattice knot burst into flames with a chain reaction and dyed Karakura Town's sky red with explosive fire. The flames illuminated the thin clouds covering the town and made it seem as though Karakura Town were lit by a second sun.

"*Whoa…!* Are you sure we should be doing this?!"

Hisagi was worrying about what would happen when the humans of the living world witnessed the spectacle from the ground, but Urahara grinned and said, "Let's hope President Vorarlberna will do something about it. Well, if it's necessary we'll use a wide-scale Kikanshinki to deal with it."

Though they had participated in several large fights in the past, excluding the decisive battle against Aizen, such showy displays as this were rare. In battles between Soul Reapers and Hollows, neither could be perceived by living humans, but in this instance, though their opponent Aura was a Fullbringer, she was also a living person. If someone on the ground were to see her, what would they think about what was going on? Hisagi considered that as he looked for Aura, but he couldn't find her. "Huh! Where did that woman go?!"

"It's likely she's hiding in the dragon or something. No, if she can make her body into smoke, I suppose there's no need for her to hide in the first place."

"Then there's no way we can fight something like that using a zanpaku-to."

"It depends on the zanpaku-to. I think the one with the most affinity in this case would be Mr. Hitsugaya's."

"You're right…"

The ice- and snow-type zanpaku-to that Toshiro Hitsugaya and Rukia Kuchiki had, or Genryusai Yamamoto's zanpaku-to, which had the ability to scorch a widespread area, would undoubtedly be able to defeat their opponent whether she was made of liquid or vapor. But Hisagi's Kazeshini, which contained physical attack at its core, had the absolute worst predisposition for this.

"Do you want to do this focusing on using kido?"

"Yes, that was what I was planning for the time being."

Hisagi hadn't noticed it yet—that Urahara had been handling things up until that point using several tactics he had used against the Hogyoku-fused Aizen.

"We can't be unwilling to try anything. Anything we can do, we must try with everything we have."

The only thing Hisagi had already realized was that the Fullbringer Aura Michibane was someone to be cautious of. As Hisagi listened to the kido chants that Urahara immediately started, he opened his eyes wide and prepared for an impact.

"Beyond the end of a thousand hands,
The hand of darkness out of reach,
The archer in heaven that goes unseen,

     Road that lights the way
     Wind that ignites the embers—
     Gather without hesitation,
     Look where I point.

Bullets of light, bodies of eight, rays of nine, paths of heaven, treasures of speed, wheels of immensity, and cannons of grey. From a distance, the bow is drawn and fades in light."

Someone as powerful as Urahara could likely have released the attack without the chant. However, he had purposefully chanted to increase its power, so Hisagi guessed that Urahara was testing something.

"Hado Number 91, Senjukotentaiho."

The swarm of lights that had spread across the sky converged in front of Urahara and turned into a dense barrage that pierced through the surrounding atmosphere itself and the red-black mob of dragons, burning them away.

Curiously, it looked very similar to the Gran Ray Cero that Grimmjow and the others had been shooting in the Rukongai around the same time. When evaluated on the basis of power, the strong kido shot absolutely wouldn't have been beaten out by a Gran Ray Cero. That is, if it weren't already stronger than one.

When Hisagi saw the kido, which showed how little of Kisuke Urahara's potential he was aware of, Hisagi unintentionally gulped. Though he had just unleashed such a massive kido, Urahara's breathing and spiritual pressure were undisturbed and he was observing his surroundings calmly.

"I see. So it seems she really can subjugate kido's reishi as well."

Then, after the smoke in front of their eyes cleared, a shadow appeared. With the ruins of what used to be the red-black dragons around her, Aura Michibane stood there with her usual intrepid smile.

"No, if I had to say which it is, she controlled the soul in nitrogen to create a barrier, it seems. Well, if she can do that in the living world where reishi is thin, then she really isn't anything to scoff at." Urahara assessed Aura as though he really hadn't expected to be able to stop her. "Though it looks like she didn't come out of that unharmed."

Though there weren't any conspicuous wounds on her body or clothes, even Hisagi felt the change. She was likely no longer able to put her spare energy into making her existence seem scarce through her Fullbring anymore. Her spiritual pressure, which had been completely diluted until then, could clearly be felt by Hisagi's spiritual perception now. On top of that, her spiritual pressure seemed to quiver as though she were exhausted, and for the first time, Hisagi determined the woman in front of his eyes had lost her cool. "Well, what a relief. If she were still unharmed after all that, then we would have had to deal with her with the same level of attack as Sosuke Aizen."

"Is this kido? I've never been hit by it directly, but it definitely isn't a skill to underestimate. It seems I miscalculated the Soul Reapers slightly."

It's not exactly like Mr. Urahara is the norm...

Hisagi recognized that misperception and decided that if she mistakenly thought Hisagi's kido was on a similar level and became cautious of him accordingly, that wasn't a problem. So he intentionally did not point out her mistake.

"Is there no way to convince you to lend us that power?" Without regard to the fact that she had been hurt, Aura gently continued to persuade Urahara.

"I'm very pleased you've extended me the invitation, but the Hogyoku...is not something I can create frivolously. And regardless of the reason, I can't undertake the task of creating one so lightly. If we were able to mass produce it and could have regulated it, I would have released it and just handed one over to Mr. Kurosaki during the last war."

Urahara was joking now, but...

"That's...a lie, isn't it?" Aura asked, still smiling.

Urahara was silent for a bit, and then replied, "If Ichigo Kurosaki were given a Hogyoku, the world would become very solid for sure. However, that is far from the result you're looking to achieve isn't it?"

"Hm?"

Not understanding what Urahara meant, Hisagi tilted his head quizzically. Urahara put on a self-deprecating smile and looked momentarily lonely as he replied, "Yes, I'm sorry. I lied. If I had given Mr. Kurosaki the Hogyoku, it would have been something entirely different, wouldn't it have?"

"Mr. Urahara?"

Ignoring Hisagi, who was dubious, Urahara asked Aura a question. "So, how much of this are you aware of?"

"Oh, are you sure you want to discuss that?" Aura snickered as she looked at Hisagi and continued, "Isn't he a journalist? I don't think this is something that we should be talking about in front of that kind."

"What's going on here? What're you trying to say?"

Hisagi interjected, not understanding what was going on, and Aura smiled thinly as she simply continued to look at Urahara. Then Urahara glanced at Hisagi and, unusually for him, said with a serious look on his face, "Since I think Mr. Hisagi would have found out about this no matter what road we took after the Tsunayashiro family got involved, I don't mind talking about it in front of him in the least."

"What are you talking about? Even I know that the Tsunayashiro family is doing something dangerous to the Soul Society and the living world."

"That's not what this is about. Mr. Hisagi, I'm sorry that this will challenge your resolve as a reporter...or really, as a Soul Reaper."

"My resolve as a Soul Reaper...?"

Hisagi was bewildered by the conversation and realized that his own hand gripping Kazeshini was oozing with sweat. His many years of experience as a Soul Reaper had likely honed his instinct so that he was aware that right at that moment, he was stepping into a conversation in forbidden territory.

"Afterward, I'll tell you what I can myself, but when that happens, will you be able to continue to pledge that you will keep with the justice of the Thirteen Court Guard Companies? That's the kind of conversation this is." Though he spoke in a light tone, his words were strangely insistent. "You can also continue to pretend to remain ignorant of these matters. Before she speaks, I might be able to force her into silence. Rather, I probably ought to do that for the sake of the Soul Society. Mr. Hisagi, should you be a part of the Soul Society, then I have no right to stop you from knowing about it."

Feeling sweat starting to ooze from his back as well, Hisagi was silent and lent his ear to Urahara.

"Had the battle with Yhwach not occurred, I would have kept it in the dark. Even I have hesitations. Aizen attempted to change the way of the world for himself. I think that was a mistake even now. However, if the world of the Soul Society itself were to seek change, I do not have the qualifications to decide whether that is right or wrong." Urahara paused at that point, then smiled gently at Hisagi. "That is something a reporter like yourself ought to be asking about the world. That is the sort of conversation this will be from now on."

"I..." Hisagi started...

"Well, let's continue to talk about this later—after we resolve the situation in front of us." In saying this, Urahara cut off Hisagi, who seemed to have been about to say something, then turned back to Aura. Hisagi had a strange feeling from Urahara that something was off.

What is this?

Mr. Urahara definitely likes talking, but was he really the type to talk like this in the middle of a fight?

Though he cracked as many silly jokes as he wanted, he wasn't one to speak in a serious tone for no reason—that was Hisagi's impression of Urahara. And it was precisely why Hisagi was bewildered that Urahara would bring up a topic "we can talk about later" right then. However, Urahara did not answer Hisagi's question and turned the point of Benihime at Aura, who was standing some distance away.

"Now then...Ms. Aura, I'm surprised by your integrity. You didn't try to attack us by surprise during that long conversation."

"How you jest." Aura quietly shook her head. "While you were talking to that assistant captain over there, weren't you also preparing your spiritual pressure and sneaking in several kido yourself?"

"That would be the same for you, wouldn't it? The dragon we just dispersed is still scattered all around this band, isn't it?"

"Huh."

Until he heard their conversation, Hisagi hadn't even realized the information that was being exchanged below the surface. *Mr. Urahara's consistently impressive... Well, this isn't the time to be dwelling on that.*

Realizing his own inexperience, he felt powerless, but Hisagi faced forward regardless.

Still, I can't let myself be a burden on him.

As Hisagi prepared himself to fight again, even though he already knew he didn't have the ability, the two preternatural people in front of him made their move.

"Turn inside out."

Just as soon as Aura muttered those words as though she were issuing some kind of command, the air around her completely transformed. The matter that Aura had been hiding in the atmosphere through Reishi Subjugation used the fragments of the dragon as an intermediary to reorganize all at once.

Instantly, gray water dominated the gray sky.

Above the skies of Karakura Town, it appeared—compared to the real thing it was tiny, but considering where they were, it was extraordinarily vast. An ocean had appeared. The two Soul Reapers who were watching the scene unfold from the ground were dumbfounded and let out cries of wonder.

"An ocean...in the sky?"

"*Ahhh!* If that comes down on us, we'll drown, Shino! L-let's run away!"

Just how much water could be up there? The ocean that had started as a lump covered the sky, eventually undulating in one direction to turn into a gigantic river that ran

freely through the air. With that vision in front of her—overwhelming, beautiful, and frightening— Hiyori jeered at the Soul Reapers, "Stop peeing your pants! Anybody with a zanpaku-to can handle that thing! Even when this Espada shark lady created something like that..."

However, at that point Hiyori stopped talking because, as a complement to the mass of seawater, a violent storm revealed itself next.

"*Ugh...*"

Tessai and the others who had been watching the scene from afar couldn't help but pause in their counterattack against the black-clad people that had appeared around them. It was that startling a scene. As though a counterpart to the flow of water, a scarlet river of lava, like a raging firedrake dragon, rushed through it.

"I think we'd better hurry up, under the circumstances..."

As though in response to Tessai's words, Jinta and Ururu both knocked out the adversaries they were dealing with.

"Seriously, what's with these guys?! They just swarmed us outta nowhere! What are they, bugs?!"

As Jinta complained behind her, Ururu stared at the sky and muttered, "There's...something else coming."

"Hunh?! What the heck?! What could come after water and magma?!" In response to the question he had just asked, Jinta had a sudden insight and yelled, "So then is it a drill and missile dragon?! That's the strongest!"

Entirely ignoring his shouting, Ururu named the flow of spiritual pressure that her own eyes captured. "It's Mr. Kisuke's dragon."

"Hado ninety-nine, Goryu Tenmetsu."

At Urahara's words, the skies parted. Five pillars of light in the form of dragons and composed of reishi had appeared. It was a type of Hado that usually created dragons from a ley line in the ground and broke apart the surrounding earth as it attempted to swallow up its target. The Hado carried a tremendous power that was fitting for the meaning of its chant: five dragon destruction.

Urahara had adapted it and hacked into the spiritual pressure of the souls flowing through the atmosphere that Aura had been subjugating, using that in place of a ley line to accomplish the Hado.

"This is more than I expected."

The composure disappeared from Aura's face, and in its place, mechanical surprise came over her.

"You've finally shown us your true face, haven't you?"

When Urahara murmured that, as though Aura were denying him, she sent the lava and magma dragons leaping at Urahara and Hisagi. Meanwhile, three of the dragons that had been created through the Hado protected Urahara and Hisagi by covering them, and the remaining two plunged at Aura to sandwich her from the top and bottom. Then, right as the dragons of three colors intersected in the air, an explosive water vapor rose up, and the entire area was blanketed in a newly created bright white light.

This battle is next level.

Hisagi, who had created the bare minimum of defense using kido but had still taken some damage from the aftermath of the explosion, cursed himself for being unable to do anything as the powerhouses several levels above his own abilities fought in front of him. However, he did not attempt to run.

He knew he was a burden. Urahara's power was tremendous, to the point that Hisagi had no idea why Urahara had suggested that they would tag team. Though he had been shown a way of battling that was great enough to make him think that the only person who could keep pace with Urahara in terms of ability was Yoruichi Shihoin, Hisagi stayed to maintain dignity as a Soul Reaper.

Had Hisagi been a Soul Reaper driven by reason, he likely would have put down his zanpaku-to as soon as he felt the fear of death. For better or worse, Shuhei Hisagi was a clumsy man. At Shinoreijutsuin he had been praised as a talented student, and though as a Soul Reaper he had actually been a heroic figure who had been better than average at most things, the illogical dignity at his core had caused him to make choices that were disadvantageous. However, it was because of that trait that Hisagi had become strong.

As a Soul Reaper, or because he had inherited the pride of an ideology from his superior as a Soul Reaper, he had continued to walk many illogical paths and had, at those times, wandered upon the line between life and death.

Though at times he had done so clumsily, he had survived in the end, and because of that unskillfulness, he hadn't allowed himself to run away. He stayed on the battleground of his own volition in this instance as well.

"Mr. Urahara! I don't know if it will work, but you could use a Binding Spell to divide her power and—"

Hisagi thought of the things he could do in his own way and tried to make a suggestion to Urahara, but he realized at that point that Urahara's spiritual pressure had disappeared from the surroundings.

"Mr. Urahara...?" The steam steadily cleared from Hisagi's vision, and Aura, who seemed to have sustained a great deal of damage and didn't appear to be doing very well, came into view. Still, he didn't see Urahara anywhere.

In front of the bewildered Hisagi, Aura once again twisted her mouth, and as though that were a signal, a voice mixed with static that seemed projected through a megaphone echoed around them. *"Scenario over. You've cleared the mission, Ms. Aura."*

"Thank you very much, President Yukio."

"With that score, I can't put you in double-S rank. You'd be B at best." At Yukio's nonchalant words, Hisagi unintentionally

raised his voice. "Hey! What's going on here?! What'd you do to Mr. Urahara?!"

"I told you from the start, didn't I, that our goal was Kisuke Urahara?"

When he examined his surroundings, in the place where Urahara had been standing before the explosion he could feel a disturbance in the spiritual pressure of the space itself, as though it had been warped.

Had Mr. Urahara been kidnapped?

That's impossible. This is Mr. Urahara we're talking about! What the hell did they do to him?!

As though ridiculing Hisagi, who was panicking, Yukio's voice continued to echo out between distorted electronic artifacts that came from the warped place. *"My preparations were complete, so I had Kisuke Urahara come to my stage. That's all."*

"Don't screw with me! Release Mr. Urahara right now!"

"Sorry, but you've got to have an event flag set to progress farther than this point."

Yukio was still expressionless as he said that, as though to tease Hisagi. Then Aura called out to Hisagi, "I'm sure that we will meet again soon."

The woman bowed politely and started to disappear again into the artifacts of noise that Yukio had created.

"I hope we meet under favorable circumstances."

"You just wait right..."

Though he raced through the sky using shunpo, he was late by a moment. Only the vestiges of the twisted spiritual pressure were left behind, though Hisagi looked for an opening for a while.

"Damn it!"

In the end, he was unable to find anything, and he let out a resentful cry while floating in the air. It was resentment aimed not at Yukio or Aura, but at himself, for being helpless in this situation. There was nothing he could do, and Kisuke Urahara had been snatched. He had no idea what that could mean and had no way of finding out.

CHAPTER FOURTEEN

IN BATTLES BETWEEN SOUL REAPERS and Hollows, to some extent being gigantic was its own advantage. Of course, in conflicts between humans and other animals in the living world, that was common sense, but in strife between Soul Reapers and Hollows, it took on additional significance. Unlike human-against-human battles, huge Hollows could be large enough to hit the heavens. Even if one could obtain an advantage through equipment or skill, for example, the Hollow would stand in the way of the Soul Reapers with a disparity that wouldn't be easy to overcome. However, the reason it was only an advantage to some extent was because it wasn't a universal superiority. A Soul Reaper who had obtained Zankensoki above a certain level could defeat a Hollow ten times larger than themselves.

Additionally, there were often cases in which a zanpaku-to might possess an ability that could oppose a gigantic Hollow.

However, even a zanpaku-to that had achieved bankai naturally had its limits. One of the Quincy king Yhwach's elite guards who had "The Miracle" Schrift, Gerard Valkyrie, was large enough that he could ward off superficial bankai and had a corresponding amount of strength and stamina.

Hollows could also grow by eating each other and in the end could turn into a large being called a Menos Grande that would stand in the way of Soul Reapers, but their growth could take several paths beyond that.

When they evolved from a Gillian to an Adjuchas, or even further into a Vasto Lorde, their stature would shrink as the reishi that had been enlarging their body steadily condensed. In the end, they would become a "high-density monster," concentrating several hundred thousand Menos Grandes' worth of spiritual pressure into a human-sized body. In other words, for part of their growth, the larger they became, the more they were recognized for being a strong Hollow—until they passed Menos Grande level, at which point the smaller their bodies were, the more they were recognized as being powerful due to their markedly condensed spiritual pressure.

However, that being the case, the *thing* that had appeared in the Rukongai was impressive enough to make them forget such practicalities. It had a gigantic body, several times larger than a Menos Grande, and was packed with a spiritual pressure density reminiscent of the Vasto Lorde class. When *it* took a step forward, the ground shrieked and tremored. When *it* cried out, the atmosphere rumbled, and all surrounding life fell into a spiral of primordial fear. When he got a look at *it*—at Hikone Ubuginu's zanpaku-to, Ikomikidomoe—Shinji Hirako let out a shocked cry from high in the sky, where he had taken refuge.

"Isn't this unfair?! You're telling us we must recognize you as king when you're not even using your own power?!"

Then the keeper of that gigantic monster, Hikone, answered in an innocent tone, "Yes, Ikomikidomoe fundamentally uses his own spiritual pressure to move, so there aren't any issues there, and if we really need to, we can combine and fight!"

"What the hell do you mean you combine with that thing?! Is it some kind of mecha?! Is that thing a giant mecha?!"

At present, Hirako was holding position a step back and observing rather than volunteering to fight directly. In normal circumstances, it would be logical for him to send packing an Arrancar that had appeared in the Soul Society, or to destroy them, but there had been a notice handed down from above: "Avoid killing Espada-class Arrancar so long as they are not hostile or rampaging in the world of the living."

The policy had been put into place to avoid an all-out war and because the overall balance of souls in the Soul Society, the living world, and Hueco Mundo had been drastically disturbed due to the Quincies' work. With that in mind as well,

Hirako intentionally did not assist Hikone and observed instead, but once he saw Hikone's uninhibited rampage, he of course had to speak up.

"What're you going to do if this gargantuan thing starts to go wild? You're sure you've got control over it, right?!"

"Yes, that's nothing to worry about!" Hikone smiled as usual as they replied, then easily snuffed out a Cero flying by with a single hand and blurted out something else.

"Because I'm just about as strong as Ikomikidomoe!"

≡

"What the hell is happening here?"

What Tier Halibel saw after opening a garganta into the Soul Society was a scene entirely outside of her expectations. She had followed Grimmjow's spiritual pressure and opened a garganta with the aim of going to the place she thought he had appeared, and Grimmjow was definitely there. But that wasn't all she found.

There were Soul Reapers and Quincies in addition to those who were neither, jumbled together and battling around *something* that was as gigantic as a small mountain.

"Is that Luppi?"

Halibel's eyes were first captured by Grimmjow's startling blue hair, but she was bewildered by the Arrancar who bore eight tentacles on his back next to Grimmjow.

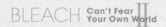

A former Espada, whom she was certain Grimmjow had killed by blowing away the upper half of his body, seemed to have formed a united front with Grimmjow and was attacking a gigantic monster. However, they had not reconciled, and the two of them were striking with high-power attacks with no regard for one another, and for a moment she watched them almost hit each other with crossfire.

"Is that the Soul Reaper from before?"

When Halibel saw the child standing on the back of the mountainlike Hollow, she distanced herself further to observe the situation, feeling unsure and surprised. Then, as though to confirm that her view of things was correct, she spoke to Nelliel Tu Odelschwanck at her side. "So Grimmjow's aim really was that Soul Reaper. But what are those Quincies doing here? They're not the ones we battled in Hueco Mundo."

"Hmm. I'm not sure... I think they're also part of the group serving Yhwach, at least. But I want to know what's going on with that monster. It looks like a Hollow, but doesn't it seem kind of odd?"

"I remember that spiritual pressure. It's the same as the one from the zanpaku-to that Soul Reaper used to open the garganta."

"So basically that *thing* is the zanpaku-to from earlier? It's shaped pretty differently. Did it achieve bankai like

Ichigo's? Or does it make more sense to call it Resurrección, since that's what we do?"

Not paying any heed to Nelliel's puzzling over something that wasn't immediately relevant to the situation, Halibel continued to observe the presences in the vicinity. However, her status as an observer soon ended.

Having noticed her, the monster that looked very much like a Hollow opened its cavernous maw and requested a conversation with her.

"Ah, new friends. Of course, I don't recognize you. It does not seem you are Barragan's mistresses."

His voice was not at all that eardrum-splitting rumble it had been. However, it still shook Halibel's and Nelliel's skulls like an eerie bass echoing directly into their heads, penetrating their guts and bones.

"You know Barragan? So that thing really is a Hollow?"

"Regardless, you thought we were Barragan's mistresses of all things. For starters, Barragan is long gone."

When the gigantic monster heard Nelliel's disgruntled response, it paused for a moment.

"Ikomikidomoe? What's wrong?"

Ignoring Hikone's question, Ikomikidomoe made the atmosphere quiver with his words. *"I see. So that crafty king has disappeared from Hueco Mundo."*

The Hueco Mundo king had lived for an eternity and ultimately met his destruction while an underling of

Aizen's. Ikomikidomoe, who muttered Barragan's name as though reminiscing, went silent for a moment, then bellowed across the Rukongai as though he were trying to destroy it all.

"—   —— —— — —— ——

—— —— — — ———— "

His voice made the atmosphere quiver, and that quiver became a gale. As the wind gathered high-density spiritual pressure, aggressive tornadoes formed one after another in the surrounding space.

It was a terrific bellow in which grief and hatred intermingled, as though he were equally intent on destroying those who attacked him, those who were spectators, those who had yet to make a choice, and everyone else.

That was the trigger that revealed yet a new level of mayhem.

≡

A LOCATION IN THE SEIREITEI, PASSAGEWAY IN A CONCEALED QUARTER

Even within the Seireitei, there was a section that only aristocrats could enter. That space, which in normal circumstances would be mostly deserted, had presently been transformed into a battleground filled with the flashing of swords and the smell of blood.

As blade crossed blade, another blade would aim for their backs, and yet another strike would block that blade, and the attackers appearing from the shadows would withdraw into the scrum. It was a battle between a congregation of the protectors and attackers—both of which were assassins by profession. It had escalated into an open melee of large groups, an embarrassment for them as assassins who normally fight by burying themselves in one shadow after another, in intimate, surreptitious struggles.

They had come under the pretext of being the guards of a member of the Four Great Noble Clans—Tokinada Tsunayashiro—in order to restrain his actions and also keep him under surveillance, and it was almost as though the attackers had targeted that time to appear.

The Punishment Force Soi Fon led was fighting a group of jet-black-clad assassins. In response to the assassins, who showed open hostility, the Soul Reapers of the Punishment Force continued to intercept attacks without so much as twitching an eyebrow, as though they were suppressing their own emotions. In the middle of that brawl, Soi Fon precisely dodged her opponents' attacks while all the time dedicating a part of her mind to keeping a constant watch over Tokinada Tsunayashiro.

Though Tokinada had insisted "these assassins are coming after me," Soi Fon didn't believe his words.

She had ascertained that in all likelihood, Tokinada had caused this so he could take advantage of the chaos that ensued, and even if the assassins were really after Tokinada, she had determined that it was certain he would take this as a lucky opportunity to hatch a scheme.

Soi Fon was aware of Tokinada Tsunayashiro's bad reputation even before he had been seated as head of the family. Though she likely wouldn't have felt any particular hostility toward him over that.

When Kyoraku had instructed her to get the Punishment Force on the move, giving a terribly hand-waving reason—"Because the Tsunayashiro family head might possibly be scheming something"—she had of course objected that that wasn't adequate rationale to take action.

"Well, it isn't just a possibility—he really is scheming something. He went out of his way to call me out and tried to have us exploit the government. He even transparently tried to butter me up by saying I was beautiful, et cetera, and pretended to be looking at me all lovey-dovey."

Then, the moment Yoruichi had wandered in to accompany them, Soi Fon had promptly blurted out an endlessly perturbing, "Let's give him the death penalty, right now, as soon as possible," and proceeded to take on the role of the villain of her own accord.

Since Kyoraku had intended to play the villain himself, he had somehow assuaged her and convinced her to promise that she would carry out her duties civilly. But under the circumstances there was no longer any point in being considerate, and instead Soi Fon continued to be vigilant of Tokinada, thinking "it would save a whole lot of effort gathering evidence if you would just hurry up and try stabbing me in the back already." However, Tokinada might have been aware of that possibility, as he didn't assault her from behind and didn't even try running away as he swung his zanpaku-to at the assassins.

He's strong.

Though she held a personal vendetta against him, Soi Fon could still calmly evaluate his abilities. She had heard he had previously been a powerhouse, as a seated officer in the Thirteen Court Guard Companies, and he went about cutting down the assassins as though he hadn't had a several centuries-long gap in work at all.

What is that zanpaku-to?

When Soi Fon observed it in the intervals between her fights, the sword Tokinada gripped only looked like an Asauchi at first glance. Though he had recited the chant for a shikai a while ago, not a single aspect of it had changed.

I've heard about the ability of the Kuten Kyokoku, the zanpaku-to that the Tsunayashiro family has been handing down from generation to generation from Captain General Kyoraku, but I would have expected that it wouldn't even change form.

However, what she had been told about its *ability* was exactly true. One of the assassins waved their zanpaku-to, and several fireballs appeared around the zanpaku-to's blade and started to assault Tokinada. It did not reach anywhere close to the level of Genryusai Yamamoto's Ryujin Jakka, and compared to Isshin Kurosaki's Engetsu, the heat of the flame was practically child's play. Regardless of that, the fireball was more than enough to burn a single Soul Reaper alive. At the same time Tokinada flashed his blade, that flame was sent flying back at his opponent like a ball rebounding off a wall. Like light hitting a mirror, the fireball reversed course and crashed into its original user. The assassin cried out and burst into flames.

Seeing this, Soi Fon's assumption was confirmed that it truly was an ability to be wary of, and that was the exact reason why she had chosen to fight without her zanpaku-to.

So he can reflect abilities, huh?

That's a lot more troublesome than I thought.

It was a technique that could simply reflect back a zanpaku-to's unique abilities. Though it was similar to Sogyo no Kotowari, which Jushiro Ukitake had used in the past, it didn't need to absorb the reishi before bouncing back, and it seemed to flick away attacks by creating a reflective wall in front of their eyes.

Given that, it was easy to determine that battling while it was in its Asauchi state would work well enough, but as far as Soi Fon could see, Tokinada Tsunayashiro's offensive was more masterful than she expected. His skill, paired with that ability, would be enough to ward off most enemies.

However... At the same time, there was doubt in Soi Fon's mind.

All it does is send back the opponent's attack...is that all the ability is?

Or is the bankai unique?

Though it was a terrifying power, it wasn't as though there weren't any ways of dealing with it. There were those who could battle without a zanpaku-to's ability. Or there were those who simply overpowered their opponents through brute strength without regard to abilities, such as Kenpachi Zaraki, or those who finished battles before even swinging a sword like Mayuri Kurotsuchi, who took advantage of the adversary's weak points. She could think of many counter-measures against it.

In fact, before Kyoraku had issued that instruction earlier, he seemed to have had the same doubts.

"It's just... I don't think that Tokinada's zanpaku-to's ability just bounces back his opponent's attacks."

He had gathered information about the zanpaku-to as the Captain General, using his connections with Central 46 and other intelligence networks. However, Kyoraku had misgivings about even getting this information from the start. *"His own zanpaku-to was forfeited. The one he is using*

now can only be held by the head of family. In other words, it's the Tsunayashiro family's power *itself that has acted as their trump card and even serves as their symbol.*

"It's the zanpaku-to that the Four Great Noble Clans have passed from generation to generation. I'd thought it would be rather like Muramas, but have the absurd power of controlling another person's zanpaku-to."

Recalling Kyoraku's words, who said that as he held up his own zanpaku-to as an example of an irregular power, Soi Fon repelled the assassins while keeping a very close eye on Tokinada at her back. Meanwhile, Yoruichi was haphazardly dealing with the assassins and sighed, lamenting, "The fact that a group as large as this has zanpaku-to without being Soul Reapers is a big problem."

In response, Tokinada snickered after he had eliminated the scrum of assassins around him. "It is because many Soul Reapers died in the earlier war against the Quincies. The thieves who took possession of those zanpaku-to when their owners went missing seem to have risen en masse."

"Oh, I merely thought that those aristocrats who didn't participate in the war had taken the initiative to openly funnel zanpaku-to illegally."

"Ha ha ha ha ha! If aristocrats like that existed, it would be a disgrace for the Seireitei!"

Tokinada laughed loudly as he, of course, bounced back a lightning strike dealt by an enemy with a swing of his sword.

He was either moving fast enough to react to lightning or he was predicting his enemy's behavior—either way, it was evidence Tokinada possessed abilities in battle that were not to be disregarded.

Tokinada easily dealt with the assassins and responded snidely to Yoruichi, who had spoken sarcastically, "Zanpaku-to and such can change hands anywhere. It is not one's origins that matter, but one's actions, isn't it? I heard that was the case with the current Kenpachi as well, right?"

"A thug who hadn't even gone to Shinoreijutsuin rose up after stealing a sword from a Soul Reaper who had died in the Rukongai."

≡

THE SEIREITEI, KUTSUWA TOWN

The yarrow plants were bent by the wind. The Seireitei had several divisions, and there were several districts that each had their own characteristics, such as the commercial district and the aristocrat's quarter. However, among those, the one that was said to be especially conspicuous was entirely unconnected to history, culture, or entertainment. It was Kutsuwa Town, which was the Eleventh Company barracks. Just as any other day, hoodlums in shihakusho acted like they owned the place as they strutted through the town's main streets waving around their Eleventh Company insignia. A man who didn't fit into the rough and tumble townscape—Yumichika Ayasegawa—walked coolly by the front of the company barracks, which was rank with the smell of blood, dirt, and booze, speaking to the man walking in front of him and to his side who fit in splendidly with the atmosphere of the town.

"Kind of seems like there's a commotion in the first ward. Wonder if something happened?"

"Since the Secret Remote Squad guys were running around and making a commotion, there might have been a big arrest. *Tsk*...If I just knew where they went, I would've gone there too. Aside from Omaeda from the Patrol Unit, the Punishment Force guys are tight lipped..."

Madarame spoke lazily as he passed through the barracks gate with Yumichika. The rough and tumble atmosphere of the town suddenly receded, and a gruff, grave spiritual pressure made the pair's skin prickle. However, they didn't let it bother them and kept walking. They had become familiar with that atmosphere, which was the very reason the two of them stayed in the Eleventh Company.

It was easy to see that the rest of the Eleventh Company members were all breaking into cold sweats over the stabbing and heavy spiritual pressure. Just being in that place made them feel as though they were rolling on the mountain of pins and needles in hell. In this district, where thugs gathered, the reason public safety did not decline precipitously—as in the Kusajishi district of the Rukongai—was likely because the owner of that spiritual pressure kept the company members under control. Then again, anyone who was surrounded by that spiritual pressure could care less about the town's public order. The source of power himself appeared in front of the two of them as they headed into the training area.

"We've come back from our patrol, Captain."

"All right…"

The Kenpachi Zaraki—that name was a symbol of pure valor in the Thirteen Court Guard Companies, and it was also a series of cursed and powerful words, the personification of a blood-drenched history. However, the man was too unrefined to be described using the word "valor." Using a torrent of vast power reminiscent of a particular type of natural disaster, he could bulldoze over an opponent's lifetime of training.

Just as indicated by that inherited name, Zaraki—which is made up of the Japanese characters for "leveled land" and "tree"—the man was like a gigantic tree that continued to stand tall even on leveled land. He was a fitting presence to bear up the meaning of the name Kenpachi—"eight swords"—as someone who never fell, no matter how many times he was cut.

When Madarame saw that the captain was unexpectedly in his captain's coat on the training grounds, he asked out of curiosity, "What's gotten into you, Captain? You're never in your captain's coat past noon when there isn't a captain's assembly."

Though he hadn't ever been one to care about coats, Kenpachi would often wear the captain's coat at assemblies, as though he were fulfilling the minimum of obligation felt toward Genryusai Yamamoto, who had picked him off the streets. Though Kenpachi wouldn't wear his shihakusho, went bare chested in the training area because it was easier to move, and enjoyed judo sparring against company members, just for today, he wasn't even attempting to train.

"Yeah, I just got word from that Captain General guy. He told me to get on my captain's coat and be ready to move at any moment."

Though it was somewhat in disrepair from the short but intense battles, his captain's coat really did have special meaning. As though he had some sort of premonition about something, Kenpachi smiled fearlessly while making the yarrow plant etched into the company badge jiggle.

"This better not be a thankless nuisance, but if there's some kind of brawl, I'm about to be thankful."

≡

THE RUKONGAI

"The heck is this?! Did we just stick our necks into some kind of ridiculous brawl?!"

These were Candice's words after she was caught up in the aftermath of Ikomikidomoe's battle, caused by the zanpaku-to that was seemingly a gigantic Hollow. Meninas responded in her usual tone, "I think we've been pretty tangled up in this stuff since the very beginning..."

"But at the start all we were doing was blowing those Fullbringer guys away and nabbing 'em! Why're we getting caught up in a fight between that distilled Menos Grande Hollow monster thing and the Arrancars?! Actually, now that I'm looking...have the Arrancars doubled?!"

Smashing a boulder that had been tossed up by the force of a thunderbolt, Candice gestured at the two new female Arrancars that had appeared.

"Like, what is with their outfits? That's way too form fitting!"

"Candice, that's like the pot calling the kettle black," Meninas said, glancing at the wide-open chests of the Quincy knight uniform. However, Candice acted as though she hadn't heard and started developing a counterattack.

"In any case, we've got to stop this goliath first, or we won't be able to do our job."

Though they could have temporarily retreated, she didn't think that Mayuri Kurotsuchi would allow them to do that.

So what they probably needed to do was take advantage of the confusion to find the Fullbringers' weak spot while battling the colossal enemy. While that may have been impossible at the moment, it would be a chance to analyze how their foes fought. Continuing to fight all the while, Candice considered this strategy and also wondered about whether Ginjo and the others would make a break for it.

"Minni! Create an opening for me!"

"Got it!"

After giving a nod, Meninas slowly moved toward the gigantic Hollow's feet and hid herself in what was likely to be the opponent's blind spot. Then she simply flexed the muscles in her arm and used brute force to lift him. That alone caused Ikomikidomoe to veer and skitter deeply into the ground in reaction.

"Hah! Good going! Leave the rest to me!"

Aiming toward where the opponent had gone off balance, Candice shot successive lightning arrows. Then, as a final blow, she drove in with an Electrocution, the same attack she had used against Ginjo and the others earlier. The surrounding area was engulfed in blinding light by the successive strikes she had launched at near lightning speed.

"That was close! What is with those people? They're not holding back even though I'm right here!" Hirako, who had narrowly dodged the lightning, felt a cold sweat break out on his face as he yelled. "Weren't those Quincies supposed to be Mayuri's footmen?! Well, right, it's not like Mayuri would care about me or the other Soul Reapers."

Having come to that conclusion on his own, Hirako distanced himself even further and turned his eyes toward Ikomikidomoe, who had been swallowed up in the flash of lightning. But...

"That's not good. Looks like it's not doing much."

Ikomikidomoe, who had been in the form of a monster until recently, had transformed into a ball, with his feet folded up. He was enshrined in the middle of the Rukongai as though he were an eerie object of art. In the next moment, just as that gigantic sphere's surroundings started to fill with white mist, countless small, winged monsters appeared from within the fog. However, they were only small in comparison to Ikomikidomoe's form; what seemed to be Adjuchas-level Hollows turned into a monster horde and began to soar through the air. Then, like an immune response, the horde leapt at those who were actually attacking—Meninas and Candice.

As he looked down at the zanpaku-to that continued to create hundreds of miniaturized "offspring," Hirako scowled and revised his opinion.

"I was wrong to think this thing was a giant mecha."

He now felt an extreme level of caution about Hikone, who controlled that zanpaku-to, and Tokinada Tsunayashiro, whom the child had received the sword from.

He continued, "He's like a whole country on legs. A frontal attack won't take down something like that."

As Hirako coolly analyzed the situation, Candice and Meninas were forced into a disadvantageous situation before they could gather their thoughts.

"What kind of zanpaku-to is that?! Can that *thing* even be a zanpaku-to?!"

"This could be bad..."

The two of them were shooting Heilig Pfeil at the monster horde heading toward them, but there were just too many of them. Meninas used her superhuman strength while Candice used her lightning bolt power to oppose them, but the attacking monsters were being continuously created with a power exceeding what they could muster, and furthermore, their opponent's main body was itself more or less unharmed.

Candice used lightning that had been combined with reishi to create a lance—a Galvano Javelin—that she wielded with both hands to cut and purify the monsters, but there were too many of them for two swords to contend with.

"Damn it! If we could just use our Voll Stern Dich abilities..."

Normally, Candice could use her wings to manage six swords using the Quincy Voll Stern Dich, but because of Yhwach's Auswählen she no longer could go into Voll Stern Dich form, and so manipulating two swords was her current limit. There was also the troublesome issue that the monsters weren't attacking recklessly—though they were a horde, they seemed to move as though they were being directed, like a single living creature attacking while aiming for an opening. Though she could annihilate them all at once through successive lightning bolts from the sky, it was like a drop in the bucket.

"*Tsk*...Guess we just poked the hornet's nest...?"

Though she was pretty exhausted from her earlier rapid fire, Candice had just started unleashing another Electrocution when something unexpected happened.

"Don't bother. You'll just end up burning through all your Blut Arterie before you get anywhere."

The familiar voice made Candice's ears quiver.

"Huh...?"

What could it mean that she was hearing that voice in this place?

Before Candice's brain could comprehend it, the voice took on a form and *ate* through the monster horde. A strange, long, narrow jaw that had suddenly appeared swallowed about a hundred of them in one gulp. The strange-looking jaw preying on the enemies sucked in the white monsters, then let out a listless sigh, and then the voice reported its impression of what it had just swallowed: "The skeleton guys from earlier were the same... Mass-produced goods just taste bland."

A girl with distinctive disillusioned eyes under a white Stern Ritter cap floated in the air. When Candice saw the

girl, her eyes opened wide and she yelled, "Li...Lil?!"

She could barely believe her eyes. The person she had been separated from half a year before, and had been trying to find some way to contact since then, appeared just now, without her even having to stir up trouble.

The girl with disillusioned eyes—Liltotto Lamperd— said to the dumbstruck Candice in an exasperated tone, "Seriously, we were planning on getting you out by taking advantage of the commotion. What were you thinking, going straight into this mess yourselves? Why do I even bother?!"

"Y-you! Why're you here?! There's no way you came here just to save us!"

"Like I just said, we came here to get you out. You've got to listen when other people are talking, you slut."

"Wait...you're really alive. I heard you betrayed his majesty, so I was convinced..."

Candice had been doubtful, thinking that in the worst-case scenario Mayuri Kurotsuchi could be lying about Liltotto and the others being alive, and she looked at Liltotto with a mix of relief and surprise.

"Don't call that ass 'his majesty.' Anyway, apparently he's long gone."

At the same time Liltotto said that, Candice heard another, different voice coming from behind. "Whoa, you're in rougher shape than I expected. Candice, how can you look so *lame*?"

Her forehead twitching in annoyance before she could even be happy about their reunion, Candice sent an anger-filled fist flying behind her.

"Gigiii!"

Easily dodging the fist, the raven-haired Quincy—Giselle Gewelle—smiled only with her mouth as she protested, "Boo, don't say it like that; you make me sound like a geezer."

"It's your own fault for making us upset, Gigi," Meninas said, as easygoing as ever, without showing any hint of emotion to indicate that they had just been reunited.

"Wait a sec! Why're you acting like this is normal, Minni?! That's weird! It feels like I'm the only one who hasn't gotten the memo!"

"If you've got complaints, I'll pretend to listen to you later, once we've gotten some grub to eat. Anyway, we've got to deal with that dangerous thing first."

The horde of monsters had continued gushing from the white mist, and as though they were analyzing the abilities of their new opponents, Liltotto and the others observed them while circling from afar. Then Giselle tilted her head in response to Liltotto.

"Huh? Why've we got to do anything? Can't we just run away?"

"That's what I was hoping for. But if we run now, it'd be useless if there are bombs hidden in Candy and Minni, right?"

"Oh!"

Candice herself had considered that possibility, but when Liltotto, who was the brains among them, mentioned it, Candice was struck with terror again. Liltotto spoke, not to Candice, but to Candice's chest, where there was sure to be someone on the other side of the communications device hidden there. She offered him a deal.

"You're listening, aren't you, Mayuri Kurotsuchi? We'll cooperate with your experiment or whatever. Just pay us back by letting Candice and Meninas go."

A distinct voice resonated from Candice's cap.

"Good grief. You must be quite conceited to believe you are in a position to be making deals."

"Whaa...?!"

Ignoring Candice, who was surprised by the voice coming from above her head, the voice on the other end of the communications device went on indifferently, *"First of all, I have not hidden a bomb or anything like that in them. Those luddites—Captain General and Central 46—informed me just the other day that putting bombs into subordinates is forbidden. Since I've called my zombies a unit, they told me to treat you as soldiers rather than as tools. Really, that's just coddling."*

"So if they haven't got any bombs hidden on them, that must mean you've put loads of other dangerous stuff in them."

"I wonder? Anyway, Quincies are antiques now. I don't intend to destroy you so casually."

"Hey! What is it with you talking in riddles?!"

Ignoring Candice's outburst, Liltotto calmly continued her exchange with Mayuri. Even as they were negotiating, she maintained her vigilance about her surroundings and the small forces of monsters that attacked her occasionally to keep her in check. Whenever that happened, she swallowed them whole and skillfully continued her conversation.

"What we want is Candice and Meninas's freedom and the guarantee of their lives. You'll be able to make a deal with some of the most battle-worthy of the Quincies—not too shabby, right?"

"That your hubris extends that far is beyond comical. It simply makes me pity you. Though you are antiques, to me you Quincies are just subjects I have finished my research on. Do you really think you are that valuable?"

"If Quincies are so worthless, then you could let go of Candy and Minni for nothing, couldn't you? Though I think they're at least worth exchanging for some chores. Plus, this is *you* we're talking about. You hid something in me and Gigi too, didn't you?"

"Huh?"

Giselle was suddenly alarmed at the topic of conversation, and Mayuri's voice was artless as he declared, *"Oh, you're a fool, but I don't dislike those who are quick to pick up on the conversation. The Quincy named Ishida had not a clue, however."*

"Sure, thanks. I'm praying you're quick to pick up on things too."

In response to Liltotto, who didn't retreat one step, the voice on the other end of Candice's cap snickered and continued, *"If I say no right now, you intend to take the negotiation up with Captain General Kyoraku, do you not? Good grief, had Shinji Hirako not been here, I could have shut you up in secret."*

"Obviously, I went out of my way to show my face because there was another company captain around."

"Very shrewd indeed."

"I already got my fill of finding out how treacherous you are. In particular, I can't help but wonder what Yhwach would've been able to do if you hadn't been fighting."

In response to Liltotto's comment, a loud sigh came from the communications device in Candice's hat.

"Obvious flattery won't bring me to compromise. Well, it is true that your ringleader had tunnel vision. Even though he could see the future, it seemed he was unable to see reality." Then, seeming in a somewhat pleasant mood, Mayuri offered a concrete proposal. *"I want as much data on that gigantic, fantastical zanpaku-to and the Soul Reaper-type research subject standing up there as you can gather. If you do that for me, I'll at least promote you from experimental subjects to mercenaries. If you're also able to catch the Fullbringers, I'll even make you taller as a special bonus."*

"Who cares about that? The bigger you are, the faster you get hungry. Basically, all we've gotta do is beat that Goliath, right?"

"I'm not expecting that much from you. If it were something the likes of you could defeat, I wouldn't concern myself with it in the first place."

"Tsk...You're underestimating us."

As though the deal were complete, after her brief complaint Liltotto posed a question to the gigantic sphere that towered high over them. "You're thinking the same thing, aren't you, Goliath?"

Giselle, who had been listening from the ground, called up to Liltotto, who was still in confrontation mode, "Hey Lil, I really don't like this. Why would we help that black and white clown?"

Then Mayuri's exasperated voice came from Candice's cap. *"Have your brains finally rotted, zombie girl? The one I made the deal with is that glutton. I never expected you to be useful in battle anyway, so feel free to fester on the sidelines."*

"I'd rather not take advice from someone who swiped another person's zombies."

"Put it behind you. He's not someone you'll win against in an argument anyway."

While placating Giselle's resentment, Liltotto looked up at Ikomikidomoe.

"We've got to shut down that giant thing before we can do anything else."

"But..."

Giselle smiled, but her eyes conveyed that she was very reluctantly acquiescing. She sighed and gave an instruction to the shade standing behind her.

"Go get him, Bambi."

"Yeah. I'll...work hard. Because Candy and Minni and everyone...is here..."

Then the battleground that had just been engulfed in the white lightning was next engulfed in explosive red fire.

"It's that bomb girl! Now you've brought in a nuisance!"

Seeing the zombie who had leapt out of Giselle's shadow, Hirako unintentionally raised his voice. His memories of nearly being blown away in the past vividly came back to him, and cold sweat formed on his forehead. The reishi bombs being let loose by the girl with reddish-black skin one after another made contact with the monsters that Ikomikidomoe was creating and transformed their bodies into bombs. Then a hot wind from the resulting chain explosion made the sweat on Hirako's brow evaporate, even though he was at some distance.

"*Ngh!* Reckless as usual. Actually, I've got to start considering my next moves..."

Hirako sighed and put his hand on his zanpaku-to, muttering in deliberation over whether to take a side in this battle or get in contact with the distant Mayuri in order to consult with him about how to settle the situation.

"Since Momo's probably told Kyoraku already, it'd be good if I saw some movement there."

"Oh, whoa... This looks like it's escalating."

Though they hadn't withdrawn, Ginjo and the others hadn't proactively jumped into the fight either. They were dodging the aftereffects while observing the situation.

"I think this would be our chance to retreat if we wanted to, wouldn't it?"

Tsukushima shrugged as he said that, and Ginjo responded, "That was what I was intending...but that kid said something about being recognized as the king, right?"

"I see. So that's what's on your mind?"

Tsukishima responded to Ginjo as though he were sympathetic. "Yeah, it's about Xcution, isn't it?"

The Xcution he mentioned was not the Fullbringer group that Ginjo had once organized in the living world, but a new religious organization that they had just heard about the other day that was throwing its weight around in the world of the living. Ginjo recalled some information he had garnered from the "new residents" of the Rukongai in the last few days and began to detail his supposition. "According to folks who recently died, the cult Xcution supposedly already has several hundred thousand believers, but...I can't help but think there's a Fullbringer or Soul Reaper involved."

They were lucky enough to be able to talk to people who had been believers while they were living, and based on

what they said, the written doctrines of Xcution regarding the afterlife perfectly matched the state of the Rukongai and the way the Soul Reapers performed Konso. Those doctrines, which referenced Soul Reapers, the Rukongai, the Seireitei's existence and even the existence of Hollows, hell, and Hueco Mundo, could have been penned by someone who legitimately knew the world of the afterlife. However, within those doctrines, there was one aspect that diverged entirely from reality. To be more accurate, there was a section about the future, which they were not yet certain would occur.

"In the shadow of chaos spanning one thousand years, a new king shall be born to reign over each of the three worlds."

At first, Ginjo had thought the religious organization was related to the Quincies and was indicating the new king would be Yhwach. However, he had heard Yhwach's goal was not to rule over the three worlds but to remove the boundary itself between the worlds and return everything to primordial soup. Thinking this cryptic and prophetic passage was the key to figuring out the group's identity, he had intended to talk to Hisagi, the self-professed journalist he met the other day, to suss out what the Soul Reapers thought. But before he could do that, an unambiguous hint had appeared right before his eyes.

"Well then, I guess it's about time for people with power like us to join in?"

Ginjo turned his eyes not to the monstrous zanpaku-to called Ikomikidomoe, but to the child named Hikone controlling it. Then he noticed it—one of the Quincies who had arrived later was approaching that Soul Reaper child, propelling herself using explosions.

"Yo, kiddo. You said your name was Hikone Ubuginu, didn't you?"

Liltotto's eyes reflected the form of Hikone Ubuginu, still unharmed and standing on Ikomikidomoe. Exasperated that not only the monster Ikomikidomoe, but also Ikomikidomoe's Soul Reaper master was unharmed after being showered by Candice's many thunderbolts, she had purposefully started a conversation to get information from her opponent. "Oh! You're one of the Quincies who was in Hueco Mundo last time, aren't you?! It's nice to see you again! It's amazing that you're eating Ikomikidomoe's followers! I'm glad I could meet you again!"

"I'd rather have *not* run into you again. So...you were saying you're supposed to become king?"

"Yes! Oh, well, to be more correct, I'm not *becoming* the king so much as Lord Tokinada is going to make me the king!"

"So on top of it being a hand-me-down, you're just a puppet king? Is there not anything you yourself want to do?"

Though she said it as though to provoke Hikone, the child didn't appear to comprehend that she was being sarcastic and innocently replied, "There is! What I want to do is be useful to Lord Tokinada!"

"So if your pal Tokinada ordered you to die a painful death, would you actually go and die?"

"Yes! And I'd do my best to suffer while I do it!"

"Uh-huh, I see..."

Crap. Just talking about this is making me feel half-witted. This kid's as crazy a fanatic as Lille is. No, the kid's a little different from him. It's not fanaticism, so what is it?

It's like the kid was made that way from the start.

Though Liltotto was dubious as to whether she could get through to the Soul Reaper, she kept asking questions. The fact was, she had a single, genuine question that was unrelated to her premise of gathering information.

"There's something I wanna ask you."

It was related to the spiritual pressure that Candice and the others had also noticed intermingling in Hikone.

"Have you heard the name Gremmy Thoumeaux before?"

Gremmy Thoumeaux: that was the name of a boy who, barring Yhwach, was said to be the strongest of the Stern Ritter—someone who could beat anybody. That he was even a boy was something he himself had contrived; in actuality, his true gender and age were unknown. He was a Quincy whose body was a single brain floating in a container and who, through the V Schrift—The Visionary—that Yhwach had bestowed upon him, had created his flesh body by "imagining" it.

He could convert what he imagined into reality, and his abilities were like a god's. In his fatal battle with Kenpachi

Zaraki, he had even materialized a gigantic meteorite and outer space itself in the Seireitei. In the end, he had imagined a power that would outstrip Kenpachi Zaraki, which had ended up bringing about his own downfall when he was unable to imagine a body that could bear that power, and because of that he had been awakened from his dream and his brain could no longer function.

Liltotto had seen the moment that Gremmy's body had collapsed and had even confirmed that his spiritual pressure had entirely ceased. She didn't know what had happened to the container holding his brain after that, and she hadn't intended to find out where it went, but...it was a different matter when she could feel Gremmy's spiritual pressure coming from the Soul Reaper in front of her eyes.

Liltotto had asked the question presuming that this Soul Reaper might have been a decoy that the living Gremmy might have made with his imagination.

"Gremmy... You mean Mr. Gremmy. Oh!"

Hikone thought for a bit and became bright-faced as though recalling something. "Yes, I do know that name! Lord Tokinada told me about that!"

"What?!"

Liltotto, who hadn't expected an actual response, opened her small eyes wide as she waited for Hikone to go on. However, Hikone's reply was the answer that Liltotto hadn't wanted to hear.

"Mr. Gremmy was one of the people used as an ingredient to create me! Yes, he was!"

CHAPTER FIFTEEN

ARISTOCRAT QUARTERS, SHINO SEYAKUIN, DIRECTOR'S ROOM

"NOW WHAT HAVE WE HERE? I never would have expected the Captain General of the Thirteen Court Guard Companies, Master Kyoraku, to pay a visit. Will falling prostrate to the ground before you just once suffice?" Seinosuke Yamada—the man who ran the pharmaceutical clinic for exclusive aristocratic use, which, though at first glance seemed extravagantly built, actually prioritized function in its design—spoke to his unexpected caller with sarcasm. The man he was talking to—Shunsui Kyoraku—had a cynical smile in his left eye as he said, "Always the same, aren't you, Seinosuke?"

"Thank you for taking such great care of my younger brother. Nothing makes me happier than to hear that the Fourth Company is doing well even after my departure."

After finishing the formal greeting, Seinosuke narrowed his eyes and said, "No, maybe I should say that I'm glad it's doing well even after Unohana is no longer there."

"Do you hold a grudge against me?" Kyoraku replied, without dodging the issue.

Seinosuke, who was the older brother of Hanataro Yamada from the Fourth Company, had formerly served for a long while as the assistant captain of the same company. Though he had occasionally rebelled against the captain Retsu Unohana, Kyoraku knew very well that they had a relationship of trust.

Unohana herself was currently nowhere in the Seireitei.

As part of Kyoraku's plan, she had sacrificed herself in order to draw out Kenpachi Zaraki's strength. Kyoraku himself understood it was likely an unforgivable act for those who adored Unohana. Regardless of that, he had prepared himself to accept all that resentment and made the decision in order to save not only the Soul Society, but all three realms, which included the world of the living and Hueco Mundo. Unohana herself had accepted that as well.

In response to Kyoraku, who acted as though he knew he would be blamed, Seinosuke quietly shook his head.

"That was just the type of person Unohana was. If she determined that allowing Kenpachi Zaraki to live would save a great number of lives, then it made sense for her, as someone who had dedicated her very being to crossing swords. Had I heard about it before, I likely would have opposed it, but, well, she likely would have carried through with it anyway. She was strong after all."

"Is that so? Well, if you have any complaints, it would be helpful if you could direct them to me, rather than Zaraki. Regardless of how Unohana felt about it, I was the one who toyed around with making the plan."

"A coward like me could not possibly complain to Kenpachi Zaraki. Why, of course, I cannot complain to you either, Captain General Kyoraku, my lord."

As Kyoraku watched this man who shamelessly called himself a "coward" remaining imperturbable in front of the Captain General, he smiled wryly and asked again, "About Unohana and Zaraki—who did you hear about that from? I was certain we hadn't released that information to the public yet."

"It was Tokinada Tsunayashiro."

At Seinosuke's quick response, Kyoraku narrowed his single eye and went silent.

"It seems he was hoping I would show some sort of grief, but all he found was disappointment. He even said, 'It is no fun teasing someone who lacks a heart.'"

"I see. He hasn't changed, it seems. But that's still a terrible thing to say."

"It is the truth, however. It seems that I am lacking in kindness and many other such sentiments."

"Not the humble type, are you? If you really didn't have a heart, you wouldn't have warned your brother, would you?"

On hearing those words, Seinosuke smiled a cynical smile and shook his head.

"I see. So that is the reason the Captain General himself has come. Hanataro, that gossip."

"Maybe it was him. Or maybe it wasn't Hanataro, but Hisagi or even others who could have told me? Regardless of who it was, weren't you expecting word to get around to me?"

"I will leave that up to your imagination, sir. So then, did you not come here in order to ask something specific of me? You didn't invite me to the barracks or to Central 46, but came on your own two feet right here to me, so you must be plotting something that cannot be public, correct?"

"I'm glad that this conversation will be quick, seeing how perceptive you are." Then Kyoraku uttered the name of a specific person. "Hikone Ubuginu. That's the name of a child who has been working around here lately, claiming to be a servant. Do you recognize the name? Surely, I don't think you can claim that you don't."

"In that case, you didn't have to ask, did you? You must have come here after discovering that the child was a patient here."

At this point in the conversation, which was like the meeting between a badger and fox, Kyoraku went a step further and asked, "Will you tell me? Where could that child possibly have come from, and who are they?"

"Though I am imperfect, I am still a medical practitioner. Are you asking me to reveal information about a patient?"

"Yes, I believe that you will tell me. You're the kind of Soul Reaper who respects life, after all is said and done, over a set of rules, or saving face, or your position. Please, if you know about the child's circumstances, that patient of yours might come out of this alive."

His face did not look all that different from his usual peaceful expression, but what Kyoraku said was still disturbing. Any Soul Reaper who had known him for an extended period of time would have known that this was not a joke or a threat, but something he genuinely believed. And Seinosuke and Kyoraku had been acquainted for quite some time while in the Thirteen Court Guard Companies.

"That you're able to express so much with just a look proves you are suited to being Captain General, and that you are an heir to the Kyoraku family as nobles of the Seireitei."

"You're giving me too much credit. This is the only way I know how to be, as I'm such an awkward man."

Seinosuke lightly shrugged and brought up a specific family. "How much do you know about the Ubuginu family?"

"I heard it was a family line that served the Tsunayashiro family, but that it died off a while ago. Officially, that Hikone Ubuginu child is said to be a distant relative, but there are no formal documents about that anywhere to be found—even in the Great Archive."

"Yes, that is exactly right. The Ubuginu family's stock is long gone. It is not as though I know the minute details of Tokinada Tsunayashiro's plot; however, it wouldn't be a stretch to interpret his request of me as treason against the Soul Society. For example, it might be considered a crime to research unspoken events and then make use of that research." Speaking about the false charges that had been imposed on Kisuke Urahara in the past, he slowly stepped to Kyoraku's side and mentioned something in a whispered voice. "*A fragment of the Reio.*"

"Huh?"

"You know what that means, don't you? Especially as Ukitake's closest friend."

"Are you saying this child Hikone also has a *fragment*?"

Seinosuke contradicted Kyoraku's guess with a thin smile. "That's not quite accurate. They used all the 'Fragments of the Reio' that the Tsunayashiro house had collected thus far as a core...and then mixed it with Soul Reaper and human konpaku. That is what Hikone Ubuginu is."

"Soul Reaper and human...?"

"Well, I was not the one who came up with the design. I do not even know for certain whose konpaku was used. It was not just one or two people. The konpaku of a Soul Reaper as well as a human from the living world, likely Quincy as well, and at least ten thousand other konpaku seem to be mixed in the child."

"That's ridiculous. The child isn't a Menos Grande—and I doubt it would be possible to condense that many konpaku together while maintaining Soul Reaper and human nature."

Though Kyoraku had denied it reflexively...*Or*...He began to consider the possibility...*Or* Kisuke Urahara, Mayuri Kurotsuchi, or Senjumaru Shutara from Squad Zero might have been capable of it. However, none of them would have worked with the Tsunayashiro family. Actually, given that it was them, they would have completed the project from start to finish themselves, and there never would have been a reason to ask for Seinosuke Yamada's help.

As though he had perceived Kyoraku's misgivings, Seinosuke spoke the truth indifferently. "Quite right. The Tsunayashiro family has no craftsman at the level of Urahara, Kurotsuchi, or Master Shutara. That is why when they first brought Hikone to me, the child was in horrendous shape."

Recalling this time, Seinosuke sighed deeply. "The child had nothing from the neck up and was missing pieces all over their body; it seemed as though their Saketsu and Hakusui were barely circulating spiritual power."

"..."

"And they told me to 'make it live.' I simply did what I could. Oh, and I won't accept any discussion at this point that it would have been better off if I had left the child to die. Even you are thoroughly aware that that is the type of man I am, aren't you?"

"Well, that's the extent of my understanding though. I doubt you would be able to elevate what is basically a meat shell into an individual with volition. Considering that it contained several fragments of the Reio, I wouldn't expect anyone with such substance at their core to so easily serve Tokinada."

"Yes. And this is why Tokinada brought it...the final component."

"What component?"

When Kyoraku scowled, Seinosuke started to delve into the crux of the issue. "Do you know of a Quincy named Gremmy Thoumeaux?"

"Yeah, I looked over the records collected at the Great Archive after the war. Wasn't that the Quincy that Zaraki battled..."

At that point, Kyoraku stopped speaking momentarily. The wrinkles on his brow furrowed all the more deeply, and he asked Seinosuke, "It couldn't possibly have been *that*?"

"Several thousands, or even tens of thousands of konpaku and many fragments of the Reio. A 'Quincy brain' that would be able to withstand the turbid waters of spiritual pressure surging like a vortex of chaotic consciousnesses. On top of that, the ability to instantaneously create outer space, with the previous owner of that brain's konpaku long gone. That thing, which had turned into a husk without life, was the last piece of the equation that had, against all

odds, been delivered to Tokinada. That is what happened."
Seinosuke grinned. "Don't you think it's ironic, Captain
General Kyoraku? Kenpachi Zaraki was strengthened
through your plan by sacrificing Unohana. Who would
have thought the corpse of the Quincy he killed—or rather
the *brain*—would have ended up right in the hands of your
enemy, Tokinada Tsunayashiro?"

Instead of replying to the sarcastic remark, Kyoraku
asked with a quiet expression, "Seinosuke, was that what you
really wanted? Weren't you in a position to sever that chain?"

"I followed my own convictions and let live what I could. I
have no regrets about that, Kyoraku. I will ask you the same
question in return—do you have regrets? Do you regret sacrificing Unohana for the sake of your conviction to protect
the Soul Society?"

Kyoraku pulled his hat down low, and a lonely, self-deprecating smile played along his lips in the hat's shadow as
he responded, "You really are quite malicious, aren't you?
Maybe you really do hold a grudge—against me, that is."

"Never!"

Seinosuke also smiled as though mocking himself, turning his face away from Kyoraku as he muttered, "I'm just
sentimental."

≡

THE PAST,
SILBERN

Silbern, the Vandenreich's base of operations. As the final battle with the Soul Reapers was quickly progressing, there had been an area with remarkably apparent spiritual pressure. Though it was a cage that had been securely sealed with a barrier that only Yhwach could make, that seal was currently undone and the intended prisoner—Gremmy Thoumeaux—was standing in a corner of the passageway.

None approached the boy who had been freed, and as though they believed they would be killed if they simply met eyes with him, the general members did not even enter his field of vision. However, there was a single figure who had approached Gremmy without hesitation.

"Yo, looks like you're doing fine, you monster."

"I wouldn't have expected you to be the one to treat me like *I'm* the monster, Liltotto."

As Gremmy spoke, a cold smile broke out on his face. Liltotto responded without a care, "Was that beyond your imagination? If you don't like monster, then I guess I could call you scum. More importantly, I ran out of sweets and I just can't stop feeling hungry. Could you whip something up for me?"

"You're pretty much the only person who would insult me and ask for stuff at the same time."

"Isn't his majesty always saying to help each other out? Stop being stingy."

"Don't call *me* stingy when you're trying to sponge candy off me."

Despite what he said, in the next moment Gremmy envisioned a mountain of donut packages. Then, at some point, a giant bag of donuts appeared in Liltotto's arms. Her eyes widened slightly as she ate one of the donuts from the bag.

"*Chomp...gulp...* Not bad, but a little too sweet."

"I don't know what your preferences are. Seems like it'd be faster for me to *imagine* that you're a sweet tooth."

"After we kill all those Soul Reapers and we're free, make sure you try all kinds of stuff. Then you'll be able to expand your imagination a bit."

"I'll think about it."

As Gremmy gave her a strained smile, Liltotto ate her donuts, smiling faintly and thanking him. "Well, you were a lifesaver. Thanks."

Then, as she was about to leave, Gremmy asked her casually, "Getting a thank-you is nice, but aren't you going to pay me back or something?"

"What is with you? You can imagine anything into being, but you still want something in return?"

"It's a matter of respect. You wouldn't feel great about being in my debt either, right?"

Liltotto muttered, "I guess you're right," in response to

Gremmy and then thought for a while before saying, "Right. When we start our thing with the Soul Reapers, if I see somebody you haven't been able to kill, I'll try hitting them while they're down."

"If I can't kill someone, then I doubt you'd be able to."

"Then when the time comes, I'll pester them in the most effective way and then run away. It's not like I'd risk my life for a bag of donuts, right? Don't expect me to be sweet to you."

Catching sight of Liltotto's grin, Gremmy wore his usual faint smile as he shook his head.

"Seriously, this whole knight's order is filled with egotists, his majesty included."

"That's a surprising thing for someone to say who's just been thrown in jail for acting like an egomaniac. So what're you gonna do after the war ends and you're actually free?"

"Right. I've never imagined that." After thinking for a while, Gremmy played it off as a joke and shrugged. "Maybe I'll try cooking? If I just try random stuff, then I might come up with something I couldn't have imagined—that seems like it'd be entertaining."

Liltotto couldn't tell whether Gremmy's words were serious, and she also answered in a way that made it difficult to tell if she was joking. "Make sure it's something that you wouldn't be able to imagine the taste of based on how it looks. If you so much as think that something looks spicy, even strawberry jam would end up like habanero sauce."

"I'll take that into account. Next time I make food, maybe I'll imagine a super high-calorie cookie that'll fatten you up with a single bite."

Liltotto pulled a new donut out of the bag and said with a sarcastic smile, "Well, I'll at least try a taste of it. I'm expecting great things, scum."

After that absurd conversation, the two of them went their separate ways. Liltotto joined up with Bambietta and the others while Gremmy took along the Quincy he had created from his imagination, Guenael Lee, and they headed into their war with the Soul Reapers.

They didn't realize that conversation would be the last words they would say to each other.

≡

PRESENT DAY, THE RUKONGAI

"You said he was an *ingredient*?"

Hikone nodded eagerly from on top of Ikomikidomoe.

"Yes! The brains in my head mostly come from Mr. Gremmy! That's what Lord Tokinada told me!"

Liltotto thought for a bit, and though only a few seconds actually passed, she wiped away the emotion in her expression as though she had come to a breakthrough. Wearing her usual somewhat sober expression, the girl hardened reishi and created a Heilig Bogen and pulled a Heilig Pfeil from the pouch on her back.

"So that's how it is. Basically, you're a completely different person who just has the same spiritual pressure as him."

"Uh?"

"Of course that's it. There's no way that scummy dude would still be alive." Though her words sounded critical, Liltotto's muttering tone was desolate. Hikone tilted their head, and Liltotto let the Heilig Pfeil pointing at the child's chest fly. "In that case, I can go right ahead and crush you then, can't I?"

"Uh!"

A roar and a shock wave was generated, and the surrounding spiritual pressure went into violent turbulence. "*Tsk*...What is that thing?"

Liltotto clucked her tongue as she looked at what was directly in her field of vision. The scene was comprised of Hikone using the palm of their hand to stop the arrow, and Blut Vene, the defensive ability particular to Quincies, spreading before her. But that wasn't all.

Though it was known only to those who had fought Arrancars and some portion of high-level Hollows, they would have seen not only the Blut Vene pattern on Hikone's hand, but also the response of Hierro, which was particular to Hollows.

The one who noticed that abnormality was Hirako, who had fought against both Arrancars and Quincies.

"Wait a sec, that can't be right."

He understood that the child had Quincy spiritual pressure intermingling within them. And because of that, Hikone's using Blut Vene wasn't surprising. However, it was something different altogether that it was accompanied by Hierro, a Hollow-specific characteristic.

Hollows and Quincies are supposed to be the least compatible! That's the whole reason why we could pump Hollow reishi through ourselves to get back our bankai!

Well, wait. To begin with, how can all of this Soul Reaper, Hollow, and Quincy spiritual pressure be all blended together?

Though blending Hollow with Soul Reaper was fairly uncommon, from Ichigo Kurosaki to the Visoreds including Hirako, it wasn't as though there were no precedents. However, without the help of a power from something like the Hogyoku, or the course of events surrounding Ichigo's birth, the reishi wouldn't have been able to retain the shape of a Soul Reaper. It should have crumbled—and this was even more the case if, in addition, Quincy, which had the worst affinity for the Hollow factor, were also mixed into the child.

Because of that, Hirako grew suspicious that the existence in front of his eyes was somehow related to the Hogyoku. But Hikone looked troubled and asked Hirako, "Umm, what is making her so angry?"

Hikone didn't seem curious so much as anxious about being in trouble for reasons they didn't understand and continued to stop the rapid-fire Heilig Pfeils with their bare hands.

"Did I make some sort of mistake?"

"I haven't got a clue. Well, you might've just stepped on some sort of land mine."

Despite Hirako's response, he could more or less guess the issue.

I thought they were just working together because they had to, as fellow henchmen...Now that I see them coming to rescue those Mayuri took on as his pawns, it looks like some of them did consider each other friends.

"That's its own kind of trouble. Seriously."

Even as Hikone and Liltotto were having their exchange, the battle continued between Ikomikidomoe's large form and the Arrancars alongside the Quincies. The winged monsters that were ceaselessly being birthed assaulted Grimmjow and the others, as they in turn took them down with Ceros and Balas and zanpaku-to, while continuing to attack the main body.

"Hey! Grimmjow! What is going on here?! Explain!"

"Hunh?! You can tell just by lookin'! I'm killin' this mammoth that dared to look down on me!"

Grimmjow *tsked* at Nelliel's words as he replied. Meanwhile, Luppi, who had been attacking from another

angle, cocked his head to the side when he saw a horde of the small monsters being mowed down by a muddy stream.

"Huuuh? You're here, Halibel? So you're still alive?"

"That's what I should be asking you. What are you doing here?"

"Obviously, I'm here to kill Grimmjow. Well, before I can do that, this huge thing is in the way, so I was just thinking of crushing it."

Luppi, who spoke casually, swung his tentacles around as he let loose a Cero and mowed down the monsters surrounding him. Halibel immediately surveyed the state of her surroundings; she noticed the blond Soul Reaper floating in the air and muttered, "Is that the masked Soul Reaper from Karakura Town?"

However, when she saw that the Soul Reaper was neither fighting nor helping the zanpaku-to that had transformed into a gigantic monster, it looked to her as though he also couldn't grasp what Hikone Ubuginu was.

"What in the world is happening in the Soul Society?"

As Bambietta's fire illuminated their surroundings, Liltotto kept shooting Heilig Pfeil one after another. Hikone narrowly evaded those while bowing quickly in between intervals.

"Uh, um, I'm sorry if I did anything wrong. I'm so sorry!"

Though the gestures only made it look like Hikone was making a fool out of Liltotto, the child was extremely serious.

Liltotto seemed to know that, and with sober eyes, she simply replied indifferently, "Nah, you haven't done anything wrong."

Then she said the words that resulted in Hikone becoming her opponent.

"But your boss, Tokinada Tsunayashiro, is going down. That's all."

"Huh?" Hikone was neither angry nor surprised—just inquisitive. "Killing Lord Tokinada is impossible."

At first glance Hikone appeared expressionless as they said that. However, beneath the bland surface was a shade of doubt accompanied by innocent cruelty, like a child who had been told not to stomp on ants. Those eyes were at the threshold of purity and ignorance—the eyes of someone who genuinely could not fathom the feelings or meaning of what another person was saying or why they were saying it—eyes that did not even attempt to understand.

Realizing that the shade in the child's depths was hollowness, Liltotto understood that for what it truly meant. She understood that the Quincy monster she knew no longer existed within that spiritual pressure.

A chill buzzed up Liltotto's spine, and an interval of split seconds passed as she blinked. In the next moment, Hikone had snuck up to her chest.

"Huh?"

The child had traveled through an intricate mix of shunpo, sonido, and hirenkyaku. Though they had been facing each

other head on, the child had appeared close to her with implausible speed that caught her completely unaware.

The moment Hikone's karate chop had broken her Heilig Bogen, Liltotto saw *it*. The hand of the child who had seemed like a Soul Reaper transformed for just a breath into a warped shape almost exactly like that of a Hollow's arm. Before Liltotto could even understand what that meant, she was blown away.

"Guh..."

It wasn't just the zanpaku-to that changed. This kid's gotten stronger too!

"Are you all right?"

Hearing this calm voice, Liltotto realized that Meninas had at some point caught her when she was blown away.

"Sorry. Didn't mean to be a burden."

Immediately standing, Liltotto glared at Hikone. Hikone looked down on the girl while also not looking down upon her and wore a simple, plain, pure smile and spoke as though stating a fact. "I'll stop anyone who tries to kill Lord Tokinada, and—"

The boy—or perhaps the girl—did not notice that their truth meant despair to others.

"Besides, Lord Tokinada is much, much stronger than me!"

≡

"I'm beat. I'm terrible at fighting."

Tokinada Tsunayashiro seemed to purposefully shake his head as he witnessed the scene in front of his eyes. What appeared before him was the entrance to the special storage area of the Visual Department—or at least the mountain of rubble that remained of it. The earlier combat continued on without change until an abrupt burst of spiritual pressure wind blew by with a golden shimmer. An echoing roar swallowed up the passageway's floor and wall, and the entrance had been reduced to powder.

"You wouldn't happen to be able to share the reason for the sudden wolfish violence, Lady Shihoin?"

Yoruichi, who stood atop the rubble, had grown winglike spiritual pressure from the tops of her shoulders all the way down her back. She looked down on Tokinada, who stood in front of the rubble, and smiled boldly.

"Calling it wolfish is so nasty of you. I'd rather you compare me to a cat than a wolf."

"So will you tell me why you stopped pretending to be a cat then, Lady Shihoin?"

"I doubt you'll correct yourself, but don't you think that was a bit forced? Well, whatever. I don't like a long slog, so in order to beat up those assassins all at once, I just exerted my true power a bit. But I wasn't expecting the walls and floor to collapse just from that. You may send the repair bill to the Shihoin family." Yoruichi paused at that point and showed off something in her hand as she continued. "Although, that's *if* you have the time to bill me."

"Wha..." Soi Fon, who had kicked away an assassin in front of her face, let slip her surprise after seeing what was in Yoruichi's hand. Yoruichi had what looked like a human fetus contained in a small cylindrical glass case, and something like a piece of a Hollow was fused to the specimen.

"I found these things together. Don't you think this is a slight deviation from the Visual Department's usual subject matter?"

"I don't recall ever seeing that. Maybe you brought it in just now?"

"I hope your hearsay works on the Central 46. It seems you already laid the groundwork, but Kyoraku has also been building up his pawn for quite a while. More importantly, those cunning aristocrats would likely prefer to set up a much easier puppet, such as a child who is a distant relative, as head of family, rather than you and your maliciousness."

Listening to Yoruichi, Tokinada did not seem flustered and simply let a nasty grin form on his face as he replied, "As far as your last opinion is concerned, I entirely agree. However...if you would go this far, may I assume that you will be rejecting my proposal concerning the Soul King and the Shiba family?"

Tokinada was referring to their three-way conversation with Byakuya Kuchiki from just days earlier, and Yoruichi replied indifferently, "Oh, that. I haven't got a clue about that kid Byakuya, but either way I don't care if the world ends up changing in the way you said it would."

"Oh…?"

"Huh?"

Tokinada narrowed his eyes in interest as Soi Fon cocked her head to the side in genuine confusion—she did not know the contents of that three-way discussion. With the other two in front of her, Yoruichi spoke openly about her philosophy of life: "Regardless of whether the ruling structure of the world of the living, Hueco Mundo, or the Soul Society changes, and regardless of what happens to the Shiba family's standing, I am still me. It might be a pain in the ass, but, well, if the Shiba family is restored Kukaku could probably fulfill the duties as needed."

When Soi Fon heard the words "Shiba family is restored," her eyes widened, and Yoruichi watched that with some amusement before folding her arms and grandly going off on Tokinada. "However, that is an entirely separate issue from whether I can forgive you for your evildoing. I never wanted that guy Aizen to stand in heaven, so what makes you think I'd approve of someone even scummier, like you? You're saying you're going to attempt to create a world with an entirely different group of people… Well, let's just see what you've got."

"I see, I see. I must say, what an honor it is to be treated as an even worse villain than Aizen."

"Did you not hear what I just said? I didn't say you were a villain—I called you 'scummy.'"

Tokinada burst out laughing.

"*Ha ha ha ha ha!* I see! That is indeed quite a difference! However, do you have any right to speak as a descendant of the Shihoin family? Can you say that to me—a member of the Tsunayashiro family—when you yourself are part of the same Four Great Noble Clans?!"

"Yeah, and I'll say it as many times as I need to. Regardless of who my ancestors were, I am still me. And you are still you. The Tsunayashiros' pedigree and past deeds have no relation to this—you're spitting on the world of your own volition, aren't you, Tokinada?"

"Yes, that's right—that's exactly it! I respect Byakuya Kuchiki for his ability to stifle his own emotions for the sake of his clan. I am not envious of him at all! However, do not forget that once you strip away the rings of the tree, even an unyielding, monolithic tree like the Kuchiki family is just as rotten inside as I am."

"Regardless of that, the Kuchiki family has become a pillar that supports the world. It's arrogant of you to compare your family to theirs when it was your family's shoot, not to mention its very trunk, that is rotten."

What...?

What is Ms. Yoruichi talking about?

Soi Fon, who had finished defeating the last of the assassins, became bewildered listening to the pair's conversation.

Obviously the Tsunayashiro family is rotten. The dark rumors about them were constant even before Tokinada became head of the family.

But why would the Shihoin and Kuchiki families also be rotten?

Ms. Yoruichi's...and the Four Great Noble Clans' ancestors—what exactly did they do?

While Soi Fon was curious about how the conversation would continue, she felt troubled that as a lesser-ranking aristocrat Soul Reaper, she should not perhaps have been privy to this conversation. Eventually, she disciplined herself with, *"Eavesdropping on the details of Ms. Yoruichi's familial circumstances out of my own interest is the lowliest of acts."* Then she devoted herself to working to erase that interest.

"Ms. Yoruichi, I have finished dealing with the attackers. I would like to return to guarding Lord Tokinada."

"Hm? Aren't you full of integrity, Soi Fon. I think we could just go ahead and arrest him though. Well, formally we're doing it as his convoy."

At that point, Yoruichi turned her eyes to Tokinada and threw some provocative words at him. "So? Where is this 'new Reio' that you were going on about? Whatever happens with you, I'd like to get a look at them with my own eyes.

They're supposedly your trump card and will do anything you say, isn't that right?"

Tokinada let out a small sigh and stared up at Yoruichi where she stood on the rubble. "Right," he said. "I suppose it's time to use my trump card."

His mouth contorted into a grin, and he pulled something that looked like a talisman from his chest pocket.

"Huh? What is that thing?"

"You can tell based on what you see, can't you? It is a trump card, just as I said."

In response to Yoruichi's doubt, Tokinada started to funnel spiritual pressure into the talisman. But in the next moment, Yoruichi, who had just been on top of the mountain of rubble, was instantaneously at his back.

"It's not as though I'd just wait idly by."

She tried to grab and twist the arm that held the talisman, but—"Too slow." As he said that, Tokinada's form and even his spiritual pressure vanished like smoke.

"Huh?!"

"Wha...? Was that an invisibility technique?!"

Shocked, Soi Fon turned her spiritual senses around to her surroundings, but Yoruichi shook her head in disappointment.

"No. It doesn't look like he used a Secret Remote Squad technique or a spiritual pressure interception cloak. It's likely that might have been a Soul Ticket."

A Soul Ticket—in the past, Kyoraku had given those to Ichigo's friends in the living world. They were special tickets that allowed one to travel freely between the Soul Society and the world of the living.

"We should check whether it was something like that and whether he escaped straight to Dangai. Though if Kisuke is around, he would go after him right away."

"But I thought that other than those given to Ichigo Kurosaki's acquaintances, they were strictly regulated by the First Company?"

"He likely stole the technique and made his own."

Yoruichi sighed deeply and let escape her cynicism about the man who was head of the Four Great Noble Clans. "Really—he's top notch at stealing the fruits of other people's labors. He likely stole that Kuten Kyokoku from his household."

Then, looking into the empty space in exasperation, she added in a small mutter that Soi Fon may or may not have heard, "You don't have to go that far in following in our ancestor's footsteps."

SHINO-SEYAKUIN

Just after he had received several documents relating to Hikone Ubuginu from Seinosuke, Kyoraku finally took a step forward and sighed.

"Well, all you did was keep an injured person alive when the Four Great Noble Clans told you to. Though the methods by which it was done are likely problematic, the ones who brought you the child were the Tsunayashiro family of the Four Great Noble Clans. From that perspective, they would be hard to refuse, and I think it would be difficult to claim that you should be charged with a crime."

"Oh my, isn't that quite lenient of you?"

"I'd rather not say it, but if I were to charge you with a crime instead and imprison you, the aristocrat big shots would likely object. Plus, thanks to you it seems there are many older folks whose lives have been extended despite only having a few years left to live."

Kyoraku put his hat back on and then thought about what would be coming in the time ahead. He let out a sigh that had a different significance than his earlier sigh.

"Who would have thought that Shunsui Kyoraku would have to govern? Being a Captain General sure is troublesome. Perhaps you should try forcing it on someone else as soon as you can?"

"I've got a mountain of stuff I'd like to do that with. I don't know how long it'll take, but there are the Court Guards that Old Man Yama left and then there's the new Court Guards. I need to find a neat point of compromise between those two."

At that point, the Thirteen Court Guard Companies' Captain General wiped the smile off his face and spoke his next words with conviction. "In order for that to happen, I need to stop Tokinada now."

"Don't you think you're a bit late for that, Captain General Kyoraku?"

"Huh? What does that mean?"

"Don't you think it's odd that you're able to meet with me like this? Why wouldn't that strategy-monger Tokinada Tsunayashiro have come up with a countermeasure to keep me quiet?"

"Huh!"

When Kyoraku realized the significance of what Seinosuke was saying, Seinosuke threw out an underhanded final blow. "If my guess is correct, *Tokinada Tsunayashiro has already finished his preparations*. That is exactly why he has overlooked what you are doing and is not intervening in any way."

"I see. That might be the case." Kyoraku seemed to brood over this for a while but answered without showing any despair. "Yes, I certainly am making the second move. But you know what, there's something I'd like to try specifically because this is the second move."

"Hm? What do you mean?"

"I just got a report from the Secret Remote Squad. Apparently there's a small commotion in the Rukongai right now. I believe it's likely related to the events that are unfolding."

Kyoraku then quickly relayed the details of that turmoil and his plan. As though showing his acknowledgement, a cheerful smile came over Seinosuke's face, and he said, "Are you sure about that? Don't you think that plan could cause problems later?"

"This is exactly the time to do it. There's a precedent for it from the Quincy war, and it's one of the better options we've got."

Kyoraku smiled quietly and spoke cynical and self-deprecating words. "It's far preferable to opening the doors to hell."

≡

"Oh…"

The fight against Ikomikidomoe's main body, which straddled the sky and earth, was ongoing. Before they knew it, the number of foot-soldier monsters being birthed had increased, and the fight was transitioning to a battlefield, but…Hikone suddenly stopped moving and pulled from their chest pocket something that looked like a talisman. The talisman was faintly glowing red, and Hikone shouted, seemingly in a fluster, "Ikomikidomoe! It looks like Lord Tokinada is calling us from *over there*! Let's go, quickly!"

Ikomikidomoe, who had continued the fight in silence for the most part, rumbled with a low voice that came from the center of his gigantic form, **"I have no interest in his welfare...but for now, I will obey."**

At the same time, the white mist cleared, and the monsters scattered around Ikomikidomoe gathered at his mouth and disappeared into it as though being devoured of their own volition.

"*Hunh?* What the hell? You thinkin' of just running away again?!" As Grimmjow yelled, the mountainous giant in front of him shrank in an instant and, after transforming back into the form of a white sword, was sheathed in Hikone's scabbard.

"Yes, we're running away!" Hikone replied and, after glancing around, yelled, "Uhh, oh, right! Is there a Mr. Kugo Ginjo around?!"

"*Hunh?*" Upon abruptly hearing his name, Ginjo had forgotten even to make himself scarce before he cried out. Though he hesitated for a moment about whether he ought to reply further, Ginjo held his breath as he came forward. "How do you know my name?"

"Oh! So you're Mr. Ginjo! Lord Tokinada told me your name! He wanted me to try comparing my strength to yours, but I think I will have to ask you to do that when we meet next time! Yes!"

"Why me? Who is this Tokinada guy anyway?"

"Lord Tokinada is my master! I heard that you are also a candidate for being the Soul King, Mr. Ginjo, but I'm going to be the one who becomes king! I won't lose to you, so I look forward to when we meet again!"

"What'd you say?"

Hikone bobbed down into a bow and turned around as Ginjo became even more confused. Hikone simply opened a small garganta and leapt in while bowing to the Arrancars and Quincies.

"I'm so sorry to do this after you went out of your way to fight all-out with me! I need to head over to Lord Tokinada's sanctuary, so if there are any of you who still do not accept me as king, then I will gladly fight with you until you do accept it!"

"Hunh? What's that kid saying? It's not like I'd let you get away."

Luppi released Ceros from his eight feelers, and the Quincies' Heilig Pfeil also aimed all at once for the void and fired, but—

"And so, if you'll excuse me."

A blue-white glitter was released from Hikone's hand as the child smiled innocently, their eyes not revealing any emotion. The glitter wasn't a Gran Ray Cero so much as a gigantic Cero that had been created by releasing dense spiritual pressure at full strength. It swallowed up all the attacks of those who had attempted to pursue the child and made them disappear. Then, after that had been unable to stop the force, it sprang at them. The Cero hadn't required any skill; it was a feat of strength that had been achieved by Hikone's simply pushing out all the spiritual pressure they had.

It became a muddy stream that made the Arrancars and Quincies sense certain death as it hurtled toward them, and while those facing it didn't have much time to react, two predators jumped out in front of the beam.

Nelliel and Liltotto had come to stand side by side by coincidence, and each of them opened their mouths wide as they *devoured* the Cero. Feasting on it using the Cero Double and The Glutton, the two women had turned the high-density Cero into their dinner.

Nelliel used the Cero she had taken in to add to a Cero of her own that she launched, but when that flash subsided the garganta's maw was no longer open.

"Looks like you've got a similar skill," Nelliel said to the Quincy girl next to her while looking at the resulting cloud of dust.

"I can't shoot it back though. Vomiting out something you've eaten is a waste anyway."

"I agree with that."

Perhaps because she had shot out such a strong Cero, a small stream of blood trickled from the corner of Nelliel's mouth.

And possibly because Liltotto had eaten the reishi of a Hollow, which did not agree with her, her breathing was rough and she looked as though she had terrible heartburn.

"So? What do we do now? You wanna continue from where we were earlier?"

Liltotto and the others had just been facing the Arrancars in Hueco Mundo the other day. Though it was possible this could end up snowballing right into combat, Liltotto figured there was a fifty-fifty chance of either side surviving if it did.

"It depends on you women. As long as you do not meddle in Hueco Mundo any more than you have, we have no reason to be hostile toward you," Nelliel replied, trying to end the battle, but another voice shouted an objection.

"How can you be so soft, Nelliel?! We already accepted the fight they started. Do you think I'll just let it end like that?" Grimmjow said. A shade standing behind him agreed for a different reason...

"You're right, a fight has already been started—though I'm referring to one from several years ago."

As usual, Luppi glared at Grimmjow with eyes full of hostility.

"Hunh? You're still alive? I thought that gigantic thing crushed you already."

Smiling wickedly and provoking each other, Grimmjow and Luppi's spiritual pressures started to gnash.

Hirako, who had been watching their situation from afar, sighed in annoyance.

"What? Are these two going to fight each other again?"

I'd like to stop them, but it'll likely just complicate things if I say anything. Maybe I should use Sakanade to make it so neither of them can fight?

No, there's that bomb girl. If things end up like they did before, that'd be the worst.

He continued to deliberate as he turned his eyes to the man who had answered Hikone's call earlier.

Is that guy over there really Kugo Ginjo? He really does look like the corpse that Ichigo took back to the living world, but...

"Seriously...why's this situation so complicated?"

Now that the common enemies Hikone and Ikomikidomoe had disappeared, the tension in the air started to accumulate again, and the situation was becoming explosive, but another voice jumped in and became the focus of attention.

"Please wait!"

It was the dignified entreaty of a young woman that echoed throughout the area. The one who had yelled as though she were leaping into the eye of a tornado was a bespectacled Soul Reaper.

"Huh?! Nanao, is that you?! Why're you here?!" Hirako shouted in surprise.

Though he had certainly anticipated some backup after reporting to Kyoraku, he expected the Secret Remote Squad

would come, not that the First Company assistant captain Nanao herself would rush directly over. He also would have understood if Kyoraku himself came for battle, but Nanao wasn't suited for fighting.

She excelled at kido, but that was an ability more suited for defense or support when it came to Arrancar-class fights. Grimmjow, prominently powerful even among the Arrancars, glared dubiously at the Soul Reaper that had abruptly appeared and said, "What, woman? What're you doing suddenly crashing the place?"

He had the glinting eyes of a beast that did not hide its hostility and was ready to go beyond the hunt, simply interested in pursuing violence toward her. It wouldn't have been odd for a normal Soul Reaper to have fainted just from his stare. Enduring that pressure from him, Nanao firmly persisted in fulfilling her role.

They were Arrancars under Aizen.

They were Quincies who had started the war alongside Yhwach.

And then they were Fullbringers who had been hunting Soul Reapers.

In the middle of a gathering of those who had formerly been hostile toward the Thirteen Court Guard Companies, Nanao Ise pushed down the resentment—or even the fear—that bubbled up from within her to the back of her chest and lowered her head to do her job as the assistant captain of the First Company.

She got on her knee and took on an air of formal decorum, as though they were her guests and, excluding Hirako, made a proposal of life or death. "Under the name of the Thirteen Court Guard Companies, I shall take everyone here under the custody of the First Company."

"Hunh? Like I said, why're you coming in here like you own the place..."

"Wait, Grimmjow."

Though Grimmjow tried to take a step forward, Halibel stopped him with her hand.

"What's the deal, Halibel?"

"Your goal is to get that strange Soul Reaper and zanpaku-to, isn't it? You should consider this discussion relevant to that."

Halibel also put Luppi in check with a stare as he tried to attack Grimmjow while the Arrancar was unaware, then simply turned to Nanao and nodded at her to urge her to continue.

Nanao was grateful to Halibel as she informed them with a humbled expression, "The Thirteen Court Guard Companies Captain General Shunsui Kyoraku has something he would like to discuss with you."

A CERTAIN PLACE IN THE RUKONGAI

"Good grief, it seems they've put a damper on things. You've gone too far now, really."

Mayuri Kurotsuchi, who had continued to observe from afar, confirmed that the combative atmosphere in the place had chilled and shook his head as though disappointed.

"It seems I should check on whether Tsunayashiro outwitted Captain General Kyoraku. Though things would have been settled so much faster had he just consulted me from the start."

Then a voice addressed him from behind. "Just how much had you already guessed from the start?"

"I'd hidden surveillance bacteria in the zombie girl. I was already observing when she fought that thing in Hueco Mundo. I tried to have the Quincies and Fullbringers fight in order to attract the Tsunayashiro family's attention, but as I said earlier, it was outside of my calculations that they would get involved directly at this stage. I should thank those Arrancars who interrupted us."

"You really are a frightening man. Were you using those Fullbringers and us as bait?"

"I am sure I have already said that obtaining Fullbringer specimens was part of the goal. More importantly, have you finished the analysis?"

In response to Mayuri, the Corpse Unit Quincy NaNaNa Najahkoop who had just returned confidently replied, "Yeah. It was difficult because that giant thing was growing while it fought, but I generally understand its spiritual pressure's pattern. The problem is that even though it's not on your level, its spiritual pressure pattern changes constantly. I think I could paralyze that, but I don't think it would last long."

After hearing this Mayuri did not specifically praise or disparage him, but coolly expressed his own judgment. "Why do you seem so proud of yourself? Of what use is it to be so proud of observation equipment producing the results of an observation? It makes me hesitate to include you in the deal I made with that gluttonous girl."

Najahkoop's lip twitched, and he recalled those who had betrayed him along with Yhwach.

"It's not the issues I've got with Bazz-B, but it's not like I haven't got a bone to pick with those guys after they just silently watched when...Actually, are you seriously letting Candice go? In that case, give me a reward for what I di... *ow ow ow ow ow*!"

An electric shock ran through him, and Najahkoop's whole body was pins and needles.

"You demand a reward before you have repaid your debt to me for elongating your life? All of you Quincies really are heartless brutes. Really, I bet you believe one can live off of sentimentality instead of money."

"*Guh*...That's no reason to shock somebody!"

Mayuri ignored Najahkoop's protestations as he muttered to himself and turned his eyes to the data he had analyzed himself. "You should know that I have collected all the data I needed on you as an experimental subject. As far as the lightning girl and the muscle girl are concerned, the outward appearance of releasing them should be enough... but since I have the opportunity, I've got another piece of work I'd like them to do. In the short amount of time remaining we will determine the power dynamic between the Court Guards and the aristocracy."

CHAPTER SIXTEEN

THE THRESHOLD

IT WAS A CURIOUS PLACE.

Compared to the world of the living and the Soul Society, the blue sky looked as though it were a few shades dimmer. Though it was filled with a pronounced amount of reishi, the atmosphere felt different than that of the Soul Society and Hueco Mundo, and the surroundings were characterized by an inorganic wasteland dotted with bare, rocky cliffs.

In part of it were two structures that did not fit with the harsh scenery. One was a building—a luxurious, Eastern-style palace like something straight from the history books. Though it was not tall, the low, sprawling, magnificent palace emitted a distinct radiance from within the rocky and sandy space. The spectacle, which looked as though someone had replaced that section of the place with the Soul Society's aristocratic quarters, was sure to provoke a reaction in anyone who saw it. Still, the other structure was even more bizarre. As though it were a single town, a gigantic royal palace that made one think of the Reiokyu and the Squad Zero Riden was floating in the sky. Though it loomed over the ground with an intense, intimidating weight from where it was in the heavens, there was no indication of a living being's spiritual pressure coming from it, and it seemed like just a container floating in midair.

Directly below the curious structure, in the courtyard of the palace rooted on the ground, a woman wearing clothes from the living world—Aura Michibane—called out, "Thank you for your work, Lord Tokinada."

The one she had spoken to, a man in luxurious Japanese-style clothing who seemed as though he were made for the palace—Tokinada Tsunayashiro—wore his usual nasty smile and said, "Yes, we had to move fairly quickly, but it seems we accomplished what we needed to in Ichigo Kurosaki's absence."

"So it seems everything went well for you then? I was expecting you at the Kyogoku much earlier. Were you out enjoying yourself all that time?"

Before Tokinada could reply, a flustered Hikone Ubuginu denied it. "No! It wasn't Lord Tokinada's fault! It was because I wasn't able to be by Lord Tokinada's side!"

"Yes, I'm sure that if Hikone had been with me, they would have been able to do something. However, I was the

one who told Hikone to go to the Rukongai. It's nothing for you to fret about."

"Ugh. I'm so sorry, Lord Tokinada."

With Hikone slinking like a beaten dog in front of her, Aura put on an inscrutable smile as she spoke to Tokinada. "But this *is* a curious place."

"You've only been to this Kyogoku three times, isn't that right?"

A Kyogoku. If the world of the living and the Soul Society could be likened to planets and the pipeline that connected them were Dangai, the void of space that surrounded those was called Garganta. Within that Garganta spaces occasionally floated up like bubbles that were filled with just enough reishi for humans and Soul Reapers to eke by in.

"Yes, it would be very interesting to know why places like this form in the Garganta in the first place."

"One theory has it that they form from what were once pitiable konpaku whose souls lost their memories entirely and failed to enter the cycle of death and rebirth. If a Hollow's final resting place is the desert of Hueco Mundo, then this is a simulated place created by humans who escaped from both Konso and the Hollows, and the souls of Soul Reapers and Rukongai residents who strayed from the flow of the cycle of reincarnation."

"So you are saying that their reishi happens to gather to create these places?"

"There are various theories. It may be just the opposite, and when the world was reborn into the form it is in now, the reishi might have simply flowed into and gathered in the spaces that spilled out from it. Well, the details of how this space came to be are not relevant now. What is important is that this is a stronghold protected by the Garganta." Tokinada snickered and said, "I do not think that the Four Great Noble Clans have been involved with Kyogoku since the Ryudoji family were cast out."

He brought up the family name of an old and esteemed aristocratic clan as he let his mind run through the deeds of Soul Society ancestors who were involved in the drama that had banished them.

"I'm sure it would have been enjoyable. It's not often that those who should consider themselves the strongest experience defeat and banishment into a Kyogoku, a place that they could not have comprehended. I cannot help but regret that I wasn't there to see that."

"I do not know anything about this Ryudoji clan, but if they are still alive, won't they eventually visit the Soul Society seeking revenge?"

"I wonder if they would. Things might have already happened that I am unaware of, and they may have been settled long ago. I cannot help but look forward to the moment I will crush them if they should attempt to come now."

"But you've already made the Thirteen Court Guard Companies your enemy and need to deal with them first, don't you?"

As she spoke indifferently of the might of those they would confront, Aura smiled thinly. Seeing that smile, Tokinada let his lips twist into another smile that had an entirely different connotation.

"Yes, that is exactly how it is. Although it's only a fraction of them. Are you frightened?"

Tokinada queried as though testing her, and Aura shook her head quietly.

"No. Kisuke Urahara was, of course, frightening, but if he is considered a top class, powerful individual in the Thirteen Court Guard Companies, then I believe I should be able to deal with the rest."

"Don't get too conceited now. Kisuke Urahara is certainly a man of infinite counterplans. However, the Seireitei is a den of thieves. Do not forget that even an ordinary soldier may hold a zanpaku-to with a power that would be most disadvantageous to you."

Though he was warning her, Aura could not miss the curiosity that tinted the back of his eyes.

If that were to happen, this man would likely laugh about it.

This noble who came to praise me for having nearly invincible power would surely sneer at me the moment I displayed shock at meeting a passing soldier who could easily destroy me.

Even understanding that, Aura still stood by the man's side.

Tokinada, understanding what was in Aura's mind, continued as though to tease her, "However, I am looking forward to it. Though you were able to obtain such power because you do not have any love or attachment in this world...in the world after we remake it anew, perhaps you will find something you are just slightly attached to... If that happens, I am genuinely, honestly looking forward to finding out whether you become stronger or weaker. Isn't that right, Hikone?"

"Yes! I don't really understand what you are saying, but if you are looking forward to it, then I am too!"

Hikone smiled innocently at Tokinada's words.

Though Aura's expression changed for just a moment when she saw Hikone's reaction, she did not reveal that to them. She pulled the conversation back to its original topic as though trying to cover up her feelings.

"Will you meet with Kisuke Urahara? He is currently being kept captive in one of our group member's powers."

After pondering this for a moment, Tokinada shook his head.

"Let's not. He is the kind of man who could kill us with one spell. We must be cautious of him, and though it was no mistake to capture him, having me meet with him directly would be like a commander running up to the front line of

a battleground. I do not intend to stain my hands with my own blood with suicidal actions."

His predatory smile distorted all the more. "We will have him create a Hogyoku after we destroy everything he was meant to protect. No, maybe we should in fact take them hostage without breaking them. However, I do have some desire to see his face the moment I kill the people he loves."

Tokinada wavered about how exactly to treat Urahara, as though it were as inconsequential as picking out a new book to read. Aura thought that this was the man's weakness as well as his greatest strength. She spoke up as though she had remembered something. "Actually, when we captured Kisuke Urahara, another Soul Reaper also fought us."

"Ah yes, I was interrupted before I was able to look at the footage directly...but spiritual pressure data other than Urahara's was observed. Since the Kurosaki father and son are gone, was it the Thirteenth Company that is currently occupying the town?"

"It was the assistant captain of the Ninth Company, Shuhei Hisagi."

"Hisagi...Hisagi? Ah, yes! Kaname Tosen's disciple!"

Recalling the face of the man whose life he had ruined, Tokinada started to speak, joy filling his voice. "*Ha ha ha!* What a strange coincidence! I was hoping to take my time making a plaything of him, but it seems that I may be breaking him earlier than intended. Though I *was* looking forward to seeing how he would report on my inauguration in the *Seireitei Bulletin*."

"He is cut off in Karakura Town. He likely cannot come here. Then again, I do not think he would have been able to come here even if he had been in the Soul Society."

As Aura casually described the current situation, Tokinada shook his head.

"No? The Soul Society people will likely come. In a few hours...no, it might only be ten minutes or so. If Mayuri Kurotsuchi is with them, he will likely immediately discern my goals and location."

"Are you fine with that? Based on Shunsui Kyoraku's personality, he will likely proceed in secrecy, but he would still send in very skilled people for the occasion."

"That is exactly why he will do what I expect him to. His coming here is a good thing, since the tricks I have used become weaker with time. If we are going to get this done, we should do it quickly."

Tokinada clapped a hand on Hikone's head to pat it, and thinking of the face of his old enemy who would be coming shortly, he spoke his desires with a joyful voice: "Now I can openly kill all of those who disturb my *entertainment* in the name of mutiny."

THE SEIREITEI, KUTSUWA TOWN, ELEVENTH COMPANY BARRACKS

Returning from speaking with the messenger that had been dispatched from the First Company, Kenpachi appeared in front of Madarame and Yumichika still in his captain's coat. He gave them a blunt order. "Ikkaku, Yumichika, we're heading out."

"Yes, Captain!"

They replied to him simultaneously, then the two started to dash after Kenpachi, who had broken into a fast run. Though they had not been told specifically where they were going or why, if a messenger formerly from the Secret Remote Squad was sent, he likely had received a secret order.

Though they had no idea whether they were heading toward certain death, it wasn't as though that would cause Madarame or Yumichika to become timid. Perhaps because Kenpachi also knew that, he didn't specifically ask them to prepare themselves for such a situation. Those who shouldered the yarrow knew by instinct that their one and only reward was the spray of blood that soaked them on the unending battlefield.

Following Kenpachi, Madarame asked Yumichika, who ran behind him and to the side, "But with the captain being called and the Second Company going on the move earlier, what exactly happened?"

Yumichika shrugged and shook his head. "Who knows? As far as strange happenings go, I guess Hisagi went to the living world too."

"He did?"

"It was to do an interview in Karakura Town. He's probably talking to Shino too, I bet."

"Shino, huh...? Wonder if she's actually doing her job right."

Thinking of his sister, who had been haggard for a while after the Quincy war, Madarame worried about her current condition.

"I saw her partner once, and he just didn't look all that reliable..."

"Yeah, he's Yuki from the Sixth Company's younger brother, isn't he?"

"Rikichi, huh? That guy was Renji's underling. Now he really had a backbone."

Rikichi Yuki was a young Soul Reaper from the Sixth Company and was famous for aspiring to be like Renji Abarai, to the point that he had gotten the same tribal tattoo over his eyebrow. In Madarame's eyes, his skills were still nowhere near Renji's, but he remembered the Soul Reaper showing some guts in the combined practices with the Sixth Company. "Well, at worst, he came from Shinoreijutsuin, and he was dispatched in a Jureichi like Karakura Town. He must have something in him."

THE WORLD OF THE LIVING,
KARAKURA TOWN, MITSUMIYA,
URAHARA SHOTEN UNDERGROUND FACILITIES

"W-w-w-what are we going to do, Shino?! H-how could Mr. Urahara have gotten kidnapped?! Maybe this is the end of the world..."

Under the painted blue sky, Ryunosuke's tearful voice reverberated in Urahara Shoten's basement, a sprawling space that seemed to defy the laws of physics. Though it was underground, that underground place that resembled outdoors was the place where Ichigo Kurosaki, Renji Abarai, and Yasutora Sado had undergone their training in the past. That space, which Urahara had created for Ichigo overnight, was called the "Study Room." Its special features were a fake sky and withered trees, and was a place where Soul Reapers could go berserk without repercussions.

In response to Ryunosuke, who was crying and yelling, Shino seized his head from behind as though performing a headlock on him.

"Why're you such a Debbie downer?! This is the exact time! When! We've got to! Be calm and collected!" Shino punctuated her words as she put her all into constraining him. "Your older brother's the third seat of the Sixth Company, isn't he?! Can't you learn to be like him even a little?!"

While suffering under her arm, Ryunosuke's eyes still had tears in them as he objected. "*Ow ow ow ow...* B-but Rikichi is terrible at taking care of the hell butterflies and he once chopped pickles with Assistant Captain Abarai's zanpaku-to and got a teacup thrown at him..."

"Who asked you to describe every episode of bad luck your brother had?! I'm saying do something about how you're always relying on Mr. Urahara!"

"*Ow ow ow ow,* but the *Seireitei Bulletin* was saying that we have no idea how many times the Soul Society could have been in ruins if Mr. Urahara weren't around!"

Hiyori Sarugaki, who had been listening to them from the sidelines, yelled in an irritated voice, "Shuddup! Any world that relies on that baldy Kisuke supporting it would be in ruins after three days, you dolt! What idiot said that?! What kind of numbskull was writing that fake news?!"

A voice addressed Hiyori from behind as she grabbed Ryunosuke's collar. "That was me."

Shuhei Hisagi, a glum look on his face, stood there. He was looking glum not because Hiyori had called his article fake news, but because Kisuke Urahara had been kidnapped before his very eyes and he hadn't been able to do anything about it.

Hiyori fixed a stare on Hisagi and moved her eyes up and down as though appraising him.

"Hunh? Who the heck are you? Weren't you Kensei's assistant captain or something? What're you doing here?"

"Well...I was interviewing Mr. Urahara."

"Don't avoid my eyes. Are you thinking 'What a troublesome person I've run into right in the middle of all this trouble?' Eh?"

"Well, yeah, half of me is..."

Hisagi, who spoke as though he weren't really there in spirit, had spoken his honest feelings. At that point, a vein throbbed on Hiyori's forehead as she twisted up the hem of Hisagi's clothes.

"You're actually telling me to my face, baldy?! Are you mocking me?!"

When Ryunosuke saw that, he thought...

She's probably actually trying to grab him by the collar. She's just too short to reach.

...but because he, of course, instinctively sensed that it would endanger his life, he didn't say it out loud. On the other hand, Hisagi, who had been caught up in this mess in such an absurd way, seemed upset for a moment until he looked like he remembered something and replied, "Th-that's right—I'm teasing you!"

"*Hungh?!*"

"C-Captain Hirako said, 'If you see Hiyori, make sure to tease her for me'!"

"Whyyy that dumb little balding eggplant! Does he think he can give orders like that just because he's got the authority of a captain?!" Hiyori turned to the empty sky and yelled, flapping both of her arms. Now released, Hisagi felt bad that he had brought up Hirako's name to avoid the brunt of the attack, and he considered apologizing to Hirako after the fact. *Actually, Captain Hirako* did *tell me to do that…*

As he was considering that, someone spoke to him from behind. "Have you and your zanpaku-to recovered now?"

"Yes, I'm fine. Thank you for your help."

Hisagi bowed his head respectfully to the giant with a characteristic haircut, Tessai Tsukabishi. Though Tessai was currently a candy shop worker, in the past he had been an influential figure in the Seireitei as the leader of the Kido Corp and had skills that rivaled Urahara's. It was even rumored that he excelled at a particular type of kido technique, which he was better at than Urahara.

Hisagi reflected upon his own pitiful state and lowered his head in front of the man who had served a prominent role in the Soul Society when he had been only a child.

"I'm sorry…it happened right in front of me. Mr. Urahara was…"

"Please don't worry yourself over it. It was the shop manager's carelessness that caused him to be kidnapped, and all it means is that the opponent was just as powerful. Based on what you said, it seems their intent was not to harm the shop manager, so in the first place we should just be happy that no harm was done to him."

Hisagi wanted to accept the man's words, but at the same time, the intense self-admonishment bubbling up from

within him wasn't so easy to escape from, even with the other man's kindness.

"No. I couldn't do anything, again."

"Why are you being so negative?"

"It's always like this. When something is essential, when it's important, I'm not strong enough. I couldn't show my face to Captain Tosen or Captain Muguruma after how they trained me." Hisagi replied to Tessai in a mumble, as though he were speaking to himself, as he gripped his hands into fists. When she heard those words, Hiyori once again got involved.

"What? What is wrong with you? Grumbling pitifully is irritating enough, but why're you calling Tosen 'captain'? You underestimating Kensei?"

The girl seemed quietly angry in a way that was different from her prior anger. Hisagi denied her assertion while also being unable to easily brush it away. "No, that's not what I mean. Captain Muguruma is an amazing captain. I'm grateful, and I'm indebted to him. But Tosen, who taught me my way of life, is someone who I feel even now is a captain to me in the same way."

"Why're you being so serious? Seriously, Kensei is being too soft on you, allowing that behavior."

Hiyori clucked her tongue and didn't pursue her attack any further. Possibly because her own past self and Shuhei as he was now had some similarities.

It was back when she was the Twelfth Company's assistant captain. She had recalled the days when she continually reminded Kisuke Urahara, "I don't accept you as my captain," because she had idolized her former captain, Hikifune, so much.

When Hiyori turned around with a docile look on her face, Hisagi had no idea how to respond.

"I..."

He couldn't get the words out since he didn't know what to say. Unable to stand by and watch, Tessai clapped Hisagi on the back and told him, "Don't debase yourself like that. You yourself are a Soul Reaper who has survived his own fair share of carnage during a long military service, Shuhei Hisagi. Though you blame yourself, your eyes still have life in them."

"That just means I'm not dead yet. I may have survived carnage, but I only just barely survived alive through luck. Treating me like a hero would be giving me undue credit."

Hisagi spoke somewhat masochistically, and Tessai quickly responded, "Yes, you certainly are different from Mr. Ichigo Kurosaki."

"I know that better than..."

"Well, that is not what I mean by it."

Cutting off Hisagi, Tessai spoke in a more serious tone than usual. When he heard Tessai's voice, which had power in it, Hisagi remembered once again that this man standing in front of his eyes had once been called the "Commander of the Kido Corp."

"Mr. Kurosaki's way of fighting is to disregard his fear. On the other hand, I can see constant, uniform fear in your eyes. But even though you hold that fear in your chest, you still choose the path of battle and are continuing to be a Soul Reaper, are you not?"

"But that's..."

Hisagi internally recalled Kaname Tosen's teachings.

"If you're really afraid of fighting...

"You've already acquired something invaluable as a warrior!"

Hisagi made a vow. If everyone had fear, he would simply walk by its side of his own volition. However, would he be able to walk alongside that fear even now?

In the first place, do I...really know what the true meaning of fear is?

Hisagi already constantly had that worry. The words Tosen had said when they faced one another were still burned cleanly into him.

"I thought I told you. Those who don't know fear have no right to fight."

"You haven't changed at all."

"Even in those words of yours, there wasn't a hint of fear lurking in them."

There was no hesitation in those words, and Hisagi had been captured by the illusion that his teacher Tosen had seen through to the very depths of his soul with his unseeing eyes, to the point that the words themselves made him fearful.

That doubt once again revived in Hisagi. As though he were seeing through that new worry as well, the former Kido Commander, Tessai, called out to Hisagi, "This is not a matter of whether you or Mr. Kurosaki is correct."

Tessai recalled the past hero and impressed upon Hisagi a truth: "Mr. Ichigo Kurosaki is certainly a hero who has saved the Soul Society, or perhaps even the world, multiple times. However, he is a novice who has not lived even a full twenty years."

"Kurosaki is impressive specifically because he's become so powerful at that age. And to think that he's supposed to be a novice compared to me…"

"This is a matter of the strength of your soul. He is still in the middle of growing. His soul is both strong and frail. If he is able to confront someone as strong as Aizen, then there must be times when he has confronted hopelessness and despair."

Those from Urahara Shoten who had watched Ichigo Kurosaki for a long time knew this. When Rukia Kuchiki had been taken away to the Soul Society, Ichigo Kurosaki wasn't able to figure out the technique for getting to the Soul Society and had lamented, "I can't do anything myself." They knew about when his close friends' pasts had been stolen by the Fullbringer Tsukishima, and how he had turned his back on that reality as well. However, Ichigo Kurosaki's soul hadn't been crushed by those events.

In the former situation, Kisuke Urahara had offered his hand, and in the latter, Rukia Kuchiki had, and Ichigo Kurosaki had waved off his fear and summoned the power to sweep aside his distress.

Though it wasn't something Tessai had been a part of, Ichigo Kurosaki had almost been seized by despair in front of Yhwach's power in the war with the Quincies. However, he had been offered a hand at that time by those he had saved, and that bravery to stand up from the pit of despair had become his power to continue fighting. Though Tessai had not seen the moment itself, he knew that was the true nature of Ichigo's strength.

"Mr. Ichigo Kurosaki is certainly a man of many qualities. However, he was neither an almighty, complete hero nor a strong, firm tree upon birth. Because of that, he was able to grow into his strength."

There was a pressure in Tessai's words, as though he wouldn't accept anything less than agreement. Hisagi felt this man had survived a great number many more carnages than he himself had during his time in the Soul Society.

"If brushing off perplexity, grief, and occasional despair and fear becomes Mr. Kurosaki's strength, then it is those who have walked alongside fear for a long time who have the role of protecting his weaknesses in the moment he is sinking in tears. What you have is strength."

"What I have...?"

"It is not that you are special. One source of fear is death. What are Soul Reapers, who are the ones that guide souls who have strayed from the path, supposed to do if they cannot protect others from fear?"

Tessai then stopped, cleared his throat with a cough, and finished what he had to say. "That is what the shop manager would likely say, in a more concise way. An oaf like myself might not have his persuasiveness."

In the next moment, Hisagi hit his face with his own fist.

"Mr. Hisagi?!"

"Tessai Tsukabishi, Kido Commander, thank you very much. You've opened my eyes."

"Right now, I am but a humble candy store employee. Please disregard that as a joke."

At that point, Tessai felt reassured by the look in Hisagi's eyes. The worry and hesitation had disappeared entirely. Hisagi, who had bowed at the silent Soul Reaper leader, had cut through his doubt and moved on in order to do what he needed to in his role as a Soul Reaper.

Jinta, who had been watching from afar, seemed fed up. "That Soul Reaper sure is simple if he's gonna get all gung-ho over a lecture from somebody like Tessai... *Bleh*."

"Don't be like that," Ururu said, karate chopping him in the head. "I think it's cool the way Soul Reapers are awkward like that."

INSIDE URAHARA SHOTEN

"If we just had a lead…"

Hisagi, Tessai, Hiyori, and the others returned above-ground and were searching for any kind of clue as to where Aura and Yukio had gone after the earlier fight. There was still a thin boundarylike film over the sky, and they were still cut off from making contact with the Soul Society. Wondering whether there was a lead there, Hisagi noticed something strange.

Since when had that been there? There was a small sphere placed on top of the store counter that released a strange reishi. It had a drawing of Urahara's face and the first character of his name marked on it. As though it had reacted to his spiritual pressure the moment Hisagi picked it up, the sphere bounced and splattered red fluid on the store's floor. The paint dripped, wriggling on its own until it spelled out a sentence.

"Whoa… What the heck is that?!"

"Please look for Ms. Aura's believers. They will likely have a 'pillar.'"

"Is this a message from Mr. Urahara?!"

It was likely something he had prepared during the earlier fight, right before giving Hisagi Gentei Kaijo.

"What's that thing about a 'pillar'? Does it have something to do with what their goal is?"

If that were the case, then did that mean in that short time, Urahara had considered the possibility that he would potentially be kidnapped? Just as Hisagi was thinking he really had to have been the most remarkable person in the Soul Society, Hiyori yelped in dismay after catching sight of the bloody sentence. "Gross! What the heck is this supposed to be?! It looks like it was written by a murder victim—with his own blood!"

After Hiyori shouted that, a supplemental bloody sentence appeared.

"P.S. To those who saw this and thought it was some written-in-a-murder-victim's-blood horror movie cliché: You have no sense of humor. Big time."

"Shut it!"

Hiyori stomped on the bloody sentence many times with the force of a Gatling gun and created cracks in the floor of the store.

Though that was curiously similar to Ichigo Kurosaki's reaction in the past, she had no way of knowing that.

"What should we do, Shino?! I thought that too, so I must have no sense of humor either."

"There's no point in talking about that."

While Ryunosuke and Shino were talking to each other on the sidelines, Hisagi was confused as his stock in Urahara fluctuated intensely.

"Don't you think that postscript was strangely long?"

Looking at Hisagi, Tessai shook his head awkwardly.

"I apologize. The last sentence was preloaded in the sphere from the start..."

≡

KUKAKU SHIBA'S RESIDENCE, THE RUKONGAI

"I see. I understand what you're saying, I do, but..." After making a humble expression, the man opened his eyes wide and yelled, "Why have you gathered at our house after all of that?! C'mon, it's just weird!"

In the reception hall of the Rukongai's pyrotechnician Kukaku Shiba's residence, Ganju Shiba's voice echoed. The heel of the residence's owner, Kukaku, came down on top of Ganju's head.

"Ow!"

"Stop making a commotion, Ganju. We have guests!"

"Aren't you being a little too generous, sis?! Are you actually going to treat all of these people as guests?!"

Rubbing his head, Ganju looked over the faces scattered around the guest room. Including Ganju and his sister, there were over twenty people gathered in the space. The number itself wasn't unmanageable; the issue was the breakdown of those who had gathered. There were the three usual freeloading Fullbringers. There were the three Soul

Reapers: Hirako, Nanao Ise, and Yoruichi Shihoin. There were the three Arrancars: Grimmjow, Nelliel, and Halibel. There were the Kurotsuchi Corpse Unit's Quincies Candice and Meninas, as well as Liltotto and Giselle who stood to their right and left, and also Bambietta who was crouching quietly in a corner of the room—this tallied up to five Quincies in total. On top of that, there were of course the Kurotsuchi Corpse Unit Arrancars Dordoni, Cirucci, Luppi, and Charlotte clumped in a corner. Then there were the two who were staying on the side, observing everyone in the room: Mayuri Kurotsuchi and Najahkoop.

The connotation may have been slightly off, but "motley crew" had the right ring to describe the people gathered there and the peculiar atmosphere in that reception area. However, unlike a crew, their relationship couldn't be described as one of camaraderie.

"Hey, stop taking advantage of the confusion to 'observe' us, you peeping tom."

At Liltotto's words, Najahkoop, who was at Mayuri's side, shrugged.

"Why're you being so self-conscious? I mean, if I were going to stare you down, then I would start with you two, Lil and Gigi. When Bazz-B betrayed me, you were complicit, weren't you? Huh?"

"How should I know? Bazz-B burning his friends from behind is normal? You were just being a dunce for not dodging it."

Liltotto ignored the fact that Bazz-B had once also hit her from behind. Going along with it, Giselle pretended to be scared as she hid behind Candice and said, "Oooh, that's so scaaary. That you'd dredge up something from so long ago is just depressing on top of being gross."

"W-why you little..."

Najahkoop scowled. Meanwhile, Luppi from the Corpse Unit glared at Grimmjow as he yelled, "How much longer do I have to wait? I wanna hurry up and tear apart this brute's guts."

Luppi tried to provoke Grimmjow with the aim of angering his opponent, but before Grimmjow could say anything in return he ended up on the receiving end of an electric current that ran through his whole body, putting him in agony.

"*AHHHHhhhh*?!"

Then, Mayuri, whose hand gripped the electric shock switch said, "Really now, can you not even read the room? Even when I gave you such a perfect opportunity, you weren't able to get it done in time. Don't embarrass me."

"*Guh*. Someday I will definitely break you..."

"It seems you have regained your rebellious spirit. I am just glad you have the ability to talk back at me like that."

When Mayuri increased the voltage yet again, it was not just Luppi who screamed. It seemed all the members of the Corpse Unit were being shocked, and they yelled in unison as they tumbled to the room's floor.

"*Gwah gah gah gah*?!"

"Why are we getting shocked too?!"

Dordoni and Cirucci were shrieking as usual.

"Ha ha. This is great. More, give me more! Make me even more radiant!"

"Ha ha ha ha ha, I can't move and it feels so strange."

Whether Charlotte and Meninas were resistant to it or simply dull, they didn't seem to be suffering much. Candice also brushed it aside with ease. "Hmph, a current like this is nothing to me."

"Hm? What is this? Wait! No way! Wait, wait, wait!"

Instead of an electric current, her attack was switched to the hallucination of centipedes crawling all over her body, and she ended up screaming too.

"As you see, regardless of whether my underlings are Quincies or Arrancars, I can have them properly disciplined, so there is no concern in that regard. Though I cannot take responsibility over the wild Quincies and stray Arrancars." Mayuri addressed this to the Soul Reapers as well as Kukaku and her brother.

Grimmjow watched Luppi rolling on the ground with faint breath and said with mixed feelings, "You seem like you've been caught up in a bit of trouble."

"*Grr.* Stop looking at me like you pity me. That's not a good look on you."

After glancing at Luppi, who tried to put on a brave face, Grimmjow's interest waned as he put his hostility on the backburner.

"Killing someone in that state isn't any fun. Hurry up and escape it or something."

"You make it sound so easy!"

With the tension mounting, the reception hall was getting out of hand.

"I've got one thing to say."

Kukaku's piercing voice resounded, and those who had been making a commotion all stopped at the same time.

"This is my house. I don't mind you being rowdy, but if you're going to cut each other up then take it outside."

Though her voice was soft, there was an energy in it that indicated she wouldn't take no for an answer.

"That woman's strong."

"Yes. She doesn't seem to be a Soul Reaper, but I suppose... I suppose there were some strong people lurking around."

Halibel could comprehend Kukaku's power through the spiritual pressure in her words, and Nelliel agreed with her.

Needless to say, those who knew Kukaku from the start, like Ginjo and the others, became quiet and subdued. The same was true for the Quincies and Corpse Unit. Other than Mayuri Kurotsuchi, that is, who marched to the beat of his own drum.

"Well, to think that you were using a firefly for lighting until now. Though you are descendants of the Shiba family, you are living quite a frugal life. You repel visitors by being too simple and economical."

"Can we kick him out first?"

There was disgust in Kukaku's eyes, but Yoruichi shook her head.

"I know how you feel, but please bear with him a little longer." Then, still sitting cross-legged, she lowered her head deeply to Kukaku. "I'm sorry. I've dragged you into trouble again."

"Don't worry about it. I told you before, didn't I? I love trouble," Kukaku replied with a cheerful smile. She suddenly noticed something. "Say, where's Soi Fon? Wasn't she with you?"

"Yeah, she's not the type to think that the enemy of her enemy is a friend. I ordered her to go check out the abnormalities within the Seireitei, so she's headed there."

"Right, I see. I don't dislike it though—working against a mutual enemy."

While they were having that conversation, they felt several spiritual pressures making their way down from upstairs and along the hallway. One of the spiritual pressures among them was more pronounced, wild and ominous. Those who noticed it opened their eyes wide when

they realized who it was—Grimmjow recalled the identity of that spiritual pressure from a memory deep within himself.

"This presence..."

It was the spiritual pressure he had encountered at the boundaries of his perception when he was near death after being cut down by an Espada named Nnoitora. It was the spiritual pressure of the man who had killed Nnoitora with an overwhelming power.

The camp of female Quincies all took on a cautious tinge in their eyes and made it known that the person who was about to make an appearance was someone they considered a threat. And Giriko Kutsuzawa, who normally seemed utterly calm, broke into a cold sweat on his forehead as his eyes roved around.

Amidst that strained atmosphere, the sliding door to the reception hall opened and five Soul Reapers appeared.

"What kind of a gathering is this?"

This dubious question was asked by the owner of the atrocious, magma-like spiritual pressure, Kenpachi Zaraki.

Madarame, who followed him, also scowled when he glimpsed the faces in the hall. When Yumichika noticed Charlotte and Giselle, he rudely let out a "*Blergh*." Additionally, Kensei Muguruma stood beside them and gazed around silently. Appearing from behind those four, the hat-wearing Soul Reaper with a particularly graceful air, Shunsui Kyoraku, revealed himself.

"Well, it seems everyone is present. What a joy it is that there are even beautiful ladies here."

Kyoraku spoke flatly, but those in the room understood his meaning. Though the spiritual pressure around Kyoraku wasn't as wild as Kenpachi's, they recognized that it was cold and keen, like a blade that had sunk to the bottom of a body of water.

"Now, how about we get started right away?"

Kyoraku clapped his hands together and said in a light tone, "It's time to supplant the Four Great Noble Clans."

CHAPTER SEVENTEEN

"OH, YOU'RE SUPPLANTING THEM? That's quite the undertaking."

Yoruichi grinned mirthfully as Kyoraku told her, "Yes, well, it's a figure of speech. It's not as though I'm trying to get flags of revolt waving in the Soul Society or planning to take over in their place. It's just that before Tokinada Tsunayashiro becomes a household name in the Soul Society through a *Seireitei Bulletin* extra, I'd like him to concede the seat of head of family."

A rebellion against the Four Great Noble Clans' head of family. Based on the reach of the aristocrats' political influence, it would not have been surprising to understand those words as an insurrection against the Soul Society itself. However, Kyoraku gently denied it. "That said, of course we can't make a move publicly. Though it is very likely they are criminals, the Thirteen Court Guard Companies cannot openly aim their bows at the Four Great Noble Clans."

"In that case, I think you were pretty hard on me when I came to save Rukia," retorted Yoruichi.

"That's because you were rebelling so openly. In comparison, we're just saying we suspect Tokinada of something. And if he boasts that it's 'all for the sake of the Soul Society,' there's a chance that his logic might win out."

Liltotto spoke up, having reached an understanding after listening that far. "In other words, since you Soul Reapers can't freely show off your firepower, you're going to try using us as pawns since you couldn't care less about us dying."

"It's not that we don't care about you. The current cease-fire is real, after all. I want to honor the bond we formed from when we took you to the Reiokyu as much as I can."

The first one to react to Kyoraku's words was Ginjo. "Based on what you're saying, I can assume you're still treating us like we're hostile forces then, can't I?"

"Right now you are formally tolerated. I want to assure you we won't lay a hand on you. But no matter how I look at the situation, it seems we've already wronged you in some way."

Kyoraku then looked at Mayuri, who answered haughtily, "I wonder if it is really possible to wrong them. I was just giving them a chance at amnesty. I mean, think about it—just having me mess them up a little will get them a good word from the director of the Department of Research and Development. I think that's a profitable decision with favorable terms."

"That sure doesn't sound like somebody who came by trying to kidnap us through brute force."

Ginjo continued to be cautious of Mayuri, the owner of the spiritual pressure that had been watching them, and Tsukishima's eyes appeared calm despite the fact he already had his hand on his bookmark. When Mayuri saw Tsukishima's move, his mouth twisted into a grin and he asked, "Are you looking for an opportunity to insert yourself into my past? Then why don't you just give it a try."

As he was speaking to Tsukishima, Mayuri approached slowly in a defenseless posture. Watching him, Tsukishima smiled thinly and shook his head.

"Naturally, I wouldn't insert a bookmark into a book that's only made up of the front and back cover."

"What do you mean by that, Tsukishima?"

Tsukishima replied to Ginjo, "He has no past to insert anything into. He probably hasn't been alive for more than a few minutes."

"What?"

Then the form that had Mayuri's shape grinned and shook his head.

"I see. So you can see the measure of someone's past before you even stick your blade into them. You've stirred my interest all the more."

As though to supplement his words, Kyoraku said, "Ahh. So that isn't your true body then, Captain Kurotsuchi?"

In fact, the Mayuri Kurotsuchi appearing in that room was not the actual Mayuri Kurotsuchi. It was a flesh doll created in his form that he was controlling from elsewhere. Kyoraku had detected it from a tiny difference in spiritual pressure. He sighed as though exasperated. There wasn't much point in Tsukishima inserting himself into the past of something that had only existed for a few minutes. To Mayuri, who had found the absolute countermeasure for the Book of the End, Tsukishima smiled sarcastically and said, "Shall I think of it as an honor that the Department of Research and Development director is wary of me?"

"Don't speak such nonsense. Obviously, anyone would create a vaccine for a virus."

While that conversation was going on, Grimmjow, who had digested the situation, clucked his tongue and said, "This is nonsense. You Soul Reapers can pick at each other as much as you want. You think we have any reason to help you?"

Spiritual pressure mixed with animosity swelled from Grimmjow, and Kenpachi Zaraki put on a wicked smile as he spoke. "I agree. As far as I see it, we've got no reason to borrow help from outsiders. If you're saying you'll become an enemy now, then it'll sure make the conversation a lot easier and faster for me."

While the heavy specter of death drifted over, a grave spiritual pressure dominated the atmosphere.

"You're the one who killed Nnoitora, aren't you?"

Grimmjow packed hostility into the glare he aimed at Kenpachi, who emitted a fiendish spiritual pressure. Kenpachi heard Nnoitora's name and raised the corner of his mouth a degree.

"Arrancars always bring up that name when they see me. What is the point? Are you stronger than Nnoitora?"

"Don't compare me to some guy who's already kicked the bucket."

"No doubt, then."

The air between the two started to quiver, and Kukaku, who observed it, developed a throbbing vein on her forehead just as Kyoraku clapped his hands together.

"All right, all right, that's enough! Enough!"

Kyoraku breezily strode between Kenpachi and Grimmjow, simply parrying and defusing their murderous intent toward one another.

"The reason I'm speaking with you is to offer a token of apology that the Soul Society...that the Soul Reapers have caused you trouble."

"An apology?"

Ginjo scowled and Kyoraku said, "Even though we're in a ceasefire, telling Arrancars, Quincies, and Fullbringers who are wanted for killing Soul Reapers to all get together and rebel against the Four Great Noble Clans is a scandal in and of itself. It wouldn't be unusual for me to get my head lopped off for something like that. Even now, you continue to hold me at my weakest point, as the Thirteen Court Guard Companies Captain General. Next time there is a dispute in the Soul Society, I think you'll be able to use this favor as a playing card."

"Can you make any guarantee that you won't just shut us up after everything's over?"

"I can declare that I won't do such a thing as many times as you'd like, but it's not as though anyone can truly make such a guarantee. However, starting now with Captain Kurotsuchi, I will thoroughly enforce the policy that none of the captains can lay a hand on you."

Hearing that, Mayuri interrupted sullenly, "How can you go and declare that on your own? You think the Captain General of the Thirteen Court Guard Companies has the authority to control the Department of Research and Development's work?"

"Actually, I'm shocked that you would think I don't. Well, please, Captain Kurotsuchi, I will plan to accommodate you whatever way I can next time."

"That doesn't inspire much confidence. What reason do I have in the first place to keep silent about what is going on?"

Mayuri asked that as though it were a logical question, and Kyoraku replied, smiling cynically, "If I'm fired as Captain General, then my successor will likely be Captain Kuchiki... Don't you think that I will put much less pressure on your 'research' than he would?"

"Really, you are a sneaky man."

Mayuri said that without hiding his irritation, and Nanao, who had been watching from behind, felt relieved.

From their behavior, those around them realized the men were not in collusion and that Mayuri was actually putting his own interests first.

"Why would you go that far, Soul Reaper?" asked Grimmjow dubiously. Kyoraku replied, "For the sake of the Soul Society and the world's future. But that's not the entire reason."

Kyoraku paused for a moment and then said, both apologetically and clearly, "A man I do not see eye to eye with is trying to do something I don't particularly like. Is it so strange that I would want to strike him from behind and hinder his progress?"

"Captain General!"

Shrugging at Nanao's flustered voice, Kyoraku added, "Yes, it would be very helpful if you understood the opinion I expressed just now as not that of the Thirteen Court Guard Companies' Captain General, but of Shunsui Kyoraku the individual."

Though he wore a gentle smile, the strain of the spiritual pressure behind it caused Grimmjow and the others to understand that the man in front of their eyes did not come to stand in this place with any normal constitution. "Hah. You make yourself pretty clear. That's way easier for me to agree with."

Then Grimmjow remembered when he had made a deal with Kisuke Urahara in the past and had one more thing to say. "When I fight to the death with Kurosaki, don't let any of the Soul Reapers get in the way. Of course I would just crush all of them, but I don't want to go to all the trouble."

"I don't think you need a promise from me for that."

Kyoraku shrugged and started to speak of one who wasn't there. "Ichigo likely also wants to fight with you one on one, I would think. I won't interfere with that."

Halibel, who had been silent until then, spoke the name of a man who no longer was in that world. "Can you swear that's the case for Stark too?"

"*Hunh?*"

Kyoraku was silent while Grimmjow raised his voice in suspicion. Though Grimmjow couldn't understand why Stark's name was coming up now, Kyoraku immediately considered Halibel's intention.

Ah, well. Even in the middle of combat, she knew the details of my battles. Of course she would be the one managing Hueco Mundo.

Remembering the battle against the Primera Espada, Coyote Stark, in which he had cut down the Espada while intruding in someone else's fight, Kyoraku nodded with his usual unchanging expression.

"*Losers focus too much on means and lose sight of winning. Captains don't have that luxury.*"

"Yeah, I'll promise you that."

As the words he himself had uttered as he had cut down that man returned to his mind, Kyoraku nodded at Halibel's words.

"But if we have another war against you, then that's a different conversation..."

"Don't try to act like a good boy. Someone may owe you or you may owe someone. But the moment you start a war, you're both evil."

"Since I think the fight that Ichigo wants is something other than 'war.'"

≡

URAHARA SHOTEN, UNDERGROUND FACILITY

"I'm not sure how to say this, but you're pretty good at that."

"That's because I've gotten used to doing this work."

In front of Hisagi, who spoke in an exasperated tone, there were several normal people lined up who had been put to sleep using kido. However, though they seemed to have the spiritual pressure of normal people both outwardly and inwardly, in actuality that was not the case.

Using a combination of Urahara Shoten's spiritual pressure sensor merchandise and Tessai's kido, the results of their investigation confirmed that there were passersby with slight disruptions in spiritual pressure numbering in the hundreds just within Mitsumiya district. Following that, Jinta, Ururu, and Tessai quickly went on the move to put several of those nearby to sleep, and brought them down to the underground space.

"Hm... It seems they are neither Soul Reapers nor Fullbringers. They do not seem to be possessed by a parasitic Hollow."

"Then why is their spiritual pressure abnormal?"

"It's likely because of this..."

Tessai pulled a necklace off of one of the sleeping people. Others had a charm of the same design on bracelets or tethered to their bags, and because of that, it was clear the people belonged to a shared community.

"Those things aren't just what's trendy these days, right?"

"No. All of these decorations bear the symbol of the religious group that the shop manager was looking into. However, more importantly, they are unique in that each one of these has been made into a small circuit that uses reishi."

"Circuits? Does that mean they're devices?"

Hisagi was dubious, but Tessai replied, "Yes. In the past, this would have been a type of prohibited technique. However, several years ago, the ban on them was lifted temporarily as part of a counterplan against Mr. Aizen."

"A counterplan against Aizen?"

Disquieting words such as "prohibited technique" and "Aizen" had come flowing out in succession, but—"Mr. Hisagi, I believe you have seen it before. Though it is not comparable in size."

At Tessai's words, Hisagi connected everything internally.

"Wait a sec...these couldn't be..."

The woman who had called herself Aura Michibane had known about Hisagi's fight against the Arrancar. How had she—or Tokinada Tsunayashiro—been able to observe that?

There had been something that the Tsunayashiro clan likely would have been interested in there. Hisagi realized it. He realized what he had been protecting during that fight. The shape of the equipment that Aura's believers had was completely different in scale, but it certainly did look very similar to...

"A Tenkai Ketchu...!"

≡

KUKAKU SHIBA'S RESIDENCE, RECEPTION HALL

"Looks like a Tenkai Ketchu."

At Mayuri Kurotsuchi's words, several people in the room reacted.

"Were those the pillars that you guys were protecting in Karakura Town?"

Kyoraku nodded in response to Halibel. "Well, to be more precise, it was actually the fake Karakura Town we had made in the Soul Society that we were protecting...in other words, you can think of the pillars that we stood up around that area as devices that switched the town out."

While speaking, Kyoraku gripped several of them in his own hand. Among the various bits of "evidence" Yoruichi had obtained from the destroyed safe at the Visual Department, there had been several cylindrical spiritual tools that looked as though they were prototypes. On the way over, Kyoraku had taken them from Soi Fon, and feeling uneasy, he had received the response he had expected from Mayuri as a result of handing them over to the man.

"It's a miniature derived from the real thing...although this is beyond the Tsunayashiro clan's skill. There are residuals that are Kisuke Urahara-like, but these do not look complete enough to be his work. I have made something similar, but of course, this does not compare."

Though Mayuri had many thoughts about Kisuke Urahara, he wasn't about to underestimate the man. When he saw the haphazard techniques that formed that small Tenkai Ketchu, he conjectured out loud: "They imitated what they saw of Kisuke Urahara's prototype and attempted to mass produce them...perhaps."

"I think you're exactly right," Kyoraku said and then continued based on what Mayuri had said. "Actually, former captain Urahara made something similar to a transportation apparatus previously... But old man Yama asked what would happen if it got into enemy hands and didn't give authorization to use it. I think old man Yama confiscated that sample and tried to put an end to it by sticking it in the vault of the central first ward..."

Hirako spoke, looking exasperated. "You think that Tokinada guy from the Tsunayashiro clan stole it then?"

"It's likely. Though he might have openly used his influence to just take it. Since it had already been leaked once, we probably should have lifted the ban and come up with a decent countermeasure against it instead... Well, I suppose we should take our time discussing something like that."

Kyoraku suddenly narrowed his left eye and dove into the main topic of conversation. "The real issue is what the head of the Tsunayashiro family is trying to do with this."

"You can't do much with just one of those. He might have been able to transport multiple people by getting four of them together. If he had a substantial number, then the conversation would be different, but of course, we would be able to tell if he had established many of these from the disturbance in the reishi. Additionally, he would need to establish them in both locations. At the very least, we know he has not put them into operation within the Seireitei."

"In that case...what is Tokinada Tsunayashiro trying to switch out with what?"

The Tenkai Ketchu could switch the location of whatever was surrounded by its multiple pillars, regardless of whether the place was in the Soul Society or the living world. The scope of what could be transported depended upon the height and depth of the pillars. Kyoraku had an inkling of where one side of the switch would take place.

"Karakura Town..."

"Hunh?" Hearing the name of the town Ichigo Kurosaki lived in, Grimmjow, who hadn't seemed very interested in the conversation until then, raised his voice. "What? You're not saying Kurosaki is involved in this thing too?"

"Just the opposite. Ichigo is away from Karakura Town today, and at the same time we stopped getting communications from Karakura Town."

Kyoraku informed them of the present situation, and Hirako, who had not been aware of it, spoke up. "Hunh? What's that supposed to mean?"

"A strange boundary was put up around the town, and we can no longer open a Senkaimon. Apparently it's also impossible to enter from the surrounding towns." He continued with more information. "At the same time that Assistant Captain Hisagi requested a Gentei Kaijo while he was heading out to Urahara Shoten for an interview, communications ceased. I think it would be impossible to conclude that those events were not related."

"Shuhei did that? I see, so that's why Kensei is here."

Hirako nodded as though he understood, and Muguruma said with a humble expression, "I was talking to Love over the Soul Pager, and apparently they haven't been able to get ahold of Hiyori after she went to work in Karakura Town. Hachi is trying to see if he can break through the boundary from the outside right now."

"What is that idiot Hiyori doing?"

Hirako held his head but calmly asked, "So, does it look like we'll be able to break through it? The boundary, that is?"

"Apparently they used something completely different from kido. He was saying it might be a variety of Fullbring."

Hearing that, Ginjo's group looked at each other.

"What do you think?"

At Tsukishima's words, Ginjo looked somber.

"Even if it's another ability that can lock things up, it's not Riruka's power. Based on what we've heard, it might be Yukio's..."

Then Giriko raised a doubt. "But I find it a bit suspicious that he has isolated an area as vast as a whole town."

"Yeah, but I doubt he's not connected to this."

If this was Yukio's work, then Ginjo could only think of two possibilities: One possibility was that he had used the last half-year to hone his abilities and could actually expand their scope around a whole town. The other possibility was that, just as when he had distributed Ichigo Kurosaki's stolen abilities, another Fullbringer had helped him.

Seeing their behavior, Kyoraku determined that their confusion was genuine and they likely hadn't been in contact with whoever had put up the barrier.

"Well, regardless of whether Yukio is involved or not, it's unlikely that Karakura Town isn't on one side of the Tenkai Ketchu. It's probable that the scope is pretty big."

Mayuri, who had been fiddling with the miniature Tenkai Ketchu in his hand—or, to be more accurate, the body that Mayuri operated was fiddling with it—added, "It seems that... the transport scope isn't focusing on the land so much as it is facing up."

"Facing up?"

"They aren't switching out the land, but the sky...that is how these have been made."

"The sky? They couldn't be thinking of transporting the Reiokyu, could they?"

Kyoraku worried that the scale of this challenge had suddenly grown much larger, but Mayuri shook his head slightly.

"I think we should view that as an unlikely possibility. That neat freak Senjumaru Shutara would not allow something like that set up around the Reiokyu."

"In that case, we should understand from this that there really is something where Tokinada ran off to... Do you already happen to know, Captain Kurotsuchi? Where Tokinada and the child Hikone have gone?"

Mayuri looked at Kyoraku as though he were genuinely mystified.

"Why are you going out of your way to ask me that when you already know the answer?"

"What?! If you know, then go ahead and spit it out, Mayuri! That's kind of the most important detail here!"

"That aside, what is far more important is that you insist on using my first name as though we were equals, even after a hundred years."

"What are you talking about?! You really are a nuisance!"

Ignoring Hirako's yelling, Mayuri simply started explaining. "Since the Quincy and the Arrancar Corpse Unit carry surveillance bacteria within them, I made the bacteria so that it automatically spreads to those that they fight. Naturally, all of you here are carriers already."

When Mayuri said those words, which made everyone in the place furrow their brows, Kyoraku quickly followed up. "Yes, and we'll have you stop observing us later. More importantly, Captain Kurotsuchi, do you know the location of the child Hikone, who is the object of our focus?"

Mayuri looked bitter when Kyoraku said he would stop the surveillance, but he managed to give a clear answer to the Captain General's question. "Though the tracking signal itself has stopped, I have a rough location based on the Binding Spell Kakushi Tsuijaku... The specimen disappeared into the largest class of Kyogoku in the Garganta."

A Kyogoku. After so casually mentioning such a terrifying place, he was of course easily able to describe his intention to fix things. "You should be grateful I am here. Normally this would be impossible, but I *am* able to create a path connecting to it."

He then pulled out two small black spheres from his chest pocket and threw them toward the end of the reception hall. The spheres instantly swelled and floated in the air after becoming as large as a human. The reishi warped between the black spheres, and an even deeper sphere, so jet-black that it seemed to swallow light, opened its maw in midair.

"I can even do it immediately, right now."

≡

URAHARA SHOTEN

"A Kyogoku?"
"Indeed."

Hisagi opened his eyes wide, and Tessai nodded deeply.

"I looked into where this Tenkai Ketchu transports to, but it is completely off the Soul Society or Hueco Mundo coordinates. If it is in the middle of Garganta, then it is likely a Kyogoku or a similar variety of space."

"A Kyogoku is one of those things—way back in the day, it was supposed to have been used as the exile location for a family that had committed a major crime..."

"Indeed, they were left behind in a place that a hell butterfly cannot reach and that Dangai is not connected to. Compared to exile in the living world, it is a harsh sentence."

"But why that place? Something as small as this couldn't possibly transport..."

After Hisagi got that far, he realized something. They had searched the spiritual pressure for humans holding suspicious objects and brought them all the way here after putting them to sleep.

"How many more people do you sense who are carrying the same objects as these guys?"

The same thought had occurred to Tessai, and he said with a humbled expression, "There are too many to count..."

Based on the number that he had heard from Aura, Hisagi broke into a cold sweat as he asked Tessai, "Supposing about seven hundred thousand people all had these things and they met up in Karakura Town...what could they accomplish?"

"Of course, I doubt that many of them are gathered in Karakura Town, but... Well, yes, if they focused on gathering in this town and deployed in neighboring towns..."

Making a calculation in his head, Tessai conjectured out loud, "When the shop manager prepared the pillars last time, he moved the whole area of Karakura Town. They wouldn't be able to get that far, but they might be able to accomplish something very close."

"That's no joke." Hisagi, realizing this was likely to become an even bigger deal than he had imagined, restlessly muttered to himself. "I don't know what they're planning, but it doesn't seem like it'll come to any good. Mr. Tessai, would you be able to use the pillars to somehow send me to those coordinates?"

"Hm..."

Hearing that, Hiyori said to Hisagi, "It's not like you'd be able to do anything by yourself."

"Even if I can't, the only option I have is to go."

"Are you going because you want to save that baldy Kisuke? Don't bother. The thing he hates the most is when the weak push themselves too hard in these situations."

Though Tessai was keeping silent, he did not refute Hiyori. In actuality, he recalled when Kisuke Urahara had told Ichigo Kurosaki something similar in the past.

"Don't use her as an excuse to kill yourself."

Those were the frank words Urahara spoke to Ichigo

when the human had attempted to go to the Soul Society without even knowing how to use his zanpaku-to in order to save Rukia. In fact, back then Ichigo would likely have died in vain if he had showed up in the Soul Society at his strength level.

In that case, what about Hisagi? He was probably stronger than Ichigo had been at that time. However, considering it in the context of the strength differential between him and his opponent, he guessed that this was pretty similar to Ichigo's situation back then. Tessai hesitated over whether to stop him, but Hisagi jumped in and said, "I know I'm out of my league. I'm not just going for Mr. Urahara, and if it comes down to it, I'll leave Mr. Urahara behind."

"Wha...?"

A vein stood out on Hiyori's forehead and she started to say something, but Hisagi anticipated it and said, "Because *I'm a Soul Reaper.*"

What he was trying to say was that his priority wasn't saving Urahara but saving the balance of the world.

"Don't say you're doing this for the Seireitei or something. Are you really going to cross this dangerous bridge because of them?"

"I'm not doing this for the sake of the aristocrats..." As he replied, Hisagi fell into thought.

Why was he attempting to go up against an enemy he was unlikely to beat? If he were doing this for the sake of peace for the people of the living world and the Soul Society, then why was he risking his life to protect that peace?

Is it my own pride, thinking that I'm the protector of the world's peace?

—No.

Am I doing this for Kanisawa, since he was killed by a Hollow, or for my subordinates, who died in the war?

—No.

Am I doing this for the people who will live in the future?

—No.

Am I doing this for the cheap sense of satisfaction that I risked my life to fight?

—No. Is that not it?

As Hisagi was deep in thought, Hiyori said in exasperation, "I just don't get it. So why are you going? Aren't you scared?"

"I am scared. To be honest, the chances of my winning in a confrontation are pitiable."

However, Hisagi had experienced that feeling many times before. The time he had most noticed the difference in power between himself and his opponent was when he had battled his teacher, Kaname Tosen. In actuality, he hadn't even been able to cross swords with him face to face. After Tosen had Hollowified and become stronger, he had managed to pierce Tosen in a vital spot after searching for an opening when Tosen wasn't able to see him.

For whom had he really fought that battle?

"But I'm definitely going."

"Like I said, why?"

"I'm not sure."

"What the heck?! You don't know? Are you even sane?"

Hiyori opened her eyes wide, still exasperated, and Hisagi tried to get her off his back by saying, "I don't have a reason or anything. It's just that if I withdraw now...if I run from being a Soul Reaper, I feel like the spirit inside me that I inherited from Captain Tosen will vanish completely."

"What's that supposed to mean? I really have no clue what you're saying. I can't believe someone like you would hold a high-and-mighty position at the *Seireitei Bulletin*!"

"I'm sorry... I know I'm being immature."

Though Hisagi was genuinely apologizing to the former Soul Reaper Hiyori, who was also his senior, there was firm resolution in his eyes. Hiyori and Hisagi stared at each other for a while. What broke that silence was the voice of a completely unexpected third party.

"Uh, um...in that case, I'll go too."

"Ryunosuke?!"

When he heard Shino's surprised interjection, Hisagi realized that the timid voice belonged to a young Soul Reaper whose presence he had forgotten.

"*Hunh?!*"

"*Eek!*"

Though Ryunosuke was frightened by Hiyori simply giving him a look, he hid behind Shino's back and whimpered, "I-I mean, Karakura Town is really going to end up in trouble, right? In that case, Shino and I won't come away unscathed anyway..."

"Aren't you scared?"

When Hisagi asked the same question that had been asked of him, Ryunosuke replied clearly with determined eyes, "Yes! I'm super terrified! If someone told me I could run, I'd take Shino and go! Oh, but we can't run since there's a barrier! What'll I do?"

"Why're you so decisive only when you're saying something embarrassing?!" Shino yelled, fed up. Though Ryunosuke went back to cowering, he continued speaking. "But if it seems we have no other possibility, I think all I can do is be a decoy while running away."

Hisagi once again looked at the boy in front of him. He couldn't even say the kid had strong spiritual pressure as empty flattery. He had heard that the kid's brother was a seated officer in the Sixth Company, but it didn't seem like Ryunosuke had much power when it came to swordplay or kido. The statement he made likely took all the courage he had to squeeze out.

"I was thinking that it'd be better for me to just go alone."

He was doing it in order to protect the girl next to him, who was his colleague and who was stronger than him.

"What're you saying, Ryunosuke?! You're weak *and* an idiot! If you're going then I'll obviously go too!"

Even as the Soul Reaper girl yelled that, it was clear she was worried about the boy.

That girl is Madarame's sister, isn't she?

I get it now. Even the young Soul Reapers have got it in them.

Hisagi smiled quietly as he felt a sense of slight relief and nodded at the Soul Reapers in front of his eyes.

"I'm glad I've got juniors like you, Ryunosuke Yuki, Shino Madarame."

"Uh! You just said...my name..."

"I-it's an honor, Assistant Captain Hisagi!"

When the famous assistant captain remembered their names and, furthermore, recognized them as members of the Thirteen Court Guard Companies, Ryunosuke and Shino were shocked. Hisagi continued to speak. "But your work is patrolling this town. I don't know what might happen around here, but there's no way to fight it if no one's around to respond. You've got to do your own job first, got it?"

"Oh! Y-yes, sir!"

"You're scolding others about it while declaring that *you're* heading over to throw away your own life." After witnessing Hisagi's exchange, Hiyori averted her eyes and muttered to herself, "That's the part about Soul Reapers I hate."

She clucked her tongue, clapped her hands on her cheeks and told Tessai, "Okay. Oh well! I can't stand being in debt to Kisuke! I'm going with you!"

Hiyori sounded triumphant, but—"That won't work." Tessai calmly and clearly refused her.

"Whaaat?! Why not, you baldy Tessai!"

Easily dodging Hiyori's enraged fist, Tessai explained as matter-of-factly as possible. "There is currently a barrier around this town, and we cannot open a Senkaimon under these circumstances. It is likely that if several hundred thousand of these small Tenkai Ketchu are activated, we could invoke a ceremony that would ignore the barrier...but using normal methods, we will not be able to push through with just a few of these."

"Then how're you saying we should do it?"

"We can see this barrier as something that alerts to Soul Reaper and kido powers. It has a muted reaction to the Hollow factor compared to other things. In that case, a good plan would be if we were to use some potent Hollow power to break through by force."

Hollow power. When she heard those words, Hiyori immediately understood Tessai's aim.

"You saying you want me to be the battery that runs that weird device?"

"Ms. Hiyori, I wouldn't mind putting in a formal request to the owner of that 'Unagiya' you work at to borrow your power."

After a brief staring contest with Tessai, who said that with a serious look, Hiyori sighed and said, "Fine. You owe me a ton in exchange though."

"I am grateful. I will set up a formation around Mr. Hisagi, so if you could load in your spiritual pressure from outside, Ms. Hiyori."

At Tessai's words, Hiyori nodded slightly and drove the young Soul Reapers as well as Jinta and Ururu, who were watching from afar, away.

"Keep back. If you get hit by my spiritual pressure, you might end up goners."

"Ms. Sarugaki. Thank you so much."

When Hisagi lowered his head, Hiyori still looked sour as she said, "I'm not doing this for you or Kisuke. It's a job—it's a gig, is all."

After Tessai made the formation, Hiyori brought her hands up to the top of her head and pulled them down as though she were tearing her face. In that instant, a white mask appeared where there hadn't been one before, and the dense presence of Hollow flowed out and filled Urahara Shoten's basement.

"Hm. It seems that this is set up not to switch out the ground, but to exchange things from the top of the barrier. I will sync the coordinates on you, Mr. Hisagi."

Tessai controlled the flow of that spiritual pressure with his kido and poured it into the miniature Tenkai Ketchu that were placed around Hisagi.

"Since we are forcing you to break through it, coordinates aside, the time it takes may range from a few minutes to half an hour. I will try to tune things to take as little time as possible."

"Thanks."

Though he was determined, he was understandably nervous about being transported by this method for the first time. While Hisagi prepared himself to freeze up the spiritual pressure at his feet at any time in case something happened, Tessai said as he put the finishing touches on the ceremony, "I'm leaving the shop owner in your care."

At that, Tessai lowered his head at the man who had claimed that he would abandon Urahara for the sake of the Soul Reapers.

In the next moment, light engulfed Hisagi's body.

As though the world were being remade, he melted into the landscape.

He disappeared without anyone knowing what reality lay before him where he was going.

CHAPTER EIGHTEEN

AURA MICHIBANE'S LIFE could be said to have been half determined by momentum. The woman who had no life purpose or attachment to the world had no particular reason to turn down Tokinada's invitation, and she accepted his proposal as an opportunity to use the one and only thing she had an interest in—her Fullbring.

At first, she did not know what Tokinada was doing.

She did as she was told, and as she was defeating Hollows and such, her senses slowly inched toward death. She might as well have been already dead from the start, her body still moving due to some error.

The more she felt that illusion, the more she simply did what she was directed to do, mechanically, day by day. However, in contrast to her enthusiasm, her foundational Fullbring powers continued to grow with the momentum of shooting bamboo stalks, and by the time she realized it, Aura had enough power that the average Soul Reaper or Arrancar could do nothing to harm her. She had turned into a human-shaped monster.

If she were to live in the living world, she had enough power to be unbound and make all serve her. Though Aura had obtained powers that could bring her money and prestige to her heart's content, she had no interest in either and instead simply continued to follow Tokinada's instructions for the simple reason that she had no reason to object.

She was brought to the Soul Society, and since she had stolen the zanpaku-to that had been passed down in his family from the head of the household, Tokinada's behavior morphed from simple fun to ambition with a clear vision.

She controlled the raging torrent of spiritual pressure to find a vast Kyogoku from inside the Garganta and offered it to Tokinada.

As for the Tenkai Ketchu that Kisuke Urahara had created, she stole a miniaturized version from the safe and offered it to Tokinada. When she was told to mass-produce those inferior devices that had been created using the Tsunayashiro clan's techniques, in the range of hundreds of thousands, she did what she was told. She created them and offered them to Tokinada.

When she was told that there needed to be a human to handle and also extol the birth of the king, she had started the religious organization as Tokinada's puppet. Then, by

displaying all kinds of "miracles," she had recruited several hundred thousand believers and offered them to Tokinada.

When she had been told that a new throne was needed to symbolize the new world, Aura created a castle even more mammoth than a skyscraper in the Kyogoku's sky and offered it to Tokinada.

When she was told he wanted a bed to look up at it, she had created a palace and offered it to Tokinada.

However, she could not make any sense of it.

Though she could do the most absurd things by controlling the reishi of objects in the living world and the Soul Society, taking them into her own body and reorganizing their structure, she could not fathom what it was that Tokinada wanted with all the things she offered to him. Though she had been told to create a throne, the one to sit in it would not be Tokinada. She was not particularly interested in knowing who, but eventually she found out.

A war between the Quincies and Soul Reapers called the Great Soul King Protection War had occurred. Though the Tsunayashiro clan of the Four Great Noble Clans had been attacked and a great number of people had apparently died, all the Quincies who attempted to attack Tokinada had the tables turned on them by Aura.

Then again, Tokinada himself hadn't been at the residence at the time, and using his own zanpaku-to's power, he had stolen a different sword from a place called Hoohden.

He seemingly hadn't been highly regarded, since not a single Stern Ritter with a Schrift showed up. When things wrapped up, she had wiped out nothing but ordinary Quincy soldiers.

However, at the time that battle ended, Tokinada's "fun" had truly started.

"I will have you give birth to the king's body."

"Do you mean you want me to have a baby?"

When Aura asked that indifferently, Tokinada shook his head, smiling.

"Of course not! Do I look like a man who thinks a woman's only purpose is to create children? In addition, I am at least faithful to my late wife. I don't see others in that way anymore. Though I do see others as playthings to have my fun with and to damage as much as my heart desires…" While saying such vile words, Tokinada celebrated a half Soul Reaper who had ended the war. "Yes, in that sense, Ichigo Kurosaki is a deeply interesting one. He is magnificent! Though he had been planned by Aizen, I cannot understand how something as ambiguous as love could create such a miracle between a Soul Reaper and a human."

Then, as Aura listened to him, she noticed it. The throne and the believers were certainly for the king. It was just that they were coming in the wrong order. Once Tokinada finished all his preparations, he was attempting to create the king to go with that foundation.

In front of her was a heap of corpses and konpaku fragments almost mountainous in size. "I recovered these from the battlegrounds. We have a mountain of Soul Reapers, Quincies, and bodies. I can have as many human and Fullbringer bodies as you need brought in from the living world, so use them as you like."

Then he gave her a component that the Tsunayashiro clan had been perfecting. It was a mass of reishi clearly different from the rest.

The thing emitted a presence that made it seem as though it had substance and intent though it was not alive, and Aura felt something within her curiously resonate with it.

Aura was befuddled by what the thing could possibly be, but Tokinada smiled and gave her an order: "Set the reishi to work and play around with it until it can wriggle around on its own. I don't mind if it isn't human shaped. I've come upon a favorable part to use as the brain, so you do not need to make one. Anyway, if the Saketsu and Hakusui can at least get to the stage where they can function, I know a genius who can make it live under any circumstances."

Tokinada smiled vulgarly as he spoke to Aura.

He spoke that way to the woman who knew nothing about children.

He told her to become a god—a mother—and create the life of a new king.

≡

KYOGOKU

"So they're here."

Tokinada, who was looking up at the floating castle from the courtyard of the palace, grinned as he sensed the disturbance of spiritual pressure from the edge of the Kyogoku.

"This spiritual pressure... Oh my, no one but the Captain General himself has graced this place with his presence directly. Old Yamamoto aside, why are the Court Guards' Captain Generals so full of youthful vigor?"

Knowing that Kyoraku was not "full of youthful vigor" at all, Tokinada spoke sarcastically.

"What do you intend to do?" When Aura asked that from the side, Tokinada told her, "First, let us see what they can do.

"After all, no matter which route we take, no one will be going home."

≡

KUKAKU'S RESIDENCE

"Don't you need to go too?"

The question was from Ganju Shiba, who had been left with the role of feeding spiritual pressure to the equipment

to keep the garganta open. Mayuri replied irksomely, "I must control the path of the garganta from here. I will at least do a decent job of making sure a path back remains open."

"That thing is like an offshoot, isn't it? Can't you leave your real body here and send your offshoot over there or something?"

"My next task is to address the fact that controlling it becomes inaccurate with distance. There is a self-destruct mechanism in it, but going out of the way to give the enemy information would be foolish."

"Giving the enemy information. Who has the time for that? If it were just the Arrancars and Quincies, it'd be one thing, but there are three captain-class people over there."

Mayuri gave a pitying glance to Ganju, who was dubious and possibly too prone to worry, as he matter-of-factly continued with his work.

"You better not be ignoring me! You're acting like *I'm* a fool—like it's no use explaining to me!"

"Oh, it seems that you *are* capable of self-awareness. You're a pretty remarkable man to challenge my conjectures."

"That's no compliment!"

Ignoring Ganju's anger, he instead indifferently offered his opinion. "It's obviously a trap."

"It is?"

"Rubbish though they may be, the Tsunayashiro clan are still the supervisors of the Visual Department. Though they are far from my level, they are more adept at gathering information than the ordinary person. Naturally, they should already know that we have gathered at the Shiba clan's residence."

"Huh?"

Rather than talking to Ganju, who was raising an eyebrow, Mayuri seemed to be talking to Kukaku, who was leaning against a pillar with her arms crossed. He continued, "I thought of the possibility that he might interfere with the garganta being opened, but instead it seems as though he would like us to jump right into the middle of his bosom. Hm."

Mayuri sensed the waver of the spiritual pressure meter he had put into his own body and said something difficult as though it were not a big deal. "As evidence of that, it seems that they will be enclosed in a barrier immediately."

"Whaaat?!"

"The moment they entered the Kyogoku, the information coming to this side entirely ceased. It seems that the doorway to return from within the Garganta has also been closed."

"Wha...?! That's super serious! Don't we need to go save them?!"

When Ganju panicked, Mayuri looked genuinely confused and said, "Why would I leap into a trap set right under my nose in order to save them?"

"Why you little..."

"In addition, I said that I had the role of ensuring they have a path home, did I not? I don't think either of you have the skills to keep the pathway to the Kyogoku open, do you?"

"Hn?"

Ganju, who felt like what Mayuri was saying was contradictory, had nowhere to put his gripped fist in his confusion.

Then Kukaku scolded her little brother, "Just leave it, Ganju."

"But, sis!"

"Yoruichi and that old guy Kyoraku definitely went fully aware it was a trap. Long story short, that guy wearing a mask like a Go game board is completely convinced that they'll crush the enemy, break the barrier, and come back."

"I have no idea who you could possibly be referring to when you speak of a Go mask, but don't you think you would have done better on his side? If we follow Tokinada Tsunayashiro's wishes, they say you may even be able to regain your aristocrat status."

Kukaku had casually heard about this situation from Yoruichi, and there was a chance Mayuri had also found this information through his own methods.

Kukaku sighed lightly and then replied as though she were genuinely annoyed, "I haven't got any interest in that. Aristocrats or not, I just do what gives me no regrets. My older brother and uncle were the same."

She was talking about Kaien Shiba and Isshin Shiba.

As she thought about her blood relatives who had done what their hearts desired, or the unceasing chain of Shiba blood going into the future, the corner of Kukaku's mouth rose as though she were enjoying this.

"It seems that that's our family's fate."

≡

KYOGOKU

"Looks like we've been sealed in. Well, I suppose this is going as expected so far."

Kyoraku and the others had made their way to a sandy place at the edge of the Kyogoku. The feel of the sand on the bottoms of their feet was dry, but a clammy and pronounced spiritual pressure seemed to cling to them and caress them.

The moment they were thrown into that place, the rift that had been opened in space until then had been forced closed by some other force. However, brushing off the dust easily, Kyoraku once again turned his eyes to his surroundings.

Hirako, who had also likewise been looking around, seemed peeved from the bottom of his heart. "So? Did you predict *this situation* too, Captain General?"

"More or less."

All around them was a horde of similarly shaped, Hollow-like monsters. He realized they were the same things that Ikomikidomoe had generated from his gigantic body in their fight earlier.

It was a horde that had grown not only to the hundreds or thousands, but somewhere in the tens of thousands.

They were divided into troops based on whether they could fly or were creatures of the ground and, in their great numbers, turned into a white tsunami as they tried to surround the group as though they were creating a gigantic cage in the wilderness.

"What is this? The main body isn't around." Seeing that Hikone and Ikomikidomoe weren't at the scene, Hirako became increasingly exasperated as he muttered to himself, "So you just made monsters and left them behind—absurd."

"That's not all. Each one of these guys has completely different spiritual pressure from the ones before."

Just as Liltotto had said, if the horde from earlier were normal Hollows, these were individually surrounded by the spiritual pressure of huge Hollows and occasionally Gillians and Adjuchas.

"In the battle at the Soul Society, that main body was 'eating' our attacks. It might be the type of thing that can take in surrounding reishi to raise its own spiritual pressure."

At Halibel's words, Nelliel sighed slightly.

"In that case, this means some trouble. This place isn't like the Soul Society—the reishi is even denser than in Hueco Mundo."

"Well, it's abundantly clear where that high and mighty Tsunayashiro is, at least."

Hirako jerked his chin to point at a gigantic structure floating in the sky that seemed much like a royal castle.

"Really now. That's basically a plagiarism of the Reiokyu. Oh well."

"Regardless, it looks like the answer has come to us easily. We know what he's planning on sending over using the Tenkai Ketchu." Kyoraku spoke in a gentle tone but beneath it was extreme caution.

In order to send over something with the mass of what was floating in the sky, he would have needed gigantic Tenkai Ketchu set up in the four corners of Karakura Town. However, Kyoraku guessed that Tokinada had likely already finished those preparations.

"It would have been better if he were sending that thing to the Rukongai or Hueco Mundo. If it's Karakura Town, as I suspect, then we should probably go pretty quickly."

While putting on his hat, Kyoraku unsheathed his zanpaku-to.

Ginjo, who had been standing behind him, attempted to test him. "We came with you, but we're going to do what we want."

"Yes. I won't go so far as to ask for your cooperation. If our goals are the same, it would be better to act separately than to make a clumsy battle formation."

Recalling their attack when the Vandenreich had remade the Reiokyu, Kyoraku nodded at Ginjo.

"It's not like I've grown to trust you. Once this is over, I've got a mountain of questions for you."

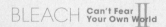

"I think that the answers you want are probably better known by Tokinada than me."

As he clucked his tongue at Kyoraku, who spoke as though he were hinting at something, Ginjo told Tsukishima and Giriko, "We're going," and kicked off the ground.

It looked as though they were heading right into the middle of the enemies, but after Giriko fiddled with something like a dial that had appeared over his clothes, spheres put together with crystals and black boxes floated around him and quivered.

"Hm... If we are hiding ourselves among this number, the three of us have exactly twenty seconds. Don't forget that if we attack while hidden, it will be a contract violation for me."

"Yeah, that's more than enough time to make a break for it."

As he replied the spheres momentarily glittered, and then, like they were melting into the air, spiritual pressure and all, they disappeared.

"Pretty handy. Can that eye-patch guy do anything he wants?"

When Hirako said that, Kyoraku smiled cynically.

"If we're being referred to by our eye patches, then Captain Zaraki and I are in for some complications. That man's name is Kutsuzawa, so make sure you call him by that."

Hirako narrowed his eyes at the Captain General, who seemed to know all the names of the Fullbringers with Ginjo, shrugged, and shook his head.

"Kyoraku, you are your hat, and Kenpachi, beyond reason, is Kenpachi. It's not confusing."

"Doesn't that make it seem like I *am* a hat?"

Though at first glance, it would have seemed like they were having an easygoing conversation, their spiritual pressure was already tuned up so that they could respond to the situation around them.

The other Soul Reapers, Arrancars, and Quincies were doing the same, and Kenpachi let his zanpaku-to hang as he tried to look for the strongest spiritual pressure around them.

"What? They're all small fry. Where's their boss?"

"They're probably in that thing that looks like a castle floating in the sky over there."

At Madarame's words, Kenpachi looked up at the multi-story structure high in the air.

"I see. Then I'm heading there. You guys can clean up the small fry however you want."

At Kenpachi's words Hirako narrowed his eyes as though he were exasperated.

"Honestly, Kenpachi is just getting more and more narcissistic. I do agree that beating the boss would be the fastest way to go about things though."

Kenpachi started to run in the direction of the castle in the sky. The white monsters reacted and tried to swarm him, but—

"You're in the way."

With a roar, his wicked blade glinted. With a light swing of his sword, Kenpachi gouged a crescent into the ground and sent it flying. Several hundred of the enemies were annihilated in the aftermath.

Faced with such power that defied logic, the Arrancars and Quincies who were supposed to be on the same side as him gulped. At that point, the white, grotesquely shaped horde seemed to switch from perceiving Kenpachi as a foreign substance that had wandered into the Kyoguku to a clear enemy, and they raised strange voices as they closed in to attack him.

In the next moment, the grotesque things thrust their arms and legs in the ground and gave birth to other monsters the same size as them from their backs.

"Self-propagation?!"

Nanao's voice was surprised, and Halibel narrowed her eyes as she muttered, "So this is the same type of power as Rudobon's."

In Rudobon's case, he created his underlings by turning himself into an Arbol, but the things in front of her eyes could each become the parent body and give birth to their own offshoot.

"They are pulling in the reishi from the Kyogoku and creating their own offshoots, I guess. They likely cannot multiply forever, but at this rate, this seems like it will become a war of attrition."

Kyoraku sighed as though this meant trouble. In mere seconds, even more of the grotesque things than had been annihilated by Kenpachi had been birthed, and they were closing in on Kenpachi like an avalanche. However, Kenpachi didn't pay them any mind at all and simply waved around his zanpaku-to haphazardly and boldly started to run.

When it came to Kenpachi's shunpo, his physical gravity was more significant than his skill. Regardless of that, his haphazard movements made him faster than a normal Soul Reaper's shunpo, and he only eased up in the moments that he waved his sword and kept cutting away the waves of white monsters that came at him.

Following after him instinctively, Madarame and Yumichika had also started running. As the strongest fire-power even within their mixed team, Kenpachi Zaraki broke through to that place using brute force.

"This won't do. There's no cooperation in this organization."

Hirako was exasperated as he realized the things surrounding them were creating a white wall as they steadily encroached in a circle.

"Well, in a situation like this, that will work." Without minding the obvious opposition, Hirako grinned. "Kyoraku, you should break through with Kenpachi. If we really engage with these guys, it'll take all day."

"But these guys are pretty fast. Even if we get through, if we fight them over there, I think they'll just chase after us and corner us."

In reply to Nelliel's concern, Hirako waved his hand lightly at her and replied, "Then I'd be a great anchor. That would be better than being at a stalemate here, wouldn't it?"

"What? Are you saying you're going to hold these guys back all by yourself?"

When Candice looked at him dubiously, Hirako sighed and said, "This isn't the time to hem and haw. Kenpachi is going to be gone soon."

"Then I suppose we will rely on your word..."

After Kyoraku met Hirako's eyes, he turned around and kicked at the ground to follow Kenpachi. Though those around him were dubious of Kyoraku's nonchalance, no one in particular opposed him.

Even the belligerent Grimmjow and others had no interest in simply mechanically hunting the masses. Glancing at the monster horde like it was a nuisance, they followed after Kyoraku without a word.

Kenpachi had already broken through the white wall that the interwoven white monsters had created. The others were leaping out of the enclosure to slip past the wall at the same moment the monsters were closing the wall back up.

Naturally, there was no way the monster horde would let them get past unnoticed. The white wall turned into an avalanche that followed after them, and they churned along the Kyogoku's ground while multiplying constantly.

They were like a mist of murder closing in on them from behind. Other than someone as strong as Kenpachi, most wouldn't have been able to make it out unscathed.

"So it's finally come. What'll we do? Should we stop them?" Liltotto made a proposal as she eyed the overwhelming mass closing in from behind. "This is your time to shine, Peeping Tom. Make them stop in their tracks."

"Don't screw with me! A hundred or two is one thing, but doing this many in one go is obviously impossible! I don't even have time to observe them!"

"*Tsk*. Useless."

Liltotto clucked her tongue at Najahkoop's angry bellow, then she started to calculate whether she and Bambietta could take any action, but Hirako eased his speed between the wall approaching the girls and said, "I'm pretty sure I told you I'd be the anchor. Hurry up and go ahead."

"You seriously doing this on your own?"

"Last time I didn't join either side and didn't do anything, right? I need to show my cool side now or Hiyori will punch me down for being the one who's always caught by surprise."

"Who's this Hiyori person?"

Ignoring Liltotto's quip, Nanao was surprised as she yelled at Hirako, "Captain Hirako! That's reckless! Even a captain like you can't stand alone against such numbers!"

Kyoraku stopped her with his hand.

"Captain General?"

Nanao looked at him dubiously, and after he smiled to show her it was okay, Kyoraku asked Hirako, "Are you intending to do *that*?"

"Yeah. It's not like it won't work in this situation."

"Got it. Once you've finished cleaning up here, make sure to follow after us right away."

With a humble expression, Kyoraku lowered his hat.

"Sorry I've dragged you into something so bothersome and entangled with aristocrats."

"I really don't mind. Well, especially now. I don't care for aristocrats who do things like this."

Grinning, Hirako stopped and stood by himself. Then, he looked up at the vast horde of monsters as they closed in on him and said his zanpaku-to's name.

"Collapse, Sakanade."

≡

"What, did they force their way through or something?"

Ginjo, who was no longer under the presence-blocking Time Tells No Lies power, muttered as he watched the tsunami of monsters that followed in the wake of Kenpachi's sword pressure.

"It *is* a savage spiritual pressure. It's exactly the right thing to be the decoy for a horde of beasts."

"Have you got something against that scary-faced Soul Reaper?"

"It's in your head. I am always placid when the flow of time is before me."

When Giriko turned his eyes away and went silent, Ginjo didn't press any further and rubbed his chin as he muttered, "Now what mess have we got here?"

"Oh? Haven't got a plan this time?"

At Tsukishima's words, Ginjo shook his head slightly.

"We didn't just separate from them without any thought. I haven't decided who to side with yet. For now, I want to collect info on this Tsunayashiro guy."

"Hm. But do you really think there will be any information you'll recognize in a place like this?"

In a wilderness that went on as far as they could see, it didn't seem as though there would be any kind of clue. However, Ginjo nodded at Giriko's question and called out to his surroundings, "I know you can hear me, Yukio!"

Then static ran through a place where there should have been nothing, and a boy appeared from the rift in space-time.

"It's been a year, hasn't it? I'm impressed you noticed."

With the boy—Yukio Hans Vorarlberna—in front of him, Ginjo said sourly, "Since I've split a part of my powers with you, if there's even a slight amount of your spiritual pressure around, I can tell."

"Uh-huh. I wonder if that's a good thing or a bad thing."

"Depends on your response."

Ginjo immediately made his pendant turn into a sword and pointed it at Yukio as he asked, "What's going on here? That religious organization Xcution that's been throwing its weight around in the world of the living...you got anything to do with it?"

"Right. I didn't have anything to do with it earlier. But now I'm in league with them."

"Do you mean individually? Or do you mean *our* Xcution is?"

"I guess that depends on your reply, Kugo," Yukio responded expressionlessly.

"What does that mean?"

"It depends on what you wish, Mr. Kugo Ginjo," a strangely charming voice resonated from behind him.

In response to the voice that came from a place where Ginjo felt no spiritual pressure at all, he instinctively swung his blade. The sword cut the air. The form of a young person seemed to be there, but Ginjo's blade slipped through her like it was cutting through smoke.

"Who the hell are you?"

Ginjo was cautious as he probed into his opponent's powers. Through his years of experience, he perceived her identity at a glance. The person who stood in front of his eyes was neither Soul Reaper nor Quincy, much less a normal human.

He realized the person who stood on the same ground as them was, in short, a Fullbringer.

"My name is Aura Michibane. It is such an honor to meet you. Should I call you the religious founder of the real Xcution?"

Then, looking at his opponent, Ginjo answered, "I was never a religious leader. Xcution isn't a creed. It's a gathering of idiots that's turning the world upside down."

≡

The giant avalanche of monsters was closing in on Hirako. They encroached on him with a force that seemed it could destroy the world. Just as the colossal mass attempted to swallow Hirako, in a moment it seemed as though they had hit a boundary, and their movements slowed.

The order in the colony that was once perfectly coordinated had vanished, and the horde hit an invisible wall. That moment came when Hirako had said his zanpaku-to's name and activated his shikai.

The sword had transformed into a strange form, the metal at the top turning into a circle. Putting his fingers on that, Hirako let his zanpaku-to's blade swing like a pendulum.

"Hypnotism doesn't work all that well on opponents like bugs. I'm just glad that the illusion is working."

With the tens of thousands of monsters in front of him chaotically scattering in all directions, Hirako smiled wryly, like a swindler who has just hoodwinked a mark.

"I've changed the directions to up, down, left, right, and front, back all over the place. Even though you were facing front, now you're facing back—frightening, isn't it? All the better when you're all jam-packed together."

Hirako Shinji's zanpaku-to Sakanade's ability was to reverse the senses of his opponents. Like Aizen's Kyoka Suigetsu, it was a hypnotism and illusion ability, and its power could be said to be unparalleled against anyone who depended on their vision—with a few troubling exceptions, that is.

"Hm?"

Hirako cocked his head to the side from where he had, at some point, ended up floating in the air upside down. The monsters started to move in a different way.

Their body parts started to creak and squeal, and they were calling to each other like insects. Then a distinct change in their movements became apparent.

The horde that had suddenly scattered into chaos steadily contained that mayhem and once again consolidated their movement.

"So they're not using their eyes..."

They started to close their eyes with something that looked like eyelids and closed off their vision to render

Sakanade's ability useless. Then, through their release of *noise*, they were able to confirm each other's location. They seemed to be communicating perfectly as though they were having a conversation and together started to adjust their movements. They sensed where Hirako was generally, using their spiritual pressure senses, and by releasing sounds in that direction, they could grasp the terrain by way of echolocation. Feeling that they were coordinating their movements, all of their mouths twisted open at once.

"Whoa, whoa. This is not really a great situation..."

As he broke into a cold sweat, the monsters all attacked Hirako at once.

"...Just kidding."

They slipped right past his side and crashed into bare rock behind him.

"Hhhhhh!"

They made strange sounds resembling shrieks as one after another they ran into the terrain around them or each other and their bodies were destroyed.

"Didn't I tell you?"

Seeing the situation around him, which was in even more confusion than earlier, Hirako smiled.

"I can also invert the sounds you hear."

Hirako calmly started walking through the gaps between the monster horde.

"I'd like to train a little more so that I can invert hot and cold too. But of course, that seems like it'll be a difficult thing to learn."

He did not follow after Kyoraku and the others, but instead headed for the center of the swarm of tens of thousands of monsters.

"Well, it'd be easy cutting you down one at a time. But doing it with so many of you seems like it'd be tiring. I should've just taken a nap at home."

Even as he complained, Hirako seemed to be enjoying himself as he continued to walk his path. While he did that, the monsters tried to attack him one after another, but he changed their trajectory, making them dodge him, and they crashed into the ground, bare rock, or each other, and their body parts scattered around them.

The monsters were not so unintelligent. They could even understand the words Hirako was saying. They were intelligent enough to think that the Soul Reaper, who had revealed his ability, was obviously looking down on them and insulting them—and they had just enough intelligence to get angry about that. However, Hirako hadn't just told them his ability for no reason. His words themselves were another weapon to confuse his opponents. Though anyone would attempt to adapt once they found out their opponent's ability was an illusion, no one had ever been able to do that in the past except Aizen. That was because the moment Hirako sensed his opponents were getting used to a line of attack, he would immediately switch the illusion on or off, or occasionally he would leave their sense of up and down alone, but only change their sense of right and left. He would fine-tune the attack repeatedly.

They would accept Hirako's words without question, and the more they tried to analyze his actions, the more the opponent would get stuck in his technique and move forward on the path of self-destruction. However, it seemed that the monsters had changed their way of thinking, and a vast number of them stopped moving at the same time.

"Huh?"

Hirako, who was suspicious, watched as they stuck their arms and legs into the ground and, just as when they had been killed by Kenpachi, started to create their own offshoots.

"I see… So that's how you do things."

The smile disappeared from Hirako's face, and he remarked with a humble expression, "Are you trying to increase the number of you that aren't under my Sakanade's powers?"

Of course, he couldn't impede the creation of new off-shoots with Sakanade's ability. Hirako sighed slightly and muttered as sweat dripped down his face, "Are you really trying to start a battle to see whether Sakanade's ability or your self-propagation is faster? Are you idiots? That's crazy."

He continued watching them with a despairing expression on his face. As though they had confirmed they had broken the spirit of their opponent, they seemed to laugh as their bodies shook and creaked, and they continued to multiply with Hirako at their center.

≡

"Hey, those guys have started to multiply real fast," muttered Liltotto when she noticed what was happening far behind her.

When they turned around, the swarm of monsters with the volume of a white tsunami really was furiously surging. In a matter of seconds, it looked as though a mountain of them had been newly created.

"Even Sakanade can't deal with that many!"

Nanao, who was thinking they really ought to send some reinforcements, felt Kyoraku lightly grab her shoulder.

"It's fine, Nanao."

"But Captain General..."

As though trying to calm Nanao, who was uneasy, he told her with a gentle tone that was filled with trust in Shinji Hirako, "This situation is still likely going just as Captain Hirako has planned."

≡

Though Hirako had stopped moving for a while as though he were frozen, his keen spiritual pressure senses confirmed that Kyoraku and the others had gone past a specific distance. The moment that happened, Hirako's sweat dried and his face broke out into the smile of a swindler.

"Well, that was really a lifesaver."

He stopped his act and was delighted that the swarm that had a certain amount of intelligence had reacted as he had expected.

"You're as simple as I thought you were."

≡

"Huh?"

Several of the people running around Kyoraku doubted his words.

Only one person knew the mystery of Hirako's Sakanade power. Kensei Muguruma was the exception. Kyoraku intentionally kept quiet about the particulars of the situation with those around him, who could potentially be enemies in the future, and simply stated it in such a way that only Nanao would understand. "You know my bankai, don't you?"

"Oh!"

Nanao, who had a good intuition, understood everything just from that. That was because she remembered something she had heard from Kyoraku before.

"My bankai isn't that easily usable. I suppose you could say it has a corresponding recoil for how strong the ability is. It has a flaw: It doesn't distinguish between friend or foe within the range the ability reaches.

"You'll find them occasionally—users of bankai that involve anyone surrounding them regardless of whether they're an ally or enemy. As for those you're aware of, Captain Kurotsuchi's Konjiki Ashisogi Jizo is one of them. It's a brutal bankai that scatters poison in its scope. Well, someone like Captain Kurotsuchi could probably modify it to distinguish between friends and enemies. There's also one more... Since he's dead I think I can talk about it. The seventh Kenpachi who used to be my friend had a bankai like that too.

"It was called Gagaku Kairo, and it was an uncommon power that could chomp up anyone—friend or foe—within a radius of several spirit miles. Because of that, Central 46 forbade him from using it within the Soul Society."

"Then the reason you left Captain Hirako by himself was because...?"

"Yes, I believe in his abilities too, but..."

Kyoraku smiled wryly as he quickened his pace heading toward the castle in the sky.

"We wouldn't even be dead weight to him...we would end up swallowed by Sakanade and actually dead. That's all it is."

≡

A hopeless scene engulfed Hirako's surroundings. In the living world, high-rise buildings are called skyscrapers, and in exactly that way, a gigantic, white multistory building that seemed to scrape the heavens formed around him.

That wall created by a swarm of several tens of thousands or even hundreds of thousands was over a hundred meters tall. Hirako himself hadn't gone to Hueco Mundo, but based on what he had heard, he could imagine that this scene would be like the entire desert itself that made up that world coming to attack him.

"Yeah, I wonder what you're supposed to say at a time like this. I'm pretty sure some guy who was stupidly gigantic said something appropriate."

While recalling a Quincy he had battled in the past, Hirako said, "Right, right—'If I reverse this situation, it'd practically be a miracle.'—was that it? I might be getting the details wrong, but that's all right."

The monsters determined that Hirako was dangerous. In a certain sense, he was even more trouble than the Soul Reaper with an eye patch who had slayed a number of them at the beginning. The colony murmured its shared thought that this was an enemy they could not allow to survive.

The only allies they had were themselves and the parent that had given them life, Ikomikidomoe. They did not consider Hikone Ubuginu, the wielder of Ikomikidomoe, to be an ally, and because of that, their solidarity as the same type of being was much stronger than any half-friend Hollows and Soul Reapers.

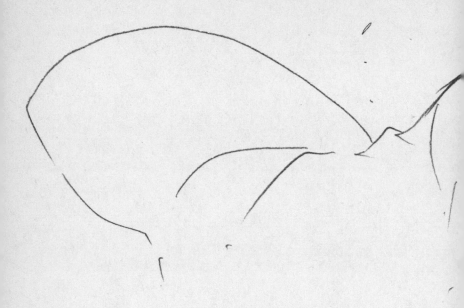

The ones that had just been born knew that instinctively. That was exactly why they determined that though there was only a single person in front of their eyes, it was a villainous existence that confused them and must be crushed with all their power.

In response to those who had been born with that unifying strength, the Soul Reaper who had stepped into

their world with a zanpaku-to of lies spoke, and they could not determine whether it was the truth or another lie: "In that case...it's almost time for a miracle. I'm going to turn things around."

Then, with the next words the man had uttered, the world once again turned upside down.

"Bankai—Sakashima Yokoshima Happo Fusagari."

INTERLUDE

HOW MUCH TIME HAD PASSED since Kaname Tosen swore allegiance to Sosuke Aizen? Before Tosen realized it, and unrelated to when he had started serving the man, Tosen had elevated Aizen to the point that the man was an absolute king in his mind.

The first few years, he remained by Aizen's side with doubts. Rather, one could even say that he viewed Aizen with hostility, thinking that perhaps he really was a Soul Reaper and a bird of the same feather as Tokinada Tsunayashiro, that there was no mistaking that Aizen claimed to have saved him only to use him as a pawn. While continuing to harbor those doubts, he firmly kept his guard up.

He also wondered whether perhaps Aizen had recruited him as an ally only because Kyoka Suigetsu did not work on him—but that doubt vanished immediately. If that were the case and Tosen were one of Aizen's weaknesses, Aizen could have just killed him.

Sosuke Aizen's power was so great that he felt embarrassed that he had even had that doubt. The more he learned about Aizen's power, the more his initial hostility waned. Aizen could not possibly be a bird of the same feather as the Soul Reapers.

The man had already overcome the limitations of a Soul Reaper, and it could be said he had the fangs to simply make those birds into one of his prey.

For the same reason, the concern that he would be used as a simple pawn also disappeared. For a man with the genius of Sosuke Aizen, a pawn wouldn't have made any difference to him. He hadn't had a reason to save Tosen at the risk of revealing Kyoka Suigetsu's power.

When Aizen had tried to compel him there to become a sacrifice for his goals, Tosen tried to stop him by killing him. However, Aizen, who lightly dodged Tosen's advance, did not even attempt to punish him.

When Tosen told him to kill him if Aizen were using him, Aizen had said this:

"Don't say something you don't mean. You're more frightened than anyone else, aren't you? Not of death, but of not being able to carry out your revenge, and of disappearing without attaining revenge.

"The path I take will likely be paved with many sacrifices. However, leaving the world in the hands of the Soul Reapers

like this would be immoral, like turning one's eyes away from a chain of perpetual sacrifices. Even if everyone else objects, I do not intend to change this theory.

"If you still condemn me, regardless of that, then you might as well sharpen your blade while you're with me, in order that someday your weapon might reach me."

After listening to these points, Tosen had asked questions.

"Why did you take in someone who could become your enemy?"

He asked what he could mean to a man like Aizen, with the grand ambitions Aizen was attempting to achieve.

"Because you are someone who knows both despair and fear. I have nothing to fear. Nothing perplexes me. However, that is exactly why I need someone to light the way."

Tosen understood. To Aizen, good and evil were equally unworthy. In order to make the world support his own path, Tosen had seen the man save the world countless times. For the sake of all he desired, Tosen had seen the man purposefully and unscrupulously stand by. Because Aizen had no reason to use good or evil as a reason, he simply grew stronger on his own and did not stray from the path that he had set out on. The path he walked was right, and he would not shy from slaughter for the sake of justice. The justice he spoke of was not at all bound by the duality of good and evil.

Tosen, who had come to understand the man named Aizen, did not doubt his intentions were any more than that.

Regardless, it would have been a lie to claim that all of his hesitations had disappeared.

He had no doubt regarding Aizen.

How he acted while walking the road of his ambitions certainly would have been viewed as treason in the world at large. However, knowing that, he was clearing the path with his own two feet for the sake of the justice he believed in.

In that case, what would become of Tosen?

Was there a right way of doing things according to his own idea of justice? Did *he* have a cause?

Was Kaname Tosen simply taking the path that the powerful Aizen walked in order to get his revenge?

As though he had seen through that hesitation, Aizen said to Tosen, "It seems you are still undecided."

"I just do not know..."

Though Tosen worried it was disrespectful, he spoke to Aizen of the fear that he had. "Because of that, I am frightened. I hate Soul Reapers. I hate the world where they have their way. But do I have the qualifications to condemn the entire world when I am acting out of a grudge?"

"That isn't the case. You and I have no need to judge the world." Aizen did not deny or affirm Tosen's fear and continued speaking about the world. "Because the world that exists now was created on top of a sin."

"A sin?"

"However, I do not approve of setting the world back to what was originally, as the founder of the Quincies who invaded the Soul Society in the past wanted. That would take away the significance of people being people. That is exactly why I will bring down the linchpin of the way of the world, the symbol of the Soul Reapers' sin, the greatest sacrifice—the Soul King in heaven."

When Aizen said it that way, Tosen spoke of his doubts about the world. "Lord Aizen, you said that you would bring the Soul King down from heaven and stand there yourself, but why is the Soul Reapers' king a sacrifice?"

At Tosen's question, Aizen spoke a word that Tosen was not familiar with for some reason. "Do you know what a Fullbringer is?"

"Hm? No... I only have a superficial education, so I apologize."

"There's no need to apologize. If anything, I am the one who should apologize for asking such an unfair question. Even in the Soul Society, those who know of the Fullbringers' existence number in the few."

Aizen then narrowed his eyes and uttered the name of the aristocratic family that tied him and Tosen together. "That is because the Tsunayashiro clan has hidden the information."

"What?!"

Once Tosen had received an explanation of the Fullbringers' existence, he still could not understand how that was connected to the Soul Society's sin.

Expressing that Tosen's doubt was natural, Aizen began to speak of what had been "before."

"Well, why do you think the unborn children's mothers are attacked in the first place?"

"Huh? So it's not by coincidence?"

Aizen quietly confirmed that, and Tosen the Soul Reaper was surprised.

"You know that I was shaving away the souls of the people in the Rukongai and offering them to the incomplete Hogyoku, don't you?"

"Yes."

"With some of them, though they did not satisfy the Hogyoku, it exhibited a very strong reaction. When I researched further I found it reacted to a certain girl whose konpaku I had taken. To be more accurate, it seemed to react to the 'nail' that was intermingling in her konpaku."

Aizen had continued to research the Hogyoku for a way to bring down the royal palace and put himself in heaven. No matter how many hundreds of souls he fed it, the Hogyoku showed no signs of becoming complete. That was why Aizen wanted the other Hogyoku that Kisuke Urahara had created, but in the process of his research, he had by coincidence noticed the existence of the "nails" and the special abilities of Fullbringers.

"Although a substantial part of her soul had been stolen, she did not die, and that girl continues to have the qualities of a Soul Reaper even now. It is likely that the 'nail' had a certain degree of influence on her. There might have been something other than her qualities as a Soul Reaper that she had lost."

"When you speak of 'nails'...is that a metaphor?"

"No. I mean a nail."

At that point, Aizen smiled boldly and gave an explanation that was beyond what Tosen could have imagined. "A part that had been carved away in the distant past *by the ancestors of the Soul Reapers*—a part of the Reio's body."

That was how Kaname Tosen came to know about it.

He found out the truth about how not only the Soul Society, but also the living world and Hueco Mundo—all three worlds—were created.

≡

As soon as he had heard everything that Aizen had to tell, Tosen had been prepared. He was prepared to become a traitor and was convinced that changing the world itself would be justice.

If it was for this cause, he would not mind throwing his life away. As the hesitation in Tosen's spiritual pressure disappeared in front of him, Aizen once again told Tosen the path that he himself was taking. "I will eventually reach the horizon of the truth and will replace the linchpin. I will likely stand in heaven, not manipulated by others into becoming a sacrifice, but of my own volition."

Aizen then purposefully offered Tosen, a man who had clear determination to serve him, a deal. "Is there anything you wish for, Kaname? I will give you a token of thanks for following me as my most loyal subject. If there is something that you wish for, you may tell me."

With words that tested his conviction, Tosen almost started to reply honestly, "My wish is for the world you create, Lord Aizen." But at that moment the image of his friend, as they spoke on the hill in the Rukongai, came into his mind.

After remaining silent for a short interval, he slowly opened his mouth to speak. "If you would allow it...I have one wish."

"Oh?"

Aizen himself hadn't expected Tosen to want something, and he squinted with great interest as he waited for Tosen to continue.

"What I wish for is—"

CONTINUED IN VOLUME III

A note from the creator
TITE KUBO

A manga artist who drew just one complete story
over the summer and felt like his job was done.
Huh?! I actually worked, so I feel like maybe I
accomplished something?!
I hope that I can continue to feel this passion.
A moderate amount of labor is such a splendid thing!!

A note from the author
RYOHGO NARITA

The second novelization author for BLEACH.
After spending several months hospitalized, I was a novelist
who wrote manga originals and game scenarios without actually
doing much work with novels.
Now that this book is coming out, I can finally declare, "I've done
my work as a novelist!" At least I think I should be able to...!

BLEACH: CAN'T FEAR YOUR OWN WORLD II

ORIGINAL STORY BY
TITE KUBO

WRITTEN BY
RYOHGO NARITA

COVER AND INTERIOR DESIGN BY
JIMMY PRESLER

TRANSLATION BY
JAN MITSUKO CASH

PUBLISHED BY
VIZ MEDIA, LLC
P.O. BOX 77010
SAN FRANCISCO, CA 94107

VIZ.COM

Names: Narita, Ryohgo, 1980- author. | Kubo, Tite, author. | Cash, Jan
  Mitsuko, translator.
Title: Bleach : can't fear your own world / written by Ryohgo Narita [and]
  Tite Kubo ; translated by Jan Mitsuko Cash.
Other titles: Can't fear your own world
Description: San Francisco, CA : VIZ Media, 2020- | "First published in
  Japan in 2018 by SHUEISHA Inc., Tokyo." | Translated from the Japanese.
  | Summary: "The Quincies' Thousand Year Blood War is over, but the embers of turmoil
  still smolder in the Soul Society...Hikone Ubuginu's mysterious origin story, and the secrets
  behind the very existence of the Soul Reapers and all their allies and adversaries, could
  be revealed to incite an all-out battle royal. Meanwhile, Urahara and Hisagi face down
  formidable enemies in Karakura Town as Tokinada Tsunayashiro's fiendish plan unfolds!"--
  Provided by publisher.
Identifiers: LCCN 2020001553 | ISBN 9781974713264 (paperback) | ISBN
  9781974718498 (ebook)
Subjects: CYAC: Supernatural--Fiction.
Classification: LCC PZ7.1.N37 Bl 2020 | DDC [Fic]--dc23
LC record available at https://lccn.loc.gov/2020001553

Printed in the U.S.A.
Frst printing, November 2020